Our Felicitations to

Father Jojayya Pudota, S.J.

on his 88th Birthday

(February 15, 1931 -)

In His Footsteps ...

Festschrift in honour of Father Jojayya Pudota, S.J.

In His Footsteps ...

Festschrift in honour of Father Jojayya Pudota, S.J.

Edited by
P. R. John, S.J.

Andhra Jesuit Province (AJP)
2019

In His Footsteps...: *Festschrift in honour of Father Jojayya Pudota, S.J.* — Jointly published by the Rev. Dr. Ashish Amos of the Indian Society for Promoting Christian Knowledge (ISPCK), Post Box 1585, 1654, Madarsa Road, Kashmere Gate, Delhi-110006 and Andhra Jesuit Province (AJP) Satyodayam, 12-5-33 South Lallaguda, Tarnaka, Secunderabad-500017.

ISBN: 978-93-88945-17-2

Explanation of the Cover design:

Life is a *marga*. We are all pilgrim people. No wonder the early Christians were called the "people of the way". It is "on this way," like blind Bartimaeus (Mk 10:52), Fr. Jojayya Pudota, S.J., heeding the call of the "Risen One" (symbolized by the pierced foot), followed the footsteps of the "Man from Nazareth," Jesus Christ. It has not been an easy journey for Fr. Jojayya, but then with the help of the Risen Saviour he walked "the way" boldly, and invites us to do the same "in His footsteps...".

Laser typeset by

ISPCK, Post Box 1585, 1654, Madarsa Road, Kashmere Gate, Delhi-110006
• *Tel:* 23866323/22

e-mail: ashish@ispck.org.in • ella@ispck.org.in
website: www.ispck.org.in

Contents

Introduction

"How beautiful are the feet of those who bring good news!" (Romans 10:14-15). St. Ignatius of Loyola and St. Francis Xavier spent a lot of time on their feet, spreading the gospel. Fr. John Calmette, a French Jesuit Missionary scholar travelled extensively during the period of *Telugu Carnatic Mission*. On 3rd January 2019, I visited Fr. Jojayya Pudota at St. Anne's Hospital, Vijayawada as he was suffering from foot injury. At the end of the visit, he asked me to pray and bless him. I felt unworthy, because in my earlier visits, it was I who sought his prayers and blessings.

Jojayya is a fine human person and a committed Jesuit priest. His exemplary life of simplicity embraced not for the sake of a rule or in conformity with the tradition, but because of its intrinsic value. At the age of sixteen, "having experienced the inner glow of inspiration," he offered himself fully to God and His Word leaving behind the plough and oxen, cotton and chilli fields, mother (Chinnamma) and father (Marayya) and three of his elder sisters. He is rooted in the (Spiritual Exercises) experience of God's unconditional love and lives a life of holiness dealing with all beings – plants, animals, and humans – tenderly and affectionately.

This year Fr. Jojayya, S.J., celebrates 88th year of his fruitful God-given life spent at the service of Jesus Christ and His Church. Down the sixty years, he travelled the breadth and width of Andhra Pradesh and Telengana bringing the good news, *'almost too good to be true'*. His numerous writings, talks, lectures, seminars, recollections, retreats and sacramental celebrations are impressive and incredible. His outstanding work stirred by Fr. John Wijngaards, MHM and written under the inspiration of the Holy Spirit is the translation of the Old Testament in Telugu. It has taken 17 long years to present the *choicest wine*, blended with Telugu idioms and in short sentences to the Catholic faithful.

The best way to honour such an incredibly creative thinker and an incessant writer on a wide variety of themes of value education and Scripture would be to publish a *Festschrift* in his honour, on the occasion of his 88th birthday, which fell on February 15, 2019. *In His Footsteps* consists of articles contributed by teachers, researchers and many theologians from India, some have been close to him and influenced by his exemplary life and some others who have not seen him or read his writings.

In the *Festschrift*, we have twenty articles honoring Jojayya. Michael Amaladoss in *"Community and Culture"* appreciates and affirms the efforts of "Jojayya's 'inculturation' 'from below' – that is, from the point of view of the people, who are trying to receive, respond to and live the Gospel in their culture".

Nagothu Sundari, enumerates the *"Contribution of Fr. Jojayya Pudota SJ for the Missionary Formation of Missionary Sisters of the Immaculate (Nirmala Sisters)"*. She recalls that "most of the Nirmala sisters have known him for the last 50 years and more, some in close collaboration with him, animating the students through leadership camps and conducting Bible Correspondence course, and others drew inspiration through his example of life, writings and teaching". The over arching argument of Sundari is that Jojayya fulfills the missionary aspiration – "the Church that goes forth" - of Pope Francis' *Evangelii Gaudium* and *Veritatis Gaudium*.

P. R. John presents a historical account of *"Two Epochs of Jesuit Contribution to the Literary Life of the Church in Andhra Pradesh/*

Telengana". He introduces *Telingana Catholic Library*. He highlights the Carnatic Jesuits and their writings during the 17th and 18th centuries. Finally, he dwells on the Second Coming of the Jesuits in 1953 to Andhra Desa and their contribution to the literary life of the Church and concludes with future orientation.

Valan C. Antony confesses: "Neither have I seen nor heard him, but what I heard *about* him drew me closer to this prodigious phenomenon-priest called Jojayya Pudota". He gladly sings the greatness of Jojayya by diving into the central theme of "Joy" in the Pauline epistle to Philippians and correlates it to Indian thinking of *ānanda*, "the self full of bliss." He ends, *Joy...Jesus...Jojayya* saying: "[Joy] is more than a mere emotion but a willful decision that strives after one quest, to be like Christ Jesus. Pauline invitation is to see God differently: seeing not just *what* God has done but *who* God is and rejoicing in Him. Jojayya does precisely this in his word and deed so graciously and gracefully".

Gorantla Johannes, in his article, highlights *"Challenges in being at the Service of Jesus Christ and His Church: Acts of the Apostles, an answer to today's challenges"*. He focuses "on the internal obstacles, challenges that the early church faced" and calls for "today's church [which] is in need of efficient leadership capable of finding swift and effective solutions, people docile to the Spirit, people committed to the common good, making sacrifices for common welfare, having a spirit of dialogue and readiness to change, better the situations".

Rudolf C. Heredia, a leading Jesuit Sociologist in his article *Science, Religion and Spirituality: Triple Dialectic to Triple Dialogue* invites his readers through seventeen sutras "to find common ground between the three [*Science, Religion and Spirituality*] for a dialogue, and turn the triple dialectic into a triple dialogue".

Rajakumar dwells on the centrality of *"Covenantal Call and Eucharistic Engagement"*. He makes a broad study on Biblical covenant and relates to Jesus Christ the Mediator of the New Covenant. Finally, he draws theological implication on "social love" – "love of neighbor and justice".

A study of Christology remains central to Christian theology. G. Jayaraj researches on *"Evolving Contextual Images of Jesus in India: The Role of the Christian Community and Theologians"*. He presents a random survey conducted in the local parishes of Pune to discover people's perception of images of Christ and their effect on their lives.

Joseph Sebastian writes: "When young men [women] encounter priests like Fr. Jojayya Pudota, S.J. and others of his ilk, they feel drawn to God and are overwhelmed, enthused and impacted with a profound respect, reverence and love for the priestly life. As a young priest, I was myself very much impressed by his exemplary life, his commitment to ministry and his own humanity. In witnessing the lived-experience of such saintly priests, we can well grasp what true formation is about and how it could grip and motivate a young man to become a priest". He links his article on, *"The New Ratio Fundamentalis Institutionis Sacerdotalis"* to Jojayya's life and ministry and poses a challenge for the priests of tomorrow in the Telugu Churches.

Peter Emmanuel argues in his article: *The Theology of Laity in the Church* that the "participation of the laity in the mission of the Church is not volunteerism in the mission of the hierarchy but a right and responsibility arising from their baptismal consecration".

Victor Edwin, *"Christian 'Trinitarian Monotheism': Conversation between Christians and Muslims"* is a joy and struggle of meeting Muslims in their homes, in universities, Islamic cultural centers, in the mosques and frequent questions, encountered in the course of conversations, of his faith in 'Trinitarian Monotheism'. He articulates the unmerited gift the Christians' faith in 'One God who is three' and the Christian theological efforts 'to make it the wellspring of our being, our life and our activity'.

Nija Vara enunciates the *Role of the Holy Spirit in the Church Today* saying that it "is not merely a uniting link between the members of the church but also a transforming and divinizing power in the life of every member of the church bestowing on him or her sublime privilege of sonship or daughtership".

Dusi Ravisekhar's article, *"The Influence of Bhakti Music of South India on Telugu Christian Hymns"* vividly highlights, the early Brahmin converts of Srikakulam, Vizianagaram, Visakhapatnam and the Godavari coast brought along with them their own rich literary and musical traditions and interacted with Christian faith. This process paid rich dividends to express "faith in the native poetic language and to compose hymns based on the native musical genre like *bhajans and kīrtanās*. This is the radical shift that took place helping the early Telugu Christian community in the 19th century to express their faith and devotion in the indigenous way".

Jerome Sylvester, in *"Khristbhakta Movement: Dialogal Mission of the Church"* shows the trajectory of Kristabhakta Movement as new way of evangelization. Khristbhaktas are seekers and followers of Christ, who accept *Yesubhagavan* as their *Satguru*. The author is of this opinion: "the spirituality of dialogue that emerges from the Khristbhakta Movement from the osmosis of faith and culture could be called as religious cosmopolitanism, for each respects not only the similarities, but the differences as well and play their role more responsibly toward whole humanity".

Amala Arockiaraj, through *"Principle and Foundation in the Ecological Context of South Asia"* invites his readers "to one of the foundational experiences of Ignatius, to discover God's project for us and cooperate with God in that project. God works with us to turn our chaos so as to make us one with cosmos! Today's ecological crisis is also an invitation from God to check our value system and set proper order".

Bala Bollineni who assists Jojayya for the past four years recalls that Jojayya's life ignites the young minds, especially in rural areas. Bala highlights four dimensions in Jojayya's work: *Becoming, Belonging, Transforming* and *Serving*. Jojayya invites all those who are engaged in youth work to be "present in the lives of young people".

P. R. John's essay, *"'You will be my Witnesses...': A Challenge and Invitation"*, shows how witnessing is more than to be as administrators in schools and colleges, parishes, social and health center and presiding over the liturgy. It is more of 'working together' and 'communing together'. If anyone wants to be a relevant 'shepherd with the smell of sheep,' (*Evangelii Gaudium*, no. 24) he/she must begin 'to know' the sheep at a 'deeply personal' and 'communitarian level'.

G.A.P. Kishore, a long standing admirer and constant reader of Jojayya's works, living in the same Jesuit community (Andhra Loyola College), reflects through his article *"Pudota Jojayya Swami Rachanavalokanam"* on the extensive writings of Jojayya. G.A.P. Kishore brings out the content and Telugu literary styles of Jojayya and makes an emphasis on reaching out to the ordinary people. The author concludes Jojayya's voluminous Christian literature is a patrimony to the generation of Telugu community.

Job Sudarshan, *"Paramahamsa Jojayya Swami"* addresses Jojayya as *Paramahamsa (supreme transcendent), Navayuga Telugu Kraistava Pravakta* (Modern Telugu Christian Prophet) and *Dirghadarsi* (seer). Sudarshan beckons his readers not to satisfy themselves in reading Jojayya's works but to carry out 'research' based on his writings and widely make them known to people.

C. V. Krishnaiah, a retired teacher at St. Xavier's School, Vinukonda, in his article titled "Loyola-Nirmala Educational Institutions, Vinukonda" expresses his gratitude towards Jesuits mission work and Jojayya's, great dedication towards value education camps both for the teachers and school children.

Sincere thanks, to Fr. P. S. Amalraj S.J., Provincial, Andhra Jesuit Province, for his message, constant encouragement in realizing this work and for his financial assistance to publish the book. I appreciate Valan C. Antony SJ, for his valuable suggestions and corrections. The views expressed in the individual articles are not of the editor but of the respective authors. I thank Sch. Gladwin S.J., of Madurai Province for the cover design. I am grateful to Rev. Dr. Ashish Amos, Ms. Ella, Ms. Whyneeta and their efficient team at ISPCK who worked wonderfully well to have this book see the light of day.

P. R. John, S.J.
Vidyajyoti College of Theology
Delhi

A Simple and Humble Jesuit Priest

Dear readers, I am glad to share some of my thoughts about Fr. Jojayya Pudota, S.J. He entered the Society of Jesus on 14th June 1955 and was ordained as a priest on 27th March 1965. He is a Jesuit for the past 64 years and a priest for the past 54 years. Fr. Jojayya renders great service to Jesus Christ and His Church through his life and mission: sharing and popularizing the Word of God. He nurtured this noble thought during his formative years and carried on faithfully as 'mission' in his priestly life.

Among his many works, the translation of 'Old Testament' stands out as unique one. He translated the Old Testament and it took 17 long years to complete the work. This quiet and unnoticed work demanded his time, energy, dedication and sacrifice. At the time of fruition of translation work, I was the Rector of Andhra Loyola College, Vijayawada. He came to my room and spoke in humble voice: 'Your servant has completed today the translation of the entire Old Testament. I request you to arrange a thanksgiving Eucharist for the community and followed by a fellowship meal'. I greeted him with much jubilation and thanked him for his work. During those days, Fr. Joseph Kallaringatt S.J., Professor of Scripture, Morning Star College, Kolkata was in Nirmala Niketan, Vijayawada. I requested him to deliver the homily. I was the main celebrant and Fr. Jojayya and Fr. Kallaringatt were the concelebrants. Fr. Jojayya's simplicity and humility were commendable that he never sought the central stage at any time of his life. Fr. Joseph Kallaringatt in his homily compared Fr. Jojayya to St. Jerome, who rendered Latin version of the Bible (Vulgate). Fr. Kallaringatt shared that Fr. Jojayya had to utilize his knowledge of Biblical languages Hebrew, Aramaic, Greek and Latin to bring out this new Translation in Telugu language.

Fr. Jojayya did not stop himself to the translation work of the Old Testament. He began a correspondence course for High School children in 1972 and a bi-monthly magazine for the daily devout reading of the Bible, *Lectio Divina*. In order to make the laity to read the Bible and to encounter Christ, he conducted seminars for the laity, catechists, teachers and nurses. He also regularly published on important Biblical themes which have a bearing on the daily life of laity. The first book brought out in this series is "Marriage and Family Life". Second is a "Collection of Scripture Services" and third is "Introduction to New Testament". Fr. Jojayya published "Chaitanya Vani," a periodical devoted to moral themes with a lot of suitable anecdotes and common examples and illustrations. A large number of non-Christian students in schools across the states of Andhra and Telangana voluntarily subscribed and benefitted from reading.

Finally, I wish that may Fr. Jojayya remains abundantly blessed by the Lord for all his services to the Church in Andhra Pradesh and Telengana States. I thank Fr. P. R. John, S.J., and all the contributors for working hard towards publication of **"In His Footsteps..."**, a *Festschrift* in honour of Fr. Jojayya.

P. S. Amalraj, S.J.
Provincial
Andhra Jesuit Province

Community and Culture

Michael Amaladoss S.J.

The relation between Gospel and culture is a topic that continues to be relevant today simply because a normal interaction between them has been made difficult for various people for various reasons. It has been considered from various different angles. The missionaries had the Gospel and sought to relate it to various cultures in the world, claiming to transform them in the process. The various groups of people who received the Gospel tried to receive it creatively and make it part of their culture. Anthropologists and theologians claimed to look at the process of Gospel-culture encounter objectively and described it in various ways. In the meantime groups of people continue to be converted in various parts of the world and their encounter with the Gospel seems to be taking various forms. The Christians in India, for example, think that they are living the Gospel in an Indian manner. The Hindus, however, consider them as practicing a 'foreign' religion and therefore alienated from Indian culture and history in some way. Efforts to make the Church Indian continue.

The process of Gospel-culture encounter in such a situation is normally called 'inculturation' today. But it is understood by various people in various ways. Some look at it 'from above' – that is, from the point of view of the missionaries, who seek to promote the rebirth of the Gospel in the various cultures of the world. Others seek to understand it 'from below' – that is, from the point of view of the people, who are trying to receive, respond to and live the Gospel in their culture. There have been and continue to be tensions between these two points of view. I think that Fr. Jojayya, S.J. represents the second point of view, though he himself may not have consciously reflected over it. I am not too sure of this affirmation, since I do not read Telugu and so have no access to his writings. But his praxis of translating the Bible in Telugu and making it reach the people involves a view of inculturation which, I think, needs to be highlighted, affirmed and promoted, since the process of inculturation remains largely an unfinished task. I think that such reflection will help us to continue the work that Fr. Jojayya started, not only in erstwhile Andhra Pradesh but elsewhere in India and abroad.

What is Inculturation?

The term 'inculturation' is patterned on the term 'incarnation'. Just as the Word of God became incarnate in the humanity of the Jewish community and culture, the same Word of God has to become incarnate in every culture and the humans who live in it. Theologians welcomed this term. In the Latin Church, for example, the Sacramental celebrations, the theological explorations and teaching were in Latin till the Second Vatican Council. The Bible too was used officially in Latin. A few translations of the Bible and the official prayers saw the light of day in the 20th century. But these were for private, un-official, use only. Though St. Jerome had translated the original Bible in Greek into Latin, further translations in other languages were not thought necessary. All the official texts of the Church too were in Latin. The other languages were thought to be ambiguous. When the missionaries came to India, for example, they did translate the Catechism into the local languages like Tamil. But other official texts remained in Latin. Luther was the first to translate the Bible in German to make it accessible to the people. But the Latin Church was not inspired to follow his example. At the level of popular devotion people did use prayers like the Rosary and Litanies in the local languages. But they had no official status, though they were allowed or rather tolerated.

Even after the Second Vatican Council, the official texts had to be in Latin and only a literal translation was allowed. This rule has been reinforced recently. The Bible – the Word of God - can have multiple translations in the same language. But the local community cannot freely translate a prayer of the Church without the approval of some Church official who does not know the language in which the translation has been made. This does not really correspond to the image of the incarnation implied in the term inculturation.

Historical Factors

An ideal image of what should happen may be imagined in this way. The Word of God comes to us in the human words of the various authors of the scriptural texts. These are not dogmatic texts but stories of God's interaction with God's people. The people to whom the good news is proclaimed and who do not share the same language retell the story in their own language. When the people listen to these stories they respond to it in appropriate ways through their own words and actions in the context of their culture. The stories must have been originally told in Aramaic which was the language of Jesus and the Apostles, though some like Paul may also have been fluent in Greek. But the stories were written down, not in Aramaic, but in Greek, because Jerusalem had fallen, the Jews were dispersed, and Church was growing in an area where Greek was the dominant language. The people also seek to respond to it in Greek in the context of Greek culture. This obliges them to interact with Greek culture which has a philosophy of its own. The impact of Greek philosophy on the simple stories of the Gospels lead to various heresies like Arianism. Categories like 'person', 'nature' and 'substance' are not Aramaic categories. The use of such categories leads to more complicated formulations of the faith. A simple comparison between the Apostles Creed and the Nicean Creed will show the differences. Corresponding to creedal expressions liturgical structures also evolved. A hierarchical community structure also seems to have evolved at the same time around the Bishops as successors to the Apostles helped by various other ministers like presbyters, deacons and probably others. Women too must have had a role among them.

In the meantime, though the Latins asserted their political power over the Greeks, the Greeks dominate with their culture and philosophy. So what develops is a Greco-Latin entity. Politically the Latins were powerful. As the Church spreads across Europe and North Africa, the centre subtly shifts from Greece to Rome and not only the faith but also the Latin culture spreads with it as a civilizational force. The Greek section gradually loses its influence and finally separates after the first millennium. In the colonial period, it is the Latin Church which spreads across the colonies in America, Africa and Asia. The missionaries simply exported the Latin doctrinal, liturgical and hierarchical structures and imposed it on the newer communities. The Bible with its good news was forgotten, except for the readings at mass in Latin. The homily perhaps referred to it. The missionaries showed more interest in translating the Catechism than the Bible. So what was really proclaimed as the Good News was not the Word of God, but a set of creeds and dogmas with accompanying theology woven into a catechism. They were accompanied by the liturgical rituals which were managed by the sacerdotal hierarchy. It is important to keep this in mind because when there was talk of inculturation after the Second Vatican Council the focus was not on the Word of God in the Bible but on the Creed and dogmas, the rituals and Church structures and discipline. There was an effort to protect these allowing some slight adjustments here and there.

Mateo Ricci and Roberto De Nobili

The world and the Church had to wait for Mateo Ricci and Roberto de Nobili in the 17th century to insist that one can be religiously Christian while continuing to be culturally Chinese or Indian. Religiously they remained very much Latin, though socio-culturally they tried to live like the Chinese and the Indians. Ricci lived like a

Chinese scholar – a mandarin. De Nobili sought to become an Indian sannyasi – respectable figures in the respective communities. But with regard to religion they remained very Latin. They had, of course, to communicate the faith in the local languages and explain and defend it. The faith referred more to the creeds than to the Bible. The basic ritual and administrative structures remained Latin-European. We had the controversies regarding the Chinese and Malabar rites.[1] But they had to do with external symbols and practices and did not touch the core of the faith with regard to doctrine, liturgy and hierarchical and ministerial structures. Fortunately, for the people, the local languages and cultures were used at the level of popular religious practices, celebrations, arts and even literature. Jesuits like Constantius Beschi and Thomas Stevens and others too contributed to the development of a Christian literature in the Indian languages. Christians could live and pray like Indians till they started anything that was an official ritual, which had to be in Latin. Songs in local languages were used. Even in Europe, mystics sang their poems and described their experiences in local languages. The other Christian Churches also made an important contribution. Martin Luther was the first to translate the whole Bible in popular German and put it in the hands of the people, asking them to read the Word of God. This situation continued till the Second Vatican Council.

From the early years of the 20th century, in a world in which the local languages, literatures and philosophies were developing, theologians had begun expressing themselves in local languages and started to dialogue with the intellectuals. Seeking to promote greater participation in the liturgy, liturgical texts were being translated and used privately. Many translations of the Bible began to appear. It is in this context that the Second Vatican Council is announced by St. John XXIII seeking to open the windows of the Church to the winds of the Spirit of God. It is significant also that the very first document discussed and approved by the Bishops in Council was the one on the Liturgy, prepared in a way by the strong liturgical movements in France and Germany focused on participation by the people. This document gives us a new insight into what will be later called inculturation.

The Vatican II Document on the Liturgy and Inculturation

The two key statements of this document are the following and both are found in one number 21 which speaks of the reform of the Sacred liturgy. The focus of the reform are the **People.** "The Christian people, as far as is possible, should be able to understand them (texts and rites) with ease and take part in them fully, actively, and as a community." Full, active and understanding participation as a community is the goal of reform. Are there any limits to this reform? The document says: "The liturgy is made up of unchangeable elements divinely instituted, and of elements subject to change. These latter not only may be changed but ought to be changed with the passage of time, if they have suffered from the intrusion of anything out of harmony with the inner nature of the liturgy or have become less suitable." The only unchangeable elements are those divinely instituted. Studies have shown that the only elements in the seven sacraments that have not actually changed in the course of history and so may be considered of divine institution are the symbol of washing with water for baptism and eating and drinking together (sharing a meal) for the Eucharist.[2] Some theologians have questioned whether the material eaten and drunk should necessarily be bread and wine or can be other material specific to and easily available in a particular place.[3] The question is what is important and central: the symbolic act of sharing or the material shared. I do not wish to go into this question here. What is important for me is the place of the community in the whole process. The document clarifies, for example, when it speaks about praying: "The prayers addressed to God by the priest who, in the person of Christ, presides over the assembly, are said in the name of the entire holy people and of all present." (33)[4] The priest may represent Christ, but prays in the name of the people. That is, the people are praying through the priest.

The document continues: "The rites… should be within the people's comprehension, and normally should not require explanation." (34) Long commentaries, therefore, should not be needed. The use of the local languages is encouraged. (35,2) What is important is relevance rather than uniformity. "Even in the liturgy the Church does not wish to impose a rigid uniformity in matters which do not involve the faith or the good of the whole community. Rather does she respect and foster the qualities and talents of the various races and nations." (37) What I want to point out here is the important role that the local community has in the reform and celebration of the liturgy. Everything else seems here secondary – except the reference to the divine institution, which, as we have seen is very limited, if we go by history.

The Vatican II Document on the Church and Local Community
The role and importance of the local community in the life of the Church is given a further boost by the document on the Church. When we think of the Church we envision immediately the hierarchy. But the Church is primarily the People of God, at whose service there are ministers. While these ministers, the Bishops and the priests, are there to guide and govern, the People of God have their own identity and dignity. They are "a chosen race, a royal priesthood, a holy nation". (1 Pet 2:9) They have Christ as their head, they being his body. The Holy Spirit dwells in their hearts as in a temple. Their destiny is the kingdom of God established by Christ and growing in history. (LG 9) In their own way, they share in the one priesthood of Christ, which they exercise by participating in the offering of the Eucharist, in receiving the sacraments and in living a life of abnegation and active charity. (LG 10) "Taking part in the Eucharistic sacrifice… they offer the divine victim to God and themselves along with it." (LG 11) The People also share in the Christ's prophetic office. "The whole body of the faithful who have an anointing that comes from the holy one (cf. 1 Jn 2:20 and 27) cannot err in matters of belief. This characteristic is shown in the supernatural appreciation of the

faith (*sensus fidei*) of the whole people, when, "from the bishops to the last of the faithful" they manifest a universal consent in matters of faith and morals." (LG 12) The Holy Spirit also distributes special graces (cf. 1 Cor 12:11) which "makes them fit and ready to undertake various tasks and offices for the renewal and building up of the Church." (LG 12)

The People of God and the Local Church

What I want to stress here is that the Church is not a top-down body, but a bottom-up one. It is primarily the People of God served – a service that can include guidance and even governance – by appropriate ministers. The various communities of the faithful are gathered together as a local church, marked by geographical or cultural factors. The universal Church is a communion of local Churches. The Bishops who serve the different local Churches constitute a college with the Pope at its head, but being "the servant of the servants of God". My purpose here is not to develop an ecclesiology, but to point out the importance of the local Church, very often rooted in and characterized by particular cultures. In this context, inculturation – the dialogue of the Gospel with a particular culture – leads to the formation of a local Church and it is this local Church that is responsible for its own ongoing inculturation. It is significant that the Office of Theological Concerns of the Federation of Asian Bishops' Conferences, when it tried to outline a theology of inculturation produced a document entitled *Theses on Inculturation and the Local Church*, it starts off with the affirmation: "The figure of the body of Christ as applied to the Church illustrates the fact that the universal Church is the communion of local Churches." (Thesis 1)[5] It goes on:

> In the Church the ministry of the Word is carried out through the apostolic teaching, the Eucharistic celebration, the Spirit-filled life and activity and proclamation of salvation. Hence these elements are generative and constitutive of the local Church. But they will be productive of the local Church only as appropriated by concrete groups of men and women in response to the Word of God. (Thesis 3)

What I would like to stress here is that a local Church is produced when a group of men and women respond to the Word of God in their life, action and celebration. In the process, they also inculturate the Word. I would also like to note that what should be inculturated is the 'Word of God', not the theological-dogmatic, liturgical and practical structures that may have been built up by other local Churches earlier in different historical, geographical and cultural locations and circumstances. But unfortunately what is inculturated are these structures and the process is also controlled by 'experts' on top with power who will block most creative efforts from below. In the name of unity, they will also block efforts from below that seek to cater to geographical, cultural and religious pluralism across the world.[6]

The Contribution of Fr. Jojayya

I would like to suggest that Fr. Jojayya, whether he was fully aware of the implications of what he was doing or not, was promoting such a dialogue between the People of God – the common people – and the Word of God by translating the Bible, especially the Old Testament, in a language that the people can understand. He also went around Andhra introducing the Bible to priests, catechists and the people so that they can read it intelligently. While he may not have launched a movement of groups of people regularly reading the Bible, he did provide the material, through his many books, necessary for an intelligent and inculturated reading of it.

Efforts at Inculturation in India

Other people in India were busy with developing an Indian rite – without much success finally, because of blocks from above and lack of careful work from below - for the Eucharist. It was, besides, a work of experts, not of the people. Theologians were developing an Indian theology in an academic atmosphere heavily controlled from above. This has remained an enterprise of a select group of people which has not yet had a wider impact among the people, who are satisfied with their popular religiosity. Some monks and religious people tried to develop an ashram way of spiritual life. It does not seem to have had the desired influence upon the larger community. Can it be that their basic mistake was not to start with the people? The only group in the wider Church who thought of the people were the liberation theologians in Latin America and elsewhere. Though they may have limited their attention to conscientization regarding their economic-political situation, they did focus on the people – the Basic (Ecclesial) Communities. The Word of God was made accessible to these groups and they were enabled to read, reflect on the Word in the context of their socio-economic life. Originally inspired by a Marxist analysis of society their theoretical and practical focus may have been narrow. But they had developed a proper method of animating and inspiring the people. The Basic Communities did read the Bible, reflect, share and pray and try to live their lives in accordance with the demands of the Word of God. It is to the credit of Fr. Jojayya that he facilitated the reading of the Bible among the people in Andhra.

The Sources of Our Problems
Reflection on Fr. Jojayya's biblical ministry in the context of inculturation has clarified for me a number of factors in the theory and practice of inculturation in India over the past 40 years. Inculturation is supposed to be an ongoing dialogue between the Gospel and culture. But the Gospel is hardly mentioned anywhere in the discussions on inculturation. The focus is on the liturgy on the one hand and theology and spirituality on the other. Here we are dealing with, not the simple, but challenging, inspiration of the Gospel, but with symbolic structures that have deep roots in a particular history and culture like the creeds with their dogmas, the liturgical, ministerial and ethical structures. The process is controlled by people sitting on top who think that inculturation is a threat to unity and 'purity' (of doctrine) and are ready with power to block anything. For example, Pope Benedict XVI said in a speech at Regensburg:

In the light of our experience with cultural pluralism, it is often said nowadays that the synthesis with Hellenism achieved in the early Church was an initial inculturation which ought not to be binding on other cultures. The latter are said to have the right to return to the simple message of the New Testament prior to that inculturation, in order to inculturate it anew in their own particular milieu. This thesis is not simply false, but it is coarse and lacking in precision.[7]

As someone engaged in inculturation in India, I find the last sentence insulting. Similarly John Paul II said:

When the Church deals for the first time with cultures of great importance, but previously unexamined, it must even so never place them before the Greek and Latin inculturation already acquired. Were this inheritance to be repudiated the providential plan of God would be opposed, who guides his Church down the paths of time and history. (John Paul II, *Faith and Reason*. 72)

So we have to dialogue, not only with the Gospel, but with a Greco-Roman tradition that sees itself as providential and mandatory and will jealously defend itself with all the power at its disposal. Fortunately we can still dialogue with the Gospel in our private prayer. But let us not waste time talking about inculturation at the level of the Church. It will be blocked by the people in power. Here Fr. Jojayya reminds us that we have to dialogue with the Gospel, not with the, apparently immoveable, structures of the Church.

Structures or the Word of God?

Looking at the process of inculturation from below, we have also focused on the structures of the faith than on the Word of God. Instead of trying to transform the lives of the people by exposing them to the Word of God and allow appropriate liturgical and other structures to emerge from below we began with trying to change the liturgy. In the process we never consulted the people. It was the work of a group of experts, who focused more on Hindu rituals that can be adapted than on the Bible. Inter-religious dialogue was mixed up with inter-cultural dialogue.

Besides, the top-down process involved experimentation. These were done not with the people in the parishes, but with some 'experts' in ashrams or similar centres. Then we were surprised that the common people and the youth were not enthusiastic about the proposals. So, on the whole it was a top-heavy process, not involving the people. Of course, whether a process involving the common people would have been acceptable by the people at the very top is also doubtful. Neither the 'authorities' at the universal nor those at the local level really worried about the people, but more about their own expertise and theological convictions and prejudices.

Conclusion

Every culture is the life of a community. When the community is neglected the culture disappears. Coming in a cultural tradition we cannot ignore the past. But the culture of the past must be evaluated not merely in terms of the present culture but in terms of a common norm. For us that norm would be the Bible, not in itself, but as it is read, meditated on and lived by the community. Our origins are more important and crucial than our history. That is what gives us our identity.

In the Euro-American countries we hear about the 'Nones' – people who believe in God, but who do not belong to any religion. This is what will happen everywhere if the religions do not inculturate but hold on to their outmoded structures. In countries in the Third World where people still seem to need religion, popular religiosity in which people's real spiritual/psychological needs are met or Pentecostal/Evangelical sects will flourish. It is time that we attended to the people than to our precious and pre-conceived structures.

Endnotes

[1] See George Minamiki, *The Chinese rites controversy: from its beginning to modern times.* (Chicago: Loyola University Press, 1985); Ines G. Županov and Pierre Antoine Fabre (eds), *The Rites Controversies in the Early Modern World.* (Brill, 2018).

² M. Amaladoss, *Do Sacraments Change? Variable and Invariable Elements in Sacramental Rites.* (Bangalore: Theological Publications in India, 1979).

³ See R. Jaouen, *L'Eucharistie du mil.* (Paris: Karthala, 1995) The author discusses whether in some African countries where wheat is not available bread made of millet can be used. I have also raised the question in my book referred to in the previous footnote.

⁴ The numbers within brackets here and in the following pages refer to the documents being referred to on the Liturgy and on the Church.

⁵ See Paper 60 on *Theses on the Local Church. http://www.fabc.org/offices/csec/ocsec_fabc_papers.html*

⁶ See M. Amaladoss, *Beyond Inculturation. Can the Many be One?* (Delhi: VIEWS/ISPCK), 1998.

⁷ Cf. http://www.catholic-ew.org.uk/Home/News/2006/Full-Text-of-the-Pope-Benedict-XVI-s-Regensburg-Lecture.

Contribution of Fr. Jojayya Pudota S.J. for the Missionary Formation of Missionary Sisters of the Immaculate (Nirmala Sisters)

Sundari Nagothu MSI

Introduction

Mission today is a multifaceted issue in the midst of emerging challenges in the Church and in the world. How can we communicate the unchanging Gospel of Jesus Christ in the changing world of today? This is one of the great missiological questions of our day. In the Apostolic Exhortation *Evangeli Gaudium* Pope Francis views mission as transformation of various realities, "I dream of a "missionary option", that is, a missionary impulse capable of transforming everything, so that the Church's customs, ways of doing things, times and schedules, languages and structures can be suitably channelled for the evangelization of today's world rather than for her self-preservation" (no. 27). More than ever, since the Second Vatican Council, Church has become conscious of its missionary nature, "the pilgrim Church is missionary by her very nature" (*Ad gentes* 2). Efforts are made to deepen the reflection on the missionary dimension and of discovering new ways of doing mission. Mission will be vibrant when all people of good will are committed to the proclamation of the Gospel in word and deed.

The purpose of this article is to pay homage to Fr. Jojayya Pudota S.J. a veteran Jesuit, an outspoken and committed religious, a renowned Scripture scholar and an inspiring missionary of our time, who has rendered self-less service to the Telugu Catholic Church for six decades. It is very vivid to many that he lives an austere and holy life. Like leaven in the dough, he was able to transform the lives of thousands across various institutions and peoples. He is renowned for his extraordinary contribution in education, formation and publication. He is a pioneer and 'innovative evangelizer' who always sought simple and creative methods to evangelize common people. The article highlights the instrumental role of an obscure Jesuit of high intellect and of extraordinary holiness, in shaping the spiritual experience of many by his lectures, writings and exemplary religious virtues.

As an exclusively missionary congregation, we, the Nirmala Sisters (MSI/PIME) have participated actively in the missionary activity in the Telugu States and have been able to contribute to the missionary dynamism of the local church. Fr. Jojayya had been a great collaborator and source of inspiration in our missionary journey. Therefore, it gives us immense joy to share our experiences with him. We are grateful to God for this charismatic and dedicated son of the soil, who has rendered almost five decades of valuable service for our missionary formation. In the following pages we recall some of the remarkable experiences, from the missionary perspective, that we cherished with him as a teacher, spiritual father, guide and mentor.

This article is outlined into three parts. The first part delineates briefly Mission as reconciliation and being merciful, integrating reflections from *Evangeli Gaudium* and Fr. Jojayya as a missionary. Second part presents briefly our missionary Charism and Spirituality, and the role of Fr. Jojayya in our missionary formation. Third part proposes some relevant means of evangelization in the context of the Telugu Catholic Church, with its challenges, drawing inspiration from the life and experiences of Fr. Jojayya.

Part I: Mission as 'being sent' to 'go forth' to Reconcile and to be Merciful

One of the important characteristics of the mission in the Bible is, 'being sent'. The Hebrew word *Shalah*, Greek *apostello* and Latin *Missio, mittere* correspond to *sending*.[1] The Old Testament contains several instances of *sending*. Mission is rooted in the nature of God, who sends and saves. The objective of sending was always to communicate the message of God to people who are in despair, suffering and in the slavery of sin. Jesus was conscious of his *being sent* by the Father and of the salvific mission entrusted to him; to establish the Kingdom of God on earth. "As my Father has sent me, even so I send you" (Jn. 20:21).

The central theme of Jesus' life and ministry was the Kingdom of God. Jesus lives his mission as a revelation of mercy towards sinners, the oppressed and the marginalised in the society. Mercy is seen as forgiveness that gives life, dignity and restoring joy (EG 3). In the heart of God there is a preferential place for the poor, so much so that he himself "became poor" (2 Cor 8:9). To those who were burdened by pain, oppressed by poverty, he assured that God brought them to the centre of his heart: Jesus identified himself with the poor, "Blessed are you, poor, because yours is the Kingdom of God" (Lk 6:20)) He taught that mercy towards the 'poor' is the key to heaven (EG 197)."I was hungry and you gave me food" (Mt 25:35). To be Church means, to be among and part of the people, to be God's leaven in the midst of humanity, a place of mercy freely given, where everyone feels welcomed, loved, forgiven and encouraged (EG 113, 114).

A Missionary Reading of *Evangelii Gaudium* - *A Church that 'goes forth'*

Evangeli Gaudium is a simple pastoral letter to "exhort" the believing people "on the proclamation of the Gospel in the present world". Pope Francis describes Church, as a 'missionary church that "goes forth" to the poor and needy' (EG 24). A church that goes forth echoes in three essential elements: *Word of God, Missionary exit* - courage to leave the comfort to go to the peripheries (EG 20) and intimacy and communion with Christ. "Communion and mission are profoundly interconnected" (EG 23). Contemplation and intimacy with the Lord can only lead us to others, to reach everyone. The Church "outgoing" is an image that can summarize the whole exhortation. The Pope invites all communities to take on to the 'path of pastoral and missionary conversion' and reminds that "mere administration" can no longer be enough. (EG 25).

Fr. Jojayya - a Servant of the Gospel and an Ardent Missionary
The image of the Church that 'goes forth' is appropriate to describe the priestly vocation and mission of Fr. Jojayya. He was born in 1931 at Kanaparru, a traditional Catholic village in Guntur diocese, Andhra Pradesh, whose ancestors were evangelized by the Carnatic Jesuit mission (1701-1773) and at a later stage by the Mill Hill Missionaries of London. Though a small Catholic community, vocations to religious life and priesthood flourished. Today nearly eighty priests/religious are serving the universal church following the example of stalwarts like Fr. Jojayya. He is one of the early vocations from the village, who nurtured deep faith and spiritual values from his parents and family members. His amazing vocation story is unique and rare of its kind. From a very young age he discerned the will of God aided by the simple faith and devotion of his parents. Being only son in the family, he comprehended well ahead the cultural implications of being a heir and what it means to hold the greatly valued inheritance of the family in every sense. He shares his vocation story in the following words. 'I received the call of God by means of illumination at various stages. I felt a strong sense of detachment from the world and its temporariness. I did not see any vision or heard any voice, but felt within me strongly that God is calling me to dedicate my life as a priest to serve him. I had a clear vision of mission,'to lead people to Christ'. In order to fulfil this mission it occurred to me

that I should become a priest'. This spark of unquenchable thirst to bring people to God deeply moved him to proclaim Christ with inner freedom and total detachment leaving behind, family, name, fame and all other securities that the world could offer. As a true disciple of Christ and obedient son of his founder father St. Ignatius, he interiorized the Gospel values, sustained a deeper union with the Lord and tried to find God in everything.

The missionary dimension of his life and activities can be defined in the following key words: intimacy and communion with the Eucharistic Lord, conscious of 'being sent', going forth, single-mindedness, detachment, and courage to leave the comfort to go to the peripheries... and so on. He is one of the few local Telugu priests who gave a striking testimony of being at the service of the Gospel totally and faithfully. He made the Gospel his daily manual, striving to put into practice the *Sermon on the Mount*, 'to be the salt of the earth and light of the world'. He was able to inspire and motivate many to follow the Gospel path. The 'restlessness' which moved him to respond to God's call ignited many Telugu Catholics, especially we, the Nirmala Sisters. With his vast knowledge of Sacred Scripture and other disciplines he published numerous books, magazines, articles and formative materials for the Telugu Catholic Church.

Mission is the action of witness and proclamation of the Good News of the Kingdom by the Church, continuing the effusive action of Trinitarian love (AG 2) as envisaged in the mandate of the Risen Christ (Mt 28, 19-20). The Church is called to be salt and light to the world and to open the heart to divine love. (EG 92,81). In the New Testament, the verb evangelize (*euaggelizesthai*) is used frequently in Luke, Acts of the Apostles and especially in the letters of St. Paul. It specifically means to "proclaim with authority and power the Good News of salvation in Jesus Christ". The Evangelizer is sent by Christ and endowed with a corresponding charism from the Holy Spirit.[2]

Deeply committed to his Jesuit motto, *for the greater glory of God,* as a true son of St. Ignatius, Fr. Jojayya embraced contemplative life and interiorization. He was able to transform the contemplative life into action through his writings and teaching ministry. His audience (Bishops, priests, sisters, the people of God and non-Christians), after attending his classes and listening to the homilies were astounded and would say, 'he spoke with authority, preaches what he practiced'. The Telugu Church is proud of this devoted son of the soil who is loved and admired by many for the example he set with his life of discipline, total detachment, a simple and sober life style.

He has been spending all his time and energy in the 'mission of teaching and writing'. First as a Telugu lecturer at Andhra Loyola College, Vijayawada, and then dedicated almost fifty years of his life to the spiritual/ human formation of priests, sisters, students, catechists and the faithful of the Telugu Catholic Church. His only passion is to proclaim the Word of God and to instil spiritual quest in others. He remained forty years in the same room, making this room a '*Manresa* experience'. It is from here, a place of solitude and contemplation that he produced master pieces of Telugu Catholic literature on various topics. One of the milestones of his works is the translation of the Catholic version of the Old Testament in Telugu, at the request of the then Andhra Pradesh Bishops Council. At a time when the Telugu Catholic Church was deeply yearning for a Bible text which is inextricably connected to Catholic Scripture and Tradition, the Telugu Catholics were fortunate to find a true son who relentlessly worked for 17 years to translate the Old Testament to its present Catholic version. The uniqueness of his translation of the Old Testament and other writings are marked by the use of the milieu, idiom, colloquial genres and cultural expressions of the common people (folklore, proverbs and parables in Telugu language), that has made great impact on the reader, conveying the message powerfully to the heart of the person. His theology is the theology of the common people and he lives it through his simple life.

Besides the translation of the Bible another important milestone is, the series of commentaries published on various books of the Bible

(*Bible Bhashyam*), which helped the Catholic faithful to read, reflect and assimilate the Word of God. These commentaries are unique and a primary source today to read the Bible with historical and theological background. There are other publications on Catechesis, moral teachings/stories, life history of saints, biographies of prominent personalities, psychology, general knowledge about the Church and the world. More than 400 books were published in the 50 years of his service.[3] He did not confine himself staying indoors, but was reaching out to others to share his knowledge and experience. He was not an "arm chaired missionary" but an itinerant missionary like Jesus, always on move, preferring common means of travel, unmindful of his ill health and age.

Part II: Contribution of Fr. Jojayya S.J. to the Missionary Formation of Nirmala Sisters

Our Missionary Charism

The congregation of the *Missionary Sisters of the Immaculate* (MSI/PIME) was founded at Milan on 8th December 1936. We are immensely grateful to God for the birth of our missionary congregation in the Church as an exclusively missionary institute, '*in the highest and most sublime sense of the word*' as quoted by Blessed Paolo Manna PIME, the *inspirer* of our Charism. India was the first Mission started in 1948 at Gudivada, where mainly PIME Bishops and Priests carried out their missionary apostolate. By God's grace our mission has continued to grow uninterruptedly, and gradually with the passing of years the MSI are spread beyond Vijayawada diocese, carrying out missionary work not only in other dioceses of Andhra Pradesh and Telangana, but also to the North-West and North-East of India and to overseas missions as well.[4]

The Charism (the grace) which gave life to our Congregation is centred on the *living passion to proclaim the Kingdom of God to all peoples* (Constitutions n.4). The Holy Spirit placed this grace in the hearts of those who prepared and realized its foundation and continues to place it in the heart of every Missionary Sister of the Immaculate.[5] Our motto '*Thy Kingdom Come*' ! describes well the goal of our life and activities. The reflections undertaken during the last three General Chapters (2006, 2012, 2018) were special moments of grace, as they were instrumental in rediscovering our Founders Charism (2006), Spirituality (2012) and to deepen our specific missionary identity - ad gentes - ad extra – ad vitam (2012, 2018).

Our Spirituality

Our Spirituality is founded on the experience of our foundresses' encounter with Jesus, the Apostle of the Father, who shows himself to them as the untiring Sower of the Kingdom and Seed that dies in order to give life. (Lk 4:42-44; Jn 12:24).[6] Jesus sent by the Father to evangelize, fascinates them and inflames the hearts with his own passion: they desire to participate in the action of the Sower who wishes that the Kingdom may spread everywhere.[7]

Based on our Spirituality, to follow *Jesus the apostle of the Father, the Sower and the Seed*, the untiring Sower, [Preacher of the Kingdom] we participate in the missionary nature (*Ad gentes* n.2) of the Church. Thus the congregation has only one mission, to proclaim Christ to those who do not yet know him, giving priority to *first proclamation,* which is the central moment of our missionary activity. It is to this end that our presence and activities are directed. (Const. n. 64)

Contribution Fr. Jojayya S.J. for our Missionary Formation

As we recall the history of the initial stages of our mission in erstwhile Andhra Pradesh, until 1963 the MSI were rendering services in the rural areas Krishna and Godavari districts. In 1963 Nirmala Convent community was opened at Patamata, Vijayawada. Since then we were being assisted for the spiritual needs by the Jesuit Fathers of Andhra Loyola College. The MSI remember with gratitude the kindness of the Rectors and various Jesuit priests who not only offered daily Mass both at the convent and the Novitiate, but also rendered spiritual services, we remember especially the Biblical instruction given by

Fr. Jojayya since 1970[8]. It is not out of obligation that he rendered various services to us, but with deep affection, concern and eagerness to orient us to actualize our missionary charism.

It was the post-Vatican period of *aggiornamento,* getting familiar with Sacred Scripture and teachings of Vatican Council II. There could not be a better person than Fr. Jojayya S.J. to explain the Bible and Catechetics. Following are some of the initiatives through which he has instilled in us the missionary passion. We are glad to share the experiences of our sisters who had been closely associated with Fr. Jojayya since 1970.[9] In one way or the other, most of the Nirmala sisters have known him for the last 50 years and more, some in close collaboration with him, animating the students through leadership camps and conducting Bible Correspondence course, and others drew inspiration through his example of life, writings and teaching.

a.   Biblical Instruction to the Sisters & Novices

Fr. Jojayya is a dynamic evangelizer, a true missionary, an ardent preacher blessed with amazing wealth of wisdom, intellectual shrewdness and tenacity of purpose. Deeply rooted in the Word of God, his person and activities are directed to the proclamation of the Good News. He imparted the knowledge of Scripture to us, explaining the deeper meanings with a specific focus on Evangelization. His teachings and instruction motivated us to deepen our missionary charism. He often reiterated the saying of St. Jerome, '*Ignorance of Scriptures is ignorance of Christ*', and stressed to make the Sacred Scripture as our companion. He ignited in us the desire to read Sacred Scripture every day, to make it our companion and to submerge ourselves in the light of the Word utilising the traditional method of meditating the scriptures, *Lectio Divina.* He created an atmosphere of freedom and space to interact with him during and after the sessions to clarify the doubts and to seek his advice. His talks, sermons and informal conversations were the pearls of wisdom. He had the gift of spontaneity, wit and humour that kept the participants engaged.

In 1968 the Novitiate was shifted from Bhimavaram to Vijayawada. From then on, until recent times every year he trained our young religious in the knowledge of scriptures especially on Prophets and book of Psalms. Being a man of contemplative prayer and mystical experiences, he inculcated in the novices the desire for prayer and inner thirst for deeper intimacy with God. His simple life style, words of wisdom, and fatherly concern made great impact on them. His vocation story made them realize the unique ways of God and to appreciate the gift of vocation in each person's life.

He understood well our missionary charism, as our formation and mission was directed and clearly reflected his dream of a *missionary Church* 'with and for the people through simple and effective evangelising methods'. We, the Nirmala Sisters have been at forefront holding 'village camps', living amidst the faithful sharing the simple food and accommodation they provided, with a transparent life style that brought them the Good News. He empowered us to reach out to the marginalised rural flocks giving prominence to the word of God. While he admired our apostolic life, he did not hesitate when necessary to remind us to rejuvenate our missionary spirit! It speaks volumes of his real love and genuine concern that we be faithful to our missionary charism.

In the recent years his special preparatory sessions to our sisters preparing for their Golden/Silver Jubilee were inspiring. The reflections with valuable insights facilitated the Jubilarians to look back to the past with gratitude and to reflect on where they have been and then to take a long view of how to be as prophetic witnesses in the future. It helped them to verify and confront oneself, not to be satisfied with what has been accomplished, not to be carried away by self-gory and worldly fame, but offered a gentle reminder to continue to commit oneself to do more. He is a tireless missionary who believes in doing maximum, he is never tired to be young, even in his 80's he says he cannot relax because there is a lot to be done! True to his

name, like his patron St. Joseph, he is silent and hardworking man
who never looks for recognition or reward, name or fame.

b.   Spiritual and human formation of Students in our Schools

Needless to say that Fr. Jojayya's spiritual assistance was not limited
to Sisters alone but to thousands of students in our as well as many
other Catholic schools, who benefitted greatly from his scriptural-
theological depth. He was very eager and enthusiastic to teach the
students about life and its good values. Every year he organized
Leadership camps in most of our schools, through which he instilled
Kingdom values in the students. Thousands of students learned
spiritual, moral and social values, and put them into practice. A great
transformation could be witnessed in the life style and character
of the students who attend his camps. His sessions also helped
the students to extract the best that was once obscure in them. It
helped them to grow in leadership qualities, self-confidence and to
overcome fear and anxiety. He is very patient and creative with the
students. His extensive knowledge coupled with his caring nature
and simplicity of heart has always captured the hearts of the young.
His unremarkable command over Telugu language with timely and
meaningful usage of proverbs, idioms and riddles attracted the
attention of many. He encouraged writing skills in the students by
publishing their articles in the magazine called CHAITANYA VANI.
Thus, he prepared the youth to have a bright future, helping them to
mould to varied situations and best respond to the signs of the time.
The beneficiaries of his service range from various backgrounds who
remain most appreciative and ever grateful.

Another method of communicating the Good News was through
the **Bible Correspondence Course** that has been conducted for many
years sharing the significance of various books of the Bible, especially
the historical and prophetical books. This prompted great interest in
the students to read the Bible, even encouraging the Non-Christian
students to do so. We are privileged and happy to have extended
our collaboration in carrying out this marvellous programme for

many years. He published many small booklets on varied topics viz., religious, cultural, social, Telugu literature, moral stories, prominent personalities, etc. These booklets are extensively used not only by students, but also teachers, catechists, sisters, priests and common people in preparing talks, prayer service and personal reflection.

c.   Contribution to Catechesis

It is a well-known fact that, besides *Samsaya Nivaarana* written by Fr. Singareddy Thomas in 1970 the only resources available on Catechesis were the series of books written by Fr. Jojayya, on Sacraments, Church, Our Lady and other themes of Catechesis (*Gnana Snaanam, Paapocchaaranam, Thirusabha, Puneetha maaatha, Kadagathulu,* and many more). These books were highly appreciated and widely made use for Catechesis in all dioceses of the Telugu States. They are the best resource books for our Catechetical and pastoral apostolate. The publication of Catechism of the Catholic Church in Telugu *Sree Sabha Sathyopadesamu* by the diocese of Warangal is very recent (2005). Fr. Jojayya is invited by Bishops, parish priests and religious congregations of many dioceses to give Biblical and Catechetical Instruction, especially during Advent and lenten seasons. He is a true catechist who catechises the faithful through his writings - articles, magazines, short stories, explanation of Biblical passages etc.

All these initiatives are commendable because, he carried out most of his work through print media and teaching even though did not have access to modern means of communications. Though his methodology may seem old or outdated, his thoughts are innovative, and the fruits produced through hard work and sacrifices are no comparison to what can be done at present with advanced technology. He is ever a student who keeps on learning, a learner to teach. He is contented, serene, peace loving, prayerful, selfless and cheerful.

Part III: Challenges of Mission Today & Creative Ways of doing Mission

The Challenges of Mission today

The challenges of mission today are very complex both at the level of Universal and local Church. Some of the challenges which are enumerated by Pope Francis in Chapter II of EG are worth considering. We recognize the ills of the Church as expressed by Pope Francis in the first months of his pontificate: competitiveness, consumerism, culture of waste, globalization of indifference, violence on the rise, lack of respect for others, economy of exclusion and inequality, individualism, denial of the primacy of the human person, deterioration of cultural values, thirst for power and possessions that knows no limits, weapons that create more serious conflicts than solutions, attacks on religious freedom, increase of relativism, etc., There are also pastoral challenges: clericalism, obsession with appearance, spiritual desertification, marriage viewed as emotional satisfaction than a commitment and responsibility towards family, secularism that proposes a spirituality without God, administrative approach prevailing over pastoral approach, etc., These challenges are a concern as they weaken the renewal in the church and the mission of evangelization.

Challenges of the Telugu Catholic Church

In 2012 the Telugu Catholic church has marked the 300th anniversary of receiving the faith (*Prabhu Yesu Mahostavam*, Mission Congress held at Andhra Loyola College Vijayawada), which was a memorable and historical event, a moment of renewal of faith. Thanks to the untiring efforts and sacrifice of the missionaries who sowed the seeds of faith, proclaimed the Good News, bringing spiritual and social transformation. Following the example of hard work and sacrifice of the foreign missionaries, many local missionaries – Bishops, priests, religious and faithful continue to sow the seed of faith and promote the growth of the local church. No doubt, prominent among them in recent is Fr. Jojayya. His life of simplicity and dedicated service to the Telugu Catholic Church carries a message to commit ourselves seriously for the cause of the Gospel.

We witness an impoverished and divided Church today. In this advanced digital world, adverse divisions based on region, caste, power and position hamper the growth and vitality of the Church. It is here, that the life and mission of Fr. Jojayya becomes an imperative to ask the following questions. Is the church - priests, religious and the people of God, are we passionate to proclaim the Good News? Do we sufficiently spend our time, energy, talents and other resources for the cause of the Gospel? What are our priorities and concerns? Can we justify that our education, healing and social apostolates fulfill the command of Jesus, to bring the Gospel to the ends of the earth - to the *peripheries*? The challenges mentioned above, call for a Church that is courageous, that does not allow itself to be overcome by "sloth" (EG 82) or by the psychology of the tomb, which gradually transforms Christians into museum mummies (EG 83). The call to the Christian communities is to grow in the missionary *dynamism* (EG 81) and face the challenges of mission with boldness and hope-filled commitment, not allowing ourselves to be robbed of missionary vigor (EG 109).

Mission today: Called to be 'missionary disciples'
The term *missionary disciples* is used throughout Evangeli Gaudium (n.120). The two terms are used to hold in tension the need both for a relationship with our Lord and the need to go to the outskirts to preach the Gospel. The approach of the missionary disciple is one of *evangelical discernment*, nourished by the light and strength of the Holy Spirit (EG 51). The Church herself is a *missionary disciple*, needs to grow in the interpretation of the revealed Word and in her understanding of the truth (EG 40). In virtue of our baptism, all the members of the people of God have become missionary disciples (Mt 28:19). In the message of World Mission Sunday of this year 2018,

addressed to the youth, Pope Francis tells the youth, "Every man and woman is a mission; that is the reason for our life on this earth. Each one of us is called to reflect on this fact: "I am a mission on this earth; that is the reason why I am here in this world" (EG 273).

At this juncture we have seen how Fr. Jojayya has been a missionary disciple, through his life and apostolate of teaching and writing. He was deeply convinced that he is commissioned with a mission in the church and dedicated all small and great things in his life for the mission of God, *Missio Dei*. We live in a church where there is declining enthusiasm towards evangelization. "Sometimes we lose our enthusiasm for the mission because we forget that the Gospel responds to our deepest needs, … if we succeed in expressing adequately and with beauty the essential content of the Gospel, truly this message will speak to the deepest yearnings of people's hearts" (EG 265). Mission today is to communicate the joy of the Gospel, born out of a personal encounter with Jesus. (EG 1) "There must be no lessening of the impetus to preach the Gospel" (RMi 34).

Relevant approaches to Mission and Evangelization from the Legacy of Fr. Jojayya S.J.

a.   Holiness of life

The Apostolic Exhortation of Pope Francis *Gaudete et Exsultate* offers a profound reflection on "Call to Holiness" in today's world with practical and simple suggestions from the Scriptures and the writings of the saints. It exhorts us not to be satisfied with mediocre spiritual lives, not to reduce the Gospel, not to despair of our own weakness, not to give up on God and the joy and gladness that he alone can bring into our lives. Mission today is about offering the church the testimony of a holy life. The Pope says his "modest goal" is to "re-propose the call to holiness in a practical way for our own time, with all its risks, challenges and opportunities (GE 2). Fr. Jojayya constantly nurtured the desire for holiness in his priestly life and mission. He was conscious that *he is a mission* in and to the Church, realized it through his life of total renunciation and being at the service of others. He was able to communicate the love of God through a life of holiness mirrored in humility, sacrifice and detachment. He is a missionary above all, because of what he is as a person, *being* rather than a *doing*; His life invites us to confirm our life with the message that, "we are missionaries above all because of what we are as a Church whose innermost life is unity in love, even before we become missionaries in word or deed" (RMi n.23).

b.   Efforts to update literature in Telugu on Scripture and Catechesis

Inculturation of the Gospel has various dimensions and areas. One of the constitutive elements of inculturation is language. A striking example in the history of inculturation often referred to is the "Cyrillo-Methodian" ideology based on the belief that the Christian faith must become incarnated or indigenized. The two Byzantine brothers saints Cyril and Methodius who during their famous mission to 'Great Moravia' were faced with strong opposition in translating Scripture and Liturgy into Slavic language. Indeed, their entire missionary endeavor was based upon the translation of the Bible and the liturgy of the Orthodox Church into a language understood by their converts.[10]

It can be said that Fr. Jojayya played the same role in the history of the Telugu Catholic Church, communicating the Word of God in a style and language that is meaningful for the common people, who found taste in reading the Scripture and other books in a style and language that is appealing to them, evoking deeper spiritual meanings and experience of God. He paid attention to various concerns of the society, church, and politics, etc., and integrated them in his writings and indicated solutions to deal with particular issues in the light of the Word of God and the teachings of the Church. These efforts of inculturation through language and culture need to be continued in providing contextual reflection on the going challenges of evangelization. Encounters of Faith and culture in and through the Word of God provide light and inspiration to the aspirations and longings of the people. This is a pressing need in today's Church.

b.   Innovative initiatives for the Animation of high school students

A lion's share of Fr. Jojayya's life was dedicated to the human, spiritual and moral formation of the young students mostly at the high school level. He knew how to communicate with any age group, young or old. He loved the young students and wanted them to lay a good foundation of spiritual and moral values at young age. He was like a father imparting spiritual wisdom and life skills, encouraging and inspiring them to be attentive listeners and not afraid of offering a loving admonition. He did not sacrifice or mince his words in communicating the truth. He instilled in them the values of courage, confidence, determination, hard work, perseverance, equality, respect, self-discipline, punctuality and time management. In spite of the new development in media and technology that give easy access to information and advanced learning, it cannot be denied that the youth of today need role models and inspiring persons who can accompany them in their spiritual and human formation.

c.   Role of the Laity and training of Catechists

The Second Vatican Council initiated a reflection on the role of the Laity in the Church both in the documents of *Lumen Gentium* and *Gaudium et Spes*. Recalling the teaching of these two documents in his message on the theme 'Vocation and Mission of the Laity' (18th December 2015), Pope Francis underlined the role of the Laity. ... *Lay people are not "second-class members" of the Church but instead are called to participate in the priestly, prophetic and kingly offices of Christ's earthly ministry ... they are "disciples of Christ who, by their baptism" and presence in the world are "called to animate every environment, every activity and every human relationship, according to the spirit of the Gospel," bringing the "light, hope and charity" of Christ to these places that otherwise would not know the "action of God" and would be "abandoned to the poverty of the human condition.*

Deeply convinced of the role of the lay people in the mission of the local church, Fr. Jojayya recognized and encouraged the role of lay people in the evangelizing mission of the local church. He took initiatives to conduct courses on Catechesis and faith formation through training programs. He motivated them to read the Word of God, Commentaries on Bible (*Bible Bhashyam)* and other books on Catechesis so as to prepare themselves well for Catechetical and Pastoral ministry among the simple people in the villages. He worked assiduously to train and promote lay involvement in evangelization. The resources and methods he developed brought new impetus for training and formation of the catechists, that also reignited the same spirit preparing them for evangelisation in the third millennium. The role of the lay person is even more essential as we witness the decrease in priestly and religious vocations. It is the duty of the church to awaken the missionary consciousness among the laity about the obligation to proclaim the Gospel. 'woe to me if I do not preach the Gospel' (I Cor 9:16)

Conclusion

Evangeli Gaudium calls for new and creative models of evangelization, from *the heart of the Gospel to the heart of people, a pastoral ad gentes.* This implies a missionary reform of the Church (EG 25-26), a true conversion, change both in the pastoral care and in the ecclesial structures (25-33). The new model of evangelization means an evaluation of the Ecclesial structures. "There are ecclesial structures which can hamper efforts at evangelization, yet even good structures are only helpful when there is a life constantly driving, sustaining and assessing them. Without new life and an authentic evangelical spirit, without the Church's "fidelity to her own calling", any new structure will soon prove ineffective". (EG 26)

It can't be ruled out that we are comfortable with the institutional church of hierarchical distinctions and our institutions unable to accommodate those most in need, especially the poor and the marginalised in our educational, healing and other ministries.

Evangelisation seems to be a hot potato as it does not fetch fame or popularity in a world that gives priority to achievements and success. It is in this context, legendries like Fr. Jojayya remain a compelling model for evangelisation filled with passion and marked with clear vision, bringing alive the message of Jesus into our evangelising ministry which is the essential mission of the Church. He has made extraordinary contribution to the Telugu Catholic Church for the last 60 years with his selfless service to the people of God. He is a legendary figure in the ministry of evangelization who toiled on this great mission land. One would be hard pressed to find a better model for mission and evangelization. In him we see a seasoned missionary, regardless of the work he was doing he has been firmly anchored by his faith with his simplicity and gentleness.

Having known him closely and collaborated with him for the past fifty years in evangelization, we the Nirmala Sisters wish to continue his legacy in serving the church through a life of holiness and unflagging zeal in proclaiming the Good News. His life of simplicity, readiness to reach out to the common people, utmost dedication in the formation of the local church through various initiatives will be the driving force in living our missionary charism. A congregation, like ours, that is exclusively missionary has a lot to learn from him. His commentaries on every book of the Bible and his infusion of the spirit of universal church have certainly inspired the Catholic Church to move to the peripheries. On this beautiful occasion of remembering his contribution to the Church, we the MSI pledge to carry forward the legacy that he has left. Walking in his footsteps is a great honour. I consider it a great blessing to pen these pages in honour of Fr. Jojayya. Definitely I call this journey a 'missionary pilgrimage' in and through which he sanctified himself and others.

As Fr. Jojayya celebrates his 88th birthday we wish to thank God along with him for the gift of his life and the fruitfulness of his service to God and the Church. May the Lord continue to bless him to be in His service for many more years, and those who had known him and profited by his teaching be enthusiastic in communicating the Word to all, especially those who do not know and are far away from God. The Spirit filled life of Fr. Jojayya resonates in the voice of Pope Francis and calls us to be prophetic Witnesses in building the Kingdom of God:

I prefer a church which is bruised, hurting and dirty because it has been out on the streets, rather than a church which is unhealthy from being confined and from clinging to its own security," he wrote. "I do not want a church concerned with being at the centre and then ends up by being caught up in a web of obsessions and procedures.

Endnotes

[1] Jacob Kavunkal, F.Krangkhuma (Edited) *Bible and Mission in India Today* FOIM series 1, 1993, Mumbai, 40.

[2] Avery Dulles, *Evangelization for the Third Millenium* (Mahwah: Paulist Press, 2009), 1.

[3] Nagothu Showri Kishore S.J., *Jesu Sabha Samaacharam mariyu Saahithya Seva* 2014,63.

[4] *History of Missionary Sisters of the Immaculate in India – Early Decades*, 2011, 9.

[5] Ibid., 23.

[6] *To the Roots of our Spirituality* Missionary Sisters of the Immaculate 2012, 5.

[7] Ibid., 45.

[8] The History of the Missionary Sisters of the Immaculate in India – Early Decades,152-153.

[9] Experiences shared by Sr. Letizia. P, Sr. Angelica Fernandes, Sr. Assunta. P, Sr. Vincent, Sr. Ursula Pinto, Sr. Marcella Giacomello, Sr.Nirmala A, Sr. Nancy D'Souza, Sr. Treasa Joseph, Sr. Cicily.K, Sr. Marina. V and the community of Jangareddigudem, Sr. Piera Mathias, Sr. Benigna Menezes, Sr. Anthonamma.M, Sr. Sundari Nagothu, Sr. Aruna Gujjula, Sr. Lucy Mary.Y, Sr. Mary Rani and Sr. Bindu Abraham.

[10] John Meyendorff, *Christ as Word: Gospel and Culture*, International Review of Mission no. 294 1985, 246.

Two Epochs of Jesuit Contribution to the Literary Life of the Church in Andhra Pradesh/Telengana[1]

P.R. John S.J.

Introduction

The battle of Talikota in A. D. 1565 was an historical landmark in the life of the Andhras. It marked the disintegration of the empire founded by Krishnadevaraya, and end of the literary movements inaugurated by him. From that time till about1850 A. D. was the period of stagnation in Telugu literature. It was during this long dark period that the Italian and French Jesuit missionaries of Madura and Carnatic Missions entered Andhra Desa. They mastered Sanskrit, Tamil and Telugu languages and rendered yeomen service to Telugu literature. They did not confine themselves to preaching gospel but made extraordinary literary and scientific contribution to the early Church in Andhra Pradesh.[2] Fr. Robert De Nobili (1577-1656), the pioneer of inculturation, took his abode at Madura, then the flourishing Nayakar Capital and the seat of the famous Sangham or Academy of the learned Brahmins gathered from different parts of India. There he lived, as a Brahmin Sannyasi, in a little hermitage situated in the very heart of the Brahmin Agraharam, and very soon his profound knowledge in Tamil, Telugu and Sanskrit enabled him to discuss freely with the learned pundits of the Sangham. Fr. J. C. Beschi learnt Telugu language and helped the Christians through his writings to grow in faith.[3] In 1598, 15th October, Fr. Simon de Sa, Rector of the college of St. Thomas Mylapore and Fr. Francis Ricio paid their respects to the emperor of Vijayanagar, Venkata Devaraya II at Chandragiri.[4] Fr. Ricio learnt Telugu language and started a Telugu school. He died in Chandragiri in 1606 and the Jesuits withdrew from Chandragiri in 1613. Eighty years elapsed before Fr. Bouchet, Fr. Pierre Mauduit, De la Fontaine and Petit in 1701 began to explore the southern districts of Andhra with two Brahmin catechists. Dressed like Fr. Robert de Nobili Mauduit carried on the mission entering into Nellore.[5] In the footsteps of these pioneering Jesuits, some about 60 Jesuits worked in Carnatic mission.

In this article, first I shall introduce *Telingana Catholic Library*. Second, I shall highlight the Carnatic Jesuits and their writings during the 17th and 18th centuries. Third, I shall dwell on the Second Coming of the Jesuits in 1953 to Andhra Desa and their contribution to the literary life of the Church and conclude with future orientation.

First Epoch: *Telingana* Catholic Library

This was an important literary treasure brought to my notice by Fr. Gispert-Sauch S.J., Vidyajyoti, College of Theology. I doubt whether even the great church historians Fr. E. R. Hambye, S. J., who wrote *History of Christianity in India* and Fr. Heras, S. J., who wrote *A Short History of the Telugu Christians* were aware of it. Telingana Catholic Library (TCL) was written in 1918 by Fr. H. Hosten, S.J., in the Catholic Directory of India with the title: "First Steps towards our Bibliotheca Catholica Telingana". Fr. H. Hosten, S. J and A. Gangloss MSFS were entrusted with the responsibility of compiling a catalogue of Catholic Telugu books and manuscripts for the use of Clergy and Religious of the Telugu country. While appreciating the great effort of Fr. H. Hosten, on the 17th June 1916, J. Aelan Archbishop of Madras wrote: "I sincerely hope that the Rev. Frs. H. Hosten and A. Gangloss, MSFS will receive every help and assistance in their laudable efforts to compile a catalogue of Catholic Telugu Literature."[6] Both these priests were successful and gathered details about 200 books or booklets. Here, from among the literature mentioned by them I mention few of the printed books either authored by Jesuits or inspired by them during the 17th & 18th centuries.

Printed Books of Jesuits or Associated with Jesuits

1. *Catechism by Jesuit Missionaries* in Badaga (Telugu), Cochin, printed before 1612.

2. *Refutation of Hinduism,* by the same, in Badaga, Cochin, printed before 1612.

3. *Paramandayaguruvula kathalu* – (A translation of the Tamil satairic story *Paramandaguruvin kathai* ascribed to Beschi.) pp 26, Madras, 1861. 8vo. Cf. Catal. of the Telugu books in the British Museum, by L. D. Barnett, London, 1912, p. 23.

4. *Mokshasadhanamu.* Arcot (?), -Later editions 1878, 1889, 1911.

5. *The Anita Nitia Vitiasamu,...* in prose and poetry, an old work, edited by the Rev. Frs. Rajanader and Balanader, Madras, 1881 – The original is said to be by Fr. J. Maynard, S.J, (in India: 1691-+1717). Cf. L. Besse, App, to Catal. Patrum... S.J. in Miss. Madurensi, Trichynopoly. 1913, p. 20.-See No. 102 infra.

6. *Vedanta Rasayanum*, a poem in 4 cantons with Commentary, edited by the Revv. Frs. Balanader and Rajanader, Madras. 1882.

7. *Month of May*, Madras. 1883-The Telugu title says the translation was made by a Sanyasi of the Congregation of Mary Immaculate, Kilacheri (who is he?), from a Tamil work by a Jesuit Father printed at Pulcheri (Pondicherry). which Tamil work? Name of Jesuit Father?

8. *Jesu Sabha sthapakulagu Archyasishta Ijnasivari charitamu adbhutamula sahitamuga,* Nellore. 1891. Translator? Original used?

9. *Hindu desapu Apostulagu Archyasishta Phramsisku Ksavarivari charitramnu...,* Nellore. 1899. Tranlator? Original used?

10. *Tobiya charitramu,* (*Sarveswara Mahatyamu*) a poem, probably old, since it is mentioned in 1840; pp. 37.-Mentioned as in the press (1881); a list of books of 1889 mentions it, or another edn., as costing 2 as.

11. The Catal. raisonne of Oriental MSS. in the Government library, Madras, Vol. 2. p. 800. No. 322 mentions a MS. copy and says it contains 84 padyas by Pingala Yellaya Kavi, in 4 arvasams or brief chapters.

Some MSS. of the Jesuits of the Old Carnatic Mission, sent to the King's Library, Paris

1. Fr. Peter de la Lane. "*Grammaire* pour apprendre la langue Talenga dite vulgairement le Badega, faite a Pontichery l'an 1729 par un missionaire de la Compagnie de Jesus de la Miison francaise du Carnate. a la plus grande glorie de Dieu." –Bibl. nat, Paris; sent in 1729. –MS., pp. 90, 4to, 183x240 mm-No. 40, fonds telinga, ancient fonds No. CCVIII, Catl. of 1739, p. 444.-A copy by Anquetil Du Perron, ibid., No. 18, fonds telinga.

2. Fr. Peter de la Lane.- "Codex chartaceus quo continetur *dictionarium Telonganico,* sen Telanganico-Gallicum, gallice Telongon-Francois, transcriptum anno 1727, in folio." Bibl. du Roi (Nation), paris, No. 206, p. 444 of the Catl. of 1739.-MS. sent in 1730.

    1. *Satya upadesham,* a big catechism.

    2. *Veda Pariksha,* refutation of Hinduism.

    3. *Irouvei Prasangamulu,* 20 discourses on the Christian virtues.-

These three must be by French Jesuit Missionaries of the Carnatic.

Sent also in 1732: *Navya Ratna mala.*-Perhaps pagan; perhaps identical with Fr. Manoel Martins' Gnana Muttu malai (Garland of Spiritual Pearls), printed at Trichinopoly in 1916.

Sent in 1733: A translation of the *Gnana opacham* (jnana upadesam) or Catechism, in Sanskrit, on olas.

Sent in 1734, and 1735: Pounar Jenma Vivecam, or metempsychosis, in Sanskrit. On both occasions the MS. failed to reach the King's Library, Paris. This is a book by Fr. de Nobili existing in several MSS. in the Madura Mission.[7]

Carnatic Jesuits and their Writings during 17th & 18th Centuries

At the service of Telugu Language

Fr. Pierre de la Lane (1669-1746) mastered Telugu so well as to be able to compile a good grammar and a lexicon. He wrote, perhaps in 1729, a Telugu Grammar, and also a Telugu Dictionary entitled Amara Simham. He was probably the author of the Telugu-French dictionary, dated 1727, now in the National Library, Paris.

Fr. Francis Ricci (d. 1604) mastered and taught Telugu language in the school he had founded and also wrote several text books for the use of the students.

Fr. Gargam in 1723 sent a list of Telugu words and explained their connection with other languages. Four years later he demonstrated somewhat elaborately the influence of Sanskrit on Telugu. He even attempted to make a comparison between Telugu, Tamil and Kannada on the one hand and Marathi and Hindustani on the other. He said: "Telugu looks to me as the most beautiful of the three (Dravidian languages) and also the purest, especially towards the north such as at Anantapur, Dharmavaram, Golaconda."[8]

Fr. Jean Calmette (1693-1739), who was outstanding in Sanskrit, sent in September 1730 a Telugu-Sanskrit translation of Christian religious terms and compared them with the existing religious terminology as he found it at Chik Ballapur.[9]

Fr. G.L. Coeurdoux (d. 1779) is the author of a Telugu-Sanskrit-French Dictionary, and of a French-Telugu and Telugu-French Dictionary, with greater emphasis on the colloquial language.

At the Service of Acquiring Four Vedas

Fr. Jean Calmette (1693-1739) came to India in 1726, and spent the whole period of his missionary life in the Telugu country. He died at Ballabaram in 1739. He could both speak and write Sanskrit and Telugu with great fluency. He was the first European scholar to succeed in getting possession of all the four Vedas, whereas Fr. De Nobili had known only three.[10] How he actually acquired them is made known in an unpublished letter of his dated Ballabaram August 25th 1732, now in the Paris National Library. This letter contains so many interesting details, proving the writer's complete mastery of Sanskrit.[11]

About the 4th or Atharva Veda he writes:

This Veda which as all the earlier missionaries in India were want to say, had been thrown by the Brahmins into the sea had in reality been carefully kept out of the common knowledge not alone of foreigners but even of all Indians not belonging to the Brahmin caste. But at last it has now fallen into our hands and the sea has been made to give back its piety. In the Sanskrit dictionary in use among Brahmins wherever there is question of, the Veda, the author admits only three, but almost all other books and poems speak of four, and yet, though there are Brahmins of the Rig Veda others of the Yajur Veda and other is of the Sama Veda nowhere are there to be found any of the Atharva Veda.[12]

The common opinion is that this Veda is but a collection of magical formulae one of which is concerned with the 'Sacrifice of Death' (a ceremony to compass the death of someone), and no one dares profess to be a followers of such a Veda. However, the fragments found in diverse hands, which I have been able to collect to the number of 12 000 Granthams - (each Grantham contains 32 syllables) form one connected whole and this - is not called Atharva Veda, but Mantra Raghassium, which may be translated the secret (treasure) of magical formulae This name is given to it in order that should the book fall into the hands of the uninitiated they may not know what it is.[13]

The first two Vedas were sent to France in 1734, the fourth only in 1738. However, they were all written in Telugu script and gave a

Telugu character to the Sanskrit pronunciation. The reading of them necessitated a scholar in Sanskrit acquainted also with Telugu. In a letter accompanying the dispatch of the 4th Veda, Fr. Calmette says:

> For this discovery of this Veda we needed a man already acquainted with such work, who would know how to piece together the scattered fragments. For in no town or kingdom is it found as a whole. We had to search for it in Mysore, in the territory of the Moors, and other neighboring kingdoms, so that I may well be said to be the only man within a radius of 100 leagues who possesses that Veda in it entirety.[14]

> And from this, passing on to the general difficulty of getting the Brahmins to communicate their religious books, he continues: Their reticence on that point is so strong that even among themselves they will not pass books pertaining to one sect to the Brahmins of another. As an instance, the Brahmin in our service having asked of a Vaishnavite the loan or sale of some volumes of his Vedantha, the latter protested, "Even were you to offer me 100 pagodas for a single sheet do you think I would consider to give it to you?"

After the perusal of such a remarkable letter, especially when we take into consideration the time when it was written, we are entirely at a loss to understand how it came to pass that it did not find a place in the series of 'Letters edifinates et curieuses du Madure Paris,' the more so as inserted, letters that would not be properly understood except by reference to it. In conclusion, and as a final appreciation of' it we shall only say that, besides revealing to us customs and manners of long past such a letter leaves us wondering at the deep and extensive knowledge of Sanskrit possessed by that missionary scholar (Jean Calmette).[15]

At the service of Theological writings
Fr. Francis Ricci (d. 1604) wrote a Telugu Catechism and a "Refutation of the Puranic Cosmology."

Fr. Etienne Le Gac (-+1711) was popularly known as Sanjeevanadha Swamy. Under his patronage, Tobiya charita or Sarvesvara mahatyam was written by Pingali Ellanaryudu. It was the first Catholic prabandham. Ellanaryudu was a Saivite Brahmin and this text was written around 1770. Prabandam is dedicated to Sarvesvara – 'Siva' and this book was written under the patronage of Thumma Rayappa Reddy. He was a grand nephew of Hanumantha Reddy who had long standing relationship with Fr. Le Gac. Rayappa Reddy hailed from Thumma vada or Tubadu and was a well respected person in the community. Sanjeevanadha Swamy handed over the prose text of Tobit to Hanumantha Reddy's first son Obul Reddy and he in turn gave the text to his brother Ananta Reddy's son Rayappa Reddy. He further passed on to poet Ellanaryudu to turn the prose text into prabandam. We could say that it was Sanjeevanadha Swamy was the inspiration in bringing out Tobiya charita prabandam. It was written in four aswas and in prabanda style. Sanjeevanadha Swamy was also responsible in bringing out prabandam on morals known as 'Jnana chintamani'. This was also considered as prabandam and belonged to the same period. It was poetical narrative of the Christianization of the first Catholic of the Gopu Reddi clan of Alamuru. Its author is another poet, Mallala Pullam Raju, who wrote it for another Rayappa, grandson of the first and lord of Siripuram in Kondavidu.[16]

Fr. Jean Calmette (1693-1739) translated the famous work of Fr. De Nobili, 'Satya Veda Sara Sangraham' into Telugu language. In 1735 he gave a text of the gospel of St. John to the palayakar of Kottakotta.[17] *Vedantarasayanam* (The essence of a True Religion - Jesus Christ, the Way to True Religion) was the first Christological epic-poem (prabandam) in Telugu literature. The popular belief was that Fr. Jean Calmette inspired Mangalagiri Anandakya Kavi, a Telugu Niyogi Brahmin to write this monumental work. There existed a lot of ambiguity as to when and by whom this kavya was written. Doubts were put to rest by Fr. Hosten in his research:

> From a note by Fr. L. Besse, S.J.: "the Catalogue raisonne of Oriental MSS, in the Government Library, Madras, by the Rev. W. Taylor, vol. 3. p. 171, No. 553 says it was composed by Anandabhi, son of Timmaya from Mandalagiri, belonging to the Atresa gotra (family), at the request of his patron, named Dasu. This Anandabhi of Ananda Rao, was a Christian Brahman, who was in the employ of Messrs. Crau

and Desgranges of Vizagapatnam." This is more precise than the note our editors, viz., that it dates from about A. D. 1700, and it makes me doubt the statement of Fr. Kroot (Hist. of the Telugu Christians, p.308) that Fr. Calmette, who died in 1740, might be the Satyabodha Swamulavaru of the Vedanta Rasayanum. When were Messrs. Crau and Desgranges at Vizag? Timmaya or Leo, the old Dasari of whom Fr. Calmette speaks in his letter of Venkatagiri, 24 January 1733, was probably Ananda's father, Cf. Kroot, op. cit., pp. 226-231.

The Structure of the Poetic Story is this: the poetic-story begins with invocation of 'Sri Sarveswaraya Namah': "I pray to Him, who resides in the hearts of good people, who is imperishable, who cannot be described by word or thought, who is without rival, who is eternal, who takes away the sins of his devotees, who is the purest light, that He may help me to bring this poem to completion".[18] Then, the poet describes the ancestor of Nidimamilla Dasaya, who had asked him to write this poem and to whom it was dedicated.

Canto 1: Parvataya, a Brahmin goes to see another Brahman called Gnanappa who asked which God one had to honour to obtain heaven (1-5). As an answer, Parvataya tells him the following story: There once lived in the town of Chik-Balapur a famous king, called Havati Baiche and a priest named Gnanabodha. (25). One day there arose in the king's council a dispute about an eclipse of the moon. Mallarasu, a very wise Brahman, said there would be no eclipse, but as the dispute could not be settled, it was resolved to ask the priest, Gnanabodha. He too, declared there would be no eclipse (25-37). Mallarasu admired the wisdom of the priest and went to see him often. One day the priest asked him: You know all about the Vedams: which then is the true God (38-41). Mallarasu explains the Hindu teaching and Gnanabodha explains that there is only one God (42-83). Mallarasu asks how he can know the true God and the priest explains the six attributes of God (84-135), and narrates the creation of angels and devils (137-158).

Canto II: Gnanabodha tells the creation of Adam and Eve, the temptation and their fall (1-40) the promise of the Redeemer to

Abraham (66) the history of Zacharias, Annunciation, and birth of St. John (108) birth of Christ up to the finding in the temple (209). **Canto III:** The preaching of St. John, fast and temptation of Christ, His Baptism, explanation of the Holy Trinity, election of the Apostles (1-88), the cure of the blind at Jericho (109), Lazarus, entry into Jerusalem (169), the last supper, the agony (226), Christ before Caiphas and Pilate (258). **Canto IV:** Jesus is nailed to the cross and dies, is buried (88), difference between limbo, hell and purgatory (95) the resurrection and apparitions, ascension, descent of the Holy Ghost (193), assumption of the Blessed Virgin (194), St. Peter, head of the Church (204), last judgment and metempsychosis (214), the ten commandments (227), Baptism, Holy Mass and Holy Eucharist (250). When Mallarasu had heard all this, he asked Gnanabodha to baptize him. The Brahmin Parvataya having finished his story takes leave of Gnanappa.[19]

Anandakya Kavi was concerned with salvific history. According to him, Salvation consisted in entering into a right religion. The way to true religion, was to experience Christ. The Church was a tangible historical body, which facilitated salvation. The gods, goddesses were human made and would not grant salvation. Throughout the *Kavya*, he maintained the humans were under sin and needed Christ to save them. He brought out the sinful nature of human beings from Adam's sin. According to him, humans were slaves of Satan, the tormenter, who kept them from acting freely. Satan impeded the human realization of freedom which God had intended. Therefore, the main work of Christ was to strive for victory against the power that held us in subjugation (Satan). Christ achieved it by pouring out his blood on the cross. In this way, Jesus Christ brought the salvation. Hence, for him, Christ is the way to true religion and it is realized by partaking in the sacraments of Baptism and Holy Eucharist.

Kandukuri Viresalingam, the Father of Andhra Renaissance, judges the poet of Vedantarasayanam to be a writer of very high eminence, worthy to be placed among the best poets of his century.

The author approaches the subject in a devotional frame of mind and gives a clear and succinct account of the life of Christ. The teachings of Jesus are not much referred to. Of the miracles, a few prominent ones are chosen- the raising of Lazarus, the cure of the blind. The Nativity stories and the events of Passion Week are narrated in detail. In the prelude, there is a disquisition on the attributes of God and in the epilogue a discourse on the means of grace. The author shows intimate acquaintance with the scriptures and the rites of the Christian Church. The kavya is remarkable as the solitary instance in which a Hindu bhakta, saturated with the thought-forms of his own country, has reverently undertaken to proclaim the life of Christ to the world.

The nature of the theme and the necessity of conveying a correct impression of the life of the foreign Guru brings out the best in the author. In handling thought-forms evidently not familiar to the Hindu mind, he shows considerable ability. For example, the phrase 'The lamb that takes away the sin' is translated without the figure, as Kalmasha Paritrana (Remover of Sins). Throughout, his writings, we come across touches of fervent Eastern imagination. 'The Holy One,' he says, 'yielding up his spirit, let fall the head on his breast, as the friend of the lotus drops behind the hill of the evening'. In one respect the book stands out as a class apart. The language is chaste and the imagery chastened. The exuberance of fancy, excess of alliteration and complexity of structure, characteristic of kavya, are all rigorously excluded. We feel in this book the earnestness of the bhakta approaching a subject too precious to indulge in the arts of mere rhetoric.[20]

At the Service of Spiritual (prayer) writings
Anitia nitia vyatyasam or the difference between the temporal and the eternal was regarded as one of the four Catholic prabandams. It was written in prose and poetry, by a Vaidika Brahmin, Samantapudi Mallyayya by name, for the catechist Marianna working in Kondavidu. The work is dedicated to a Neopolitan Jesuit Fr. Georgio Manente, and therefore belongs to the last two decades of the 18th century.[21]

Fr. Georgio Manente was a charismatic leader who led in 1787 the exodus of a large number of Christians from Oleru to the Chengelpet district and established the great Kilachery mission.[21] The Telugu Catholics, especially at Kilachery, Pannur etc. revered two writings: a history of the Old Testament, called *Purva Vedam, Rajula Charitra Amrutam Bhavam*, and the life of Christ. It is claimed by tradition that they contained the teaching of Fr. Etienne Le Gac.[23]

The *Vedanta Saramu* is of a higher order of writing. The title means 'essence of theology'. Two works called *Veda pariksha* (refutation of Hinduism) and *Satya Upadesha* (catechism), although published much later under the combined title of *Moksha Margamu* (way to heaven), go back to about 1754. The copy of *Satya Upadesha*, kept at the Paris National Library, is dated 1729. The old cook boy of the Oleru missionary seems to have brought from there a manuscript book titled *Moksha margam* or the Way to Heaven, written on thick paper, kept by his descendents as a precious heirloom. On the last page of the book it is written: "this book was written at Oleru in 1746 when Fr. Gnanaprakasam was in charge." This might possibly have been the missionary who led the Kammas from Gandikota to Oleru. He was a French man named Fr. Cordey, Gnanaprakasam being his Indian name. He died in 1755.[24] To the homiletic genre belongs the Iruvai Prasangamulu, a collection of twenty sermons by an unknown author.[25]

Popular poems on the life Christ, on that of his Mother Mary, religious dramas, recitals, all in verse, were often used by those early Telugu Catholics. Nanya dasham depicts as examples the lives of three saints: Tecla, Cecilia and Agatha. Gnana Muthiyala Mallika, or Collar of Pearls, is the Telugu adaptation of a Tamil work by Fr. Emmanuel Martins who worked in Madurai and died in 1656. There is also a collection of short poems by Polavarapu Rayanna of Ravipadu. In the National Library, Paris is preserved a manuscript entitled Gnana Kavita.[26]

Fr. L. Bazou commenting on the Christian writings mentioned above says:

> It can be said that all those works and many more that were once popular, are now either lost or forgotten. Written in the simple style of everyday life in the village, they did help to preserve the Catholic spirit of the people. Typically Telugu in their inspiration and background, they were such as could be understood and enjoyed even by the ignorant; they brought the teachings of the Christian faith to the level and comprehension of all. In the Marriage of Samson, for example, the Bible story is narrated in a genuine Telugu village setting. Here are other poems that deal with the village worthies such as the karnam, the priest, and other local officials. Each of them renders the local colour in a masterly manner.[27]

Other books written during carnatic mission: *Satya veda sara sangrahamu, Atma nirnayam, Ajnatavasa dhyanalu, Vedantasaram, Nistara ratnakaram purva vedam, Suvishshapu bata, Veda pariksha, Divyavatara padyalu, Kanyadasam.*

Second Epoch - Coming of the Jesuits to Andhra Pradesh in 1953
Bishop Mummadi Ignatius made a request to the then Superior General of the Society of Jesus Rev. Fr. Jansens to send Jesuits to Andhra. In 1953 the Jesuits from Madurai Province came to Andhra Pradesh and began Andhra Loyola College. Then onwards the Jesuits moved into many apostolates and literary apostolate always found a place. Fr. Jojayya Pudota (1931 -) has been a silent and hard worker in the vineyard of Jesus Christ. He is a creative pen in the hand of God for the past 45 years. It is not an exaggeration if I were to say that most of the Catholics in Andhra either heard the name of Fr. Jojayya or read his writings. He had a command over Telugu language and he could express his thoughts in a poetic manner. He initiated the reading culture in the catholic community and in particular among the pastors, nuns and catechists who carry the evangelization work in interior villages.

Telugu Catholic Bible

His outstanding work was Catholic translation of the Old Testament into Telugu. In 1904 one Fr. Rolla of Nadigama wrote a complaint to Examiner (p. 1001), stating that he could not find any Telugu Catholic Bible.[28] In Kilachery mission Christians were using three big volumes, edited by Frs. J. E. Balanader and T.J.Rajanader, 2 on the O. T and 1 on the N.T. However, the truth was there was no Telugu Catholic Bible in single volume. Recognizing the need of the faithful, Andhra Pradesh Bishops Council entrusted the herculean task of writing a Telugu Catholic Bible to Fr. Jojayya. Singlehandedly, with utmost devotion, sincerity and sacrifice he slogged for about seventeen years to complete this monumental work. Today, one can find Telugu Catholic Bible in Catholic families and parishes. I am sure that generations of Telugu readers will appreciate the chaste and poetic Telugu that emanated from this deeply spiritual person.

Other Writings of Fr. Jojayya

Fr. Jojayya published pamphlets, booklets and the magazines Chaitanya Vani, Bible Bashyam as a guide to the students, teachers and catechists. The purpose was to disseminate the Biblical knowledge and Christian faith to the Christian faithful. He brought out booklets on various themes in Christian theology: liturgy, sacraments, social/moral teachings, Christology, patristics. Late Fr. Thanam Marreddy compiled the works of Fr. Jojayya under ten volumes:

1. Bible Parichayam	2. Bible Bodhanalu
3. Bible Vakyamrutham	4. Prarthana,
5. Thandri-Christu	6. Kristu Jivita Paramartham
7. Pavitratma	8. Divya Satprasadam-Jnanasnanam
9. Jnanavivaham-Tirusabha	10. Devamata-Antyagatulu

In preface to these volumes writes Bishop Mallavarapu Prakash: "Fr. Jojayya is a well known priest in the Church of Andhra Pradesh through his writings. His hard work, service, the desire to write in chaste Telugu is praise worthy. Fr. Jojayya is a big blessing to those who are interested in Catholic Church, Bible and its doctrines. His relentless search for truth and the desire to disseminate the knowledge helped the church in Andhra Pradesh to forge ahead."

Future Orientation

1. Much of the early Jesuit missionaries success was due to their sympathy with the people for whom they worked, their knowledge of the people's language, religion, philosophy, customs, manner and prejudices. They even went so far to adopt native dress and social habits.

2. The legacy left behind by the Jesuits of Carnatic mission unleashed the wave of Christian publication in the form of books, dramas, burra-kathas and yakshaganas.

3. The rich Telugu Christian theological vocabulary is drawn from the two traditions: Tobiya charitra (Sarveswaramahatyam) emerging from a Saivite tradition and Vedantarasayaman emerging from Vaishnavite tradition.

4. On the foundations of Carnatic Mission, later Telugu Christians adopted literary methods, available from *bhakti* movement, to express their devotion and attachment to Jesus Christ. As a result, there emerged immense Christian prose and poetry, which brought richness to the Telugu culture and literature. The poets and hymn writers beckon us for new images of Jesus. An "image" of Jesus Christ implies more than a Christological statement. An image functions like a complex symbol that fuses together intellectual understandings, emotional responses, and relational styles. The reality of Jesus Christ expressed is not merely at the conceptual level but more at the relational level.

5. We find close resonance with Ignatius of Loyola, who speaks of "Contemplation to Obtain Love" and "All for the greater glory

of God". I am sure that this patrimony is given to the Church in Andhra by the hard work of evangelization by the Carnatic Jesuits.

6. The images like Jesus, the *Sadguru* and Jesus, the *dalit*, are attempts to articulate the experience of Telugu peoples in Telugu language.

7. Fr. Jojayya Pudota in his article on "Dalita Christu" shows us how the present church in Telugu states must integrate sub-altern tradition along with Saivite and Vaishnavite traditions.

8. Hence, there is a need on the part of church in Telugu states (bishops, religious, priests) to invest its personnel and resources for to create a vibrant Telugu Christian literature in the modern world. The early missionaries engagement with the poets and writers beckons the present church to pay due attention to lay Christian poets and writers and even patronising them.

Conclusion

The church that has no regard or appreciation for its history is like a directionless ship. This can be applied to most of our Catholics, clergy and religious with regard to their sources of 'Faith History'. We the Catholics should know how catholic faith came into our region, at what cost and pain our ancestors accepted to live by it and who were the Missionaries who made it possible for us to inherit this faith. *Lumen Fidei*, the first encyclical of Francis' papacy says: "In God's gift of faith, a supernatural infused virtue, we realize that a great love has been offered us, a good word has been spoken to us, and that when we welcome that word, Jesus Christ the Word made flesh, the Holy Spirit transforms us, lights up our way to the future and enables us joyfully to advance along that way on wings of hope" (n.7). "The life of the believer becomes an ecclesial existence, a life lived in the Church... Christians are 'one' (cf. *Gal* 3:28), yet in a way which does not make them lose their individuality; in service to others, they come into their own in the highest degree" (n. 22). The thought of Christians are one is a shared memory which contains a promise and that shared memory begins with baptism. The Church has to be at the service of humanity's kinship. That is why the early Christians addressed each other as brothers and sisters. "...They called the church together and reported what God has done with them and how he had opened the door of faith..." (14:27). I conclude with the visionary words of Fr. Jojayya Pudota: "We have to create catholic literature. Catholic theology has to be disseminated in a scientific way through theological journal. We must overcome our socio-economic problems through the principles of social teachings of the Catholic Church. Christian music, painting and art forms have to be nurtured. For such ventures, we need to depend on our personnel and resources instead on foreigners and foreign resources."[29]

Endnotes

[1] This was a paper presented at the Bicentenary celebrations of the Restoration of the Society of Jesus in Hyderabad on 21st September, 2013.

[2] E. R. Hambye, *History of Christianity in India, Vol III* (Bangalore: The Church History Association, 1997), 336.

[3] H. Hosten, *Menology of The Indian Missions Part I, Jesuit Missionaries in India* (1542-1800), 328.

[4] A. Kroot, *History of the Telugu Christians*, (Trichy: St. Joseph's Printing Press, 1909), 25. Cf. P. Jojayya, *Jesusabha-Samacharam*, (Vijayawada: Andhra Loyola College Publication, 1965), 14.

[5] D. Gordon, "Our Roots: The Carnatic Mission," in *Andhra Jesuits*, (Belgium: 1991), 2.

[6] H. Hosten, "First Steps towards our Bibliotheca Catholica Telingana," in *Catholic Directory of India*, 1918/1., 23.

[7] Ibid., 41-42.

[8] E. R. Hambye, *History of Christianity in India, Vol III*, 336.

[9] Ibid.

[10] Stephen Neill, *A History of Christianity in India 1707-1858* (New York: CUPress, 2002), 92.

[11] J. Castets, "Pioneers in European Sanskrit Scholarship," (further details not available).

[12] Ibid.

[13] Ibid.

[14] Ibid.

[15] Ibid.

[16] E. R. Hambye, *History of Christianity in India, Vol III*, 339.

[17] Ibid., 337.

[18] Mangalagiri Anandakya Kavi, *Vedantarasayanam: A Poem in Four Cantons* (Nellore: St. John's Press, 1969), Stanza., 6.

[19] Cf. M. Anandakya kavi, *Vedantarasayanam: A Poem in Four Cantos* (Nellore: St. John's Press, 1969), 15.

[20] http://archive.org/stream/historyoftelugu l00chenuoft/historyoftelugul00chenuoft_djvu.txt

[21] E. R. Hambye, *History of Christianity in India, Vol III*, 338.

[22] R. C. Paul, *History of the Telugu Christians* (Madras: Good Pastor Press, 1929), 35.

[23] E. R. Hambye, *History of Christianity in India, Vol III*, 338.

[24] H. Heras, "Jesuits of Old Days in Andhra Desa," (published in June 1955).

[25] E. R. Hambye, *History of Christianity in India, Vol III*, 339.

[26] Ibid., 340.

[27] As cited in E. R. Hambye, *History of Christianity in India, Vol III*, 340.

[28] H. Hosten, "First Steps towards our Bibliotheca Catholica Telingana," in *Catholic Directory of India*, 1918/1., 19.

[29] P. Jojayya, *Jesusabha-Samacharam*, (Vijayawada: Andhra Loyola College Publication, 1965), 17.

Joy... Jesus... Jojayya

Valan C. Antony S.J.

Introduction

Neither have I seen nor heard him, but what I heard *about* him drew me closer to this prodigious phenomenon-priest called Jojayya Pudota. "...[B]e not afraid of greatness: some are born great, some achieve greatness, and some have greatness thrust upon 'em," says Malvolio, the pompous steward of Olivia's household, in Shakespeare's *Twelfth Night* (Act II, Scene V). Acclaimed and applauded as a scholar, writer, veteran, teacher, counselor, pastor, and translator, Fr. Jojayya would fit into the third category ("some have greatness thrust upon 'em"). Generations of Andhra Jesuit Province scholastics whom I have taught here in *Vidyajyoti* have shared with me about Fr. Jojayya, his towering personality, his love for God and the Word of God and his zeal for proclaiming both in words and deeds his Master, Jesus who fills his life with *joy* that is deeply divine. His love of the Society, his deep pastoral sense, strong commitment to social justice, and a special love for the poor are all archetypally exemplary. The more I got to know about Jojayya Pudota, the more do I discover the striking semblance he has with Paul, the Apostle: his love for God, Christ Jesus and his Church, his missionary zeal, indomitable courage, and robust optimism that one finds in *Philippians*.

Philippians is a very personal letter.[1] Among other themes, Paul's attitude to suffering and how he is able to rejoice under trying circumstances are remarkably impressive. That joy is a dominant motif in the letter might be challenged but, as a recurring motif, can scarcely be ignored since a note of joy rings throughout the letter.[2] What is it that lies at the heart of Pauline serene disposition that makes it essentially an epistle of joy? This study shall show how it all depends on Pauline optic, his way of *thinking* and viewing life from the point of view of his knowledge and intimacy with Christ.

Context of the Letter

Philippians is one of the captivity epistles of Paul. During his imprisonment in Rome, Paul is not reduced to total inactivity. Acts 28:30 tells us that he has his own lodgings, and friends and coworkers are permitted to visit him. He is, for example, visited by Epaphras and Onesimus from Colossae, and served by Epaphroditus from Philippi. Probably, from Epaphroditus, Paul would have learnt that "the Philippians are in a life-and-death struggle for the gospel in Philippi, and if their present unrest goes uncorrected, it could bid fair to blunt, if not destroy, their witness to Christ in their city."[3] In prison, uncertain whether he would be befriended or beheaded by Caesar, Paul could have been whining, instead he is exhorting his addressees "to rejoice in the Lord," on all occasions (*pantote*) irrespective of circumstances, trials and burdens. He sends a letter in which he updates his beloved Philippians with news about himself, his trial, and also about some of the troubling issues that divide the congregation in Philippi. He encourages them to "rejoice in the Lord" (4:4-6) and stand firm in faith despite persecution and warns them to be on constant guard against threats posed by Judaizers.

Joy, the Refrain of the Letter

Of the 326 occurrences of words for joy in the NT, 131 are found in the 'authentic' letters of Paul (i.e., nearly forty percent).[4] A consistent emphasis (16x) on "joy" (*khara*) and "rejoicing" occurs in this letter (1:4, 18[2x], 25; 2:1, 2, 17[2x], 18[2x], 28, 29; 3:1; 4:1, 4[2x], 10). It almost acts as a refrain in a hymn, making the letter essentially an epistle of joy by the theologian of joy.[5] The verb *khairein* in classical Greek, J. Reumann observes, was a greeting and "in the philosophers an object of reflection…; in Stoics, negatively as an affection, positively as a "good mood" of the soul, for the wise, the *telos* (goal or supreme good) in life…; In hellenistic religious texts, festal joy."[6] But to Paul, joy comes with the gospel through the Spirit and is connected with hope. Thus, joy, in this brief letter, is more than a keynote. The table below recounts the occurrences of joy (noun - *khara*) / rejoice (verb *khairō*) in *Philippians*.

References to joy/rejoicing in Philippians		
Noun **khara**	1:4	….constantly praying with *joy* in every one of my prayers for all of you.
	1:25	….I will remain and continue with all of you for your progress and *joy* in faith.
	2:2	….make my *joy* complete: be of the same mind…..in full accord and of one mind.
	2:29	Welcome him then in the Lord with all *joy*…
	4:1	my *joy* and crown, stand firm in the Lord in this way, my beloved.
Verb **khairō**	1:18 (2x)	What does it matter? Just this, that Christ is proclaimed in every way, whether out of false motives or true; and in that I *rejoice*. Yes, and I will continue to *rejoice*…
	2:17(2x)	But even if I am being poured out as a libation over the sacrifice and the offering of your faith, I am **glad** and *rejoice* with all of you-
	2:18(2x)	and in the same way you also must be **glad** and *rejoice* with me
	2:28	I am the more eager to send him, therefore, in order that you may *rejoice* at seeing him again…
	3:1	Finally, my brothers an d sisters, *rejoice* in the Lord.
	4:4(2x)	Rejoice in the Lord always; again, I will say, **Rejoice**.
	4:10	I *rejoice* in the Lord greatly that now at last you have revived your concern for me.

The gospel of Christ and the community "in Christ" motivate Paul's outbursts of joy: he is joyful when he prays for the community (1:4); his joy increases at their progress in faith (1:25); he is joyful at the advancement of the gospel (1:18), at the price of his own life (2:17); he urges the community to make his joy complete by being like-minded and of one mind (2:2); he tells them to welcome back Epaphroditus with all joy (2:29); in 3:1 "rejoicing" acts as a safeguard against the Judaizers, who enforce the mosaic law upon the new converts; he commands them to rejoice (4:4); and finally he rejoices over the gift the community has sent him (4:10).

It must, however, be pointed out that on the one hand Paul says that joyful disposition cannot be affected by external circumstances like imprisonment or the possible violent death (1:18; 2:17), on the other hand, it appears that joy *can* be affected by the externals: if the Philippians "stand firm in the Lord" (4:1); at Epaphroditus' recovery (2:28, 29) etc. Now, how does Paul reconcile these apparent contradictory affirmations? It is here that we come to the heart of Pauline secret for his rejoicing-disposition.

The secret lies, for Paul, in the mind-set, attitude, optic or perspective characterized by "peace," a disposition that viewed life with all of its ups and downs with equanimity.[7] It is a confident way of looking at life that is rooted in faith, in who God is and what he has done through the person and the redeeming work of Jesus Christ. Joy for Paul, in other words, is more than a mood or an emotion. It is a decision and a deliberation. Such joy is possible because it is based upon *how one thinks* (Phil 2:6-11). After all what goes on in one's mind, affects how one feels. The 'lost archangel' in Milton's *Paradise Lost* seems to be aware of that. Thrown out of heaven, he proclaims:

... hail, horrors; hail,
Infernal world, and thou, profoundest hell,
Receive thy new possessor; one who brings
A mind not to be changed by place or time.

The mind in its own place, and in itself
Can make heaven of hell, a hell of heaven. (Book I)

The key revelation in *Philippians* is the mind-set/optic, or attitude. In this context, the verb *phronein* is an important word in Pauline diction. It includes the notion of thinking, "to form or hold an opinion" about someone or something, "to set one's mind on, to be intent on something," and "cannot simply mean that Paul here pleads for drab uniformity of thought or that he insists on everyone holding in common a particular opinion—a demand that by its very nature would contribute to dissension,"[8] but "a total inward attitude of mind or disposition, that strives after that one thing."[9] Of the 23 occurrences in Paul's letters, 10 are found in *Philippians*: (1:7; 2:2 [2x], 5; 3:15 [2x], 19; 4:2, 10 [2x]):

phronein in Philippians	
1:7	It is right for me to think this way about all of you, because you hold me in your heart, for all of you share in God's grace with me, both in my imprisonment and in the defense and confirmation of the gospel.
2:2 (2x)	make my joy complete: be of the same mind, having the same love, being in full accord and of one mind.
2:5[10]	Let the same mind be in you that was in Christ Jesus.
3:15(2x)	Let those of us then who are mature be of the same mind; and if you think differently about anything, this too God will reveal to you.
3:19	Their end is destruction; their god is the belly; and their glory is in their shame; their minds are set on earthly things.
4:2	I urge Euodia and I urge Syntyche to be of the same mind in the Lord.
4:10 (2x)	I rejoice in the Lord greatly that now at last you have revived your concern for me; indeed, you were concerned for me, but had no opportunity to show it.

Such a consistent recurrence simply goes on to prove how important it is, for Paul, to view and think with the right mind-set: the same mind that is "in Christ Jesus" (*en Christō Iēsou,* 2:5). The Philippian hymn (2:5-11) highlights how Jesus was not attached to his status: [11] "though he was in the form of God, did not regard equality with God as something to be exploited (2:6)." On the contrary, he 'humiliated' himself "taking the form of a slave," and was "obedient to the point of death-- even death on a cross." It is interesting, at this juncture to note also how closely Luke resembles Paul when the former, in the words of D. Balch, "announces crucial aspects of God's character in the Magnificat (Lk 1:46-55). A distinctive cluster of terms signals God's acts: humility (*tapeinosis,* 1:48), slave woman (1:48), proud (*uperephanous*), powerful (1:51-52), exalt the humble (*hupsosen tapeinous,* 1:52), rich (1:53)."[12] Such is the attitude or mindset that Paul exhorts the Philippians to embrace, to have "the same mind in the Lord (2:2, 5; 4:2)": a disposition that marks self-emptying, and altruism. In other words, the 'thinking' that Paul alludes to involves social relationships and is defined by humiliation (modeled on the *encomium* to Christ) and love: "having the same love" (*tēn autēn agapēn ekhontes* cf. Phil 2:2). This is what Christ did (humiliated himself and showed his love), unlike Coriolanus (of Roman antiquity) who refused to do; something the Romans knew to be ideal and necessary. It is this mindset after which the Philippians are to pattern their relationships, and this will enable one "to rejoice in the Lord."

Joy: a defiant 'nevertheless'?

Joy can be stifled and muffled surely and effectively by triviality, routine and extreme suffering. In fact, Paul has travelled his *via dolorosa* (Rom 8:18; also, Col 1:24; 2 Cor 11:22-33). But for him, joy does not mean the absence of sorrow but the ability to rejoice in the midst / in spite of it. Philippians were discouraged because of Paul's imprisonment, the possibility of his death, Epaphroditus' illness, the attacks from legalists (Judaizers), the "heretical libertinists with gnostic tendencies,"[13] and friction among certain female members of the church. To counteract this predicament, Paul prescribes rejoicing "in the Lord."

Joy, according to Paul, is a quality, and not simply an emotion, of which God is both the object and the giver. Is Paul just being naively optimistic? Is he inviting the believers to see a bright 'rainbow' in the midst of negativities and opposition? Not so. The appeal to joy is made with the realization that a believer's faith is "in the Lord," the "governing factor in the exhortation,"[14] especially when one is faced with situations marked by difficulties. In Paul's case, to quote Barth, it "is a defiant 'nevertheless.'"[15] This explains why he exhorts the Philippians "to rejoice in the Lord," not in themselves as recipients but in him as source.[16]

Paul invites the Philippians to see God in a different way. It is God, not merely God's blessings, for which one gives thanks; a radical change from being thankful *for* to simply *being thankful*. It is about changing the object of gratitude from God's blessing to God's very character, nature and promise (as revealed in the *encomium* to Christ). Such an understanding of joy in Indian thinking is often translated as *ānanda*, "the self full of bliss." G. Gispert-Sauch notes:

> A metaphorical poem about the tree as a symbol of a human being at the end of chapter 3 of the Brhadāranyaka Upanisad, probably composed about the time of the early Israelite prophets, concludes with the proclamation that the human being is rooted in Brahman itself, who is "Grace for the giver, the Goal of those who stand firm, knowing It." Here this Brahman is defined as "consciousness and bliss": *vij nānam ānandam brahma!* The theme of bliss as the essence [of] Brahman appears often in the Upanishads.[17]

Though the possibility that suffering can produce joy is anticipated in the Old Testament, Pauline call to rejoice in adversity is distinctive in being affected through the suffering and vindication of Jesus himself (2:5-11). It is no mere gaiety or jollity that knows no gloom but is the result of the victory of faith that enables us to experience God even in adverse circumstances. This "joy" in Paul's thought is his *"ground for boasting or glorying"* (*kaukhēma*). The emphasis is *not on the action itself*, but on the basis for it (1:26).

Conclusion

In prison, Paul is not pining and pouting, but rather penning words of encouragement and asking the Philippians "to rejoice in the Lord." This rejoicing is more than a key note; it is the axis around which the letter revolves. It is the secret of Pauline outbursts and is the result of an attitude, or perspective that views life in faith. Therefore, it is more than a mere emotion but a willful decision that strives after one quest, to be like Christ Jesus. In short, Pauline invitation is to see God differently: seeing not just *what* God has done but *who* God is and rejoicing in him. Jojayya does precisely this in his word and deed so graciously and gracefully.

Endnotes

[1] That Philippians was written when Paul was in prison in Rome and that the letter is a composite one is assumed in this paper. See G. F. Hawthorne, *Philippians*, WBC (Waco: Word Books, 1983), 12-15.

[2] Cf. J. J. Muller, *The Epistles of Paul to the Philippians and to Philemon* (Grand Rapids: Eerdmans, 1955), 21.

[3] G. P. Fee, *Paul's Letter to the Philippians*. The New International Commentary on the New Testament (Grand Rapids: Eerdmans, 1995), 32.

[4] W. G. Morrice, "Joy," in *Dictionary of Paul and His Letters*, ed. G. F. Hawthorne, R. P. Martin, D. G. Reid (England: Inter-Varsity Press, 1993), 511-512.

[5] W. G. Morrice, *Joy in the New Testament* (Exeter: Paternoster Press, 1984), 113-116.

[6] J. Reumann, *Philippians: A New Translation* (New Haven, Conn: Yale University Press, 2008), 105.

[7] G. F. Hawthorne, *Philippians*, 18.

[8] G. F. Hawthorne, *Philippians*, 67.

[9] Ibid., 67-8.

[10] That Phil 2:5 is defined by Phil 2:6-11 is something to be taken note of.

[11] J. Reumann, 635.

[12] D. Balch, "Accepting Others: God's Boundary Crossing According to Isaiah and Luke-Acts," *Currents in Theology and Mission* 36:6 (December 2009): 422.

[13] R. Jewett, "Conflicting Movements in the Early Church as reflected in Philippians," *NovT* 12 (1970): 362-390.

[14] R. P. Martin, *Philippians*, NCB (London: Oliphants, 1976), 154.

[15] K. Barth, *The Epistle to the Philippians*, trans. J. W. Leitch (Richmond, VA: John Knox Press, 1962), 120.

[16] Peter T. O'Brien, *The Epistle to the Philippians*, *NIGTC* (Grand Rapids: Eerdmans, 1991), 485.

[17] George Gispert-Sauch (ed.), *Gems From India* (Delhi: ISPCK/VIEWS, 2006), 44.

Challenges in being at the Service of Jesus Christ and his Church:

Acts of the Apostles, an answer to today's challenges

Gorantla Johannes OCD

Introduction

The Gospel of Luke and the Acts of the Apostles is a unified literary work that describes a single large story in two volumes. It is agreed beyond doubt that both these volumes were written by the same author called Luke, of whom St. Paul speaks in his letters (Col 4:14; 2 Tim 4:11; Phm 1:24). Both the volumes are loaded with clues about the character, circumstances, purpose, and thought patterns of the writer.[1] The narrative unity of these two works is manifested in its unfolding of a single dominant purpose, of one theological project. The single dominant purpose is at work both in the ministry of Jesus and in the ministries of Jesus' witnesses. John the Baptist, Jesus, the Apostles, all share in the same purpose of God found in Lk 3:6 - *that every flesh shall see the salvation of God*. All the individual episodes in both the works serve to the realization of this purpose. The two volumes are to be read in sequence as the same theological project binds both the works.

Narrative unity of Luke – Acts: God's Purpose

Jesus, the central character of Luke's Gospel has a mission, which he must fulfill. In Lk 4:18-19 Jesus himself reveals the purpose of this mission. His mission consists of preaching Good News (Prophet), proclaiming liberty to the captives, sight to the blind, freedom for the oppressed (King), and finally proclaiming the Lord's year of mercy, building the bridge between the Father and mankind, a mediator (Priest). This salvific mission has a point of departure and a point of arrival. The point of departure is the bosom of the Father. This purpose comes to an end when every flesh experiences the salvation of God. Jesus carries out his mission in person for few years and entrusts his followers to carry forward until it reaches its culmination. Hence he called Peter, James, John, and others. He constituted them into disciples, the Church, the mystical body of Christ. He is still present in the world through the Church to continue the mission entrusted by the Father. The driving force of the mission of Jesus while he was physically present in the world, and the driving force of the mission of the mystical body the church, is the same: the Spirit. The same spirit that anointed Jesus anointed also the disciples on the day of Pentecost (Lk 3:22; 4:18; Acts 2:1-4). Empowered by the same Spirit, the disciples, the Church, the mystical body of Christ continued the same mission of Jesus fulfilling his promise and a wish in Acts 1:8 *"But you will receive power when the Holy Spirit comes on you; and you will be my witnesses in Jerusalem, and in all Judea and Samaria, and to the ends of the earth."* However, at the end of the Acts the purpose of God is only partially fulfilled. Church continues the mission of Jesus and of the apostles today through each and every member. Every disciple is called to partake in the mission of Jesus and continue his presence and his mission in the world today.[2] This is how the purpose of God reaches its completion.

Narrative unity of Luke – Acts: Description of a Journey

Gospel of Luke is a description of the journey of the word of God from heavens to the womb of Mary (Lk 1:26-38). It was born at Bethlehem (Lk 2:1-7), grew up in Nazareth (Lk 2:39-40). At the baptism, the age of 30, this word has been consecrated, anointed by the Spirit (Lk 3:21-22). After the Baptism, the Word journeyed through villages and towns proclaiming the Good news, and doing good to people in Galilee (Lk 4:44; 5:15; 8:1), when the time drew near takes up the journey passing through Samaria and then Judea (Lk 9:5152;), and finally reaches Jerusalem (Lk 19:37). The word is crucified by the powers of this world (Lk 23:46), an effort of Satan to block this journey, a journey that enlightens people living in darkness[3]. Darkness tried to overpower this Light.[4] However, the story proves that the journey does not end with the death on the cross. It continues. The powers of darkness could not prevail over it. Because there was a driving force within the Word, the power of the Spirit fueling, propelling the journey of the word. The story of continuation of the journey of the Word after the death is narrated in the Acts of the Apostles.

Acts of the Apostles is a description about the re-birth of Jesus in a different format: the birth of the Mystical body of Christ, the church and beginning and expansion of this mission to the ends of the earth. The first chapters of the Acts describe the expansion of this Word in Jerusalem, and from chapter 8, after the death of Stephen, the further expansion begins, to Judea, to Samaria and to the gentile world. Luke concludes his work when the Word reaches Rome. So added to the purpose of God that unites both the works, the journey of the Word also is a strong point of narrative unity.

Spirit at the root of the Mission
Another prominent factor that binds the two works of Luke is the presence and the action of the Holy Spirit. Of the 89 times that the word Holy Spirit (*Pneuma hagion*) appears in the New Testament, 54 instances are found in the works of Luke (13 times in the Gospel and 41 times in the Acts). Of the 379 occurrences of the word Spirit (*Pneuma*) in the New Testament, 106 are found in Luke (36)-Acts (70). Of the 70 occurrences of *Pneuma* in the Acts, more than 40 refer to the Holy Spirit. Obviously, Luke has more to say about the Spirit than any other biblical writer does. He portrays the Spirit as

the activity and presence of God (Lk 4:18). For Luke, Jesus was a man primarily of the Spirit. And in becoming and being guided as followers of Jesus, experience of the Spirit was of utmost importance. That is why the key turning points in Luke's two-volume work are initiated by the Spirit: Jesus' birth (Lk 1:35), baptism (Lk 3:21-22), temptation (Lk 4:1-2), and the start of his ministry of speaking and healing (Lk 4:18). The beginning of Acts (Acts 2:4) and the story of the beginning of the mission to the Gentiles (Acts 10,44-48) are also marked by experience of the Spirit.

The Holy Spirit plays a key role in the Acts of the Apostles. From the start, in Acts 1,2, the reader is reminded that the Ministry of Jesus, while he was on earth, was carried out through the power of the Holy Spirit and that the "acts of the apostles" are the continuing acts of Jesus, facilitated by the same Holy Spirit. Acts thus presents the Holy Spirit as the "*life principle*" of the early Church and provides five separate and dramatic instances of its outpouring on believers in 2:1-4, 4:28-31, 8:15-17, 10:44 and 19:6.

Rejection of God's purpose; Obstacles on the Journey

The journey of the word in the Gospel as well as in the Acts was never easier. In both the books the powers of this world did everything possible to reject God's purpose, block this journey. However, the story again reveals that the powers of this world cannot prevail over the power of the Spirit. In spite of relentless efforts of the enemies of the Word, the Word continued its journey until what Isaiah prophesied is fulfilled that *every flesh shall see the salvation of God*. In chapter 28 of Luke the word of God reaches Rome and Paul was preaching freely to all those who came to him.[5]

In both the journeys, in Luke as well as in Acts, the rejections and obstacles are described. In the Gospel, the Pharisees, Scribes and the Jewish authorities rejected the message. They tried to criticize every word, move of Jesus. Finally they even succeeded to crucify and kill him. However, they succeeded only to kill the physical body of Jesus. But they never knew that they have no power to stop the journey of the Word.

Luke describes in the Acts of the Apostles on one hand the journey of the word of God and on the other, the continuous rejections and obstacles from their own people, from the temple authorities, from gentiles etc. Luke does not forget to mention the internal conflicts within the church during this delicate time of expansion. However, in spite of the external and internal rejections the mission triumphs. The story that Luke narrates is not a monologue of God but seem to be a dialogue between God and a recalcitrant humanity. However, the final victory is always for God. Since the purpose of God is that of universal salvation as Luke portrays in the Gospel and Acts, the story cannot be brought to completion in Acts. Luke leaves it wide open. The story continues. The same dialogue continues even today.

Purpose of the Article
The purpose of this article is to highlight the challenges faced by the early church and the manner in which the early church dealt with these challenges as described by Luke. I would like to focus only on the internal obstacles, challenges that the early church faced. They could easily overcome the external enemies by the power of God but in some occasions, the internal challenges posed a greater threat to the very unity of the early Church. Luke takes utmost care to describe these problems and the manner in which the early church or its leadership resolved them. What Luke describes in Acts are not the challenges faced by Church or the disciple of Christ two thousand years ago, but they are challenges faced at all times and in all places. The author of the Acts tries to give solutions to problems for all contexts and for all places and for all times. I strongly believe that the problems that the church faces today are not different from that of the early church. Hence, the solutions proposed in the Acts might offer a ray of hope to solve the modern challenges.[6]

Interweaving of two narratives: Major and Minor

If we read attentively, there are two narrative lines in the Acts of the Apostles: the major and minor. The major line is about the journey of the word of God under the guidance and the action of the Holy Spirit. How it began, how it progressed, and how it reached the ends of the earth is described progressively and systematically. From Jerusalem to Judea, then Samaria, and then to Rome thus to the ends of the earth. The minor line narrates the challenges faced during this journey. There was a force within the church as well as outside trying to block the journey. However the powerful presence of Spirit guarantees the progress. The end is a manifestation of the power of the Spirt over the malicious plans of the evil force trying to block the journey. The minor line is trying to distract, obstruct the major line but does not succeed.[7]

Major narrative line

Under the guiding action of the Holy Spirit, the Word makes its journey from Jerusalem until it reaches Rome. This is the major line of narrative in the Acts. The powerful and active presence of the Spirit paves way for the journey and expansion of the Word. This is evident every time that Luke repeats the phrases: *The word is spreading and the number of disciples increasing day by day* (Acts 2:41; 4:4; 5:14; 6:1; 6:7; 8:7-8; 8:13; 8:38; 9:42; 10:48; 11:18; 11:21; 13:12; 13:48; 16:5; 16:33; 17:12; 17:34; 18:8; 19:20). The Spirit of God pervades throughout the Acts of the Apostles. It is the Spirit of which Jesus promised who guides in first person. At the same time Luke demonstrates in the same line of narration that this journey was not easy. It was marked by continuous rejection. All the obstacles that Luke speaks in the major narrative are external: Jews, Pharisees, other political authorities etc. The conspiracies, arrests, threats, persecutions and murders (4:1-22; 5:17-42 - arrest of Peter and John; Chapter 7 - Death of Stephen; Chapter; 9:1-2: evil intentions of Saul; 12:1-3: Persecution by Herod, death of James, arrest of Peter; 16:22-23: flogging, imprisonment of Paul and Silas; 17:1-15 and 19:9

- Opposition and difficulties caused by the Jews; difficulties faced by Paul...) all form part of the major narrative.

Minor Narrative line

From time to time, Luke takes a small deviation from the major narrative and almost like a parenthesis often very brief, makes a short note on the internal problems of the early church. These frequent parentheses are found in Acts 1:15-26; 5:1-11; 6:1-7; 8:9-24; 15:1-33. Luke presents them as the threats to the journey. Although they seem to be internal, they have threatened the very unity of the early church. Luke not only describes the existing problems, but also explains how the early Christian community led by the apostles was able to find adequate solutions to overcome these challenges and let the journey move forward unhindered. This is what I call here the minor narrative.

Internal Challenges in the Early Church

I wish to treat here the five important problems faced by the early church as described by Luke and explore how the problems were addressed and solved by the early leadership. Through these episodes Luke proposes solutions to various problems that the church of all times and all places might face.

Sede Vacante: Acts 1:15-26

The first internal challenge to be faced by the followers of Jesus is that of finding a replacement for Judas Iscariot. After the death and resurrection of the Jesus, even before the descent of the Holy Spirit, the early Christian community had to face a challenge: replacing Judas Iscariot. In 1:15, "Peter becomes the leader of the church"[8], takes initiative and explains the situation to the disciples gathered around. He sets an objective criterion for substituting Judas. He gives a clear definition of the requirements for membership of the twelve in terms of 'being with Jesus throughout the ministry, death and resurrection until his being taken up (Acts 1:21-22)[9].

"The community responds by doing as Peter recommends. Peter's faith inspires the faith of others"[10]. They proposed two, they prayed, they drew lots (1:23-26). Although there could be several disciples who must have wished to replace Judas in the apostolic ministry, the objective criteria has excluded majority of them. Peter has not proposed the names. This must have come automatically from the assembly as the criteria set are clear. The members accepted the criteria, they agreed upon the method of choosing among the two. In this way, the problem is solved easily. This episode certainly highlights Peter's responsiveness to Jesus' commission and ability to guide the church in its new task and also indicates the church's willingness to support and collaborate with Peter's leadership.

The fraud of Ananias and Sapphira: Acts 5:1-11

The second internal challenge that the early church had to face and resolve was the fraud of Ananias and Sapphira. This episode must be read with the background of what Luke repeatedly states regarding the nature of the early Christian community at Jerusalem.

"*They devoted themselves to the apostles' teaching and fellowship, to the breaking of bread and the prayers. And all who believed were together and had all things in common; and they sold their possessions and goods and distributed them to all, as any had need*" (2:42, 44-45). Again "*now the company of those who believed were of one heart and soul, and no one said that any of the things which he possessed was his own, **but they had everything in common**. There was not a needy person among them, for as many as were possessors of lands or houses sold them, and brought the proceeds of what was sold, and laid it at the apostles' feet; and distribution was made to each as any had need*" (4:32, 34-35). Immediately after this statement Luke cites the example of a certain Joseph whom they call Barnabas later, who sold his field and handed the proceeds to the apostles. Luke presents as an example of a man who dedicates himself totally and sincerely for the welfare of the community. This is immediately followed by the episode of Ananias and Sapphira (5:1-11). Like Joseph, they too sold a piece of land. But they put aside some of the proceeds and handed over the rest to the apostles. Repetition of similar phrases in both the accounts encourages us to read both the episodes side by side[11]. Obviously, Luke uses the story here as a contrast between types, between the open, honest, generosity of Joseph Barnabas and the secretive deceptive avarice of Ananias and Sapphira.

Contrary to what Barnabas did, Ananias retained part of the sale price with his wife's knowledge.[12] This was certainly a calculated deception. In the conception of Luke all the community life was empowered by the Holy Spirit. Any action against the spirit of the community will be considered an action against the Holy Spirit and not just against the apostles as the human organizers of the collection.[13] Rightly Peter calls it lying to the Holy Spirit. The outward act of Ananias appears to represent a heart and soul united with others in mutual care, but hidden motives are at work. They are mocking the community's spirit of unity.[14] Ananias wants to be part and not to be part of the community, to be and not to be of one heart and one mind at the same time. Sapphira not only shares in the deceit but also in the punishment. The rebuke is followed by the immediate death. Thus, showing no compassion toward Christians who lack complete commitment. The double death clearly emphasizes the seriousness of the threats to the church represented by Ananias and Sapphira. It is a threat of a particular kind, one that arises from inside, is deceptive and attacks a central aspect of the church's life as presented by the narrator. The heartfelt devotion to others demonstrated in the community of goods.[15]

The example of Ananias and Sapphira teach us that even a Christian, spirit filled community can become tainted by counterfeit and deception. When that happens the judgment is swift and severe.[16] God does not tolerate a deceptive heart. His action would be swift and severe. God does not tolerate people that live double lives, people that deceive the community. It is a deceit against the Holy Spirit. It is a warning to the disciples of all times. "When we are dishonest and when we do not use our material resources for common good, we become part of a chain of values and behaviors that eventually collapse. Lying creates distrustful relationships. Failing to share destroys the community. When groups engage in deceit and hoard resources, they create climate of distrust and hostility that eventually lead to downfall."[17] This episode, a cautionary tale, recalls the situation of members of Christian community or religious community today, where often people tend to live double lives. Pope Francis considers living the poverty as one of the greatest challenges of religious life and the church today.[18]

Divisions in the community: Chapter 6:1-7
According to 4:35, the apostles have a direct role in administering the distribution of goods. Proceeds from the sale of the property are placed at the feet of the apostles and then are distributed presumably by the apostle. Acts 6:1-7 describes the ideal of this unity quickly giving way to factionalism. We hear of a complaint, a grumbling that disturbs the very unity of the church in Jerusalem. The threat to the unity appears precisely in the area of church's life where unity had been most clearly demonstrated the sharing of the wealth with the needy. The Hellenist widows complained that they did not receive an adequate amount in the daily distribution whereas Hebrew widows received plenty.[19] The conflict implies that Hebrew widows were more privileged than the Hellenists. We can compare to the modern problems of favouring one's own groups.

When the problem is brought to the table, the apostles did not write off the problem. They accept that a problem exists. This is the first step towards a solution. Then they summoned the whole body of disciples to reflect, discern and decide. The twelve act with dispatch to solve the problem and restore the unity. The apostles understand that this is a problem of excessive centralization, for they are unable to attend to the material needs of the people as they are involved in the spreading of the word. So, they found a solution. By decentralizing the system, by delegating the powers and authority, and by 'sharing the community leadership' in other words the Apostles find a solution to the impending challenge.[20] They begin to think realistically and distinguish the two kinds of services. They draw clear distinction between two types of service, serving tables and serving the Word, because they believe that the former is now interfering with the latter. Hence, the twelve propose a decentralization or a division of labour. They will now concentrate on prayer and the word and let others distribute food. This sounded reasonable to everyone in the community, and consequently accepted unanimously by the whole community (6:5). This demonstrates clearly that when the proposals are objective and are not selfish, self-promotive, it is always easier to find consensus. Excessive centralization or power in the hands of one or very few give rise to problems.

Money and Power corrupt religion Acts 8:9-24

In chapter 8 of the Acts, Luke presents an interesting episode of a certain Simon living in one of the Samaritan villages. He was a magician by profession. When he heard the preaching of Philip, like many others he too was baptized in the village. Apostles Peter and John visit this Samaritan community to confirm them in their faith. Peter and John imparted the Spirit through laying on hands upon the newly baptized. Simon the Magician was impressed by it, and desired this gift for himself. He is still damp from the water of immersion and wants to buy the power of the Holy Spirit. Simon wants to use the spirit to enhance his own privilege. Simon must have been a rich man to make this offer to the apostles. He is not asking the Spirit for himself but the power to confer it on others through his hands. This would make him equal to the apostles, and let him be paid more for his magic. Simon believes that he could make more money from such power and hence is ready to invest money in it. This can be deduced from the way Luke presented Simon in this episode. Although his magic is not described, Luke gives him two negative characteristics: He claims that he himself is someone great (8:9), and he thinks that he can obtain by money the power to control the Holy Spirit (8:18-19). *"when Simon saw that the Spirit was given through the laying on of the apostles' hands, he offered them money, saying give me also, this power, so that anyone upon whom I lay my hands may receive the Holy Spirit."* Peter replied, *"May you and your money perish, for thinking that the gift of God could be bought with money"* (8:20). The request reveals the core of Simon's motivation and his modus operandi. Peter reacts decisively and cuts to the heart of Simon's problem[21]. Peter sees in his request a wrong way of thinking. Peter sees him poisoned with bitterness and as gripped in sin (8:22-23). Simon's proposal to pay evokes strong rebuke from Peter making clear that this is a serious error and immediately calls him to repentance[22]. *"Repent therefore and may God forgive you"* (8:22). For the growing church, Simon's attitude clearly represents serious dangers that the mission must avoid[23]. Such behavior leads to social destruction. Simon would have perished had he not repented.

What is the impending danger for the church of people with such attitudes? In this new territory being claimed by God, the demonic powers in Samaria find their representative in the magician Simon[24]. Simon is the representative of people and groups who seek inappropriate power in the community. Occasionally people may even try to buy their way into power through money. Money can corrupt religion. This passage makes clear that whenever religion is used to make its leaders seem great and powerful and whenever a religion becomes a commodity by serving the interests of those who have or want money it has become corrupt. The tendency towards self-promotion and the use of religion for financial benefits makes a religion corrupt. The religious leaders must make it clear whenever the crowd gets false ideas that they themselves are neither divine nor great. Because this is a human tendency, Luke rings the bells of caution to the church of all times and all places.

Division of Churches: Acts 15

Chapter 15 of Acts is generally titled the Jerusalem council. The narrative discourse of this passage in Acts is often called the turning point in the missionary drama of acts. The issue narrated in this chapter is the most contentious internal matter faced by the young church. 15:1-35 recounts a pivotal meeting in Jerusalem that completes the authorization of the mission and clarifies its terms[25]. I do not wish to enter into the details of the contention, for it is long and complex, however, I would like to highlight the content of the challenge and how early church faced this problem and how it resolved it.

What was the dispute? The whole issue begins when some persons from Judea come to Antioch and teach that Gentile Christians must be circumcised in order to be saved (15:1). This is exactly in contrast to what Paul told the people. Paul did not demand circumcision, passing through the law of Moses but told them to remain as they were when they embraced this new faith (15:2). This new teaching produces lot of dispute. Consequently, the Antioch church decides to send Paul, Barnabas and some others to Jerusalem to resolve the dispute. If the Jerusalem church supports the demand for circumcision, and if no resolution of the dispute can be found, then the communion and friendly relation between the churches in Antioch and Jerusalem will be gravely threatened. Such is the seriousness of the dispute. The Gentile mission of Paul and Barnabas has widespread support outside Judaea but the support of the Jerusalem church is now in question. The early and the young church is in a great crisis. There is a great danger of a split. How did the church manage to come out of this crisis? Luke takes much space focusing on the role of the Apostles, their openness to the Spirit, and their readiness for dialogue to bring a happy end to the dispute.

How was the dispute resolved? Chapter 15:7-21 contains three discourses: that of Peter, Paul and Barnabas, and James. These speeches are presented by Luke as the necessary means of persuasion. These three speeches together present a single persuasive interpretation of

God's purpose. They relive the past experiences and try to find in them the indications of God's purpose. Peter begins with his experience through the Cornelius' episode. He learned from that experience that God makes no distinctions and gives the Holy Spirit equally to Jews and Non-Jews. Hence burdening the Gentiles to go through the Mosaic Law would be equal to testing God (15:7-11). Then Barnabas and Paul interpret their recent mission. They recount the miracles and wonders that done among the gentiles (15:12). Finally James tries to shows that scripture agrees with the experience of the church in its mission. "Adequate clarity comes when the experience of those active in the mission correlates with those aspects of the biblical tradition that present saving purpose of God in its widest dimensions"[26]. The speeches are a manifestation of the apostles' openness and docility to the action of the Holy Spirit in their life and mission. They were all coherent and revealed beautifully the plan and purpose of God towards the Gentiles. This clarity of the apostles makes a solid foundation for the church to make a decision. The rest of the participants also prove to be open, dialogical, and that they have not come to the council with prejudices, prefixed ideas or pre-made decisions. The decision was made collegially. (15:22).

This meeting confirms the freedom of the Gentiles from the law. However, the meeting also proposes that the Gentiles should be asked to abstain from some of the practices offensive to the Jews and their religious culture (15:19-21). The assembly as a whole will accept this proposal and make it part of their letter. Then it will be joyfully accepted in Antioch (15:31) and actively promoted by Paul. Acts 15:30-33 indicates that a harmonious and supportive relation between the churches has been restored by the decision in Jerusalem. The Antioch church accepts the rules of abstinence gladly. Thus, a major crisis in the new community of Jews and Gentiles has been resolved.

The following steps can be traced in the whole dispute: the existence and the awareness of a dispute, fierce arguments, readiness to resolve through a dialogue, a dialogue made in utter openness and docility to the action of the Holy Spirit and in coherence with the Scriptures, proposing solutions acceptable to both the parties, collegial decision, acceptance with joy, and finally the restoration of unity and communion. Such a conclusion was possible because here is a group of people filled with the Spirit, seeking exclusively the welfare of the community, ready for an open dialogue, readiness to sacrifice personal, selfish ideas for the common good, through give and take attitude. When there is a sincere desire to find a solution, people should be ready to be open and ready to change their opinions.

Conclusion

Threats from internal corruption, suspicion, and conflict endangered the communion and unity in the early Jerusalem community. Luke foresees similar problems, hindrances and challenges in the history of the church because the church is composed of human beings. So Luke proposes effective and adequate solutions -if adapted - for all times and places. The early church had problems, but according to Acts, it also had leaders who moved swiftly to ward off corruption and find solutions to internal conflicts supported by people who listened to each other with open minds and responded with good will. After almost two thousand years, today's church problems are same: struggle for higher positions, groupism, favouritism, partiality, corruption, division, suspicion, conflictual relationships etc. There is nothing to be surprised about because even the Jerusalem community, in which there were Apostles who had the personal experience of Jesus, was not spared from such evil tendencies. Today's church is in need of efficient leadership capable of finding swift and effective solutions, people docile to the Spirit, people committed to the common good, making sacrifices for common welfare, having a spirit of dialogue and readiness to change, better the situations. In the service of Jesus

Christ and his Church, without leaders and believers with these above mentioned characteristics, the church will always be ineffective and weak. Luke reminds us even today that internal challenges are more dangerous than the external.

Endnotes

[1] Shillington, V. G., *An Introduction to the study of Luke-Acts*, *T&T Clark approaches to Biblical Studies*, Bloomsbury, 2015 (2nd Ed.) 2.

[2] Tannehill, Robert C., The Narrative Unity of Luke-Acts, *A literary Interpretation*, Vol I: The Gospel according to Luke Philadelphia (1986), 1-9.

[3] Is 9:2: The people who walked in darkness have seen a great light; those who lived in a land of deep darkness— on them light has shone.

[4] John 1:5: The light shines in the darkness, and the darkness has not overcome it.

[5] Acts 28:30-31: And he lived there two whole years at his own expense, and welcomed all who came to him, preaching the kingdom of God and teaching about the Lord Jesus Christ quite openly and unhindered.

[6] Cfr. Maggioni Bruno (ed.,), Il Nuovo Testamento, *Conoscerlo, Leggerlo e Viverlo*, Torino (2013) 55-63.

[7] Tannehill Robert C., The Narrative Unity of Luke-Acts, *A literary Interpretation*, Vol II: The Acts of the Apostles, Philadelphia (1990), 1-6.

[8] Tannehill, Robert C., The Narrative Unity of Luke-Acts, *A literary Interpretation*, Vol 2: The Acts of the Apostles; Philadelphia (1986), cfr. 20-21.

[9] Mullins, M., The Acts of the Apostles, Dublin (2013), 65-68.

[10] The Narrative Unity of Luke – Acts, Vol. II,–21.

[11] Mullins, op. cit. 85-86.

[12] The story of Ananias and Sapphira resonates the stories of Adam and Eve, story of Achan in the book of Joashua, (7:19-26). This man also kept property for himself from the fallen city of Jericho, which was supposed to be consecrated to the Lord. He too was sentenced to death. And also that of Judas Iscariot in the Gospels

[13] Mullins, op. cit. 86.

[14] Parson, M., Acts, *Paideia Commentaries on the New Testament*, Grand Rapids, (2005) 75.

[15] The Narrative Unity of Luke – Acts, Vol. II, 79.

[16] Shillington, op. cit. 95.

[17] Allen, R. J., Acts of the Apostles, *Fortress Biblical preaching commentaries*, Minneapolis (2013) 54.

[18] Pope Francis, La forza della vocazione, *Conversazione con Fernando Prado*, Bologna (2018) 94.

[19] The Hellenists were Jewish women who did not speak Aramaic, the everyday language of the Jewish people in Palestine. They spoke Greek for various reasons. The Hebrew widows were Jewish women who did speak Aramaic.

[20] The Narrative Unity of Luke – Acts, Vol. II, 79.

[21] Mullins, op. cit., 101.

[22] Allen, op. cit., 73-74.

[23] The Narrative Unity of Luke – Acts, Vol. II, 105.

[24] Johnson, T. L.,The Acts of the Apostles, Collegeville, MN (1992) 152.

[25] Allen, op. cit. 122.

[26] The Narrative Unity of Luke – Acts, Vol. II,-184.

Science, Religion and Spirituality:

Triple Dialectic to Triple Dialogue

Rudolf C. Heredia S.J.

Truth as satya, reality, is many-sided, anekantavada as Jaina philosophy rightly affirms. There can be many perspectives on it and no single one alone can be so comprehensive as to grasp all of it. However, it cannot be contradictory, and neither can science, religion and spirituality be in contradiction in so far as these pursue truth. Their apparent differences arise from their different perspectives and methodologies. These are contraries not contradictions and result in a dialectical tension between the three not a negation of one by the other. A more nuanced understanding of such contraries would resolve them into complementarities that can be the basis for resolving these tensions: science as reason-based and religion as faith-based, as also a spirituality that could be premised on one or the other. We need to find common ground between the three for a dialogue and turn the triple dialectic into a triple dialogue.

The pursuit of science always opens to new frontiers in its domain. When it exceeds its limitations of its own discourse, it loses its way and betrays its pursuit. Beyond those frontiers are ever receding horizons of other realities beyond the discourse of science, to which science can point to but never really pursue. These are the ultimate human concerns and anomalies of human life. Religion ventures into this domain to unravel this reality and relate humans to it. Spirituality too engages with it.

But religion too can lose its way, when bad faith displaces good faith, and transparency and trust is compromised for security and certainty. The dilemma between charisma and institutionalisation demands a delicate balance to stay the course. In its effort to appropriate and internalise the truth whether of science, or religion or even art, spirituality helps stay this course. Least spirituality too looses its way, it must balance withdrawal and detachment, which could lead to esoterism and exclusiveness, with engagement and concern, which could become superficial and populist.

The necessity of this triple dialogue is well illustrated by our present ecological crisis precipitated by climate change. We need a new science with an alternative technology to replace the old ones. For what caused the problem in the first place is unlikely to provide an appropriate solution to it. It will only be more of the same rehashed and disguised. Moreover, the crisis is embedded in our consumerist culture and the market economics that sustain it. We need a radically new worldview which is not likely to come from within the perspectives of old sciences. A change of world view and mind-set is imperative.

Clarifying the terms of Discourse

There is an ennui regarding the debates on "science and/or religion". Sometimes 'religion' is replaced with 'spirituality' but this seems to skirt rather than confront the deeper issues involved. The starting premise here is that the three terms are intimately related and the tension between them must be addressed with a more nuanced understanding of the terms. Only then can the dialectic between these be opened to a dialogue about them.

The anomalies in the relationship between these three can be addressed with a dialectic or a dialogue. Dialectic is used here in the sense of a tension between two opposing antagonisms that is resolved into a tertium quid, a third alternative. It is premised on a rational understanding. A dialogue is a conversation that seeks understanding between the participants so to find common ground between protagonists and then move together to higher ground together. It is premised on a hermeneutic interpretation. Thus "dialectics is the optimism of reason. Dialogue is the optimism of the heart." (Panikkar 1983: 243) We can speak of a 'dialectical dialogue' which would be premised on reason and rationality which would pertain more to reason-based science and spirituality; while a 'dialogical dialogue' would be premised on relevance and meaningfulness and would pertain more to faith-based religion and spirituality.

'Science' and 'spirituality' have meant very different things to diverse peoples. At the outset we need to agree on how they are to be understood at least for the purpose of this discussion to make consensus and disagreement the more credible and useful, or else we will talk past each other. Science here is used to signify a systematic study of the world to create an organised body of knowledge about its structure and functions. Spirituality is used in the sense of a vision and way of life. Moreover, both these terms are intimately bound up with another, which must also be brought into the discussion: "religion as "what ultimate concerns man". (Tillich 1958:2)

Secularisation is a complex and multidimensional social process beyond the scope of this essay. Here we will understand it as a process of 'rationalisation', in Max Weber's (1968) understanding of the term, as a systematic application of reason to realty. In society this transforms mores into laws, social relationships into institutions and organisations into bureaucracies, nations into states, … A secularised world claims to be premised on rationality, just as science claims to privilege reason. Thus, there is an obvious affinity between a secular world and a scientific worldview, a "universe of meaning". (D'Sa) Rationalisation demystifies our world and can free us from our oppressive traditions. But it also disenchants our world as well, making it a place where humans feel strangers in their home, for humans do not live by reason alone. As Pascal famously said: "the heart has reasons that reason does not know." (Pascal, 1958 N.277)

Science and technology based on it have a logic of their own and without human values and humane concerns, this can alienate and destroy rather than liberate and serve. But there are limitations as well, too often neglected if not denied. Reason is not the only human faculty with which we need to live in our world. We also need meaning and motivation, purpose and value. Nor is logic the only way to investigate our world. We need intuition and imagination, insight and understanding as well.

Both science and religion are quests for truth, though with different methodologies each with its own limitations: science more experimental, religion more experiential. Scientific experiments are objective, validated by their replicability. Religious experience is subjective, authenticated by its meaningfulness. Spirituality seeks to appropriate this truth in a vision and express it in a way of life. It is in a quest for human fulfilment. The relationships between these are essentially compatible and complementary, though they can become opposed and antagonistic.

This quest for truth could be more rationally objective and/or experientially subjective, or both if there is no real contradiction between the two. The relationship between science and religion can be either opposed and antagonistic: rationalist, positivist science versus fideistic, dogmatic religion; or compatible and complementary: the quest for truth through reason and experimentation along with the same quest through testimony and experience. Rationalism and positivism have their intellectual and methodological limits, which when exceeded, misdirects the scientific quest; fideism and dogmatism have their psychological and sociological compulsions, which if not overcome, betray the religious quest.

Spirituality, as a quest for human fulfilment, endeavours to appropriate and internalise this truth in a vision and way of life.

As a vision, it expresses meaning and motivation, as a way of life it affirms purpose and value. The vision must necessarily be derived from a worldview which could be more reason-based or faith-based, or once again both, if there is no contradiction between them. In either case such a spirituality would be more intensely religious in its worldview or less so, depending on how close this connection was. It could also draw on a more scientific worldview, in which case the consequent spirituality would be more rigorously secular or less dependent on the closeness of this connection. Also, the worldview could derive from a single religious tradition or from multiple ones in for an inter-religious vision, if these traditions are inclusive and fluid, in which case we could speak of an 'inter-spirituality', combining many sadhanas.

As a way of life, a spirituality must be practical. It would be quite inadequate to merely articulate an abstract, intellectual understanding of this vision in terms of ideas. It must further be expressed in concrete practises and norms for human beings living in a materiel world. Spirituality is often more concerned with practice than belief. Inevitably, such practices get ritualised and the norms standardised in a community following the same spiritual path. These are two elements of a religious tradition, and depending on how far this process goes, the way of life will begin to resemble a religious tradition and eventually even become one or at least similar to one, even if it is more rather than less secular. This is how ideologies become functional homologues for religion and spirituality.

However, Spirituality has a natural affinity with religion, certainly with a more open, less ritualist religion. Both are concerned with personal quests for a reality beyond the everyday mundane world, and as such can reinforce one another. Only when science negates any reality beyond the material is there a contradiction with spirituality and religion. Science then becomes a functioning discipline and mind-set, for the lab and for life.

Science, Religion and Spirituality

Symbol Systems

Science communicates in precise concepts that are defined as univalent and expressed in 'signs' for to facilitate communication. If all truth is to be restricted to the empirical and all knowledge to be derived from inductive or deductive logical, then clearly in such an empirical-rationalist frame of reference, there is no room for a faith-based religion or spirituality in this such a worldview. Religious language is necessarily symbolic, for that is the only way the transcendental in ultimate concerns can be approached. This can be through words, as a scriptural text, or actions, such as rites and rituals. A spirituality premised on a vision of the transcendental will better communicate in symbols, as a practical way of life this can also be done in concepts and signs.

Symbols are quintessentially multivalent and to interpret them literally is to misread them and betray the communication or worse. A symbol system demands a hermeneutic to bring out not just the meaning but the meaningfulness of a symbiotic communication. This follows not so much the logic of reason but rather seeks a meaningful interpretation to bring out the 'surplus of meaning' beyond the communication. The explanatory power of the interpretation is what authenticates it.

Symbol systems are shared in society and across groups and communities. Strong emotions cathetic onto social symbol systems, particularly religious ones. As such they necessarily exist in the public domain. They cannot be isolated in a private one, for the public and private domains are in constant and interpenetrative interaction. When symbols systems overlap and with each other and collective interests in society, they reinforce each other and result in collective myths that are constructed into social identities. These can be open and inclusive, or closed and exclusive; ennobling and transforming or chauvinistic and oppressive.

Two Worldviews

Symbol systems always exist within a worldview, within a horizon of meaning. When differing worldviews meet and interact there can be either a clash of horizons and a mutual alienation, or a fusion and reciprocal enrichment. We need an authentic hermeneutic to critique these worldviews to find commonalities from which to bridge differences and find common ground and move to higher ground.

Science too has its worldviews. That of Newtonian science was a closed system of cause and effect, of action and reaction. Einstein's relativity theory has pried this open and Heisenberg's quantum mechanics and introduced an indeterminism, that has now left physics still searching for an integrated theory to make sense of the anomalies and contradictions that still remain within a receding horizon. But it remains a secular-rational worldview, though less intransigent and arrogant than earlier ones. A religious worldview can be fideistic and dogmatic but under the pressures of secularisation, is opening to more relevant and less dogmatic understandings. Spirituality has a smorgasbord of alternative 'visions', worldviews to chose from, depending which is chosen, the way of life will follow accordingly.

A critique of the scientific-secular and a humanist-religious worldview will help further this discussion. A dichotomy between science and religion results in a dialectic rather than a dialogue between the two. Thinking in such binary opposites is more characteristic of Western than Eastern thought, where faith and reason are complementary, not opposed ways of seeking the truth, *satya*, reality. Both must be included in a more comprehensive understanding that opens to a genuine dialogue, not just between science premised on reason and religion premised on faith, but between religions as well.

After a corrosive rationalism rubbished religion, postmodernism now undermines our confidence in the earlier modernism. A backlash of religious revivalisms and fundamentalisms is spreading like inkblots across countries and continents. To address such issues, we need to understand the limits of positivist science based on the experimental method, and the horizons of religious faith based on an experiential quest. Each must be able to interrogate the other's truth in a constructive conversation rather than in an antagonistic debate. However, faith must respect the legitimate domain and methods of reason, which in turn must be sensitive to the belief convictions and value commitments of faith. We must steer clear of both a fideism that reject reason in the domain of faith, and a rationalism which displaces faith with reason.

Ways of Proceeding
Beyond the incremental progress of the experimental method, from time to time science crosses a threshold with a 'paradigm shift', (Kuhn 1970) that is, an intuitive leap of imagination a breakthrough to a new model of interpreting data and resolving old contradictions and opening new perspectives. This is not based on experimental logic, though it is post factum authenticated by it. An exaggerated faith in the experimental methodology remains blind to such imaginative intuitions. At most the method will bring you to the end of the road, but not help make the imagination leap beyond.

The popular use of scientific technology is without much understanding of the theories and techniques that underpins it. It is pragmatically accepted because it works. This is an uncritical use of science quite alien to the scientific mind-set. It is analogous to 'faith'. Such uncritical pragmatism eventually instrumentalises and dehumanises science and leads to its misuse, as most obviously in modern warfare.

Religions are founded on the experience of charismatic persons whose teachings are institutionalised and experiences ritualised into a tradition. This is meant to give later believers access to the original experiences and teachings across history and geography. But these must be critiqued, interpreted and discerned to contextualise them in changing life-situations. A living religious tradition must be renewed and contextualised to remain meaningful and relevant, or it ossifies and regress into blind faith. Unfortunately, much of popular religiosity gets distanced from such good faith and mixed with superstition and magic. People seek assurance and certainty in their insecure and fluid world. This is faith with no *Cost of Discipleship*. (Bonhoeffer 1970) It easily blinds itself to dogmatism and fundamentalism which eventually this consolidates into religious extremism, even fanaticism. When politicised into a religious ideology, this can precipitate horrific violence, especially when religion is put on the defensive, as with a belligerent secularism or rationalism.

Ashis Nandy (Nandy 1992:80) distinguishes between 'religion as ideology' and 'religion as faith'. All ideologies can help to interpret a social situation. The closed, rigid ones can be dysfunctionally aggressive and exploitative: whether religious fundamentalism or cultural nationalism, liberal capitalism or socialist Marxism. We need liberating, open functional ones, to open our world to understanding and intervention. Religious faiths too and can be oppressive or liberating, extremist or moderate. We need to recover "religious tolerance from everyday Hinduism, Islam, Buddhism, and/or Sikhism, rather than wish that ordinary Hindus, Muslims, Buddhists and Sikhs will learn tolerance from the various fashionable secular theories of statecraft." (Nandy 1992: 86) Tolerance in both domains, ideology and faith is needed to make dialogue viable. And we need charismatic persons to help with the breakthrough to sanity before an apocalypse overtakes as all.

Thomas Kuhn's *The Structure of Scientific Revolutions* (1970) demonstrates how the scientists are reluctant to abandon old theoretical models, and marginalise those that do so, until forced by a paradigm shift that overtakes them. In such cases when scientific theories resist change, they function like an ideology, refusing to accept the limits of its own methodology and models and so denying a self-critique and compromising the open-endedness of a scientific worldview. The institutionalisation of science can create vested which can commercialise the scientific quest, displacing the pursuit of truth for that of profit or power, and an ideology will develop to rationalise this.

The vision of the truth that spirituality seeks and tries to appropriate and internalise may not be pertinent or valid for changed personal social contexts. The way of life chosen may be a rationalisation of psychological needs with their unconscious compulsions and project a hidden agenda for false security in comfort zones. Discernment and discretion are always necessary. Some external point of reference can help towards a reality check, and yet guides and gurus are not always guarantors of authenticity. For this transparency with oneself and in one's spiritual community is imperative.

Thus, spirituality as a faith-based vision and a reason premised practise can straddle both: science as reason-based and religion as faith-based. In exploring the three-way relationship between these, it imperative to address the apparent dichotomy between faith and reason and turn an oppositional dialectic into an al opposition and be turned into an enriching dialogue.

Faith and Reason

Bridging the Divide
Perceiving faith and reason as binary opposites rather than as two alternate ways in our quest for truth is more typical of Western thought, where this readily leads to an impassable divide, as between fideism and rationalism. "What has Athens got to do with Jerusalem?" asked Tertullian (c160–c220 CE) at the beginning of the Christian era when confronted with Greek philosophy. But if believers would privilege faith, rationalist would reverse the hierarchy, and never the twain would meet. The resulting dualism between faith and reason would seem to leave each in an independent domain of human experience and knowledge, compartmentalising our lives and impoverishing them into bargain, even as philosophers and theologians attempted to accommodate each other across the divide.

However, our contention here, as with Eastern thought more generally, is that faith and reason are complementary not contradictory ways of seeking the truth, since truth itself, *satya*, as ontological reality even more than just epistemological truth, cannot be contradictory, otherwise reality itself would be absurd. What is needed is to include both in a more comprehensive understanding, which in fact would thereby be the more human for being the more inclusive and holistic. However, we must first refine our understanding of what we mean by 'faith' and 'reason' so as to explore more incisively the relationship between the two.

If faith and reason is conceived as contradictory, the relationship between the two can only be oppositional and leads to an antagonism or alienation between them. Considered as contrary, the relationship would be dialectical, which implies reading one pole against the other and vice versa. Seen as complementary the relationship is then dialogical, which implies a conversation between different points of view to come to a consensus. For such a dialogue, we must begin with a basic question: *what does being 'reasonable' mean to faith, and again what does the being 'faithful' to reason require?*

For, though ours is an age, which at the global level may be characterised by secularism, there are as yet strong pockets of religious resistance, at times even provoked by this very challenge of globalisation. (Beyer 1994) There is an increasing religious revivalism and fundamentalism. The Enlightenment an age of reason which seemed to have undermined the traditional age of faith. Today a postmodern age is putting to question all the grand narratives that once seemed to epitomise the cutting edge of our evolving rationalist optimism.

A binary opposition between faith and reason easily leads to an unbridgeable divide between fideism and rationalism, which all too easily deteriorates into a schizophrenia between religious intolerance or withdrawal, between rationalist dogmatism or indifference. A more inclusive understanding is expressed in our *first sutra: faith and reason are complementary not contradictory ways of seeking the truth.*

Towards a Phenomenology of Faith

More conventionally faith is understood as giving one's assent to a truth on the testimony of another. This is what makes belief credible, that is, worthy of being believed. Thus, understood faith is a matter of belief that focuses on the content and its credibility. In so far as this testimony is external to the believing person, its trustworthiness would rest on the credibility of the one giving the testimony and its transmission, and not only on the content of the belief itself. Thus, what I believe is the *content of faith*, whom I trust is the *act of faith*. Hence our *second sutra: what we believe depends on whom we trust.* Thus, if *I believe you*, it is not just because I accept what you say as true, but more so because *I believe* you are a trustworthy and truthful person.

This opens up the inter-personal dimension of faith that focuses not on our relationship to things as to objects, but to persons as to subjects, an I-thou, not I-it relationship. This is the faith that gives me access to the other person as a self-disclosing subject. For Martin Buber (Buber 1958) such I-thou relationships are possible with things as well. i.e. with nature. Gabriel Marcel's personalism (1952) would accommodate this, but an empiricist worldview constrained by a reductionist methodology cannot but discredit such 'knowledge'.

It is then the authority of the testimony, moral or formal, that legitimates belief. However, as this testimony gets institutionalised in a tradition it can get even more distant from the original founding experiences and events themselves. Thus, oftentimes claims of divine inspiration for the authority of religious testimony made by such institutional traditions, or at times the author of this testimony, the testifier, is seen to have claimed divinity itself. This would seem to put such testimony beyond human scrutiny. However, any communication, and most certainly a revelation of the divine to the human, must inevitably involve filters. Indeed, even the immediacy of a mystical experience, in its very first and necessary articulation to oneself, and in its later communication to others, necessarily involves the mediation of thought and language. This already implies an inescapable distancing from the original experience itself and the inevitable need for a hermeneutic understanding if the experience is to be relevant and meaningful /reasonable. In sum then:

"To believe is, formally, to know reality through the knowledge which another person has of it and which he communicates by his testimony; between faith and reality there intervenes the person of the witness, who communicates his knowledge so that the believer may share in it and thereby attain to the reality itself." (Alfaro 1968: 316)

Articulating a Critique of Reason

The term 'reason' derives from the Latin '*ratio*' and its more restricted sense "absorbs the meanings of 'giving an account', 'ordering things' or 'laying things or ideas out in a comprehensive way'. Other terms in which it may be contrasted with are *muthos* ('tale' or 'story'), *aisthesis* ('perception'), *phantasia* ('imagination'), *mimesis* ('imitation'), and *doxa* ('belief')." (Finch 1987:223)

Logic, deductive and inductive, the experimental method, ... are among the various ways that have been proposed to systematise the use of such reason. Thus, assent to truth here is 'reasoned', not dependent on testimony, but on evidence that can be verified, and which leads to conclusions that can be tested. This then is a rational method of investigation that leads not to 'belief' but to 'knowledge'. The acceptance of such knowledge is based on intrinsic criteria, and not on any extrinsic testimony or authority.

So far, the focus is very much on the method of rational knowledge not on its content. In practice much of what we accept as reasoned knowledge, scientific or otherwise, is not something that we have tested or verified for ourselves using any kind of rational investigation. Often it is merely on the authority of someone who "knows better".

In other words, on the authority of wiser, more learned, more knowledgeable persons, or sometimes it seems simply because of the compulsions of the formal position the person holds. For a bit of information in our lives cannot be traced to source and verified before it is being accepted. It is not just a practical impossibility, theoretically it would lead to an infinite regress, because the very methodology of any rational knowledge rest on basic premises, like the reality and intelligibility of the world we live in, which cannot be logically proven. They are experienced existentially.

'Rational knowledge' then has an element of 'faith', which is often neglected. But once again this refers to its content. What needs to be examined is the methodology by which such knowledge is arrived at. For even when such knowledge is accepted in 'faith' in principal at least it can be tested and verified. However, even while acknowledging the limitations of a methodology, one must also accept its validity where this applies. And so, our third sutra: *a rational methodology transgressing its inherent limitations can never yield 'rightly reasoned' knowledge.*

In this context Karl Popper's distinction in his *Open Society* (Popper 1962) between classical rationalism and critical rationalism is pertinent here. The first seeks secure knowledge from axiomatic premises, the second accepts given knowledge as 'hypothetical' and through critical testing seeks to further refine and extend it. Thus, Euclidean geometry is completely rational within the constraints of its own premises, but the non-Euclidean ones start from different assumptions and has extended geometric applications substantially.

A critical examination of the methodology involved in these rationalisms would arrive at certain limitations that are often neglected and even violated by their proponents for reasons that are external to the methodology itself. This is precisely what the sociology of knowledge has drawn attention to and has convincingly demonstrated, how the underlying presumptions, which inevitably are socially derived, prejudice our presumed rational and impartial objectivity. These presumptions and pre-judgements are beyond the investigative methodology of such reasoning itself. How then do we critique such presumptions and prejudices? For if the ideal of the Enlightenment, of an unbiased, autonomous subject, must be abandoned, how does this become a positive constituent of any interpretation, and not a limiting one? It is precisely here once again that the relationship between faith and reason must be interrogated.

Thus, we have the Kantian 'a priori's that are accepted as methodological imperatives if such empirical/experimental knowledge is to be possible at all. However, there are pre-judgements and presumptions that must ground any rationality, as the hermeneutic tradition would insist. Moreover, when non-empirical/experimental sources of knowing are involved, other methods of ascertaining truth are required. Dilthey's (1991) understanding of an interpretive discipline, and Weber's (1968) *verstehen*, empathetic understanding, do offer such viable methodologies, while hermeneutics and deconstruction have today demonstrated the limits of the old Enlightenment rationalism and have offered alternative analytic approaches. In making, then, this distinction between the content and method of reasoned knowledge, we discover not just the limitations of the empirical-experimental methodology, but we once again uncover the 'faith' element that is more often than not decisive in the content being accepted.

For the prejudgements and prejudices that hermeneutics and the sociology of knowledge emphasise are not subject to reason so much as to the interests and status, the "unconscious ideologies" and fundamental options of those involved. For Hans-Georg Gadamer, the present situation of the interpreter is not something negative, but "already constitutively involved in any process of understanding." (Linge, 1977: xiv) We can never be entirely rid of our prejudices, or more literally our 'pre-judgements', or in communication terminology our 'filters'. For "the historicity of our existence entails that prejudices in the literal sense of the word, constitute the initial directedness of our whole ability to experience." (Linge 1977: 9) It follows there can be no pre-suppositionless interpretation, since there is no pre-judgementless experience! Consequently, our *fourth sutra: where we position ourselves influences how we reason.* To conclude then:

"There has been a marked decline in the prestige of reason in the twentieth century, due to a changing awareness of the conventionality of what passes for reason. But the present age does not suffer so much from a want of rationality as from a too arrow conception of what constitutes rationality. To some present-day critics, rationality has been purchased at the cost of human meaning and human understanding." (Finch 1987: 224)

Faith as Constitutive of the Human

As with content and method we need now to make a somewhat similar distinction with regard to faith. Too much attention has been focused on faith as content, that is, 'belief'. We need to examine the faith as act, and what precisely makes such belief possible. Why in fact do we accept the testimony of others? Once again, the capacity to make this act of faith is certainly an *a priori* condition for the necessarily interdependent lives we live. Moreover, if we grant that we are not the ground of our own being, then this "faith" must transcend and reach beyond the horizons of the human. But if all truth is to be restricted to the empirical and all knowledge to be derived from inductive or deductive logic, then clearly in such an empirical-rationalist frame of reference, there is no room for faith, or as Paul Tillich says, for "what ultimately concerns man". (Tillich1958) Hence our *fifth sutra: whether or not we believe depends on our self-understanding.*

In this sense Panikkar rightly insists that faith becomes a "constitutive element of human existence". (Panikkar 1971: 223 – 254) And it is precisely as such, that we must test any content of faith. For a content of faith that does not fulfil the human dimension, i.e., to make the believer more human, cannot be "good faith". And so, our *sixth sutra: if to believe is human, then what we believe must make us more human not less!* The test of good faith then would be whether the act of faith gives assent to a content that is in fact humanising. And this is precisely what an experiential self-reflective rationality can do. This is where and how we must seek the reasonableness of our faith.

So too with blind faith; here the act of faith becomes compulsive rather than free, and 'catechs' on a content that promises security and perhaps even grandiosity, rather than one that expresses trust and dependency. But only when we accept that faith is a constitutive dimension of human life, do we have a framework for making such an investigation. Thus, *sutra seven: faith that is 'blind' is never truly humanising; faith that is not humanising, is to that extent 'bad faith'.*

Language as Distinctive of the Human

But if faith is a constitutive dimension of human existence, certainly we must say the same of reason. The classical definition of 'man' we have come to accept from Aristotle is "anthropos logicon", translated as rational animal. But this does not quite integrate the elements of faith and reason together. It is a one-sided definition that stresses only a single dimension, which certainly might help to identify humans, as opposed to animals but it does very little to help to a more comprehensive and inclusive understanding of what is distinctively human. Panikkar instists "we are more than rational animals and we are certainly more than mere machines." (Panikkar 2013: 4)

In fact, the original Greek word used by Aristotle was "*logicon*" from '*logos*', which in its more restricted sense means "word". Hence, Aristotle's definition would more correctly be translated as man is a "verbal animal", or "speaking animal". In other words, it is language that becomes the distinctive and defining characteristic of human beings. This of course implies reason but much more than that as well. Anthropologically this makes sound sense. And it is precisely because language implies inter-communication and inter-relationship, that is expresses so well the inter-dependence of humans, for there is no such thing as a private language. It is only such a comprehensive understanding of the human that gives us a framework in which faith and reason can be included, as distinct but complementary dimensions of the human.

Unfortunately, however, reason is often used to investigate, challenge and even rubbish the content of faith, by applying a rational-empirical methodology. This is precisely to misunderstand the language of faith, which is not at the level of rational-empirical discourse but always a symbolic one. What is needed rather is an interrogation that derives more from a hermeneutic investigation that contextualises content, and to interpret the content at the various levels of meaning that are often present therein, from the literal and the direct, to the symbolic and the metaphoric. For when it comes to the act of faith, an experimental methodology with its objective emphasis, is quite inadequate to such a subjective act. What we need is a more self-reflexive and experiential methodology, which while being subjective is neither arbitrary or irrational, but one which focuses on symbolic "meaningfulness", more than literal meaning and rather than just on measuring quantities and determining cause and effect. Thus, our *eighth sutra: only a self-reflexive, experiential methodology is meaningful to the discourse of faith; a rationalist, empirical one is alien to it.*

Besides inductive and deductive logic, there are many kinds of rationality as Max Weber has emphasised, but they are other complex ways in which reason can impinge on human life as when it rationalises or 'orders' it on the basis of law, bureaucracy, tradition or charisma. (Weber 1968) Instrumental and value rationality are just two classics examples of this from Weber. Broadly he understands rationality as the application of reason or conceptual thought to the understanding or ordering of human life. This is articulated in our *ninth sutra: in so far as there can be many understandings and orderings of human life and society, there must correspondingly be many kinds of rationality as well.*

Institutional Dilemmas

The institutionalisation of religion involves fundamental dilemmas that must be lived in tension since they cannot be resolved or wished away. For as Thomas O'Dea (1969) so insightfully points out: *religious experience needs most yet suffers most from institutionalisation*. This is our *tenth sutra*. Precisely because such experience is so fragile and impermanent it needs institutions to preserve it through historical generations and spread it across geographical spaces; and yet it is so ephemeral and ineffable that it cannot but be distorted and alienated by this very institutional process. In Max Weber's phrase, the "routinisation of charisma", is both necessary and subverting. There is a correspondence here between the charismatic experience that is more a matter of faith, and routinised institutionalisation that is more a concern of reason. Hence our *sutra eleven: 'experience' is necessary to vitalise institutions, and vice versa, 'institutions' are needed to preserve experience*.

For even as new experiences precipitate new understandings, they can alter our consciousness in radical ways, which then demands a renewed faith. For "on the one hand, there is an interpretation of the faith conditioned by one's view of reality and on the other there is a view of reality nurtured by one's interpretation of revelation." (Libano, 1982: 15) Echoing W.I. Thomas, we have *sutra twelve: while it is true that faith does not 'create' reality, it does make for a 'definition of the situation' that is real in its effects; and vice-versa, our experience of reality affects our faith-understanding*. (Thomas 1928: 571-572)

Religious traditions that have stressed 'orthodoxy' (right belief) tend to focus more on the content of faith, whether this be the intellectual content of the beliefs taught and accepted or the moral values and norms. The first focuses on intellectual truth, the second on moral goodness. However, such orthodoxies tend to neglect the act of faith, which as a constitutive dimension of our life represents precisely an internal critique, an intrinsic guarantor of a content of faith, which ought to fulfil our deepest human desires and hopes.

For this a religious tradition must emphasise 'orthopraxis' (right practice), where the focus is on the act of faith. For here the crucial emphasis is neither on belief in the true or the good, but rather a commitment to the true and the good, to authentic human living, an existential engagement with, and a critical reflection on living. It is at this fundamental existential level that the relevance and meaningfulness of faith must be sought. For it is at this level of living praxis, that truth, intellectual or moral, must be internalised to have meaning and motivation. Rationalist logic best pursues the truth it investigates within the limits of its methodological discourse. Beyond these boundaries it becomes reductionist and invalid.

For the relationship between faith and reason to be very fruitful, reason must critique faith for its fidelity in humanising our life, with meaning and motivation; just as faith that must commit reason to serve this same humanising project, affirming its validity within the domain of its own discourse. Hence a constant search in an ongoing religious tradition for an ever deeper and more relevant 'orthopraxis' and 'orthodoxy', rather than an uncritical, unchanging faith; as also the continuing scientific quest for a more adequate and pertinent 'rationality' beyond the rationalism of the Enlightenment. And so, our *thirteenth sutra: faith and reason must complement and critique each other in an ongoing humanising dialogue.*

A Humanising Dialogue

Our hermeneutic suspicions can now become the points of departure for us to initiate and continue this dialogue across the apparent divide between faith and reason. But we must first be clear with regard to the horizons of understandings in which it takes place. Only then can there be a 'fusion of horizons' which can give the dialogue "the buoyancy, of a game, in which the players are absorbed," (Linge 1977: xix) as the later Wittgenstein had observed. (Wittgenstein 1962) And it will happen as in "every conversation that through it something different has come to be." (Linge 1977: xxii)

In making a distinction between the content and the act of faith, we realise that the content may vary across various cultural and religious traditions. However, the act of faith in so far as it is constitutively human, will necessarily have a great similarity across cultures and religions because at this level we begin to touch on the most fundamental aspects of the human. Here again it is our faith, both as act and content that can help us discern the human authenticity of these pre-judgements and presumptions.

This precisely becomes the basis for an enriching inter-religious dialogue, which can begin to bridge the divide between religious traditions, and in which one can recognise oneself in the other and the other in myself! Because the act of faith is constitutively human, it will necessarily have a common basis across varying cultures and traditions. This then is our *fourteenth sutra: the act of faith rather than the content of faith must become the primary basis of interfaith dialogue.*

Today the revivalism of faith traditions justifies the unreasonable and even the irrational in the name of faith, while a rationalist secular science dismisses all faith-based beliefs as irrational and unscientific. This merely turns the dilemma between faith and reason into an irresolvable dichotomy not an enriching exchange. We must embrace both as expressed in our *fifteenth sutra: an inclusive humanism must embrace both 'meaningful faith', as well as 'sensitised reason'.* The 'hermeneutics of suspicion' must eventually yield to the 'hermeneutics of faith'. (Ricoeur 1973) For it is only thus that we will be able to bring a healing wholeness to the "broken totality" of our modern world, in Iris Murdoch's unforgettable phrase. This gives us *sixteenth sutra: the relationship between faith and reason must be pursued in the context of a hermeneutic circle as a dialogue or it will degenerate in a debate across an unbridgeable divide.*

It was Jonathan Swift who said that we have enough religion to hate each other but not enough to love each other. This can be rephrased in our last and seventeenth sutra: *we seem to have so much 'dogmatic belief' we become intolerant of each other, and not enough 'human faith' to appreciate and learn from each other*! Indeed, once a tradition gets locked into and becomes as ideology, whether religious, spiritual or even scientific, boundaries get fixed, borders are closed. There can be no 'fusion of horizons' only a clash of worldviews, and worse a 'clash of civilisations' once these are premised on antagonistic ideological worldviews, often masked as religious.

Triple Dialectic to Triple Dialogue: A Cosmotheandric Solidarity
For the triple dialectic to yield to a triple dialogue, we need to envision a more holistic universe in which the three are engaged in a mutually enriching interlocution. The domain of science with its reason and experimental method is the material cosmos. Humans are a *part of* this cosmos, not *apart from* it. The domain of religion is the transcendental beyond the material, the ultimate human concerns intrinsic to conscious human beings. Faith and experiential reflection stretch this domain beyond the just the human to the divine, whether this is conceived as a personal ultimate 'Thou', a saguna Brahma or an impersonal reality beyond the material, the Real of the real, a nirguna Brahma. Spirituality brings this together with its vision and way of life.

Thus, the cosmic, the human and the divine can come together in a cosmotheandric vision. (Panikkar 1977: 125) This is crucial to address the multiple crises overtaking our world today. The ecological crisis inflates them all and anticipates a disastrous catastrophe that could overtake our species and our planet. To address this effectively we must harmonise the material cosmos, human consciousness and integrate them all in a cosmostheandric solidarity, (RaimonPanikkar, http://www.infinityfoundation.com/mandala/i_es/i_es_panik_dharma.htm) underpinned by reason-based science and faith-based religion, and an eco-spirituality adequate to this task.

Pope Francis has attempted to sketch this in his encyclical *Laudatio Si* ('Praise be' the first words of Francis of Assisi's "Canticle to the Sun") The encyclical is subtitled: On Care for Our Common Home. It echoes the plea of the UN's Earth Summits: Only One Earth: Care and Share more emphatically and lyrically than the staid matter of fact UN Climate Change Agreement Conference, Paris 2015. (Ghose 2016: 201) The Pope refers to the patron saint of the environment: "Francis helps us to see that an integral ecology calls for openness to categories which transcend the language of mathematics and biology, and take us to the heart of what it is to be human." (Laudato Si No 11) Indeed, if we do not get our act together and bring science, religion and spirituality on the same platform, we might sleepwalk through the Great Derangement overtaking us (Ghose 2016) and precipitate an already looming apocalypse, a pralaya.

References

Alfaro, Juan, 1968, "Faith", *Sacramentum Mundi*, ed., Karl Rahner, Herder and Herder, New York, 313 – 322.

Beyer, Peter, 1994. *Religion and Globalization*, Sage, London.

Buber, Martin, 1958, *I – Thou*, Charles Scribner, New York.

Dilthey, Wilhelm, 1991, Selected Works, Vol 1, ed., Makkreel, Rudolf A', and Frithjof Rodi. Princeton Univ Press, Princeton.

D'Sa, Francis X. S.J. "*Art and Spirituality*", unpublished manuscript.

Finch, Henry Le Roy, 1987, "Reason", in *The Encyclopaedia of Religion*, ed., Mircea Eliade, Vol. 12, Macmillan, New York, 223 – 224. 16.

Gadamer, Hans Georg, *Philosophical Hermeneutics*, 1977, trans. and ed. David E. Linge, Univ. of California Press, Berkeley.

Ghosh, Amitav, 2016, *Great Derangement - Climate Change and the Unthinkable,* Penguin, India.

Kuhn, Thomas, 1970. *The Structure of Scientific Revolutions*, Univ. of Chicago Press, Chicago.

Libano, J.B., 1982: 15, *Spiritual Discernment and Politics: Guidelines for Religious Communities*, trans. Theodore Morrow, Orbis Books, New York.

Linge, David E., 1977, "Introduction", pp. - ix – lv. in Gadamer, op.cit.

Marcel, Gabriel, 1951, *Homo Viator: Introduction to a Metaphysic of Hope*. H. Regnery Co.,Washington, D.C..

O'Dea, Thomas, 1969. *Sociology of Religion*, Prentice-Hall, N. Delhi.

Panikkar, Raimondo, 1977, "Colligite Fragmenta: For an Integration of Reality" in *From Alienation to At-oneness,* eds. F.A. Eigo and S. E. Fittipaldi, Villanova Univ. Press, Villanova, Penn.

Panikkar, Raimon, 1995, *Cultural Disarment: The Way to Peace,* (trans. Robert R. Barr, Westminster John Know Press, Louisville, Kentucky.

Panikkar, Raymond, 1971. "Faith-A Constitutive Dimension of Man", *Journal of Ecumenical Studies*, V.8, N.2, pp. 223 – 254.

Panikkar Raimon, 2013, *The Rhythm of Being: The Unbroken Trinity*, The Gifford Lectures Edinburgh University Panikkar, Orbis Books, NY.

Pascal, Blaise, 1958, *Pensées, E.P. Dutton and Co., NY.*

Popper, Karl, 1962, *The Open Society*, Routledge and Kegan Paul, London.

Ricoeur, Paul, 1973, "Ethics and Culture: Habermas and Gadamer in Dialogue", *Philosophy Today*, Vol.17, Summer, pp. 153 – 165.

Thomas, W.I. and D.S. Thomas, 1928, *The child in America: Behaviour problems and programs.* Knopf, New York.

Tillich, Paul, 1958, *Dynamics of Faith*, Harper and Row, New York.

Weber, Max, 1968, *Economy and Society: An Outline of Interpretive Sociology,* New York, Bedminster Press.

Weber, Max, 1964, *Sociology of Religion*, Beacon Press, Boston.

Wittgenstein, Ludwig, 1967, *Philosophical Investigations*, (trans. G.E.M. Anscombe) Basil Blackwell, Oxford.

Covenantal Call and Eucharistic Engagement

Rajakumar Joseph S.J.

Covenant is a central Christian concept that binds and defines our understanding of God and our relationship with God. The covenant is an expression of God's grace and unconditional love for his people. It is a bond between God and his people, which makes us heirs to God's promises and blessings. "When Christian theology speaks about the covenant, it is speaking about God's gift of revelation and salvation."[1] The covenant is the sign that Christianity is part of God's plan and Salvation. It is a sign of God's fidelity to his people. The initiative to invite the covenant partner comes from God himself. We become God's chosen people, sons and daughters of God, "the two partners become blood relatives"[2] and they enter into a relationship which necessarily involves promises.[3] In other words, through covenant Israel became "literally the son of God and somehow shared in the divine nature."[4] The covenant, thus, paved way for adoptive sonship, a deep partnership with God and a special relationship with God. The significant element of a covenant was "a demand or approach (negotiations) and a response visibly accepting the demand as finally defined. Such a sequence created a known relationship because it was defined and visibly accepted. And this is covenant."[5] Thus covenant was an event, an action and a state of life, a relationship, not a word.[6]

Biblically the idea of covenant relationship can be traced from Genesis onwards with its complex and evolving history. The Hebrew word that refers to covenant in Old Testament is *Berit* (*Berith*). Many scholars are of the opinion that the word *Berith* is most likely derived from an Assirian word or Accadian *"bari"*, which means to bind or fetter, in the sense of a bond or treaty.[7] It brings about a legally binding relationship of solidarity with God and human beings mutually.[8] The word *berith* occurs nearly 300 times in the Old Testament, to refer to the meaning that there is a bond of union being established between two parties. "*Berith* had a "secular" meaning, that is, a non-transcendent comprehension, as well as a religious significance."[9] In its secular meaning, it stands for social relationship between two groups or parties or two persons, who make an agreement and seal it through a symbolic ritual act.[10] The symbolic ritual act is the concrete expression of the deeper bond envisaged by both the parties. When the covenant is made by God with his people, it takes a religious - transcendent sense that God becomes their protector and provider, while the subjects are expected to be faithful to his commandments. The ritualistic and cultic signification of the concept 'berith,' gives it a religious insight.[11]

When the word 'berith' was translated into Greek in Septuagint, the authors used the word 'diatheke' and not 'syntheke.' "If 'berith' was understood by LXX writers as a 'contract', 'treaty' or 'covenant' (in the simple sense), the obvious Greek rendering would have been 'syntheke.'"[12] But the New Testament writers did not perceive God's covenant as a treaty between equals, but as "a divine provenience, a grace. It was a result of a choice."[13] Therefore they view it as a "benevolent disposition, like that of a man making his will (*diatheke*)."[14] Hence they chose the Greek word, 'diatheke,' which implies a disposition, a relationship, an arrangement, a testament or a will made by one party with plenary power, which the other party may accept or reject, but cannot alter.[15] In a nutshell, the word 'diatheke,' not only implies an agreement made by God to protect and provide for his people, but also a benevolent disposition which is revealed in God's mercy and unconditional love for his chosen people.

Covenant in the Bible

In the Bible we read about a number of different covenants between human beings. The covenant between Jacob and Laban to settle their family hostility (cf., Gen 31: 44-45) is an apt example of a covenant between human beings. They piled up stones as a witness to their mutual oath and offered sacrifice and ate a covenantal meal together. So also David and Jonathan entered into a covenant to seal their friendship (cf., 1 Sam. 18, 20). Bible also describes various covenants between tribes (cf., 1 Sam. 11:1; Judg. 2:2; Ex. 23:32), between a king and his people (cf., 2 Kings 11:4; 2 Chron. 23), between kings themselves (cf., 1 Kings 20:34) and also between a king and his vassals (cf., 2 Kings 11:4).[16] The marriage contract between a man and his wife was also viewed as a covenant (cf. Mal. 2:14).

Nevertheless, what captures our attention in this article is the covenant made by God with his people. Indeed the first covenant is the '**covenant of works**,' which God made in the context of creation (cf., Gen. 3:15).[17] It was followed by the promise that God made to Cain that no one would slay him (Gen 4:15). But the concrete and visible covenant was found in the promise of God to Noah. **Noah's Covenant** - God tells Noah, "I will establish my covenant with you," (Gen. 6:18). Here we notice, "God comes to Noah and his sons and announces that he will establish his covenant with them and with every living creature. The scope then of this promise is not limited to Noah and his seed, but is universal."[18] It is applicable to the whole human race. The rainbow becomes the sign of God's intention that envelopes history from creation to new creation, which will be made through the blood of Jesus Christ[19] and will become the everlasting covenant.

Abraham's Covenant: The universal nature of the covenant develops into an eternal one, when God makes his covenant with Abraham

(Gen. 15 and 17). In this covenant of grace, Abraham received three promises – "a great posterity, a special relationship with God, and the land of Canaan."[20] God promised to give Abraham the Land and had made him the Father of "a multitude of nations" (Gen 17:4). In this God pledged an everlasting covenant and went to be God of Abraham and of his offspring (cf., Gen 17:7). Then God went on to say, you and your offspring 'shall keep my covenant,' (cf., Gen 17:9). He extended the same covenant later with Isaac and Jacob (cf., Gen 26:3, 28:13-15).

Mosaic Covenant: The Mosaic Covenant is very significant in the history of Israel. It takes place on Mount Sinai and there God declares his general terms of the covenant. *"If you obey my voice and keep my covenant, you shall be my treasured possession out of all the peoples. Indeed the whole earth is mine, but you shall be for me a priestly kingdom and a holy nation"* (Ex. 19:5-6). The people replied, *"Everything that the Lord has spoken we will do"* (Ex. 19:8). Though the Mosaic covenant looks like a Suzerain-vassal relationship[21] between God and his people, it is beyond Suzerain approach. A Suzerain is the conqueror, who makes unilateral treaties and the vassal is obliged to swear allegiance and loyalty to the Suzerain. The Suzerain in turn will help and protect the faithful vassal. But in God's covenant, "the people are also adopted into a filial relationship with God (Ex. 4:22; Deut. 8:5). He was not only their suzerain; he was their Father."[22] The Sinaitic covenant, which is sealed in blood (Ex. 24:8) contains **five divine promise**, (1) Israel is God's treasured possession, (2) Kingdom of Royal Priests, (3) A Holy Nation, (4) God will defend Israel from all her enemies and (5) God will be merciful, gracious and forgiving.

The Mosaic covenant reveals that the foundation of covenant is grace and steadfast love. The Israelites in turn love God, more than anything else. Due to this love, they obey His word and keep his covenant. Therefore, the obedience of the people is not to earn God's grace, instead overwhelmed by God's grace and love, they obey and trust his words. They experience forgiveness by trusting the one who forgives. However in weak moments, the Israelites did not keep the covenant. They broke the covenant. In a normal course of action, God should be punishing the Israelites. But God revealed that covenant is based on grace and he renewed the covenant, saying, *The Lord, the Lord, a God merciful and gracious, slow to anger, and abounding in steadfast love and faithfulness, keeping steadfast love for the thousandth generation, forgiving iniquity and transgression and sin, yet by no means clearing the guilty, but visiting the iniquity of the parents upon the children and the children's children to the third and the fourth generation* (Ex. 34: 6-7). God, thus, demonstrated himself as a merciful and gracious God.

Davidic Covenant: The Covenant with David resembles in much the same way as that of Abraham's covenant. "In David, the promise to the patriarchs is fulfilled, and renewed."[23] However the newness in the Davidic covenant is the offer of Kingdom and his rule over it. God tells David, "I will raise up your offspring after you, who shall come forth from your body, and I will establish his kingdom" (2 Sam. 7:12; 1 Chr. 17:12-13). Thus God promises them the land and his rule over that land, by choosing his servant to bring justice to the nations. Though the usual word for covenant '*berith*,' is not found in the Davidic references in 2 Samuel 7 and 1 Chronicles 17, the word used is *hesed* and it functions almost as synonym for *berit*.[24] Keeping this promises in mind the prophet Isaiah refers to Israelites as covenantal community, which is called to be a light to the nations, "I have given you as a covenant to the people, a light to the nations" (Isa 42:6). In spite of these promises, the Israelites experienced the fall of Israel, Judah and the destruction of the temple. On account of the devastation of all outward symbols of God's covenant promises, people begin to lose hope in the covenant.

Jeremiah's New Covenant: In the light of destruction of all covenantal symbols and people losing hope, Jeremiah prophecies, God is not giving up on his promises. It is God who made the covenant and he "will win out because of his own fidelity, his *hesed*."[25] In order to emphasise God's fidelity and hope in steadfast love, the prophet Jeremiah proclaims a New Covenant of God. He writes, *The days are surely coming, says the Lord, when I will make a new covenant with the house of Israel and the house of Judah.... I will put my law within them, and I will write it on their hearts; and I will be their God, and they shall be my people. No longer shall they teach one another, or say to each other, 'Know the Lord,' for they shall all know me, from the least of them to the greatest, says the Lord; for I will forgive their iniquity; and remember their sin no more.* (Jer 31:31-34). The New Covenant underscores the interiorization of the law and inscribing of the law of love in their hearts.

Ezekiel's New Covenant: Nearly about twenty years after Jeremiah comes prophet Ezekiel and reiterates the coming of the New Covenant as internalization of Torah and an inner renewal involving a heart transplant and the conferral of a new spirit.[26] According to him, "A new heart I will give you, and a new spirit I will put within you" (Ez. 36:26-27). The new spirit is God's own spirit and hence they will know the Lord internally and perceive him through his own Spirit. Hence Yahweh is not only speaking of physical regeneration, but also of spiritual renewal to bring about a new attitude towards God. Thus the covenantal concept of God has evolved: from old covenant to a new covenant with significant developments in their nature and character.

Significant Features of the Covenant

1. Yahweh established the covenant with Israelites because of his unconditional love for them. The Hebrew root word that expresses the **unconditional love is 'ahabhah**. In the Old Testament context, it expresses the relationship with Yahweh and Israel (Dt. 10:12; 11:13, 22; 19:9, Jer 2:2) and thus indicates total love which demands all of one's energies.[27] The unconditional love not only presupposes an inner disposition, but also includes a conscious act on behalf of the person, who is loved. Therefore the axis of

God's covenant is unconditional love. The best example from the biblical figures is found in 1 Sam. 18:3-4 – "Jonathan made a covenant with David, because he loved him as his own soul. Jonathan stripped himself of the robe that he was wearing, and gave it to David, and his armor, and even his sword and his bow and his belt." They, thus, seal their friendship with a covenant (*berith*)[28] and Jonathan demonstrated his faithfulness to their loving friendship. God's **covenant-love (*hesed*)** is much more than this and hence God is infinitely merciful and calls Israel as *Kahal Yahweh* (treasured possession - Ex. 19:6).

2.   The result of this covenantal love is ***shalom***, meaning peace or wholeness. Pedersen writes, *shalom* or *berith*, peace or covenant,

> Do not designate different kinds of relationship. *Shalom* means the state of prevailing in those united: the growth and full harmony of the soul, *berith* the community with all the privileges and duties implied in it. Therefore both the words may be used together, a "covenant of peace" (Ezek. 34:25; 37:26; Ps. 55:21), and if it does not appear from the context, we cannot see whether mention is made of kinship or friendship.[29]

Hence to enter into a covenant also implies enter into a relationship to bring about peace. Peace is a rich positive word, it denotes mutual confidence, and harmony of the community. The peace that flows from the covenant is one that wells up from the depth of mutual trust. According to Pedersen, "*Shalom* is the full manifestation of the soul, and if souls are united, then their *shalom* consists in their acting together for the common prosperity."[30] When the souls are united, their wills are also united to work for growth of the community. The state of *shalom* is the ideal ambience for fellowship in every relationship.[31] The deepest aim of the covenant is to set Israel on *shalom* status, where they experience protection, love and prosperity.

3.   The blend of 'unconditional love and shalom' results in God's unbreakable fidelity (Emet). It is this unbreakable fidelity that keeps the covenant forever. God's fidelity does not depend on

human fidelity to the promises they make. God's fidelity is anchored on Love, Truth and Integrity. God is truthful to his love. In spite of Israel's doubtful fidelity, God remained unwavering in his faithfulness to renew and restore the covenant. The divine stubborn fidelity to his promise stems from God's gratuitous grace, which is not the effect of the covenant, but precedes and causes it.

4. **The blood** of the Sinaitic Covenant is the sign of "**communion sacrifice**." According to Ex. 24:6-8, "Moses took half of the blood and placed it in cups; with the remainder of the blood he sprinkled on the altar...." When people agreed to practice the covenant, "Moses took the blood, sprinkled the people with it, and said: Here is the blood of the covenant, which Yahweh has made with you on the basis of all these prescriptions." In this act God is represented by the altar, and the people are sprinkled by the same blood and therefore they communicate in the same life. This unity of life is not a sign or suggestive, but operative.[32] The blood sacrificed here plays a **Unitive function**. It becomes an instrument that unites God and his people. The two ritual actions of sprinkling the blood on the altar and on the people function like a dialogue that bridges both the parties and symbolizes a covenant of communion.[33] It is on account of this covenant communion that Yahweh says, "I shall be your God and you shall be my people"(Jr. 7:23, 31:33; Ex 6:7; Gen. 17:7-8; Ez. 36:28).

Secondly, blood for Israelites is the **symbol of life**. In Deuteronomy we read, "Be sure that you don't eat the blood, for the blood is life," (Dt. 12:33). Israelites always remember, how the smearing of blood on the lintel protected them from death and gave them a new lease of life in the Passover from Egypt to the Promised Land. They also knew that "any person or object signed by the blood of the altar (cf., Ex.36 ff) is drawn into the sphere of the holy, of divine favour, and thus is withdrawn from disaster."[34] Blood thus is the sign of life and holiness.

Thirdly, from their own experience of atonement sacrifices, Israelites were aware of the **Purificatory role of blood**. According to Leviticus, "For the life of the flesh is in the blood; and I have given it to you for making atonement for your lives on the altar; for, as life, it is the blood that makes atonement" (Lev. 17:11). Thus blood had an expiatory function in forgiving sins and restoring life and people to God. God's covenant brought about union, provided them with a new lease of life and made them Holy people of God.

5.   **The New Covenant**: The New Covenant, according to Jeremiah, first underscores the redemptive and restorative act of God in his love and mercy. Secondly it is no more external, but places the law within the heart, so that there is no need to teach each other 'know the Lord', but they will know the Lord personally. It insists on personalization and interiorization of the law, made possible by the Spirit.[35] The law is now the very spirit of the Lord and he gives himself in his Spirit.[36] The Spirit is a gift from the risen Lord. Thirdly, the expression, 'know the Lord' (Jer. 31:34) indicates the type of binding relationship caused by the Covenant fidelity.[37] Hence they remain faithful to the New Covenant. Fourthly, the new covenant remits their sins and removes their uncleanness (Ez. 36:25). In this way, they receive a new heart, through which God himself lives in their heart and enables them to produce fruits of holiness within their hearts.[38] Finally, the new covenant is a continuation and fulfilment of all that was promised in the old covenant. It is an everlasting covenant (Is. 61:8 and Jer. 32:40). In the light of Isaiah and Jeremiah, the new covenant is a spiritually renewed relationship with Yahweh and it will be sustained forever. Jesus Christ is the ultimate mediator, who would establish this New and everlasting Covenant.

Jesus Christ the Mediator of the New Covenant

The true meaning of the old covenant is revealed in Jesus Christ, who is the mediator and fulfilment of the new covenant. "Jesus Christ is the mediator of the new covenant because of his sacrifice on the cross. The necessity of the death of Christ is emphasized on the ground that a covenant requires a blood sacrifice (Heb. 9:15ff)."[39] In the Exodus covenant event (Ex. 24:1-11), Moses took half of the blood and sprinkled it on the altar and he took the second half of the blood, which was called "the blood of the covenant," and sprinkled it on the people. The 'blood of the covenant,' here symbolized union and a true sharing in the blessings of the covenant.[40] In the same way, Jesus takes the Mosaic Formula, makes it his own and articulates it in the first person of the personal pronoun: 'my blood of the covenant.' Like the blood of the Mount Sinai under Moses, the blood of Jesus at Calvary unites God and his people and brings infinite blessings to people, who participate in it.[41]

Jesus anticipates the infinite blessings of the New Covenant and symbolically places it in the Last Supper context and paves way to be remembered for generations to come. Jesus, who instituted the last supper in the Upper Room, initiated the process of new covenant, by inviting his disciples to 'take, eat and drink. Through this prophetic symbolism, "Jesus offered to his disciples a life of fellowship with God, represented in their 'eating and drinking' the bread and the wine."[42] According to the Antiochene tradition, "By drinking of the cup the disciples enter into the covenant instituted by Jesus, they thereby make real the oneness symbolized by the single cup: oneness with Jesus, oneness among themselves, and therefore oneness with God himself."[43] The oneness with God and God's people is substance of the New Covenant. The blessing of 'the blood of the new covenant,' is fellowship with God and once again becoming 'children of God.' The blood at Sinai covenant was of animal and external, but Jesus sheds his own blood at Calvary and makes the New Covenant to be internal and eternally binding.

According to the Gospel of Matthew, "the covenant presupposes the forgiveness of sins."[44] Jesus says, "Drink from it, all of you; for this is my blood of the covenant, which is poured out for many for the forgiveness of sins" (Mt 26:28). Matthew draws inspiration from the Suffering Servant text of Isaiah (cf., Is. 53: 10, Heb. 9:22) and emphasizes that the forgiveness of sins is one of the main characteristics of the mystery of the death of Jesus and the New Covenant. St. Paul writes, Christ was sent by God as a sacrifice of atonement, by his blood (cf. Rom 3:25). It means, "Christ's offering has the character of atonement. Those who unite themselves with him and are sprinkled with his sacrificial blood will really be cleansed internally."[45] Christ's blood and death not only reconcile the people with God but also make forgiveness possible for them. In fact, the crucifixion is the beginning of the New Covenant; for through his death, he broke the power of evil and replaced all Old Covenant sacrifices by his once and for all sacrifice of himself (Heb.10:12ff). Though the Gospel of Mark and Mathew use the words, 'For the multitude' and 'For many' respectively, the intended meaning according to Semitic anthropology is 'for all.' According to Semitic understanding, "the human race is not a crowd of individuals but, a *single* reality that is created by God."[46] The blood of Jesus, thus, is shed for the forgiveness and salvation of the entire humanity, which reaches the entire humanity through the disciples. However, the drinking from the cup is not merely to purify and expiate the sins alone, but more so to nourish themselves and live more fully in abundance.

In fulfilling the prophecy of Ezekiel (cf., Ez. 36:27), Jesus by his death gives his own Spirit and "the Spirit makes the covenant a personal reality in each believer."[47] The new covenant, due to its internal and personal fidelity is unbreakable. Moreover the blood of the new covenant is not externally sprinkled on the people who receive it passively, but the 'cup' must be taken and 'drunk' in accordance with the command of Jesus.[48] In the context of Israelites, cup symbolized passion, destiny and suffering. Hence the disciples were invited to join in the mission of Jesus Christ, by drinking his own blood from the same cup. When Jesus offered the cup in the context of Last Supper, he was indeed offering participation in the salvific passion, death and resurrection. By our communion in the body and blood of Christ, we are appropriating the mystery of the paschal mystery and we are invited to enter into the same self emptying mission of Jesus Christ to give life in abundance.

Eucharistic Covenantal Mission and Social Love

"A sacrament is always an act that establishes a covenant community."[49] The celebration of the Eucharist is therefore a covenantal act wherein the participants accept the gift of Jesus as sustenance for their lives, with a sense of being one community, which is united by social love. In the Eucharistic covenantal community all are brothers and sisters belonging to the same family of God. Jesus as the source of sustenance for all, the Eucharist brings with it the responsibility of becoming ourselves, with Jesus, a source of sustenance for others who are in need of bread and social acceptance for survival. Thus the Eucharistic community comes out with a message of unity to heal the divisions, bridge the gulf between high and low caste and build an inclusive covenantal community. Hence, "to enter through the Eucharist into the covenant is to accept far more seriously the brotherhood, the common destiny of mankind, and the obligations toward the needy among all mankind than any state has ever been willing to do."[50] The Eucharist covenantal love, thus inculcates in us a deep sense of social love.

The encyclical *Mysterium Fidei*, emphasizes the theme of 'social love' as the spring board and the consequence of our participation in the Eucharist. It says;

> The worship paid to the divine Eucharist strongly impels the soul to cultivate a **"social love,"** by which the common good is given preference over the good of the individual. Let us consider as our own the interests of the community, of the parish, of the entire church, extending our charity to the whole world, because we know that everywhere there are members of Christ.[51]

The encyclical makes it explicit that the worship of the Eucharist is always a call to give priority to the common good over one's individual choices and likes. In other words, 'social responsibility' takes priority over the individual needs. Hence any meaningful Eucharist has to result in a strong experience of 'social love' and 'social responsibility.' Without this crucial depth our Eucharist will remain a meaningless cultic celebration.

Nonetheless, the concept of 'social love' that emerges from our participation and communion in the Eucharist has to culminate in our efforts towards social justice in our neighbourhood, in our ministries and in our apostolates. The social love is the reflection of our love of God. The document *Justice in the World,* affirms that the love of neighbour is essentially linked to the love of God, and connects this love with justice. Thus faith and justice are related in building a just society. It says:

> According to the Christian message, therefore, man's relationship to his neighbour is bound up with his relationship to God; his response to the love of God, saving us through Christ, is shown to be effective in his love and service of man. Christian **love of neighbour and justice** cannot be separated. For love implies an absolute demand for justice, namely, a recognition of the dignity and rights of one's neighbour. Justice attains its inner fullness in love.[52]

Thus this document makes two vital points: 1. love of God springs from the love of neighbour, and 2. the dignity of the human person demands social justice. These two are integral to any theologizing process and have a strong inner unity: justice reaches its fullness in love of God and love of neighbour. The Eucharist is central to both and leads from one to the other. Therefore a total participation in the Eucharist implies our total participation in the struggle for a just society seeking its actual transformation.

Addressing the Hierarchy in America, Pope Paul VI said: "The Eucharist is of supreme relevance to our people in their Christian lives. It is of supreme effectiveness for the transformation of the world in justice, holiness, and peace."[53] Thus the Eucharistic celebration is a mission of transformation of the world and not just a pious activity that is at peace with the status-quo and is satisfied with a few charitable and developmental activities. The Eucharistic mission entails that we take the oppressed people seriously and fight for justice that they may have life in its fullness. It is in this struggle for the suffering masses that we become holy and in bringing fullness of life to them that we seek peace. We are not mere passive peace lovers satisfied with the existing unjust situations, but peace makers,[54] who live a life of a prophet challenging the existing unjust structures.

From the Altar of the Lord to the Altar of the world[55]
Leon Dufour says that the Eucharist is a challenge that enables us to cross over to the other shore[56] (cf. Mk 4:35). In essence, our participation in the Eucharist cannot but be a moment of both inner and outer transformation and crossing over. In our mission to cross over to the other shore, the table fellowship, as a school of charity, justice and peace, liberates each one for taking initiatives to alleviate hunger, to care for the marginalized, and to help out in social activities. Consequently the Eucharistic covenantal mission stands as a challenge to the racist, ethnic, and caste based groups. According to Aloysius Pieris, such a challenging Liturgy is the 'liturgy of life'[57] welcoming the dawn of a *full humanity.*[58]

The Eucharist is an experience of God and neighbour through the vertical and horizontal axis. The Eucharistic communion with the Lord culminates in our covenantal communion with one another in social love to serve and sacrifice ourselves for the mission. The social love that constitutes the Eucharistic mystery reminds us of our social responsibility to commit ourselves for the cause of the Dalits, Tribals and other oppressed sections of the society, who are truly and equally members of the Eucharistic body of Christ. Hence, the Eucharistic mission today is to respond to the covenantal call of self-emptying and radical availability for social commitment and solidarity, to bring integral liberation and wholeness to the broken people and to build inclusive communities.

Endnotes

[1] Joann Spillman, "The Image of Covenant in Christian Understanding of Judaism," in *Journal of Ecumenical Studies,* Vol. 35, No. 1, (1998), 67.

[2] Bouwmeester, *The Bible on the Covenant,* Trans. Ingrid Van Ladesteyn, (Wisconsin: St. Norbert Abbey Press, 1966), 13.

[3] Cf. Paul R. Williamson, *Sealed with an Oath: Covenant in God's Unfolding Purpose,* (Illinois: Inter Varsity Press, 2007), 35.

[4] Dennis J. McCarthy, "Covenant in the Old Testament: Present State of Inquiry," in *The Catholic Biblical Quarterly,* Vol. XXVII, no. 3, (July: 1965), 217.

[5] D J. Mecarthy, *Treaty and Covenant,* Analecta Biblica 21 A. (Rome: Biblical Institute Press, 1978), 21.

[6] Cf., Ibid., 14.

[7] Cf., Cf. Paul R. Williamson, *Sealed with an Oath: Covenant in God's Unfolding Purpose,* 37.

[8] Joseph Kottackal, "Deuteronomy: The Book of the Covenant," in *Bible Bhashyam,* Vol. XV, No. 2 (June: 1989), 77.

[9] Charles LaFontaine, "Sacrament as a Sign of Covenant," in *Review for Religious,* Vol, 34, No. 4 (1975), 559.

[10] Cf., Ibid., 559.

[11] Paul Palatty, "Discipleship and the Covenant," in Bible Bhashyam, vol. XIII, No. 3, (September, 1987), 200.

[12] J.C. Hindley, "The Translation of Words for 'Covenant', in *Indian Journal of Theology,* Vol. 10, (1961), 19.

[13] Albert Gelin, *The Key Concepts of the Old Testament,* Trans., George Lamb, (London: Sheed and Ward, 1955), 38.

[14] Ibid., 38.

[15] Gerhard Kittel, Edit., *Theological Dictionary of the New Testament,* Geoffrey W. Bromley, Trans., Vol. II, (Michigan: Eerdmans Publishing comp. 1968), 128.

[16] Cf., William G. Morrice, "New Wine in Old Wine-Skins", in *The Expository Times,* vol. 86, (1974-75), 132.

[17] Cf. Paul R. Williamson, *Sealed with an Oath: Covenant in God's Unfolding Purpose,* 69.

[18] William Dryness, *Themes in Old Testament*, (Virginia: The Paternoster Press, 1979), 116.

[19] Cf. Paul R. Williamson, *Sealed with an Oath: Covenant in God's Unfolding Purpose*, 68.

[20] William G. Morrice, "New Wine in Old Wine-Skins", 133.

[21] Cf. Paul R. Williamson, *Sealed with an Oath: Covenant in God's Unfolding Purpose*, 121. He writes, "A 'father-Son' relationship between suzerain and vassal (also known as the suzerain's servant) creates a legal basis for the gift of an enduring dynasty. The suzerain guarantees protection for vassal or his heir by promising to annihilate a common enemy, so long as loyalty to the suzerain is maintained. The Suzerain guarantees protection of the vassal's people, with whom a subsidiary agreement is sometimes made."

[22] William Dryness, Themes in Old Testament, 119.

[23] George Mendenhall, "Covenant," in *Interpreter's Dictionary of the Bible*, Vol. I, (Nashville: Abingdon Press, 1962), 718.

[24] Cf. Paul R. Williamson, *Sealed with an Oath: Covenant in God's Unfolding Purpose*, 121.

[25] Xavier Leon-Dufour, *Sharing the Eucharistic Bread*, (New York: Paulist Press, 1987), 149.

[26] Cf., Cf. Paul R. Williamson, *Sealed with an Oath: Covenant in God's Unfolding Purpose*, 167.

[27] Cf., G. Johannes Botter weck and Helmer Ringgen, Edit., *Theological Dictionary of Old Testament*, Vol.I, Trans. John T. Willis, (Michigan: William B. Eerdmanns, 1974), 103. It also uses the Greek word *agapao* to refer to this Hebrew word *ahabhah*.

[28] G. Johannes Botter weck and Helmer Ringgen, Vol.I, 105.

[29] J. Pedersen, *Israel: Its Life and Culture*, Vol. I, (Atlanta, Georgia: Scholars Press, 1970), 285.

[30] Ibid., 287.

[31] William G. Morrice, "New Wine in Old Wine-Skins," 132.

[32] Bouwmeester, *The Bible on the Covenant*, Trans. Ingrid Van Ladesteyn, 27.

[33] Cf., Leon Dufour, *Sharing the Eucharistic Bread*, 144.

[34] Bouwmeester, *The Bible on the Covenant*, Trans. Ingrid Van Ladesteyn, 27.

[35] Cf., Paul Palatty, "Discipleship and the Covenant," in Bible Bhashyam, vol. XIII, No. 3, (September 1987), 204.

[36] Cf., Leon-Dufour, *Sharing the Eucharistic Bread*, 150.

[37] Cf., Paul Palatty, "Discipleship and the Covenant," in *Bible Bhashyam*, vol. XIII, No. 3, (September, 1987), 204.

[38] Cf., Leon-Dufour, *Sharing the Eucharistic Bread*, 150.

[39] William G. Morrice, "New Wine in Old Wine-Skins," 134.

[40] Cf., Ibid., 135.

[41] Cf., Vincent Taylor, *Jesus and His Sacrifice: A Sturdy on the Passion Sayings in the Gospels*, (London: Maccillan and Co. 1937), 136.

[42] William G. Morrice, "New Wine in Old Wine-Skins," 135.

[43] Leon Dufour, *Sharing the Eucharistic Bread*, 154.

[44] Ibid., 148.

[45] Bouwmeester, *The Bible on the Covenant*, 99.

[46] Ibid., 148.

[47] Ibid., 152.

[48] Ibid., 147.

[49] Monika K. Hellwig, *The Eucharist and the Hunger of the World*, (New York: Paulist Press, 1976), 55.

[50] Ibid., 66.

[51] Pope Paul VI, *Mysterium Fidei: The Mystery of Faith*, (3rd September 1965), No. 69.

[52] Synod of Bishops, *Justice in the world*, (30th November,1971), 3.

[53] Paul VI, "The Eucharistic sacrifice as center of the Church's unity," Address to the Bishops of Regions I and II of the United States, in *DOL* no. 189, (15 June, 1978), 433.

[54] Cf. Willian Barclay, *The Daily Study Bible: The Gospel of Mathew*, vol. 1 (Bangalore: Theological Publications in India: 1981), 108.

[55] John Paul II, *Ecclesia De Eucharistia*, no.8, Supplement to *Petrus*, vol.25, nos. 5-6, (May-June 2003): 8.

[56] Xavier, Leon-Dufour, *Sharing the Eucharistic Bread*, 300.

[57] Cf. Aloysius Pieris, *An Asian Theology of Liberation*, (New York: Orbis Books, 1988), 4-6.

[58] Ibid., 126.

Evolving Contextual Images of Jesus in India

The Role of the Christian Community and Theologians

Ghattamaneni Jayaraj S.J.

Introduction

The Christological question is at the epi-center of Christian living and theology. When I study theology (in specific Christology), I come across many images of Christ explored and enunciated by theologians. In the process of academic discussion about these Christological images, I often wondered by a recurring comment 'it takes time to explain these images to the faithful'. This astonishment triggers me to actually delve into the pastoral significance of the Christological images proposed by theologians by exploring whether they evolved from the Christian community's experience of Jesus Christ or not. I see the pressing need to respond to the questions: Is there correspondence between the images of Christ proposed by theologians and the images of Christ emerging from existential and experiential encounter of the faithful? How do Christological images make the Community and how do Christological images evolve within the community of faithful in India?

Seeking answer to those questions, I propose that every intellectual theological endeavor sees to it that any Images of Christ proposed by theologians in the Indian context of socio-political-cultural-religious plurality emerge from Christ experience of the community of faithful consolidated by personal experience so that owning those images as their own, the faithful shall be guided to lead a committed Christian life of witnessing to love and justice in their actual, living context.

I reach this horizon by first exploring the status of Christian community in the present Indian context of religious fanaticism, political vagueness and economic looting. In the second part, starting with a brief overview of Jesus' images from Children of light from India, some images of Christ proposed by Indian theologians like Michael Amaladoss and Sebastian Kappen and their significance and influence on the community will be explored. Having explored those images, I present the conclusions from a random survey (in the form of a questionnaire) conducted in the local parishes to discover people's perception of images of Christ and their effect on their lives.

Indian Christians - Challenges and Dilemmas

The Indian census shows that the Christians make 2.30% (2.78 crores) of Indian population.[1] Christianity is the third highest practicing religion in India. It is a negligible minority in comparison to 79.8% of Hindus and 14.23% of Muslim population.[2] Though minority in number Christians in India boldly proclaimed Christ and lived the values envisaged by the Gospel of Christ. Stanley Jones (1884-1973), a 20th century Methodist Christian missionary and a theologian comments that in India Christ is taken without Western civilization.[3]

After having grappled with Western influence in their practice of faith for so many years, Christians now make Christ their own in their Indian context, culture and community. Through centuries of its presence Christianity influenced various aspects of Indian society. Addressing the 30th Plenary Assembly of the Conference of Catholic Bishops of India (CCBI) of the Latin Church, in Bangalore on February 4, Cardinal Oswald Gracias said, "The Catholic Church needs our nation and India needs the Church."[4] This clarion call exposes the deep rootedness of Christianity on Indian soil and in

Indian hearts. However, being a minority, the journey with Christ on Indian roads has not always been smooth sailing. Christians in India are continuously exposed to varied and complex challenges and confused amidst irresistible dilemmas.

The Challenges

With the rise of Hindutva and implementation of the ideology of *gharvapasi* by the religious fundamentalists, the presence of the Church in India is at cross roads. The fact is that 10 years ago, India stood at 87% religious. Now, it has dwindled to 81%. There is a clear shift from belief to lack of belief in the Indian subcontinent.[5] We cannot blame the changing trends in the postmodern scenario. The Church needs to introspect and truthfully look within. Looking at the life of the teachers of the Church, the faith of the common Christian is weakened. There is incompatibility of beliefs and practices. The link between faith and life is missing. Vatican Council II rightly calls everyone to overcome, 'the false opposition between professional and social activities on the one hand, and religious life on the other' (GS 43). One of the serious errors of our age is, 'the split between the faith which many profess and their daily lives' (GS 43). It is also said that "The fault lies with us: we do not go to the fountain like the Samaritan woman or keep the lamp on the lamp stand as a faithful disciple should."[6] Christians seem to fail in allowing their image of Jesus to penetrate and permeate their lives.

The Dilemmas

Indian Christians find themselves at another cross road and are frozen in the face of the crises and the moment of decision. The vigorous resurgence of fundamentalist Hinduism or 'Hindutva' in our times has created an atmosphere of suspicion, if not open hostility, toward Christianity.[7] Combined with this is the strong nationalistic feeling which regards Christianity as foreign, alien, and symbolic of colonialism. The question is no longer how best to propagate the Gospel, the question has become how to survive.

The Christian community is drawn primarily from the socially and economically weaker sections of society and has yet to be liberated from the psychological, social and economic handicaps particularly in the rural area.[8] The Indian Christian has further to contend with divisiveness within the Church rendering it politically and economically weak in facing the crisis that confronts the Church today.

Another dilemma before the Indian Christian is to what extent s/he can merge her/his identity with general society and yet remain true to her/his faith and be an active member of her/his Church. We have a fear that conformity to the general pattern will lead to criticism from the Christian community and refusal to conform will be misconstrued by our Hindu hosts. The dilemma is, "merging the Indian Christian personality with the danger of losing his identity versus the refusal to adapt to the Indian culture and remaining isolated from the culture of our nation."[9] Christianity even after many years of its existence in India is not yet firmly rooted in the Indian soil and still depends for its sustenance – material, organizational, and spiritual on foreign help.

At this juncture, exploring and proclaiming the experiences of encounter with the person of Christ is the need of the hour. India needs Christ. Christianity in India should primarily be an expression of the Christ experience of the faithful and their genuine and prophetic response to the person of Jesus Christ. E. Stanley Jones calls himself an introducer to Christ when it comes to proclaiming Christ of the Indian Road.[10] He acknowledges that the task in India is, "to know Him, to introduce Him…to trust India with the Christ and trust Christ with India." [11] Jesus is his own witness. The person of Jesus will be irresistible to India today. Some of the Indians who found Christ on the Indian soil would create a spark on meeting Christ and frame Jesus' images.

Jesus' images from Children of Light in India

A glimpse at a few 'Children of light in India'[12] like Pandita Ramabai (1858-1952) from Maharastra, Ganga Dhor Sarroji from Orissa, Venkayaa from Andhra Pradesh, Sadu Sundar Singh (1889-1929) from Punjab elucidate how Christ captured the lives of Indians. Their image of Christ arose from their personal encounter with Jesus of the gospels.

Pandit Ramabai was captivated by the Gospel according to Luke. She was moved by the transformative power of Christ and exclaimed, "My heart is drawn to the religion of Christ."[13] In her fight for the upliftment of women, she realized that she had accepted Christ but had not found Christ completely. This indicates her search for Christ. She experienced Jesus as an emancipator from social alienation and suppression experienced by women in India. Christ was exalted in the life of this devoted daughter of India. His love was made manifest in her committed action of uplifting the widows and the orphans.

Ganga Dhor Sarraoji was the first Orissa convert. He too encountered the truth of Christ through the gospels. In speaking of Christ's great sacrifice, he exclaimed, "Men of wisdom, tell me where you find such love, and I will sit and listen!... Ah! you cannot find it anywhere on earth; this heavenly love. He who formed you has died in your stead. He who gave you life parted with His own to redeem you and give to you eternal life."[14] He experienced Christ as a lover who sacrificed his life to save every one.

Pagolu Venkayya of Krishna district, Andhra Pradesh, from his early life, was searching for a true God. He went to every temple and every *poojari* to seeking answer to his prayer: "O Great God, show Thyself to me!"[15] When he heard about Jesus from a Christian missionary, Thomas Y. Darling, Venkayya exclaimed: "This is my God... I have long been seeking Him, and now I have found Him. He is my saviour, I will serve Him."[16] He was baptized in 1859 by

Thomas Y. Darling and died on September 19, 1891. Jesus was a true God and Saviour to him. They sought Christ and found him. Their convinced proclamation of Christ through Indian voice influenced many others to embrace Christ and form their own images of Christ. This leads us to revisit the Jesus' images by two contemporary Indian theologians.

Images of Jesus: Indian Catholic Theologians

Indian theologians draw inspiration from the New Testament Jesus' images in order to locate their positions in terms of their faith and further to express their personal images of Jesus to a believing community.[17] They give shape to their experience of Jesus by attributing to him various titles that arise from their faith experience and their encounter with *Sitz im Leben* of the Christian community.

Michael Amaladoss

Michael Amaladoss explores images of Jesus in the light of the Gospels and in a multi-cultural and multi-religious context of India (Asia).[18] He looks at Jesus and understands his significance for India through images which are at work in their own culture and religious tradition. Jesus' encounter with Indian culture will give birth to some images that appeal to Indian people. He evokes the following images of Jesus: Jesus, the Sage; Jesus, the Way; Jesus, the Guru; Jesus, the Satyagrahi; Jesus, the Avatar and Jesus, the Dancer.[19] Each image evolves from a context and from diversity of experience. Consequently, an image might have its own pros and cons when we probe into it for establishing its authenticity either theologically or culturally. Here, I make no effort to explicate limitations of those images.

Sebastian Kappen

Sebastian Kappen explores images of Jesus in the poverty stricken and justice seeking context of India. The alarming instances of injustice and social alienation in India and within the Church make him present an image of Jesus, the prophet of a new humanity and the prophet of a counter culture.

Kappen's interpretation of the person of Jesus mainly concentrates on the function of Jesus as a prophet of a new humanity. He refers to the prophets in the Old Testament saying that "the more intense their longing for the future, the more vehement was also their criticism of social evils."[20] It is in the line of these great prophets that Jesus stands. Jesus as the Prophet of the New Humanity lived at a time when cult, law and apocalysptism had supplanted prophecy.[21] He created hope for a New Humanity by announcing the kingdom of God (reign of God) and by unfolding a horizon of hope.[22] Jesus, the prophet of hope is also an emerging image for Indian context seeking social-religious-political liberation.

The evangelists portrayed Jesus in response to the prevailing situation of the community. Jesus' images explored by Michael Amaladoss emerge out of multi religious-cultural set up of India. Familiarity with Indian or Asian cultures seems to be the prerequisite to understand these images. Similarly, Sebastian Kappen's image of Jesus erupts as a response to oppressive structures of India. There are various images of Jesus portrayed by many theologians, spiritual writers as well as well corporate writers.[23] Their effort is to present Jesus meaningfully to Christians as well as to the people of other faiths.

Now, I analyze what are the images surface from the Christian community's encounter with Christ and how many of these images, both from the Gospels and from the theologians, are appropriate to the community.

A Survey: Jesus' Images and the Christian Lay Faithful

The task before me is to determine whether there is meaningful conversation between the images of Jesus born out of the empirical reality of lived experiences of individual Christians and academic or systematic presentation of images by the theologians.

Grappling with this task at hand, I conducted a survey among the faithful with the following objectives: (1) to find out the images of Jesus emerging from individual Catholics; (2) to know how the images of Jesus are appropriated in the daily lives of ordinary believers; (3) to know the familiarity of the Christians with the images of Jesus from the theologians to see what creative and critical insights emerge; (4) to know what kind of images of Jesus, Catholics would envisage for India today. This study expands scholarly knowledge about the perception of Jesus Christ present among the ordinary Christians and helps to fill a gap in knowledge about Jesus among the ordinary Christians and the theologians.

Survey Method

The survey is conducted among the adult and educated Catholics of 17 years and above, chosen at random from the parishes in the city of Pune namely Dapodi (St. Thomas Church), Hadapsar (Mother Teresa Church), and Camp, Yerwada (Divine Mercy Church), Sainikwadi (Christ the King Church) and some individual Catholics are also surveyed randomly. The survey consists of a total 320 respondents. They were stratified into four groups according to their age: 17-30 years, 31-45 years, 46-60 years, 60 years and above. The respondents were given a questionnaire consisting of 9 closed-ended questions and 3 open-ended questions. A printed questionnaire was administered to them either by the researcher himself or by others who are well informed about the purpose and the details of the research. The questionnaire begins with probing into an individual's image of Jesus and his/her experience of Jesus Christ. Then, his/her familiarity with the images of Jesus from the Gospels and theologians is enquired which follows probing into his/her image of Jesus for India. A Statistical software (SPSS: Statistical Package for the Social Sciences) is used to analyze the data.

Survey Analysis

The total number of individuals surveyed are 320 of which 132 (41.25%) are males and 188 (58.75%) are females. Figure (1) clearly indicates the contribution of female participants is significantly higher than the male participant in all the age groups.

Table - 1

		Gender		Total
		Male	Female	
Age	17-30	50	70	120
	31-45	50	75	125
	46-60	19	33	52
	60 above	13	10	23
Total		132	188	320

Figure - 1

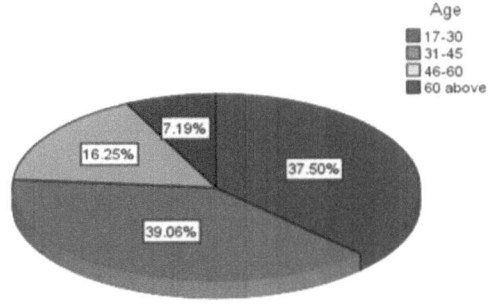

Initial Experience of Jesus

It is evident from 85% (107 Males 165 Females) of the respondents that they first learn about Jesus 'at home'. The next place where they first learnt about Jesus is at Catechism classes but only 9% of them. This is a clear sign that family plays a vital role in imparting the knowledge of Jesus to the children.

The image of Jesus, the Saviour, is very dominant among 42.5% of the faithful. The image of Jesus, the Healer, is also preferred by

18% of them. The other images among in the order of preference are Jesus the Immanuel, the Son of God, and the Friend respectively. They personally come to know about Christ from reading the Bible (56.9%) and from the sermons (21.9%). The analysis also indicates that very insignificant number of them come to know about Christ from book, hymns and other sources.

There are certain devotions that bring the individual Christians closer to Jesus like Holy Eucharist, Rosary, Family prayer and Sacred Heart devotions and others. For 51.9% of the respondents, it is Holy Mass and for 25.3% of them the family prayer plays a vital role to experience and come closer to the person of Jesus Christ. The other devotions like rosary and Sacred Heart devotions and others also help them.

The early Church was busy to determine the true nature of Jesus by raising questions about the nature of Jesus Christ whether he is fully human or fully divine; fully human and fully divine. When the respondents were asked about how they understand Jesus in the light of those terminologies, 186 (58.1%) of them expressed that Jesus is fully human and fully God and 85 (26.6%) of them said that they understand him as who is fully God (Figure 2).

Figure - 2

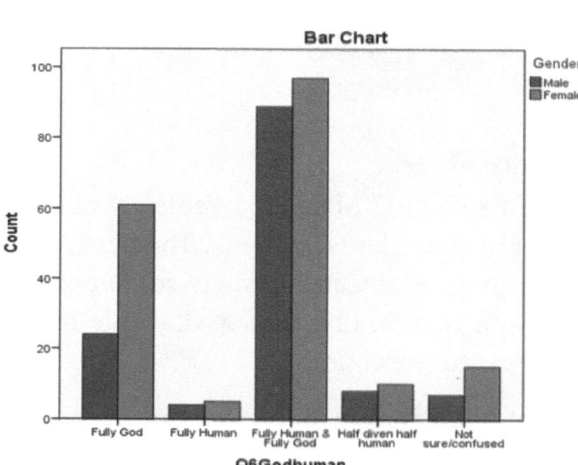

Conformity with the Images of Jesus from the Synoptic Gospels
We have seen that in the synoptic gospels the evangelists presented
Jesus the Son of God, the Son of Man, the Crucified Messiah, the
New Moses, the Immanuel, the Liberator, the Saviour, the Great
Reconciler and Healer. But when people read the Bible they create
an image of Jesus. These images either resonate with the images
proposed by the evangelists or new images might arise depending
on the context of an Individual Christian. The following images
recurred in many of the respondents: Jesus the Saviour, the miracle
worker, the teacher (referring to the Sermon on the Mount), good
Shepherd, the compassionate God, the forgiving God, the merciful,
the crucified Saviour. The images are not formed merely by reading
the Gospel but when they also encounter Jesus in their daily lives.
The majority of respondents experienced Jesus when they are facing
troubles and difficulties in life. They see him as a Saviour, a comforter,
a helper. Similarly, most of them also experience him as Healer
because they believe in the healing power of Jesus. So, the image
of Jesus as Healer is more prominent among the faithful who have
the personal experience of Jesus. The majority of the respondents
are familiar with the images of Jesus from the Gospel and it is also
clear that they accept the appropriateness of those images of Jesus
to their lives.

Table - 2
Saviour of All

		Frequency	Percent	Valid Percent	Cumulative Percent
Valid	Highly appropriate	272	85.0	85.0	85.0
	Appropriate	12	3.8	3.8	88.8
	Less Appropriate	2	.6	.6	89.4
	Not Appropriate	34	10.6	10.6	100.0
	Total	**320**	**100.0**	**100.0**	

Table - 3
Son of God

		Frequency	Percent	Valid Percent	Cumulative Percent
Valid	Highly appropriate	283	88.4	88.4	85.0
	Appropriate	9	2.8	2.8	91.3
	Not Appropriate	28	8.8	8.8	100.0
	Total	320	100.0	100.0	

It is evident that 272 (85%) of the respondents agree that Jesus, the Savior of all, is highly appropriate (Table 3). We also observe that 283 (88.4%) of the respondents agree that Jesus, the Son of God is also highly appropriate (Table 4). The images of Jesus, the New Messiah (61.3%) and the suffering servant receive approval of 61.3% and 51.9% from respondents respectively. We understand that individual Christians consider Jesus as Son of God and as their Saviour. It resonates with respondents' opinion when they say that they experienced Jesus mostly in times of difficulty and in times of despair.

Appropriateness of the Images of Jesus from the Theologians

The analysis establishes that the following images of Jesus are highly appropriate to Jesus: the Compassionate (79.1%), the Way (60%), the Prophet (56.9%), the Guru (56.3%), the Servant (51.3%), and the Reformer (45.1%). On the contrary, the appropriateness of the following images is under debate as some of the respondents show their disagreement: Jesus the Sage (16.6%), the Satyagrahi (22.2%), the Dancer (5.9%), the Pilgrim (16.9%) and the Avatar (15%). The bar chart indicates that around 55% say the image of Jesus as the Avatar is not appropriate and 78.3% of them say the image of Jesus as Dancer is not appropriate. Though the ordinary Catholics always refer to incarnation of Jesus as Avatar (in their vernacular), they seem not quite at home in looking at him as merely an Avatar.

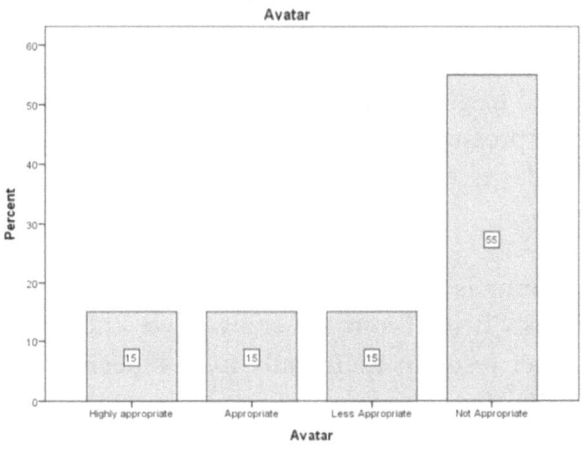

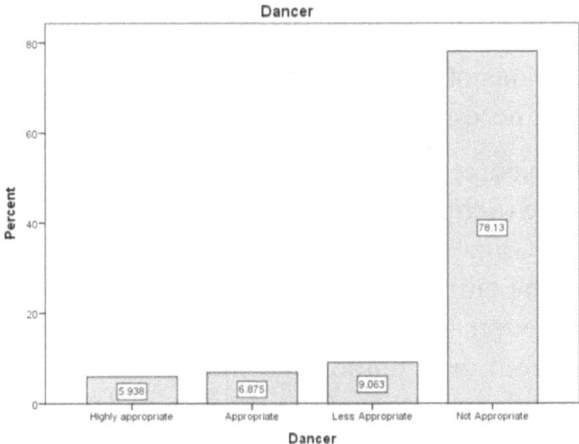

Having seen the appropriateness of the images we turn to the image of Jesus that Pope Francis witnesses to the people. From the options placed before them (Jesus the Shepherd, the Merciful God, the Peace Maker), 58.1% of the respondents chose Jesus the Merciful God and 25.6% of them chose Jesus the Shepherd. The results surely reflect the influence that Pope Francis makes on individual's life to get closer to Jesus, the Merciful God. We know that witnessing to Jesus plays a vital role in framing a proper image of Jesus in the minds of the faithful.

The question arises: what kind of images of Jesus do we Christians need to give witness to him in India today? Most of the respondents expressed that India needs Jesus, the peace maker, the good Shepherd, the Healer, the merciful, the reformer.

Inferences

An image of Jesus is born out of an existential encounter with the person of Jesus Christ. From the analysis we know that individual Christians meet Jesus in their daily lives especially in their daily struggles of life. Jesus becomes a response to their struggles. He becomes a companion and a friend. The images they are familiar with and meaningful to their lives are: Jesus the healer, Jesus the rescuer, Jesus the miracle worker, Jesus the Saviour. We could infer that they do not embrace Christ explained through concepts but through concrete situations of life. Therefore, familiarity with the struggles of people is the necessity to present Jesus' images to the community.

Another resource where an individual Christian meets Jesus is the word of God (Scripture). The Church and the theologians need to emphasize the Gospel stories of Jesus Christ during the days of faith formation of the faithful (for example at Catechism classes and in sermons). Moreover, the majority of respondents first came to know about Christ from their home. This emphasizes the importance of family in the faith formation of the children and in helping them to form an effective image of Jesus.

In a study of these images three worlds are made clear: "the situation in the life of Jesus, the life of the Early Church and the life of the evangelist (three *Sitze im Leberi).*"[24] The Gospel writers created, defined and wrote from a third *Sitz im Leben. The theologians make efforts to build bridges between two worlds of the evangelists and the faithful. The study reveals that the efforts are not in vain but further recommend that they need to highly consider the experiences of the faithful to suggest any images of Jesus.* They are to continue to study, interpret and create images relevant for the situation in the lives of Christians today. They have a responsibility to translate and interpret it faithfully, joining a work that began thousands of years ago at the beginning of time in Jesus and is still being painted, being written and being proclaimed until his return. Christians embrace, live and become a part of the Gospel when they listen, create and speak out meaningful images that are true to who Jesus was and what he came to do and true to their lives.

Conclusion

A Christian community evolves and creates images of Jesus Christ and an image moulds the community because Jesus' images emerge from an existential and experiential encounter of the faithful with the person of Jesus Christ. In the current multi-religious context of striving to respond to the challenges of religious fundamentalism, divisiveness within the Church, atrocities against its 'minority community' status and dilemma of its identity, the Indian Christian community is made to reflect and respond to the question: Who is Jesus for her?

Some of the Indians who experienced Christ personally like Pandita Ramabai, Ganga Dhor Sarroji, Pagolu Venkayya and others showed a way to meet Christ upon Indian soil. Moreover, their exemplary lives proved that Jesus is extremely attractive and indispensable to India. India needs Jesus, the Peacemaker, the good Shepherd, the Healer, the Merciful One, the Reformer and the Prophet, Pope Francis too gives powerful witness to the images of Jesus as a merciful God and a good shepherd.

The study showed that the lay faithful continuously seek for Jesus in their daily lives. It has also shown the importance of the role of family to introduce Jesus to children and to initiate them into personally relating to him. There is also great responsibility on the clergy to present stories of Christ during the faith formation of children taking place through catechism classes. The emphasis should be on the word of God in Scripture and the person of Jesus Christ.

Further, in their search for Jesus, Indian Christians look up to the Jesus of the Gospels and frame their images of Jesus Christ. The images from the synoptic Gospels (the Son of God, the Son of Man, the Crucified Messiah, the New Moses, the Immanuel, the Liberator, the Saviour, the Great Reconciler and Healer) and the images of Jesus explicated by two Indian theologians Michael Amaladoss and Sebastian Kappen (Jesus the Way, the Servant, the Compassionate, the Prophet of a New Humanity) continuously guide them to make Jesus the exemplar and essence of their way of living. Moreover, experiencing Jesus mostly during the times of struggles they experience Jesus as their healer, their Saviour, their help and their friend. The images of Jesus Christ born out of their lives are: Jesus, the Healer, the Friend, the Companion, the Rescuer, the Saviour and the Joy-giver.

The study poses a challenge to theologians to listen to what the people are saying and to seriously take into consideration the experiences of the lay faithful so that they suggest meaningful images of Jesus in such a way that people can understand, believe in the new way shown by Jesus Christ, and commit themselves to building up an Indian Christian community of faith, hope and love. Besides being a service-minded and outward looking community, such a community must also be a 'servant' to society, at large. Thus, as a result of their faith experiences and their close contact with Indian contextual realities, the theologians and the lay faithful should constantly strive to respond to Jesus' question: 'Who do you say that I am?'

The Church as pilgrim is always in search for an answer to Jesus' question, "Who do you say that I am?" (Mk 8:29). This exploration of answering the question is continuous amidst the changing modes of cultural, social and political scenarios of the world because Jesus meets the faithful in their own contexts. This study of knowing the bridgeable gaps between academic Jesus' images and practical images of Christ will enhance Christian living of witnessing love and justice in their context. Every image is born out of a mutual interaction between Jesus and a community or an individual. Community makes an image and an image makes the community.

Endnotes

[1] The Census Organization of India, https://www.census2011.co.in/religion.php, under "Religious Census, 2011," (accessed February 12, 2018). The Census presents that 2% (1.67 Crore) of them are in rural India and 2.96% (1.12 Crore) in urban area.

[2] Ibid.

[3] E. Stanley Jones, *The Christ of the Indian Road* (New York: Grosset & Dunlap, 1925), 9.

[4] Vatican News. "Card Gracias: Indian Christians should become fully Indian and fully Christian," http://www.vaticannews.va/en/church/news/2018-02/cbci-meets-in-bangalore-india.html (accessed February 21, 2018). The Conference of Catholic Bishops of India met in Bangalore on February 4, 2012 for the 30th Plenary Assembly.

[5] J. D. Brucker, "*Religious Beliefs down Globally,*" May 30, 2013, under "Religious beliefs," http://natskep.com/religous-belief-down-globally (accessed January 30, 2018).

[6] Joseph Francis, "Porta-Fidei-Door Way to Faith, an Extended Commentary," *The Divine Shepherd's Voice* 4/1 (2013): 8.

[7] Yeager Hudson, "Christian Dilemmas: Disaster or Opportunity?" in *The Indian Christian's Dilemma Disaster or Opportunity*, eds. Yeager Hudson, Joseph Barnabas et al. (Poona: Israelite Press, 1968), 1-8.

[8] S. K. Hulbe, "The Dilemmas before the Indian Christian," in *The Indian Christian's Dilemma Disaster or Opportunity*, eds. Yeager Hudson, Joseph Barnabas et al. (Poona: Israelite Press, 1968), 39.

[9] Hulbe, 43-44.

[10] E. Stanley Jones, *The Christ of the Indian Road* (New York: Grosset & Dunlap, 1925), 223.

[11] Ibid., 14.

[12] Arthur Parker, *Children of Light in India* (London: Fleming H. Revell Company, 1929). The author presents portraits of Indian saints as children of light.

[13] Artur Parker, 45.

[14] Ibid., 75.

[15] Ibid., 96.

[16] Ibid., 99.

[17] C.I. David Joy, *Christology Revisited: Profiles and* Prospects (Bangalore: ATC Publications, 2007), 113. It is evident that the synoptic gospels present various images/titles of Jesus. He is called the Son of Man, the Crucified Messiah, the New Moses, the Emmanuel, the Liberator and Saviour and the Great Reconciler and Healer. These images demonstrate that Matthew, Mark and Luke have made their unique contributions to portray the picture of Jesus.

[18] Though Amaladoss explores 'Asian' images of Jesus, I would like to address them as 'Indian' images of Jesus because India upholds many aspects of Asian culture.

[19] Michael Amaladoss, *The Asian Jesus* (Delhi: ISPCK, 2005).

[20] S. Kappen, *Jesus and Freedom* (New York: Orbis books, 1977), 52.

[21] S. Kappen, *Jesus and Cultural Revolution: An Asian Perspective* (Bombay: A Build Publication, 1983), 25. In this book, Kappen also evokes the image of Jesus, the prophet of a Counter-Culture.

[22] Kappen, *Jesus and Freedom*, 56.

[23] Some of the images of Jesus among Asian (Indian) Believers: Jesus as a Moral Teacher by Raja Ram Mohan Roy (1774-1883); Jesus as an *Avatar* seen by Ramakrishna Paramahamsa (1836-1886); Jesus, the *Satyagrahi* by Mahatma Gandhi (1869-1948); Jesus, the *Advaitin* by S. Radhakrishnan; Jesus, the *Bodhisattva* by the Buddhists. There are 50 images of Jesus enumerated by Anslem Grun in his book *Images of Jesus* translated by John Bowden (Mumbai: St Pauls, 2002). In the corporate world Laurie Beth Jones presents an image of Jesus CEO in her book, *Jesus, CEO: Using Ancient Wisdom for Visionary Leadership* (New York: Hyperion, 1994).

[24] William Joel Lock, "The Synoptic titles for Jesus," *Master's thesis*, Mc Master Divinity College, Hamilton, 2005),136-150.https://macsphere.mcmaster.ca/ *bitstream/11375/15568/1/Lock%20Joel.pdf* (accessed on 26 January, 2018).

The New Ratio
Fundamentalis Institutionis Sacerdotalis
Joseph Sebastian S.J.

Introduction

Formation of priests is one of the most significant 'services of Christ and his Church'. The priesthood constitutes the backbone of any Local Church. A stable and solid priestly life and ministry presupposes a sound, substantial and sustainable formation of the aspirant for this unique way of life of a priest. A superficial and a dissipated formation will de-stabilize the life and ministry of a priest, sooner than one imagines. We have been witnessing to this worldwide phenomenon in the local churches, in the last five decades. There has been a long exodus of priests leaving priestly life and ministry officially and unofficially, the innumerable scandals and the consequent shelling out of the fortunes in the dioceses and the congregations, and the resultant mediocrity that has robbed the authentic joy of a fulfilling priestly life in general.

When a young man hears the call of God and desires to respond to it adequately, he banks largely on his own personal experiences of the priesthood as lived and witnessed to in the lives of holy priests he had encountered in his life. If the seminarian decides to go forward in his priestly call, this affirms the impacts of the good priests made on him, even though they might be a minority, but mighty and overwhelming.

When young men encounter priests like Fr. Jojayya Pudota, S.J. and others of his ilk, they feel drawn to God and are overwhelmed, enthused and impacted with a profound respect, reverence and love for the priestly life. As a young priest, I was myself very much impressed by his exemplary life, his commitment to ministry and his own humanity. In witnessing the lived-experience of such saintly priests, we can well grasp what true formation is about and how it could grip and motivate a young man to become a priest. Instead of formulating the principles and procedures for true priestly formation in the abstract, we can as well evolve the same, from our witness of the lived-lives of such priests. This is what they bear witness to a true process of priestly formation. Fr. Jojayya's life and ministry bear abundant testimony to the profundity and solidity of his own priestly formation and what it should be for the priests of tomorrow in the Telugu Churches.

In the past, a seminarian who sought admission into the seminary was perhaps a physically grown up young man but psycho-spiritually still a child who needed to be tutored into all the nitty-gritty of a psycho-spiritual-intellectual life. For him, it became yet another experience of his own childhood now, in the seminary to cope with all the imposed injunctions of the formators. He had to go through the entire spectrum of his priestly formation with the mind-set of a child, all the time accepting and living up to the expectations of the formators. In the process, he bracketed his human personality and tried to spiritualize everything, aspiring to be divine before becoming authentically human. Such an orientation was even extoled as normal, ideal and angelic!

But the young men who come to the seminary today are not as innocent, ignorant and naïve as were their predecessors in the past, instead, they are very much the product of the modernized and globalized world of today with its new set of values, attitudes and mentalities. The diverse societal impacts and influences, mass communication, and social media have such an over-whelming grip on the young man of today that he comes to the seminary with a heavy burden of his many prior exposures, experiments, experiences, habits, hang-ups and compulsive addictions that have to be identified and addressed.

Conforming to and complying with the outmoded ways of priestly formation of the past neither appeals to nor helps the seminarians of today. It is a Himalayan task to accompany such men who are coming with the mind-sets of a child/adolescent with a barrage of questions, and a series of doubts, uncertainties, ambiguities, fear and guilt. To accompany them, it needs altogether another formative paradigm than the traditional one, where the young man is helped to be himself first, to face himself squarely, and then to be encouraged and guided in his personal questioning, searching, seeking, felt-needs, aspirations and human fulfilment. The approach of the formators telling him: "I know everything, and do what I tell you", is far from forming him as an autonomous person, a self-affirming individual and this will adversely affect his character and personality. He will not be a man of courage, conviction, character and commitment. The poor quality of his formation will be self-evident when he will have to stand on his own legs, to direct himself and to lead and guide others in the future, as a priest.

It is to form such men of today that the New Ratio envisages its new thrusts, orientation and proposals, keeping in mind all the evolution of thoughts on formation since the Vatican II. The basic insight of Vatican II: the priestly formation now in the seminary has to be closely related to the pastor's life and ministry in the future, is the kernel of this new document. This New Ratio was published in 2016 by the Congregation for Clergy, marking the Silver Jubilee Year of the release of the monumental document of Pope John Paul II: *Pastores Dabo Vobis* in 1991. Integrating the thrusts of the Vatican II and its documents, the directives of the Post conciliar era and especially, the new pastoral thrusts and insights of Pope Francis, this document portrays a new vision of formation for the shepherds of tomorrow.

This New Ratio bears in mind i) the mind-sets and the contexts of the seminarians today, ii) the challenges of priestly life in the evolving modern world moving into the unknown future, and iii) the existential situations of the church and the world today.

Developments prior to the New Ratio

1, "Optatam Totius" (that is, Opting totally) on Oct., 28, 1965 by Paul the VI: "Decree on Priestly Training" in the light of Vatican II; 2. "Presbyterorum Ordinis" on Dec. 7, 1965 by Paul VI: "Decree on the Ministry and Life of the Priests"; 3. Ratio Fundamantalis Institutionis Sacerdotalis issued on 6th Jan., 1970, by the Congregation for Catholic Education. (The First Ratio); 4. Updating of the previous Ratio: after the proclamation of the New Code of Canon Law in 25th Jan., 1983, the previous Ratio was amended and updated and published on 19th March 1985; 5. Pastor Bonus, (Jun 28, 1988) of John Paul II, the Seminary formation transferred from the Congregation for Education to the Congregation for Clergy. 6. Post-Synodal Apostolic Exhortation: Pastores Dabo Vobis, of John Paul II, on 25th March 1992 (25 years after the two Vatican II decrees, as above); 7. Apostolic Letter of 'Moto Proprio' of Benedict XVI, Ministrorum Institutio on 16 Jan., 2013, which shows how formation in the Seminaries finds a natural continuation in the On-going Formation. 8. The New Ratio: Pope Francis' perspective of Pastoral-ness or the 'pastorality' of the priest gave a new impetus to re-formulate the priestly formative process in this new Ratio. It has been prepared, signed and published by the Congregation for Clergy on 8th Dec. 2016. At the preparatory stage, this document went through 14 drafts and the present one is the 15th and final version, after consulting various other Congregations, Pontifical Commissions and other related Bodies.

The Plan of the Document: There are 210 Numbers in 8 chapters.

Introduction

Ch. I: General Norms: Nos 1 -10;

Ch. 2: Priestly Vocations Nos 11 – 26;

Ch. 3: The Foundations of Formation Nos 27 – 53;

Ch. 4: Initial and On-going Formation Nos 54 – 88;

Ch. 5: The Dimensions of Formation Nos 89 – 124;

Ch. 6. The Agents of Formation Nos 125 – 152;

Ch. 7: The Organization of Studies Nos 153 – 187;

Ch. 8: Criteria and Norms Nos 188 – 210

The chapters three, four and five are the central and substantial part of this document. Chapter III deals with the foundations of formation and elaborates under six themes: a) the seminarian as the subject of formation (R 28 & 29; b) the basis and purpose of formation: the priestly identity (R 30-34); c) the journey of formation as the Configuration to Christ (R 35-40); d) A formation for Interior life and communion (R 41-43); e) Means of formation (R 44-52) and f) the unity of formation (R 53).

In chapter IV, the first part treats of the four stages of initial seminary formation (R 54 – 88), *the propaedeutic* (R 59, 60) forming the seminarian, a good and formed Christian based on Christian values and principles; the *discipleship (philosophic) stage* (R 61 - 67) where the goal is to root the seminarian in the *sequela Christi;* the *theological* or the *Configuration stage* (R 68 – 73), where the seminarian's goal is to be configured into the person of Christ and the *pastoral or vocational synthesis stage* (R 74 – 79). In the second part (R 80-88), the Ratio makes a strong plea for the absolute need of an ongoing updating that is urgent and essential for a priest in the modern world of knowledge explosion, research and specialization. Without the ongoing formation, the priest will become an obscurantist and an irrelevant person.

Chapter V makes its own substantial additions and complementary suggestions to the previous document of *Pastores Dabo Vobis*. In general, every chapter has a new thrusts, or foci or emphases which give a depth and a pastoral charm to the earlier treatments.

In June 2017, the Sacred Congregation for Clergy organized a two-week seminar in Rome for 120 English speaking formators from America, Canada, England, Ireland, Australia, New Zeeland, and Philippines and I had the privilege of being one of its participants, representing Collegio Urbano in Rome. There were 20 well-thought and solid presentations on different aspects of the Ratio and each one was followed by a group discussion and a plenary session. It was a very enriching and enlightening learning experience indeed! At the end of it, I could not believe myself when the participants expressed spontaneously and honestly on how inadequate and un-'aggiornamented' was our present formation programme and how it should be remedied in the future. I wish to share with the readers through this article, some of those highlights and insights that deeply touched me.

My presentation here has three parts: i) The specific thrusts, emphases and accents in the New Ratio, ii) Humanity as the foundation of the other three dimensions of formation and iii) A personal reflection on formation.

Part I: a) Initial comments and observations on the New Ratio
It is vitally important to look at the ecclesial vision of the Holy Father Pope Francis to understand the import of this document. The essential features of a priest and his ministry are derived from the Pope's understanding of the Church: as the People of God in continuous journey. A new way of being the church today is the overall horizon in which the life and the ministry of the priest today are posited and envisioned. A new way of being the church in the modern world of the Vatican II and as a consequence, a new way of being a priest today will lead to the new way of being formed for his pastoral life

and ministry, with all the these new ways mutually enriching each other. This pastoral character of the life and the ministry of the priest of tomorrow has to determine the quality and the density of his formation today and has to set a tone for his formation prior to his ordination. Formation is conceived in this new Ecclesial and Pastoral vision. The *pastorality* as envisioned and implied here has greater repercussions to theology itself, where the pastoral theology has been relegated to the periphery of the systematic theology.

- Accompaniment as an important component of 'Pastorality' (R nn. 44 – 49): The accompaniment of the priest in the life-journey of the Christians and his close proximity to them characterize the 'iter' (the journey) of his own formation. The formation is seen as a journey to be configured into Christ, the Good Shepherd. The Pope, the bishops and the priests are basically pastors of souls and their dignity and role is to accompany the faithful in their life's journey. The pastors have to be always open to and available for the people and they should not expect them to come to them where they are (R n. 29). Instead, like the true Shepherd who went out to find the lost sheep, they have to go out of themselves to encounter the people where *they* are, in the circumstances and contexts of their lives. This in turn implies a new way of relating with and serving the people.

- Any directive for priestly formation should reflect this ecclesiological vision of 'pastorality', reaching out, collaboration and accompaniment as well as the need for the appreciation of the condition of the Local Churches. Such a vision of ecclesiology and priesthood flows from the priesthood of Jesus Christ himself. The context in which the priesthood unfolds itself will always be the changing situations of the Church at any given time. In today's world, the signs of the times call for a new way of 'gospelling' to peoples, cultures and nations.

Hence, we need priests, who are *new* evangelizers. Every priest is called to be the face of Christ and his mercy, and to be an embodiment of Jesus, the Good Shepherd. Here, we have to take note of the Pope's insistence on the 'being' of the priest determining his 'doing'.

- This document speaks of a three-level development of this Ratio: at the Universal level (*Ratio Univeralis*), the Local Church (National/Regional) level (Ratio Nationalis) and the Seminary level *(Ratio Seminaris)*. The New Ratio flowing from the Universal Ratio, strongly recommends a National Ratio, at its respective local level, (R nn. 3-8) after which, the particular seminary will further deliberate and formulate its own way of proceeding in order to realize both the universal and national Ratios.

b) New accents and emphases of the New Ratio: Four specific characteristics of the formation: unique, integral, communitarian and missionary.

Unique: The formation of priests is the continuation of a single "discipleship journey", which begins with baptism, perfects itself with the other sacraments, and is welcomed at the center of one's life. There is the unity between the common priesthood (of all believers) and the ministerial priesthood of the pastors (R nn. 31, 53)

Integral: Training in different dimensions has to be included in an integral vision, which takes into account of the four dimensions proposed by 'Pastores Dabo Vobis': the human, the spiritual, the intellectual and the pastoral. It is necessary that the whole journey of formation does not identify itself with any single aspect, but is always an integral path of discipleship with a synthesis of all the four dimensions (R n. 28).

Communitarian: Formation has an eminently communitarian character from the beginning; the vocation to the priesthood is discovered and welcomed by the family and the Christian community, and is formed in the seminary. The seminary is a family of all the seminarians to become a family of priests, serving a specific parish and diocesan communities. Formators and seminarians must consider themselves and act as a true formative community, which shares a single responsibility (R nn. 32, 41, 50 - 52).

Missionary: Since the seminarian comes from the Christian community and returns to serve and guide it as its pastor, formation is naturally characterized in a missionary sense of 'being sent'. Since formation has as its aim the participation in the one mission entrusted by Christ to his Church, that is, evangelization in all forms that will be characterizing and determining the priest's missionary actions. Seminaries form missionary disciples "in love" with the Master, to become the shepherds "with the smell of sheep" who live in the midst of them to serve them and bring them to the mercy of God (R n. 32).

- Formation is based very much on the interpersonal relationship and this must mature every day. Formation is accomplished through daily interpersonal relationships (R 41). Each seminarian must strictly strive for forming a formative community. Integrated training comes from a formative community. Human relationship is the vehicle for this training (R 50-52).

- The role of the seminary family in training. The seminary is a family, a fraternity, a fellowship, a communion and an intimacy of the disciples of Jesus. These elements have great values in this family. The growth in formation and the growth in relationship/ friendship go together. Thus friendship and fellowship have a very significant role in the seminary formation. If a seminarian has not cultivated a friendship consciously or has no friends at the end of his formation, he should not be ordained (R 52, 90-92).

- Formation is an intimate relationship between God and the seminarian fundamentally. God is the true formator.

Basically, formation fundamentally is a self-formation in intimacy with God. Parents, friends, teachers, formators are merely facilitators, companions who help the seminarians to form themselves. The formators' role is a catalytic one, but an important one (R 42).

- Graduality and progressivity (progressiveness) of formation is like every other growth. Graduality is a fundamental part of any educational pedagogy. Graduality of various stages, gradualness in each stage, and the graduality of each person and group are presupposed.

- When seminarians are aware of the scandals of priests, they may be discouraged or scandalized and may even think of leaving the seminary. If only they had been deeply impressed by, met with and touched by some or even one holy priest, they will certainly continue. Even one experience of an authentic life is enough to inspire and sustain one's vocation. God calls us not extraordinarily but through the lives lived and witnessed to by the holy priests.

- Proximity and accompaniment are fundamental aspects to maintain closeness with believers in our pastoral ministry and with the seminary family during formation. There is a great emphasis on the aspect of accompaniment and closeness to the seminarians by the formators in this document. The formators must accompany the *formees* like a mother and father with their son, with kindness and firmness (R nn.44-49).

- Formation is similar to an experience of Pentecost. Before the descent of the Holy Spirit, the apostles were gathered together in the upper room, and were filled with great fear, timidity, inferiority... and they did not dare to go out. When the Holy Spirit descended upon them, they became courageous and daring heroes and they left the room and went out to meet the people. Getting out of oneself and to reach out to others is the most important formative paradigm of this document. Those who live for themselves, instead of being mediators, may settle down to becoming intermediaries, CEOs, and purely administrators. The band of very sad, disillusioned, frustrated priests belong to this category.

- The priest makes his message a very happy one with his own life. When he preaches joyfully, his action is a witness that God has touched and transformed his life. Joy exudes through his entire life. (The central theme of *Evangelii Gaudium*).

Part II: Human Dimension: the Foundation for the other three

After having commented and highlighted on the general thrusts and specific accents of the New Ratio, now we turn our attention to focus on the foundational nature of the human dimension. Pasores Dabo Vobis has crystallized priestly formation under four dimensions or aspects. Human dimension is the basic and foundational one, on which the other three aspects are constructed. In the past, we have extolled both the spiritual and the intellectual dimensions rather too one-sidedly, relegating the human and the pastoral to a secondary level. In this document, the human and the pastoral dimensions are recognized for their due roles and put on par with the other two and they are foundational. If the human dimension is the point of departure, the pastoral dimension is the destination of priestly formation. In the past, we were proud 'to be spiritual and intellectual' but were reluctant and grudging and condescending to be human and pastoral. This document affirms authentically the legitimacy of the human nature for priestly formation and one cannot be spiritual without being human.

a.   The Human Dimension in the New Ratio – (Nos 93 – 100), A Summary:

No. 93: The Seminarian has to grow to his authentic maturation as a human person, and not outside of his humanity. He is called to develop his personality on the pattern and model of Christ, the perfect human person. N.T. refers to this transformation: Mt. 28:20; I Pet. 5: 1-4; Tit 1: 5-9. The Church Fathers developed and practiced the care of the man. They were convinced of the profound need for human maturation. A sound, balanced and harmonious spirituality demands a well-developed humanity. That is why St. Thomas called: "Grace builds on nature" (Ref on p. 53, Notes no. 10). This means grace does not supplant nature but perfects it. Hence, we need to cultivate humility, courage, common sense, magnanimity, right discretion, judgement, tolerance, transparency, love for truth and honesty.

No. 94: Human formation is the foundation of all priestly formation. We should not want to become divine before we become human. True human formation is the basis of the integral formation and growth of the person. We need to cultivate different qualities and aspects, physically, psychologically, morally, aesthetically and socially. To achieve the above growth, the seminarian has to be aware of his own life-history in his various stages of his growth, so as to establish well-balanced and interpersonal relationships and the capacity to handle positively the moments of his solitude.

No. 95: The development of the personality of the Seminarian has to be evidenced by his mature capacity for relationship with both men and women of various ages and social conditions. Sound relationship with women is pastorally very important for a Seminarian. Women play a complementary and a collaborative role in the growth of the human person at different levels.

No. 96: The Seminarian must be aware of his weaknesses, inadequacies and limitations in his personality: his temperament, complexes, compulsions, habits, addictions, and negative mind-sets and behaviors. He must constantly evaluate his vocation journey critically, and desire to grow and to improve in the future.

No. 97: Human formation is also a necessary component in the evangelization and proclamation of the Gospel. Mediated by his humanity, he is to go to "the ends of the earth" which has been expanded through mass media and social net-works. Today, it is in this public forum or piazza, where opinions, ideas and information are exchanged and new relations and communities come into being. The future pastors cannot stand aloof from this existential and evolving situation. To handle the social media and the digital world with ease, becomes the integrating part of the development of personality of the seminarian. He must learn to use these technologies with proper theological insights.

No. 98: New possibilities are offered by the digital world to accomplish the mission of Christ today. He must discover 'new places' through which many are moving daily to the 'digital peripheries' (not merely the geographical territories of the past). Media can help us to feel closer to one another, creating a sense of closeness, harmony and unity of the human family, and effective communications to know better and to go closer to one another.

No. 99: Attention must be paid at the same time, to the inevitable risks coming from the digital world and the various forms of compulsions and addictions. The seminary is a school of humanity and faith. Jesus as the Good Samaritan tried to heal the wounds and injuries by pouring a balm; we too must be like him.

No. 100: Social networks must be integrated into the daily life of the seminary community, as 'places' that offer new possibilities in interpersonal relationships and engagements.

b.   Some Observations on the Human Formation in the New Ratio

This section dealing with Human Formation: a) lays out the essentials from the New Ratio and b) addresses other theoretical and practical issues.

- Human formation must be considered in the context of the entire Ratio.

- It is a spiritual document with a vision and not juridical in nature.

- Basis: development of theology of priesthood from Vatican II: Optatam Totius (11), Presbyterum Ordinis (3) and Pastores dabo Vobis (43- 44).

- Essential principles on human formation in the New Ratio:

    + Sound Biblical and theological foundation for human formation.

    + Rooted in the reality of the Incarnation (R 120).

    + God intervenes in human affairs: from Creation to Revelation, God reaches out to humanity extending salvation.

    + Human formation is essential and is the foundation for other dimensions. (R 89). This is the first of the four dimensions (R Intr. No 1, 84c 91, 130 189).

- PDV: 43. "The whole work of priestly formation would be deprived of its necessary foundation, if it lacked suitable human formation". Human formation is the foundation for all types of formation.

- Human maturity is distinctively related to the spiritual serenity (R 41). Being at peace with oneself is its basic openness to the Spirit. Only when we are comfortable with ourselves, can we attend to others.

- It calls for systematic work on the development personality of the seminarian (R 63). The holiness of the priest is built upon it.

- Human formation must be attended to, at each level of priestly formation (R 60, 62, 64) and approached appropriately, adapting to each level.

- Challenges for the young men of today: The young men today have to face the new challenges and deal with them realistically. The Cultural reality of divorced parents and dysfunctional families psychologically affect the growth of the seminarians. Cuddled, defended and pampered by overtly protective parents have deep consequences for the seminarians. The difficulty for making permanent commitment has its influence on the youth of today. None of these disqualifies a seminarian in his early years of formation. Adequate attention, guidance and care should be extended to the seminarians.

Part III: Personal Reflections on Formation, Formator & *Formee*
I wish to make the following comments and reflections on the process of formation with their positive or negative consequences for the formators and the *formees.*

The Process of Formation: The process of formation is very similar to the process of growth, or maturation or conversion or transformation. Formation implies a process of both education (information) and formation. Education largely focuses on the gathering of information, learning of skills and techniques and acquisition of knowledge simple and advanced, organized and systematized. One can be informed and instructed about anything, which can fetch the learner a diploma, a degree, a qualification which may help to make a living and be considered a knowledgeable or a qualified person.

While, formation implies yet another process of a person being enriched by the moments of reflection, inner silence, to be at peace with oneself, the ability to face and accept oneself, self-evaluation, self-responsibility, personal options, character formation, value acquisition, affected by the knowledge one has acquired and allowing oneself to be shaped by them. All these will lead one to a mature, integrated and convinced human person with a strong sense of personality and nobility of character. The information, skills, techniques and knowledge acquired are useful but what has to result from all these is the emergence of the mature human person, the blossoming of the humanity of the person. Such a person will be better tuned for a human and spiritual formation which is basically to be a God-centered person, living a vibrant life of profound faith. Such a formation for a Christian will make him a wise person, endeavoring to see how God had been operative in human life and history. Theologizing is to facilitate such a person to grow into that wisdom, which God alone can give. A wise person is deeply human and spiritual.

The Positive role of a Formator

The formation journey is both a gift and a task, a call and a response. Let us take the parable of the seed: the life and potentialities it contains within it will flow to its natural culmination, as it lets God to have his own way with it. The seed benefits by the preparedness of the earth, the water, the manure, and the pruning and digging by the gardener to bloom to its destiny. So also, if the seminarian is well disposed like the earth, open-minded and large-hearted, he can benefit by all the facilities and opportunities provided and the accompaniment by the formators in the seminaries.

Although formation implies the auto-formation of the *formees* with the grace of God, still the formators do play a facilitative and catalytic role by their accompaniment. As the seminarians begin their life in the seminary, their fast and effective growth will depend on their awareness of their past human history and their willingness to share with the formators. All the efforts that the formators make to reach out to them can go to waste, if they are not aware of their own inner controllers or conditioners which are not allowing them to go forward spontaneously. It is at this stage, the seminarian feels the need to cut deep into his inner life. He realizes the conflict between the inner and outer faculties that God has endowed us with. The exterior life captures and monopolizes the consciousness of the seminarians and they find it very hard to enter into their inner sanctuaries where the human and divine realities will coalesce and where they can experience the harmony of the inner-exterior confluence. If one is finely tuned humanly, one can easily get tuned spiritually. The human and the spiritual dimensions are not our opposing enemies but collaborating and complementing friends. When the seminarian experiences this inner harmony, every spiritual activity will be self-transforming, heart-warming and soul-filling.

When the interior life is tightly locked up, there is a deep human deficiency. One easily feels lonely, unloved, rejected, unwanted, empty and frustrated. When this prevails over a period, the Ego seeks to fill the void with seeking for possession, power, position, prestige, sex and addictions, thinking that it is the outside reality that will make one feel fully human and happy. The real power is internal and from within, which determines the personality and character of the person. If the formator does not help to heal his brokenness, wounded past and human deficits, a profound growth will not be in the offing either at the human or at the spiritual level.

As per the parable of the sower, seeds that fell on rocky soil, amidst the thorns, and on the walking pathways, they could not grow and thrive because nobody could help them to grow. Rocky situations of their humanity, thorny bushes oppressing and suppressing their legitimate growth and the pathway seeds which felt trampled upon, humiliated and dehumanized, the seminarian needs good gardeners (formators) who will facilitate their growth, liberate them from all his negative packages of the past and point to their infinite potentialities for growth from within.

Our spirituality will always limp, and will be extrinsic to our human growth, if our humanity is not adequately prepared for it or if spirituality is not rooted and grounded in our humanity. Spiritual life can easily become an ongoing fighting with the ghosts, when our humanity is blocked and locked up in our own complexes, wounded pasts, inhibitions, habits, addictions, unhealed memories, habitual repressions and suppression. These realities have largely originated already from our own families, schools, parishes, from all our relationships with our parents and family members, teachers, priests and others; all these impacts were made before we entered the seminary. Similar negative experiences in the seminary can also aggravate and reinforce them further. These are all to be faced realistically to deal with them adequately. The growth and blossoming of the seminarian depends on the preparedness of his humanity to warmly welcome the call of God and to respond to it wholeheartedly, but ably facilitated by formators, the God-sent gardeners for our growth and formation.

The Theology of Laity in the Church

Peter Emmanuel

Introduction

The role of the laity in the Church is being questioned and discussed since the Second Vatican Council. A closer look at the present reality of the Church shows that many Christians do not fully feel a sense of belonginess to mission of the Church. Pope John Paul II says that "There is so much need today for mature Christian personalities, conscious of their baptismal identity, of their vocation and mission in the Church and in the world".[1] Whereas Pope Francis reiterates "there is clear awareness among the laity about their responsibility in the Church grounded in their baptism and confirmation, but it does not appear in the same way in all places."[2]

The participation of the laity in the mission of the Church is not volunteerism in the mission of the hierarchy but a right and responsibility arising from their baptismal consecration. In this background, we shall look at the teachings of the Church, which mentions that laity drive their vocation by virtue of baptism and play an essential role in spreading the good news. In order to understand the theology of laity, we need to understand certain basic terminologies such as people of God, laity and clergy.

The People of God

St. Peter addresses to followers of Christ "You are a chosen race, a royal priesthood, a holy nation, God's own people, chosen to declare the wonderful deeds of God" (1 Pet 2:9). It clearly shows that in the Early Church, there was no division between Christ's faithful as laity and priests. St Peter uses the Greek word '*laos*' to mean the people as God's own people.[3] The books of Pentateuch manifest the fact that God chose a community at Mount Sinai "You are my people and I am your God" (Ex 19:5-6). *Alvaro del Portillo* says that the Christian community used the term 'faithful' to mean membership of the people of God acquired through the sacrament of baptism.[4] St. Paul also describes the Church as the Body of Christ (Rm 12: 4-5, Eph 4:4-6), which indicates that there is no division between the children of God.[5] The differentiation is based on the diversity of ministries.[6] Whereas all participate in the priestly, prophetic and kingly mission of Jesus Christ and the Church.[7]

Therefore, *Lumen Gentium* clearly states that mission of Christ is given to the people of God and in the Church, there is diversity of ministry but unity of mission.[8] Thus in the New Testament, we find that Christian community grew up as community of believers, who enjoyed same dignity irrespective of their states of life and the same idea is rediscovered and reiterated in the teachings of Second Vatican Council.[9] Therefore pope, bishops' priests, religious and laity, are equal members of the Church as people of God.[10]

The Laity

The word laity does not occur in the whole of bible.[11] *Yes Conger* says that "there is no vocabulary to express the distinction of clergy and laity in the New Testament".[12] *Karl Rahner* defines laity positively and negatively. A lay person is negatively looked as one who does not have a position in the hierarchy of the Church, whereas positively speaking, he mentions that layperson is commissioned and blessed as co-operator of God's grace in and through the Church's life because of baptism and confirmation.[13] *Lumen Gentium* speaks about 'all the faithful' except those in Holy Orders and those who belong to a religious state of life approved by the Church.[14] The laity is called to live in a world and make their apostolate a leaven in the world and share in the three-fold mission of Jesus Christ by virtue of baptism.

The Clergy

The term clergy is derived from the Greek word *kleros* meaning a lot or inheritance and it refers to the whole people of God in the New Testament.[15] A clergy is considered to be religious official, belonging to a religious order or a pastor of a Church or denomination.[16] *Paul Steven* says that in the Bible the word *kleros* is inclusive and was never used to describe a special group of believers set apart from the whole people of God to hold any religious office in the Church as we see today.[17]

The Historical Background of the Laity

It is necessary to look into the historical background of the laity in the Church. It will enable us to have a panoramic view of all the issues involved and will facilitate our efforts to arrive at the contemporary understanding of the theology of the laity.

The Laity in the Apostolic Period

We have seen that the term laity is unknown to the New Testament but the concept of people of God as community of believers provides the scriptural basis for the theology of laity.[18] The understanding of Israel as the People of God is also found in the New Testament.[19] The people gathered together by Jesus Christ are called '*laos*' (1 Pet 2:9). The word '*laos*' is equated with the Greek word *Qahal*, which means the people of God. Thus, the real implication of the term laity is the whole Church and the *laos* of God or the laity of God.

In today's context, the term *kleros* is applied to sacred ministers but in the New Testament, the term *kleros* is applied to the entire people of God.[20] Therefore during the time of New Testament, all

Christians were considered as *kleros*, a people set apart to build up the Christian community.[21] we can say that all the members of the Church were treated with dignity and equality in the New Testament and during Apostolic time.

The Distinction Between laity and Clergy

During the time of Apostles, there was no distinction between clergy and laity (Acts 8:4) but after their deaths changes began to take place, which deepened a gap between the laity and the clergy.[22] The Second and third century marked a division between clergy and laity, which led to the clericalization of the Church.[23] By the third century, there were ordained ministers to celebrate the sacraments, which marked a functional division between laity and the clergy.[24] Within few years, the institutional Church was dominated by the clergy and the laity only just participated in the liturgy and teaching as passive participants.[25] Therefor what divided the laity and clergy is the conduct of the worship.

The Communion Ecclesiolgy of Lay Participation

Inspite of the new vision of the Church as people of God, there exists a great divide between laity and clergy. The reason for such division is because of the two Ecclesiologies prevailing in the Church, namely pyramid ecclesiology and Church as the people of God.

The Role of Laity in the Pyramidal Ecclesiology

The pre-Vatican ecclesiology is called the pyramidal ecclesiology because it has a structure in the Church like a pyramid.[26] It emphasises on the absolute of powers of the pope, who in turn delegates his authority to bishops, bishop to the priest and at the bottom level of pyramid, we have the laity, who have not authority or no role to play according to pyramidal ecclesiology.[27] The impact of such ecclesiology was such that laity who were majority in the Church were reduced to minority as mere spectators in the Church without having any positive role to play.

The Role Laity and Second Vatican Ecclesiology

The change from hierarchy to people of God was brought by the Second Vatican Council in the light of New Testament. It emphasised the equality among all the members of the Church as brothers and sisters, where there is no fundamental difference between clergy and laity apart form a functional difference.[28] Thus, Second Vatican Council asserts equality and dignity of entire people of God and elaborates their roles in the Church and the world as priest, prophet and king.

The Priesthood of all the believers: Baptismal Participation

The idea of people of God is closely related to the idea of the priesthood of all the believers. The basic equality and dignity among the members of the Church is expressed in baptism, which is common to all (Heb 2:7, 1 Pet 2:9). Thus, the priesthood of all the believers, lay and ordained is derived from the one, holy and eternal priesthood of Christ and all the ministry is Christ's ministry in which the faithful are privilege to participate according to their gift.[29] The Vatican Council affirms in *Lumen Gentium* that the common priesthood is a consequence of baptism and the common priesthood of all the believers is derived from the priesthood of Christ.[30] Therefore, the lay people are incorporated through baptism in Christ as people of God and share in the priestly, prophetic and kingly office of Christ. Though there exists a functional difference between the clergy and laity but the fact remains that both have common identity as priestly people of God.[31]

The Laity and the Documents of the Second Vatican Council

We have seen so far that how the Second Vatican Council brought a change in its understanding of the laity. Now, we shall briefly examine five documents of the Second Vatican Council to study that how these documents provide enough opportunities to the lay people in the exercising their ministries as a lay person.

Sacrosanctum Concilium

According to *Sacrosanctum Concilium,* the participation of all the faithful in the liturgy finds beautiful expression in the Eucharist.[32] The expression 'faithful' does not mention about clergy and laity separately but collectively as active members of the Church, who play active and vital role in the liturgy.

> Mother Church earnestly desires that all the faithful should be led to the full conscious and active participation in liturgical celebrations.[33]

The Church wants all the faithful to participate actively in the liturgy so that it can appear a worshiping community in the celebration of the liturgy.

Lumen Gentium

Lumen Gentium highlights priesthood of all baptised, whether ordained or non- ordained, share equally.

> Though they differ from one another in essence and not only in degree, the common priesthood of the faithful and the ministerial or hierarchical priesthood are nonetheless interrelated: each of them in its own special way is a participation in the one priesthood of Christ.[34]

The Church is not to be seen as body of hierarchy but as a living community where laity play equal role in building the community (1 Pet 2:9-10).

Ad *Gentes Divintus*

Ad Gentes Divintus mentions about the communitarian dimension of the Church, where laity plays a significant role in collaboration with the clergy and religious in the field of evangelization and forming Christian communities.[35]

> Therefore, missionaries, the fellow workers of God (1 Cor 3:9), should raise up communities of the faithful… they might carry out the priestly, prophetic and royal offices entrusted to them into one people.[36]

The document highlights that chosen people of God are called to carry out the mission of God and the mission is not seen as a duty incumbent upon the Christians but very nature of being a Christian.

Gaudium Spes,

Gaudium Spes, express the relationship of the Church with the world.[37] It highlights that laity being in the world has a prominent role to play in carrying out the mission of the Church.[38]

Apostolicam Actuositatem

Apostolicam Actuositatem expresses that laity participates in the three-fold mission and plays an active role in the world.[39]

> The apostolate of the laity derives from their Christian vocation and the church can never be without it. Sacred scripture clearly shows how spontaneous and fruitful such activity was the very beginning of the Church (Acts 11:19-21; 18:26).[40]

All the above documents show that the Second Vatican Council has given due importance to the laity in the Church and in the field of evangelization.

The Understanding of Laity in the Church from Pope Paul VI to Pope Francis

Pope Paul VI did not issue any major document specifically dealing with the laity, however, in *Populorum Progressio*, he appreciates the laity for their missionary work.[41] Whereas in *Evangelii Nutiandi*, he says that laity have a specific role to play in world and they are in charge of the temporal task and for this reason they exercise a special form of evangelization.[42] Pope John Paul II in *Christifideles Laici,* on the vocation and mission of the lay faithful in the Church and in the world highlights baptismal dignity as a framework to define the status of the laity. He says that laity is called to participate fully in the Church's life as communion and its mission in the world.[43] Pope Benedict XVI following footsteps of his predecessor clearly affirms that it is the duty of the people of God to proclaim the always and everywhere the gospel of Jesus Christ.[44] He even says that we need to educate Catholic laity in the social doctrines of the Church.[45] According to him, laity should take a critical role in the life of the Church, alongside of the Clergy, and to fully participate in her mission to the world.[46] Pope Francis says that we need well-formed lay people, whose life has been touched by the personal and merciful love of Christ Jesus.[47] All the teachings of five Popes encourage the laity to take active part in the mission of the Church.

The Laity in the Context of Asia

Although in Asia, Christians are only a minority but their vocation and mission have been one of the primary concerns in the mind of the Asian Bishops specially in the overall context of evangelisation.[48] The bishops of Asia consider that the lay people, as the disciples of Jesus Christ, who are called to share in Christ's mission according to their lay state in the Church.[49] Even the bishops of India have expressed that laity have the advantage of going to places where the clergy cannot go.[50] Thus we find that Bishops of Asia have expressed that mission of the Church is not just the duty of bishops, priests, religious men and women but is the concern of all the faithful.

The Participation of the Laity in the Mission of the Church

The mission and vocation of the laity is situated within the call of people God.[51] It is a call to Christian discipleship to follow Jesus.[52] Pope Francis also exhorts all Christians to be missionary disciples in the work of evangelization.[53] The laity along with clergy and religious as people of God participate in the mission of the Church to proclaim the Good News to the whole world.[54] The Church calls every member to become aware of the responsibility, which is entrusted everyone as a unique task and which cannot be done by another and which has to be fulfilled for the good of all.[55] Thus, laity as people of God are called to fulfil their mission as individual or part of the community.

The Participation of the Laity in the Structures of the Church

The Church exhorts the laity to be active member of the Church. Within the Church, we have structures such Diocesan Pastoral Council, Parish Council, the Diocesan Synod Assembly and Parish Finance council recommended by the Vatican Council for the better participation of the laity, clergy and religious to assist the bishop and priests in matters relating to pastoral activity.[56]

> The lay faithful participate in the life of the Church not only in exercising their tasks and charisms, but also in many other ways. Such participation finds its first and necessary expression in the life and mission of the particular Church, in the diocese in which "the Church of Christ, one, holy, catholic and apostolic, is truly present and at work. The same Council strongly encourages the lay faithful actively to live out their belonging to the particular Church, while at the same time assuming an ever-increasing Catholic Spirit.[57]

In the Archdiocese of Delhi, we have all the structures to felicitate better participation of the laity.

The Lay Empowerment in the Archdiocese of Delhi

In the Archdiocese, we have some ministries, which are by the lay people as their lay initiative but always encouraged and supported by bishops and priests of the Archdiocese of Delhi. We have 'Table Ministry' by the lay volunteers which is an attempt to reach out to thousands of visitors, who come to Cathedral. The Small Christian Communities to empower the participation of the laity in the Church. The *Kirpa Satsang* movement, a special prayer service organized for people of all faiths on every Friday evening at the diocesan community Centre by the lay people under the guidance of a priest. We have Jesus Youth Movement to reach out to college students. The Archdiocese is also blessed with '*Santana*' community, which is basically made up of families, staying together and carrying out the work of evangelization as a family. Jeevan Dham: The Centre of Life is a house run by family and is visited by so many non- Christians to listen to the Word of God, for prayers and healing. Delhi Charismatic Renewal Service is also managed by the lay faithful of the Archdiocese.

The Challenges

The formation of the laity is a big concern in the Church as many of them are busy with their daily affair of life whereby they don't get time to participate in the ongoing formation programme. There are laity, who play a role of prolonged arms of the parish priest to collect church support fund, organise parish feast and so forth only. The challenge to encourage the laity to be missionary comes also comes from priests and religious, who only like to see the faithful coming for Sunday mass only and keep up the pious association of the parish going on.

Conclusion

We began our journey by looking at role of the Laity in the Mission of the Church. The teachings of the Church clearly define the role of the laity that they derive their vocation from the baptismal call and as people of God, they along with priests and religious have responsibility towards the mission of the Church. From the beginning Popes have emphasised the significance of the laity in their teachings that without them Church can't accomplish her mission. They are the life line of the Church in spreading the mission of God. The laity also plays a vital role in the structures of the Church.

In the Archdiocese of Delhi, we have various ministries by the lay people such as 'Table ministry', 'Jeevan Dham', 'Jeevan Jyoti Ashram' and so forth, which are started by them and fully supported by the bishops, priests and religious as part of the evangelization in the Archdiocese of Delhi. Though, we are faced with many challenges, yet clergy and religious with the help of active laity do not leave any stone unturned to empower the laity at the parish and archdiocesan level.

Endnotes

[1] John Paul II, "Message for the World Congress of Ecclesial Movements and New Communities", on 30th May 1998.

[2] Pope Francis, *Evangelii Gaudium, The Apostolic Exhortation on The Joy of The Gospel, 24 November 2013*, 102: *AAS (2013) 1019-1137* (Trivandrum: Carmel International Publishing House, 2013), 86. (Hereafter referred *Evangelii Gaudium*).

[3] A A Hagstrom, "Theology of Laity," *New Catholic Encyclopedia* (Washington, D.C: Thomas Gale, 2003), 290.

[4] Alvaro Del Portillo, *Faithful and Laity in the Church*, trans. L. Hickey (Shannon, Ireland: Irish University Press, 1972), 15.

[5] Vatican Council II, "*Lumen Gentium*, Dogmatic Constitution on the Church, 21 November 1964, no 32, in *AAS* 57 (1965) 5-7," in *Vatican Council II the Conciliar and Post conciliar Documents*, ed. Austin Flannery (Mumbai: St. Paul Publications, 2004), 354–355. (Hereafter referred as *Lumen Gentium*).

[6] *Lumen Gentium*, 11, 329–330.

[7] Vatican Council II, *Apostolicam Actuositatem*, Decree on The Apostolate of Lay People, (18 November, 1965), 2: *AAS* 58 (1966), 837-864, in *Vatican Council II the Post Conciliar and Post Conciliar Documents*, ed. Austin Flannery (Mumbai: St. Paul Publications, 2004), 677. (Hereafter referred as *Apostolicam Actuositatem*).

[8] *Lumen Gentium*, 32-33, 354–355.

[9] The documents of Second Vatican Council such as *Lumen Gentium*, Dogmatic Constitution on the Church, *Apostolicam Actuositatem*, Decree on the Apostolate of Lay People, *Gaudium et spes*, Pastoral constitution on the Church in the Modern World focus on the role of the laity in the Church.

[10] Kuncheria Pathil, *Theology of the Church New Horizons* (Bangalore: Dharmaram Publications, 2006), 35.

[11] Kenan B. Osborne, *Ministry: Lay Ministry in the Roman Catholic Church: Its History and Theology* (New York: Paulist Pr, 1993), 7.

[12] Yves Marie Joseph Congar, *Lay People in the Church: A Study for a Theology of Laity* (London; Westminster: Christian Classics, 1985), 4–5.

[13] Karl Rahner, *Theological Investigations, Volume II: Man, in the Church.*, trans. Karl Kruger (New York: Helicon Press, 1963), 319–30.

[14] *Lumen Gentium*, 31, 353.

[15] Paul Lakeland, *The Liberation of the Laity in Search of An Accountable Church* (New York- London: Continuum, 2003), 10.

[16] R. Paul Stevens, *Abolition of the Laity: Vocation Work and Ministry in Biblical Perspective* (London: Send the Light, 2000), 31.

[17] R. Paul Stevens, *The Other Six Days: Vocation, Work, and Ministry in Biblical Perspective* (Grand Rapids, Mich.: Vancouver, B.C: Eerdmans, 2000), 32.

[18] Lakeland, *The Liberation of the Laity in Search of An Accountable Church*, 11.

[19] Stevens, *Abolition of the Laity: Vocation Work and Ministry in Biblical Perspective*, 30.

[20] Ibid., 32.

[21] K T. Sebastian, *Towards a Theology of Laity the Era of the Lay People* (Bangalore: National Biblical Catechetical and Liturgical Centre, 1999), 29.

[22] Anne Rowthorn, *The Liberation of the Laity:* (Eugene, Or: Wipf & Stock Pub, 2000), 27–31.

[23] Herbert Haag, *Clergy and Laity: Did Jesus Want a Two-Tier Church?* trans. Robert Nowell (Tunbridge Wells: Burns & Oates Ltd, 1998), 100.

[24] Christopher M. Bellitto, *Ten Ways the Church Has Changed: What History Can Teach Us About Uncertain Times* (Boston, MA: Pauline Books & Media, 2006), 35.

[25] eds Stephen Charles Neill and Hans-Ruedi Weber, *The Layman in Christian History* (Philadelphia: Westminster Press, 1963), 28–59.

[26] Alphonse Thainese, *Participatory Communion: An Ecclesiological Inquiry on Lay Participation in the Local Church Based on the Documents of the FABC (1970 - 2006)* (Indian Society for Promoting Christian Knowledge, 2008), 97.

[27] Pathil, *Theology of the Church New Horizons*, 123.

[28] J Patmury, "Laity and Mission," in *Mission Trends Today Historical and Theological Perspectives*, ed. Joseph Mattam and Sebatian Kim (Mumbai: St Pauls, 1997), 147.

[29] Rowthorn, *The Liberation of the Laity*, 12.

[30] *Lumen Gentium*, 10, 329.

[31] Ibid., 10 & 31.

[32] Vatican Council II, *Sacrosanctum Concilium*, The Constitution on the Sacred Liturgy, (4 December 1963), 2: *AAS* 56 (1964), 97-138, in *Vatican Council II the Conciliar and Post conciliar Documents*, ed. Austin Flannery (Mumbai: St. Paul Publications, 2004), 21. (Hereafter referred as *Sacrosanctum Concilium*).

[33] *Sacrosanctum Concilium*,10, 27.

[34] *Lumen Gentium*, 10, 329.

[35] Vatican Council II, "*Ad Gentes Divinitus*, Decree on the Church's Missionary Activity, 7 December 1965: 5, AAS 58 (1966), 947-990," in *Vatican Council II the Conciliar and Post conciliar Documents*, ed. Austin Flannery (Mumbai: St. Paul Publications, 2004), 718. (Hereafter referred *Ad Gentes Divinitus*).

[36] *Ad Gentes Divinitus*, 5.

[37] Vatican Council II, "*Gaudium et Spes*, Pastoral Constitution on the Church in The Modern World, 7 December 1965: 1 AAS 58 (1966), 1025-1120," in *Vatican Council II the Conciliar and Post conciliar Documents*, ed. Austin Flannery (Mumbai: St. Paul Publications, 2004), 794. (Hereafter referred *Gaudium et Spes*).

[38] *Gaudium et Spes*, 31-32, 818–820.

[39] Ibid, 10, 685.

[40] Ibid.

[41] Paul VI, *Populorum Progressio, Encyclical on The Development of People, (26 March 1967), 81 AAS 60 (1968) 612-623.*

[42] Pope Paul VI, *Evangelii Nutiandi, Post Synodal Apostolic Exhortation on Evangelization in the Modern World, 8 December 1975, 70 AAS (1976): 5-76* (Bangalore: National Biblical Catechetical and Liturgical Centre, 1980), 61. (Hereafter referred *Evangelii Nutiandi*).

[43] Paul John II, *Christifideles Laici, The Apostolic Exhortation on the Vocation and the Mission of the Lay Faithful in the Church and the World, 22 December 1988,10: AAS 81 (1989), 427-479* (Mumbai: St. Paul Publications, 1989), 24–25. (Hereafter referred *Christifideles Laici*).

[44] Benedict XVI, *Motu Proprio Ubicumque et Semper, Apostolic Letter on Establishing the Pontifical Council for Promoting the New Evangelization (21 September 2010) AAS 102 (2010) 788-792.*

[45] "Message of Pope Benedict XVI to Cardinal Peter Kodwo Appiah Turkson, on the Occasion of the Plenary Assembly of the Pontifical Council for Justice and Peace, on 3rd November 2010.

[46] "Message of His Holiness Pope Benedict XVI on the Occasion of the Sixth Ordinary Assembly of the International Forum of Catholic Action, 10 August 2010).

[47] "Address of Pope Francis to the Participants in The Plenary Assembly of The Pontifical Council for Laity, 17 June 2016.

[48] Franz Josef Eilers, *For All the Peoples of Asia: Federation of Asian Bishops' Conferences Documents from 1992-1996*, vol. II (Quezon City, Philippines: Claretian Publications, 1997), 119–120.

[49] Ibid., 211–212.

[50] Conference of Catholic Bishops of India, *Report of The Thirteenth Plenary Assembly of the CCBI* (Barrackpore, Kolkata: CCBI Secretariat, 2001), 8.

[51] Ibid, 8, 326–327.

[52] *Apostolicam Actuositatem*, 3, 678.

[53] *Evangelii Gaudium*, 120, 96.

[54] Ibid, 5, 322.

[55] *Evangelii Gaudium*,120, 96–97.

[56] *Christifideles Laici*, 25, 67.

[57] Ibid.

Christian 'Trinitarian Monotheism'

Conversation between Christians and Muslims

Victor Edwin S.J.

Introduction

I meet Muslims in their homes, in universities, Islamic cultural centres, in the mosques that I frequent and in the Sufi shrines. I am often questioned, in the course of conversations, of my faith in 'Trinitarian Monotheism'. Clearly aware of the intense conversations around the topic in the past, I share with them the unmerited gift the Christians' faith in 'One God who is three' and the Christian theological efforts 'to make it the wellspring of our being, our life and our activity'.

Further, I point out to them that we believe that this one God, who is our creator and our judge, reveals God's self as Father, Son and Holy Spirit in the salvation history on human kind. This affirmation, I found is very important in the outset, since, some Muslims seem to think that Christians are not monotheists. I stress on the relation between revelation and salvation. This connection between revelation and salvation if not stressed, the Trinitarian doctrine will be in danger of becoming additional information about God's inner life separated from God's salvific presence. If it becomes simply additional information about God, then Muslim will let us know that their suspicion is true and that Christians have corrupted their faith! In our conversations around the this theme, I tell my Muslim friends that Christians believe in One God and entrust themselves to God who is present here and now with a deep faith that not only are we of and for God with all we are but God is ours with all that God is.[1]

I further point out to my Muslim friends that the Church in her traditions has grown in the awareness of the mystery of the three persons who are One God. In other words it is a vision of faith in motion by its theological unfolding. Various ways of approaches to the mystery testify at once to the continuity and progress between the revealed message and the faith of the Trinitarian Councils. This affirmation of 'continuity and progress' in faith articulation is essential as often many Muslims tend to think faith in Triune God is a mere Christian philosophic speculation of later centuries.

It is my experience, Muslims respond to Christian articulation of faith in Triune God in mainly two different ways: some out rightly reject since the 'Qur'an rejects the Trinity', and point out that we, Christians, have 'corrupted the original message of the revelation given to Jesus'; and others though do not articulate clearly, seem to express that Christian faith in Triune God is confusing and irrational. Rarely sometimes I have also come across some Muslims who call Christians to abandon their faith in the Triune God and insist that we must embrace the faith in One God whose nature is not known as believed by Muslims.

Looking back into the history of Christian-Muslim relations, we may find many such debates between Christians and Muslims. In this essay, I investigate and present the Muslim thinking on the Trinity during the early centuries of Islam. It will be shown that two major factors influenced Muslim theological thinking on the Christian belief of the Trinity in that period. First, that the Qur'anic teaching as explained by the exegetes had an effect on Muslim theological thinking. Secondly, that the Arabic-speaking Christian theologians' articulation of their faith in the Trinity also affected and shaped Muslim theological thinking. Reading through texts on exchanges between Christians and Muslims during this medieval period encourages us to delve deep into the present context that is marked by complexity due to social, political, cultural, and religious underpinnings.

The teaching of the Qur'an

The Qur'an makes several observations about different aspects of the Christian faith. Some of these observations, Muslim exegetes claim, deny the Christian teaching on the Trinity. The Qur'an seems to challenge Christians on three important aspects of their faith with regard to the triune nature of God. 1. Is Jesus God? 2. Is God, the third of three? 3. Does God have a son? A closer look at different passages elucidates this.

The following passage is said to address the first question:

> They indeed have disbelieved who say: Lo! Allah is the Messiah, son of Mary. (Q. 5:17).[2]

The following Qur'anic verse is said to concern the second question:

> They surely disbelieve who say: Lo! Allah is the third of three; when there is no God save the One God. If they do not desist from so saying a painful doom will fall on those of them who disbelieve. (Q. 5:73).

The following Qur'anic verse is understood to concern the third question:

> O People of the Scripture! Do not exaggerate in your religion nor utter aught concerning Allah save the truth. The Messiah, Jesus son of Mary, was only a messenger of Allah, and His word which He conveyed unto Mary, and a spirit from Him. So believe in Allah and His messenger, and say not "Three" – Cease. (it is) better for you! - Allah is only One God. Far is it removed from His transcendent majesty that he should have a son. (Q: 4:171).

Following the exegetes, Muslim theologians debated with their Christian counterparts on above mentioned questions.

Theological exchanges between Christians and Muslims on the Trinity in the early centuries of Islam[3]

One of the early Christian theologians, John of Damascus (d. 753 CE),[4] dismissed Islam as a heresy.[5] He believed that the Qur'an was an ignorant imitation of the Bible.[6] However the Arab Christian theologians, who came after John of Damascus, quickly realised that Islam cannot be dismissed as a heresy and it needed to be answered theologically.[7] The question relating to the nature of Trinity could not be avoided.

The Arabic-speaking Christians used *kalām* categories,[8] which were familiar to Muslim theologians in presenting their faith in the Trinity.[9] The debate between *Mu'tazilīs* and *Ash'arīs* itself, some scholars believe, was the fruit of their interaction with Christians.[10] This view does not go uncontested.[11] *Mu'tazilī* scholars argued that God's essence is undifferentiated[12]and therefore the attributes have no real existence. *Ash'arīs*, on the other hand argued "that unless God's attributes are real, and derived from entities within the being of God, he cannot be endowed with them in any meaningful way."[13] Ammâr al-Baṣri (d. 850) who lived before Abu al-Ḥasan 'Ali al-Ash'arī (d. 935/6) argued that God has real attributes,[14] and presented the Son as the knowledge attribute and the Holy Spirit as the life of God attribute. Ammâr al-Baṣri neither uses the Bible to defend the Trinity nor dismisses Islam as a heresy. He engages with Muslim theologians intellectually with the categories of Islamic *kalām*. In his writings Christian dogmas and ideas are expressed in Arabic which Muslims (esp. *Mu'tazilīs*) could appreciate.[15]

The dialogues between the Nestorian Catholicos Timothy I of Baghdad and Caliph al-Mahdi,[16] and between Hishām ibn al-Hakam and a Christian patriarch Bariha[17] also show that Christian belief in the Trinity was questioned by Muslims and defended by Christians. Timothy I explained that God's Word and God's Spirit endow God's essence with the characteristics of reason and life. There is no separation between God, God's Word and God's Spirit.

God is wise and living through God's Word and Spirit and they are integral to God's being.[18] Timothy I emphasised that God knows and lives through his Word and Spirit. It should be remembered that the debate between Hishām ibn al-Hakam and Bariha was probably not historical, though it may reflect late 8th and early 9th century Muslim views of the Trinity. Both Caliph al-Mahdi and ibn al-Hakam in their arguments against the Trinity; "focus on what they identify as the contradiction within the Godhead between Persons who are both distinct from one another and also equal and identical."[19] While Caliph al-Mahdi asked Timothy I "to explain how on the one hand he does not worship three Gods (*sic*), and yet how on the other the three Persons are not confused?"[20] Ibn al-Hakam forced Bariha "to concede either that the Father and Son differ in their actions and so cannot be equal in status, or that they are completely identical and so are not in reality distinct."[21]

The Muslim authors use the same *kalām* categories to demonstrate that the Christian explanations were far from satisfactory. 'Alī b. Rabbān al-Tabarī is one amongst them. In his work *Radd 'alā al-Nasārā* (*The Refutation of the Christians*), he makes two important charges against the Christian belief in the Trinity.[22] First, he argues that titles like Father and Son "are deprived of their meaning when Christians claim that the Son is both like the Father in being eternal and unlike him in being generated, for the two titles then become interchangeable."[23] Secondly, "if Father and Son are both almighty and omniscient, as the Creed states, they lose the characteristics of superiority and inferiority implied in their relationship, and the Father will no longer have the authority to send the Son to earth."[24] His conclusion is "that the language used by Christians does not afford any real description of God."[25]

Another contemporary Muslim theologian al-Qāsim ibn Ibrahīm in his *Radd 'alā al-Nasārā* makes his point loud and clear: "God is one and so Jesus must be human, and that the divine God cannot be in relation with a human being."[26] He too reflects on the titles 'Father' and 'Son': saying that if these titles are to be taken seriously then it is logical to say that one being brought the other being into existence in time, consequently "the doctrine of the Trinity cannot provide an accurate means of comprehending God, since the titles upon which it rests arise from an act that occurred at a particular time."[27] Al-Qāsim ibn Ibrahīm knew exactly the nuances of Christian explanations of the Trinity and attacked it logically.[28] Both these theologians placed stress on the relationship between God and Jesus in their refutation of the Trinity. In their arguments, they "demonstrate the overriding influence of the Qur'an on the Muslim side of polemic."[29]

Abū Yūsuf Ya'qūb b. Ishāq al-Kindī, another 9th century theologian, subjects the Trinitarian formula to the logic of Aristotle and shows the doctrine of the Trinity "as contradictory either with itself or with the precept that God cannot be composite."[30] He has three arguments against the Trinity: first, since he understands that hypostases are composed of the substance as a reality and a distinguishing property, he concludes, "everything which is composite must be caused, and nothing that is caused can be eternal."[31] Secondly, he shows that if individuals (in the case of the Trinity, three individuals) are eternal, they cannot be restricted only to three, because "individuals are part of a species and bear accidents, and since a species is composed of a genus and a difference, it naturally follows that there will be more than three eternals."[32] Thirdly, using the philosophical system of Aristotle, he shows the contradiction in the proposition: three are one and one is three.

In this discussion, so far it is clear: first, that dismissing Islam as a heresy did not last long. Secondly, Christian thinkers who wrote in Arabic, realised the intellectual challenge of Islam and engaged with it on its own terms. Thirdly, some Muslim theologians had a clear understanding of the ways in which Christians defined the doctrine of the Trinity. Fourthly, some of them, like 'Alī b. Rabbān al-Tabarī and al-Qāsim ibn Ibrahīm, focused upon the Father–Son relationship and demonstrated the weakness of the doctrine. While on the one hand, Muslim theologians kept the Qur'an as the basis for their discussion, on the other hand, people like Abū Yūsuf Yaʿqūb b. Ishāq al-Kindī used Aristotelian philosophy to oppose Christians. Fifthly, the Trinity was an important element in the anti-Christian polemical treatises composed by Muslim theologians in the early Muslim centuries. Several of these arguments are developed in the treatises of the three important theologians that are examined in some detail in the following section.

Muslims Theologians: Christian faith in the Trinity cannot be rationally sustained

Abū ʿĪsa al-Warrāq, Al-Nāshiʾ al-Akbar, and Abū Bakr al-Bāqillāni (all 9th century) have been chosen for consideration in this section. Before discussing their views on the Trinity it is necessary to establish that there is sufficient reason for choosing these particular scholars. All three showed in their discussions to their satisfaction that Christian faith in the Trinity cannot be rationally sustained. They felt that the doctrine of the Trinity was not only irrational but also challenges the Islamic doctrine of God.

Al-Warrāq (d. after 864 CE) was an extremely influential scholar and a provocative thinker who had a great expertise and interest in the religions known to him. He acquired a considerable knowledge of the Christian sects. He showed rigorous academic objectivity in his approach to understanding as well as attacking Christian faith. His work was the result of the most painstaking examination of the teachings of the Christian groups he encountered.[33] His "Against the Trinity" is an important work in the history of Christian-Muslim relations. In his work, al-Warrāq attacks the doctrine of the Trinity in a sustained manner. He is a *Shīʿite* scholar.[34] Al-Akbar (d. 906 CE) though cannot be regarded as a major *Muʿtazili* theologian - he was scorned even by Muslim contemporaries - his value is that he reflects late 9th century Muslim rationalist attitudes towards the Trinity. Al-Bāqillāni was a leading theologian from the *Ashʿari* tradition.[35]

Abū ʿĪsa al-Warrāq

Al-Warrāq in his *Al-Radd ʿalā al-Tathlīth, al-juzʾ al-awwal min kitāb al-Radd ʿalā al-Thalāth Firaq min al-Nasārā* (hereafter *al-Radd*)[36] set out to "expose the shortcomings in Christian teachings, and to show Christians that their faith was riddled with inconsistencies."[37]

It will be helpful to present briefly the deals with the Trinity in his work. The first section of *al-Radd* (§16-69) examines the interpretation of the Trinity by Nestorians, Jacobites and Melkites. This major section has several sub-sections. In the first sub-section (§16-29), he questions the claim of Nestorians and Jacobites that there are three hypostases and one substance. In the next sub-section (§ 30-69), he examines the Melkite claims that the hypostases are identical with the substance but substance is not identical with them. He splits up this sub-section into three smaller parts and argues for the incompatibility of all possible alternative forms of this relationship: substance is identical with all the hypostases in all respects (§ 31-43), in some respects (§ 44-55) and in no respect (§ 56-69).

The second section (§ 70-125) examines the relationship between substance and hypostases; (§ 70-88) examine how the hypostases though uniform can be differentiated; (§ 89-105) scrutinize how they can possess different characteristics; (§ 106-118) attack the Christian groups' tendencies to explain the Trinity based on analogy with created things; and (§ 119-125) use philosophy to counter arguments that suggest that hypostases exist necessarily. The third section goes from (§ 126-150). In this section he discusses the distinction between the hypostases (§ 126-128), shows the internal contradiction in hypostases as attributes of other hypostases (§ 129-131), discusses the generation of the Son from the Father (§ 132-140), and concludes by examining the various terms employed to explain the hypostases (§ 141-150).

Al-Warrāq uses two kinds of arguments in *al-Radd*.[38] Both are effective and show his intellectual ability to employ philosophy and his knowledge of Christianity. The first kind of argument seeks to identify the incoherencies in explaining the Trinity and to show that the Christian opponents' logical conclusions directly contradict their fundamental beliefs. He shows that if the Melkites believe the substance is completely identical with the hypostases it will contradict their faith. He argues that this faith conviction would lead to any one of the following conclusions: "either the comprehensive substance must be three specific substances like the hypostases and so three hypostases, or it must be a single specific substance like each one of them and so no longer the comprehensive substance, or hypostases must be a comprehensive substance like it, making two comprehensive substances." The second kind of argument involves the demonstration of how the Christian presentation of the Trinity is incompatible with logic and common sense.

In both arguments, he lays emphasis on the three hypostases as three separate entities. These three hypostases are three separate actualities within one Godhead; i.e. three entities within one Godhead! He wonders how these three separate entities could be one? Moreover, he argues that substance if real is a fourth member of Godhead.[39] His preoccupation is to show that there would not be any fruitful discussion on the unity of God if Christians continue to hold on to their idea of the Trinity.

Al-Nāshi' Al-Akbar

Al-Nāshi' al-Akbar presents his refutation of Christian doctrines in his *Al-Radd 'alā al-Nasārā min Fī al-Maqālāt* (hereafter *Fī al-Maqālāt*). In *Fī al-Maqālāt*,[40] al-Akbar "shows no interest in exploring the structure of the doctrine in itself, insisting only that it does not make sense."[41]

Al-Akbar ridicules Christians for saying that the three hypostases are identical and distinct from one another at the same time. He also points out "that if two things are utterly identical, as the Christians say the hypostases are, one cannot be the cause of the other. He underlines the ridiculousness of the Christian claim by showing that they both make distinctions between the three Persons and also insist there is no distinction between them."[42] Al-Akbar insists that hypostases that are distinguished by causal relationships cannot be equal. He appears to miss a delicate nuance in presenting the relation between Father, Son and Spirit before criticizing it. Already in the time of al-Akbar, Christians explained the relationship between Father and Son in terms of generation. They term the relationship between Father–Spirit and Son–Spirit in terms of procession. Al-Nāshi' appears to reduce this fine distinction to a simple causal relationship. He then presents two major arguments against the Trinity. Each argument counters the Christian thinkers' presentation of the Trinity. These arguments indicate to the atmosphere of intense polemics surrounded any discussion on Christian faith in one God. We shall look at these arguments.

Argument 1: Hypostases and accidents
As indicated above Christians use Muslim *kalām* categories to present the Trinity, showing how the hypostases can be entirely identical with one another while at the same time keeping their distinction.

Christians argued that accidents in themselves are undifferentiated. However, when they inhere in a material, they bring about distinction. Black and white become black and white when they inhere in a material thing. One can distinguish between white paper and black paper. White paper gets its whiteness when the accident inheres in paper, and so also with black. White and black as accidents can be distinguished only in respect of being accidents of different qualities. Christians argued, "like accidents the divine hypostases can be considered both distinct and uniform." Al-Akbar presents three-counter arguments.

- The accidents are formally different from the material bodies in which they come to inhere. If hypostases are analogically compared to accidents, they are different from the substance

(Godhead) and that would lead to multiplicity within the Godhead.

- If hypostases, as accidents, are both uniform and distinct, then uniformity and distinction should arise from within themselves (that is not possible) or from a cause outside themselves, but in the case of hypostases it would entail an additional causal entity within the Godhead.

- Hypostases can only be said to be uniform and distinct by an external agent. It would bring multiplicity within the Godhead.

Argument 2: God's attributes

The Christians argued that it is evident from the design of the universe that it has a maker. The maker of the universe should be knowing and living, since all intentional beings have these qualities. In Muslim circles the qualities of knowing and living were considered as God's attributes. In section 1.3.2, it was noted that the *Mu'tazilīs* and *Ash'arīs* clashed on this point. The *Mu'tazilīs* maintained that such attributes are human descriptions of God and such attributes are not integral to God. They opposed such attributes because in their opinion they would compromise the oneness of God. The *Ash'arīs* on the other hand used these attributes to say positively something about God.

Following 'Ammâr al-Baṣri, the Christians in the time of al-Akbar, made use of the *Ash'arīs's* interpretation and suggested that God's attributes of knowledge and life were in fact the Son and Holy Spirit as endowers of the qualities of knowing and living upon the being of God.

Al-Akbar rejected this argument with the following six counter-arguments. In the first four counter-arguments, he showed that divine attributes cannot be limited to two. It will be recalled here that 'Ammâr al-Baṣri had already counter-argued that the divine attributes may be many but life (Holy Spirit) and knowledge (Son) are pre-eminent ones. The next two counter-arguments appear to be weightier than the first four.

- If the creator is three hypostases and one substance, al-Akbar, following al-Kindi, argues that the hypostases must inhere in one substance and since they are differentiated the substance must be composite. The unity of God is violated. It brings God into the realm of a composite being.

- In a second counter-argument he showed that if God is explained in terms of substance (the human person too is made of substance), it will bring God into the realm of contingent being.

- Al- Akbar argues essentially that the doctrine of the Trinity is rationally unsustainable since it entails beings who are distinct in themselves and yet uniform with one another.

Abū Bakr al-Bāqillānī

Al-Bāqillānī presents a good picture of the *Ashʿarī* tradition in his writings.[43] In his treatise, *al-Tamḥīd*, he discusses the Trinity along with other doctrinal issues that came up in Christian-Muslim theological discussions.

Al-Bāqillānī first of all aims at rejecting the idea that God is a substance. He believes that if the idea of God as substance is eliminated, then the foundation of Christian faith is destroyed.[44] Secondly, he questions why Christians restrict hypostases to three?[45] Christians, in their discussions with Muslims, from the early 9th century onwards presented their faith in the Trinity in terms of one divinity that posses two attributes: knowledge and life. Knowledge and life are traditionally equated with Son and Spirit. However, al-Bāqillānī cites power as another attribute. When Christians argue that it is identical with life, he disagrees with them. He argues that it is like knowledge and it should be fused together with knowledge or it should be considered as a separate attribute, as an additional hypostasis. He finds that to restrict hypostases only to three is arbitrary. Like the other two scholars discussed here, al-Bāqillānī also focuses his critique on the Christian faith in one God.

Final Comments

First, it is clear in our discussion that the Arabic-speaking Christian theologians used *kalām* categories to present their doctrine of the Trinity to Muslims. This had two consequences. The first consequence was, since the Christians used theological terms that Muslims understood, they were able to enter into dialogue with Muslims on an equal footing. This is a positive consequence. Carefully reading and reflecting on the conversation between Muslims and Christians, one come to recognise that finding a common ground for the intellectual articulation of one's faith is essential even to this day.

Secondly, the Muslim theologians had a good grip of Christian understanding of the Trinity. In their response, there are two different approaches. Al-Warrāq made every effort to understand the Christian presentation of the Trinity. He perceived how different groups present the doctrine. Then he went on to show that it was riddled with inconsistencies. Al-Akbar appears to respond differently. He made serious efforts to understand the Christian arguments but did not show interest in exploring the structure of the doctrine itself. Though both these scholars differed in their approach, they both conclude that Christian faith in the Trinity is rationally unsustainable. My conversations with Muslim friends have shown that there is a hesitation on their side towards understanding the structure of the doctrine, in the sense of finding this faith conviction as theological unfolding of the mystery of the One God both they along with Christians worship. In other words there is a lack of interest in trying to understand 'what Christians really believe in'. I often thought at those moments that there is a hesitation to receive from other 'matters that are pertaining to faith of the other'. I humbly recognise that I too am eager quite often to share, but not that open to receive. In matters of faith, it appears it is quite easy to give not that easy to receive. Deeper engagements in dialogue teach me that if one 'shares and receives' in dialogue one deepens one's own faith and enter into others 'sacred territory' with deep respect and humility. In other words, one takes roots and take wings.

Thirdly, the Muslim theologians appear to have concluded that the doctrine of the Trinity compromised the strict monotheistic unity of God (*Tawḥīd*). The Christians' language of Father, Son, and Spirit did not provide any real description of God. The alternative version of God which the Christians tried to present in opposition to the Qur'anic presentation was riddled with errors. Christians and Muslims could not really find a common ground in their explanations about God. The implication is if Christians and Muslims want a common ground then Christians have to abandon their faith in Trinity and accept *Tawhīd*. One may find such positions even today. Such positions do not lead one to deeper forms of dialogue.

As a conclusion, it must be said that the One God which Christians and Muslims worship, albeit in different ways, need not be a source of conflict between these two sets of believers. We must keep engaging with one another and sharing our faith with one another. Individuals and groups that keep doing such 'faith sharing' will recognise that the one God that they worship guides both Christians and Muslims in their respective faith convictions invite them to know and love one another. Certainly, as such faith engagement shaped Muslim and Christian theological thinking in the eighth and ninth centuries will continue to shape the theological thinking of both Christians and Muslims in the pluralistic world of today.

Endnotes

[1] Piet Schoonenberg, "The doctrine of the Trinity: empty dogma or fruitful theologoumenon?," *Theology Digest* 39 [1992]: 23-31.

[2] See also: "They surely disbelieve who say: Lo! Allah is the Messiah, son of Mary." (Q. 5:72).

[3] Students of Muslim writings on Trinity are hugely indebted to the long-term work of Prof. David Thomas who has prepared critical English

translations with footnotes and introductory essays on the key writers. These are the only accessible editions and therefore we are confined in the choice of both textual material and critical analysis.

[4] John of Damascus was an important official in the administration of the Umayyad Caliphs who retired from his position due to the diminishing influence of non-Muslims in the administration. See: G. Hawting, *The First Dynasty of Islam* [London & New York: Routledge, 2000], 61-65.

[5] H. Goddard, *Islam: Towards A Christian Assessment* [Oxford: Latimer House, 1992], 13; J.W. Voorhis, "John of Damascus on the Moslem Heresy," *The Moslem World* 24 [1934]: 391-398.

[6] D.H. Sahas, *John of Damascus on Islam, the "Heresy of the Ishmaelites"* [Leiden: Brill, 1972], 132-133.

[7] D. Thomas, *Christian Doctrines in Islamic Theology*. [Leiden: Brill, 2008].

[8] *Kalām* is the "formal, intellectual exercise in the systematic defence of the credibility of religious doctrines". See: S.H. Griffith, *The Church in the Shadow of the Mosque*, 46; See also: G.D. Newby, *A Concise Encyclopedia of Islam* [Oxford: Oneworld, 2004], 120.

[9] R.M. Frank, "The Science of Kalām," *Arabic Science and Philosophy* 2 [1992]: 9-37. See also: M. Cook, "The Origins of Kalām," *Bulletin of the School of Oriental and African Languages* 43 [1980]: 32-43.

[10] H. Wolfson, *The Philosophy of Kalām* [Cambridge, MA: Harvard University Press, 1976], 58-64.

[11] S. Rissanen, *Theological Encounter of Oriental Christians with Islam during the Abbasid Rule* [Åbo: Åbo Adademis Förlag-Åbo Adademi University Press, 1993], 11-17.

[12] "...therefore that the qualities listed in the Qur'an and deducible by reason, such as God's knowledge, power and life, could not derive from any really existent attributes that might be identified in addition to God's essence itself... God is knowing did not mean that he possesses an entitative attribute of knowledge, since this attribute would have to be eternal and formally distinguishable from God's essence, rendering his unity only relative..." (D. Thomas, *Christian Doctrines in Islamic Theology* [Leiden: Brill, 2008], 4).

[13] D. Thomas, *Christian Doctrines in Islamic Theology* [Leiden: Brill, 2008], 4

[14] ...that the defenders of God's absolute unity were illogical because when they denied he had an attribute of life they implied he was lifeless, and when they denied he had an attribute of knowledge they implied he was ignorant. Thus God must possess real attributes... life and knowledge had priority as

constitutive parts of his being and as the origins of all his other attributes...
(D. Thomas, *Christian Doctrines in Islamic Theology* [Leiden: Brill, 2008], 4).

[15] J.M. Gaudeul, *Encounters & Clashes: Islam and Christianity in History II Texts*, 39.

[16] N. A. Newman, ed., *The Early Christian-Muslim Dialogue*, 163-268; W. G. Young, *Patriarch, Shah and Caliph* [Rawalpindi: Christian Study Centre, 1974].

[17] D. Thomas, "Two Muslim-Christian debates from the early Shi'ite traditions," *Journal of Semitic Studies* 33 [1988]: 63-65.

[18] A. Mingana, "The Apology of Timothy the Patriarch before the Caliph Mahdi," *Bulletin of the John Rylands Library* 12 [1928]: 159.

[19] D. Thomas, *Anti-Christian polemic in early Islam: Abū 'Īsā al-Warrāq's "Against the Trinity"* [Cambridge: Cambridge University Press, 1992], 31.

[20] Ibid., 31.

[21] Ibid.

[22] 'Alī b. Rabban al-Tabarī's treatment of Trinity is not complete. Ibn Taymīyya reproduces al-Tabarī's arguments in his *Al Jawāb al-Sahīh liman baddala Dīn al-Masīh*, [Cairo, 1905], vol. II, 312 – vol. III, 3.; See also: T. F. Michel, ed., and trans., *A Muslim Theologian's Response to Christianity: Ibn Taymiyya Al-Jawab Al-Sahih* [New York: Caravan Books, 1984].

[23] D. Thomas, *Anti-Christian polemic in early Islam*, 32.

[24] Ibid.

[25] Ibid., 33.

[26] Ibid., 34.

[27] Ibid.

[28] H. Wolfson, *The Philosophy of the Kalam* [Cambridge: Cambridge University Press: 1976], 320.

[29] D. Thomas, *Anti-Christian polemic in early Islam*, 35.

[30] Ibid., 37.

[31] A. Abel, *Le Livre pour la refutation des trios sects chrétiennes* [Brussels, 1949], 4.12-17. This reference is cited by D. Thomas in *Anti-Christian polemic in early Islam*, 37.

[32] Ibid., 10. 5-8. As cited by D. Thomas in *Anti-Christian polemic in early Islam*, 37.

[33] D. Thomas, *Anti-Christian polemic in early Islam*, 3, 57.

[34] W. Madelung, "Abū 'Īsā al-Warrāq über die Bardesaniten, Marcioniten und KantÓer" in H. Roemer and A. Noth, eds., *Studien zur Geschichte und Kultur des Vorderen Orients* [Leiden: Brill, 1981], 210-224.

35 D. Thomas, *Christian Doctrines in Islamic Theology*, 31.

36 This work has two parts: the first part deals with the Trinity and the second deals with the doctrine of the Incarnation. The first part of his exposition dealing with the Trinity is particularly relevant in the context of this dissertation.

The English translation of *al-Radd* contains 150 paragraphs (D. Thomas, *Anti-Christian polemic in early Islam*, 3). The first 15 paragraphs contain teachings about the Trinity. In these paragraphs "Abū 'Īsā gives an impressive demonstration both of his knowledge about Christianity and of the ease with which he can deploy his sources (D. Thomas, *Anti-Christian polemic in early Islam*, 55)." He also expects that his arguments could be of use to other polemicists of the era (See: S.H. Griffith," 'Ammār al-Basrī's Kitāb al-Burhān: Christian Kalām in the first Abbasid century," *Le Muséon* 96, [1983]: 155f).

37 D. Thomas, *Anti-Christian polemic in early Islam*, 3.

38 Ibid, 59.

39 D. Thomas, "The Doctrine of the Trinity in the Early Abbasid Era," in *Islamic Interpretation of Christianity*, ed. Lloyd Ridgeon [Richmond: Curzon, 2001], 85.

40 *Fī al-Maqālāt* like *al-Radd* shows both interest in explaining how Christians presented their arguments in defence of the Trinity and employs vigorous counter-arguments to demolish any such claims. In the foregoing section al-Warrāq made every effort to understand the doctrine as it is presented by different Christians. He also explored the structure of the doctrine itself in order to understand and then debunk it. His long and complicated discussion revealed his efforts to understand the Trinity. It would not be an exaggeration to say that he approached his opponents with fairness and made every effort to seek the truth itself.

41 D. Thomas, *Christian Doctrines in Islamic Theology*, 31.

42 Ibid.

43 Ibid., 119.

44 He argues that Christians claim that God is substance. But, if God is substance, then he must be a noble and supreme substance. He pushes this a little further and concludes that if God is noble and supreme, he should be the highest instance of a series of beings. This conclusion implies a continuity of identity between God and the created order. However, he affirms that there is no continuity between the phenomenal world and the transcendent world. He argues that if Christians believe in some continuity of identity between God and the created order, then God must be temporal, and like

all known substances, God's substance too must bear accidents. Moreover, in the phenomenal world the agent of action is not a substance but a composite body in which substance inheres, so accordingly God must be a body. His argument appears to undermine the Christian idea of God as substance.

Al-Bāqillānī, appears to miss two important distinctions that Christians make when referring to God as substance. First, Christians affirm that *God exists because of himself* rather than because of *anything outside him;* God is not contingent. Al-Bāqillānī, however, appears to conclude that God exists because God can be observed. Secondly, when the Arabic-speaking Christian theologians used the term *'jawhar'* for substance, they use it to refer to a self-subsisting agent, whereas Muslim theologians understood substance as the basic element of the material world out of which constituent parts of physical reality are constructed.

[45] The full text is translated in D. Thomas, *Christian Doctrines in Islamic Theology*, 169-171.

The Role of the Holy Spirit in the Church Today

Nija Vara, MSGN

Introduction

The age and movement of the church is remarkably attributed to the Holy Spirit while expressing the tremendous significant-activities in the church in terms of her formal founding on Pentecost and her functioning through the sacraments as the continuation of the experiential presence and the salvific work of Christ. The Holy Spirit is labeled as the soul of the church and unifying principle of the church. The Spirit is not merely a uniting link between the members of the church but also a transforming and divinizing power in the life of every member of the church bestowing on him or her sublime privilege of son ship or daughter ship.[1] On the other hand, we have not emphasized sufficiently on the role of the Holy Spirit in the church. Therefore, there is the obscurity of the Holy Spirit which can be seen in the context.

Context: To speak about the Holy Spirit, it is not easy because the terms, such as Father and the Son are applied to the first two persons of the Trinity and which help us understand in a very personal and very familiar way. On the other hand, the Holy Spirit is described neither in personal nor Trinitarian terms. Therefore the obscureness could be firstly the very doctrine of Trinity by which the early Christians were speaking about substance and nature of the Holy

Spirit saying where the Spirit will fit into because it has character of moving or causing things to happen. Secondly, the more emphasis is given to Jesus Christ than Holy Spirit. Thirdly, symbols are used to describe the Spirit. As a result, this obscure definition of personal character and thus the personhood of the Spirit are under concern. If the Holy Spirit is a person and thus a divine people then we are deprived of the due worship, faith, surrender and love because we don't understand the personhood in its entirety. It is essential that one knows the Holy Spirit as a person. Many people testify to the blessing of the Holy Spirit as a real person like Christ himself rather than as a gracious influence or mysterious power. Holy Spirit is ever-present, loving friend, constant companion and mighty helper.[2] Hence, there is a need to emphasis on the significant role of the Holy Spirit in the Church today.

The Holy Spirit in the Life and Mission of the Church

The Church is Born of the Spirit
The giving of the Spirit to the disciples marks the beginning of the church. The Spirit brings the church into being. Three main texts are relevant here.

John 19:30
Here Jesus' death is described. "…and He bowed his head and gave up His spirit." We understand here that Jesus entrusted his spirit to the hands of his Father. The promise of Jesus is fulfilled at the time of his death. His heart was opened and from it came out blood and water (Jn 19:34), the streams of the living water. For John, living water is the spirit (Jn 7:37-39). So 19:30 would mean the communication of the Spirit of Jesus to "his own" (Jn 13:1)

John 20:22
According to this verse, the Risen Lord communicated the Spirit to his disciples. And when he had said this, he breathed on them and said to them, Receive the Holy Spirit. It is evident from verse 21 that

the disciples are given Holy Spirit in view of their mission: Just as the Father has sent me, so I send you. This shows that Jesus equips them for this ministry by giving them the spirit.

Acts 2
According to Luke, it is on the day of Pentecost that the Holy Spirit is officially given to the Apostles. The Spirit came upon them when they were all in one place. (Acts 2:1) The Spirit came upon the group as they were living together in prayer.[3]

On Pentecost, the Holy Spirit was sent by the Father and by the Son precisely to vitalize the structure and finality of the Church. When the work which the Father gave the Son to do on earth was accomplished, the Holy Spirit was sent on the day of Pentecost in order that he might continually sanctify the Church, and thus, all those who believe would have access through Christ in one Spirit to the Father.[4]

The Church is led by the Spirit
The coming of the Spirit sets everything moving. The church resolutely sets out to fulfill her mission. But the book of Acts makes it clear that the church does it in the power of the Spirit. Two points must be noted here according to the Acts of the Apostles.

The primary human agents in the spread of the word of God are all men and women filled with the Holy Spirit. The twelve apostles were filled with the Holy Spirit on the day of Pentecost (2:4). In 4:8, Peter speaks to the Jewish leaders filled with the Holy Spirit. The same is said of the entire Christian community in 4:31. The seven members, chosen by the community as deacons, were full of the Spirit and of wisdom (6:3). The most important among the seven was Stephen who was full of wisdom and Spirit (6:10), and just before his death full of the Spirit (he) gazed into heaven and saw the glory of God (7:55). According to 9:17 Ananias asks Paul to get baptized that his sight will be restored and he will be filled with the

Holy Spirit. Later right at the start of his first missionary journey, we find Paul speaking filled with the Holy Spirit (13:9). Barnabas who played a decisive role in the shaping of Paul (9:27 11:25-26, 30; 12:25) and who became later his companion especially during the first missionary journey, was also a good man, full of the Holy Spirit and of faith (11:24).

There are important turning points in the spread of the word, in the growth of the church. She is confronted with pressing challenges. She has to take momentous decisions. She does under the guidance of the Holy Spirit, sometimes under real pressure from him.[5] In all the events, we see the church is led by the Spirit.

The Spirit Achieves the Mission of the Church

As the church marches forward, she bears witness to Jesus by preaching the Gospel under the guidance of the Holy Spirit and thus prepares herself for the final destiny. The transformation of the believers is also the work of the Holy Spirit. The inner transformation of a human person is always seen in the Bible as the work of the Spirit of God. It was described thus in the Old Testament (1 Sam 10:6) that Saul "turned into another" man by the Spirit; In Ezek 36:24-32; 37:1-14, we read about the inner transformation of the people of God by the Spirit. It is also applied to the people of the New Testament. For example, the Spirit dwells in them according to Rom 8:9, 11; I Cor 3:16; 1 Cor 6:19). It is the "Spirit of son ship or daughter ship" (Rom 8:15) and makes them children of God (Rom 8:16). The Spirit introduces the believers "into Christ" (Rom 6:3-4; Gal 3:27). The Spirit helps the believers to be obedient to God (Ezek 37:14.24) and to find God's will in prayer (Rom 8:36-37; 1 Cor 2:10-11). It helps them to confess Jesus as the Lord (1 Cor 12:3) and to serve him (Rom 12:11).

The believers on their part should make themselves be transformed by the Spirit. They should let themselves be "filled with the Spirit" (Eph 5:18). They should not "grieve the Holy Spirit" (Eph 4:30), but instead, should "live by the spirit" (Gal 5:25), "walk by the Spirit" (Gal 5:16.25) and should allow themselves to be led by the Spirit (Rom 8:14)

They can be sure of this final fulfillment because they have been given the Spirit as the "first fruits" (Rom 8:23) and a "guarantee" (2 Cor 1:22; 5:5; Eph 1:13-14). The presence of the Spirit in the church, in the believers, is a promise and a foretaste of this final achievement.[6] It is God's Spirit who unites us together in supernatural life. The Spirit works for the holiness of heart and life in his people and sets them apart from the world forming them into a community for his mission to the world.[7]

The Signs of the Holy Spirit in the Life of the Church

There are some signs of the Spirit in the church which complement the church and sometimes our treaties and volumes on ecclesiology will be lacking such descriptions of the signs of the church. The following are the signs:

Joy

St. Paul writes the Galatians the theme of Joy. Accordingly, it is one of the most authentic signs of the presence of the Holy Spirit of God and no one will take away from us (Jn 16:22). This joy is the breath of the Spirit resting on the poor of the beatitudes. Sergius Bulgakov contrasted rationality as characteristic of the grace of the *Logos* with the revelation of the Holy Spirit as the following signs.

Beauty

Thus, the revelations of the Spirit cannot be perceived by pure reason, but by other faculties of the human spirit, where they resound as ineffable words which human beings are not permitted to express. The hypostasis of the Spirit is the hypostasis of beauty and we understand that his action in nature fills it with beauty, which is already a foreshadowing of the kingdom of God through the Holy

Spirit.[6] To conclude in the words of Sergius Bulgakov: "The beauty of the world is the I effect of the Holy Spirit, the Spirit of Beauty, and Beauty is Joy, the joy of being."

The Gift of Prophecy

Among the gifts of the Spirit described in the New Testament, Sergius Bulgakov gives priority to that of prophecy. He distinguishes between the specific gift of prophecy bestowed on the ecclesiastical hierarchy and the general gift of prophecy accessible to all as a result of Pentecost. The gift of prophecy is thus an intrinsic dimension of the new life in Christ, where human beings deny themselves, take up their cross and realize their divine-humanity in Christ. Not only do they receive the Spirit but they create in and through the Spirit.

Life in Christ

This gift is more than a particular gift amongst others; it specifies the Church's very being, for this is the life of God himself communicated in its fullness. Thus, the church is above all a life, not an institution or a doctrine or even a system. Ivan Kireevsky had already discovered this certainty in the faith of his wife, who was a spiritual daughter of the *staretsi* of Optino. Everything in the church depends on love. The church's soul is the Holy Spirit, the grace of God living in a multitude of reasons enable the creatures.

Love

The third great gift of the Spirit in the church is the gift of love. Human beings participate in the divine life, being bound by the Holy Spirit into the love which unites the three persons of the divinity among themselves. Sergius does not hesitate to speak of spiritual eros as the quest of human beings for their Creator. Thus, just as the living persons are united in love, so is with the church on earth, in which human beings are united with one another in love through the gift of the Holy Spirit in the church.[8]

Ecclesiology of vat-II

Understanding of the Church according to Vatican II

The church was undoubtedly the central theme of the Second Vatican Council. All the sixteen documents of the council primarily deal with the church. The council wanted to read the opening phrases of the two main documents on the Church as: *"Lumen Gentium"* meaning "Light of the Nations" defining the Church, the body of Christ as the light to all nations; and *"Gaudium et Spes"* meaning "Joy and Hope" defining the Church as a community whose mission is to give joy and hope to the world today.[9] Thus, the Second Vatican Council has made a valuable contribution to the development of a new ecclesiology.

The aspects described above are only a help to understand the council's ecclesiology. Since all those aspects cannot be described here, I shall highlight some of the insights of the Second Vatican Council which are significant for us in India today. The main ecclesiological thrust of the council is characterised by seven shifts which as a whole constitute a substantial advance in the theology of the church.[10] The council has not provided a blueprint for this new church but has given some orientations as to what the mission and the shape of the church of the future should be. In short, I can say that the new church should be a God - centred and a people - centred church. As rooted in a deep experience of God in Christ Jesus, it should manifest and meditate this experience to others. The church of the future should be a servant church that is a church at the service of the people and should work for the creation of a new society in India[11] where all will be equal in dignity and freedom.

The Specificity of the Work of the Holy Spirit in Vatican II

Vatican II was a call by the Spirit addressed to the church for an overall renewal. This is evident from the context of its convocation and the methods used for its implementation. The setting was not the need for a defence against errors in dogma and morals. Pope John

XXIII called it a pastoral council, that is a council meant to make the church fulfill her function more effectively and relevantly in the world. After the council, the implementation affected the whole of ecclesial life and not merely a particular aspect.

The work of the council seen in this perspective may be compared to an overall overhauling of a machine. Today many industrial and other concerns do this. They dismantle, e.g. an aeroplane, take out its parts, recondition them and then reassemble these parts so that the plane may function perfectly well. Similarly, in the church, during this post-Vatican II period, we have been renewing the various aspects of the church's life. In fact, I would say, that we have done it quite well. Now is the moment to reassemble these parts with a view to make them function effectively and relevantly. In the spirit of Vatican II, we can say that this new way of being Church will have its central trust in being a community of mission; only then can we assume that the church has experienced a new Pentecost through Vatican II as envisioned by John XXIII. Then each part of the church will contribute towards the creation of a Church that is conscious of her identity as an evangelizing church.[12]

Church as the Temple of the Holy Spirit: Pneumatological Dimension of the Church

Jesus Christ not only lived on earth for a short time, established the Church and elected his followers but more than enough care had also been taken for the Church. As the exalted Lord, Jesus Christ poured out the Holy Spirit and this remains present the in Church and in the world. The doctrine of the Church can only be dealt within the doctrine of the Holy Spirit.[13]

The apostle Paul expresses the lasting efficaciousness of the exalted Lord in the Holy Spirit in the concise formula: 'the Lord is the Spirit' (2 Cor 3.17). It is in the Holy Spirit that the process of transforming the world into the kingdom of God which is justice, peace and joy in the Holy Spirit (Rom 14.17). The transformation begins in the

Church and happens through the Church. Hence, Paul describes the Church as building, house and temple of the Spirit (1 Cor 3.16; 2 Cor. 6.16; Eph 2.21; 1 Pet 2.5). It is the Spirit who unites the Church and holds it together. All statements about the Church as the people of God and body of Christ are only possible in the Holy Spirit.[14]

The image of the church as the temple of the Holy Spirit expresses the constitutive element between the church and the Holy Spirit. The Christian community at its earliest stage considered itself as the fulfillment of the eschatological expectations promised through the prophets and brought about by Christ. The first Christian community came to the realization of who they were through the outpouring of the Spirit which is the gift of the risen Lord. The experience of the Holy Spirit is so powerful that Christians regarded their new existence as anew creation in the Holy Spirit.[15]

In Spirit, the Church is One, Holy, Catholic and Apostolic
The one mediator, Christ established and ever sustains here on earth his holy church, the community of faith, hope and charity, as a visible organization through which he communicates truth and grace to all people. This is the sole Church of Christ, which according to the creed we profess, is One, Holy, Catholic and Apostolic, which our Savior, after his resurrection, entrusted to Peter's pastoral care (Jn 21:17), commissioning him and the other Apostles to extend and lead it (Mt 28:18) and which he raised up for all ages as "the pillar and mainstay of the truth" (1 Tim 3:15), (LG no. 8).

The Church is One in the Power of the Holy Spirit
"We have been baptized in the one Spirit to be one body" (1 Cor 12:13; Eph. 4:4). Cyril of Alexandria says, "Since we have all received the one and the same Spirit, we are all mixed with one another and with God." In the decree on Ecumenism, the Church takes up this teaching and states, "It is the Holy Spirit, dwelling in those who believe, pervading and ruling over the entire Church, who brings about that marvelous communion of the faithful and joins them

together so intimately in Christ that He is the principle of the Church's unity (UR 2)." The Spirit is the principle of communion because the Agape, which is poured out into our hearts by the Spirit of its very nature 'Unites' (Rom 5:5).

The Church is Holy in the Power of the Holy Spirit

The unity of the Trinitarian communion constitutes the sanctity of the Church, which is 'holy' because she participates in the Trinitarian nature of God and more especially in the sanctity of the Holy Spirit.

The New Testament describes the sanctity of the Church by calling her the holy temple of God (1 Cor. 3:16; Eph. 2:21; Jn. 14:15) whose faithful are "a spiritual house, a holy priesthood, a holy nation" (1 Pete 2:5). Just as the Spirit, during the baptism of Christ sanctified and consecrated Christ's body of flesh, similarly during Pentecost, the Spirit sanctified *and* consecrated his mystical body, the Church. Thus, all members of the Church are sanctified.[16]

The unity created by the Spirit is a holy unity. This is holy because it is a unity with God, a unity brought out by the Holy Spirit, holy love, God's love.[17] Therefore, "all in the Church, whether they belong to the hierarchy or are cared for by it are called to holiness according to the Apostle's saying: 'For this is the will of God, your sanctification' (1 Tim. 4:3). This holiness of the Church is continuously shown forth in the fruits of grace which the Spirit produces in the faithful and so it must be a striking witness and example of that holiness" (LG 39). Thus, a call to be a true Christian symbolizes a call to lead a holy life that is to be perfect as the heavenly Father is perfect (Mt 5:48).

The Church is Catholic in the fullness of the Spirit

The word 'Catholic' means universal, total, entire etc. The Catholicity of the Church expresses a dimension of qualitative, vertical fullness primarily and only subsequently also the dimension of quantitative, horizontal and intensive fullness. The Church was Catholic on the day of Pentecost and will always be so until the day of the Parousia

(CCC 830). The Church is one irrespective of different nations, languages and cultures. This oneness is the result of the act of the Spirit. The Holy Spirit not only ensures the internal Catholicity within the Church but also Catholicity in the extensive sense, reuniting in a single body, human beings of different sexes, races and nationalities. The Church cannot confine the Spirit within her limits and constrain the action of the Spirit. On the contrary, the Spirit opens up the Church towards an encounter with the world through the mission. It is the Holy Spirit who "opens the eyes of the mind and makes it easy for all to accept and believe the truth.

The Church is Apostolic in the continual sending of the Spirit

On the day of the Pentecost, the Spirit descended on the Apostles and on those who were gathered around them. From that original nucleus, the Church has multiplied up to the present day. It is the Holy Spirit who caused the Church to be Apostolic. The Holy Spirit will be the counselor of the apostles and the Church always present in their midst as the teacher of the same Good News that Jesus proclaimed. The church is Apostolic also through the apostolic succession. The *Holy Spirit* is continuously at work in the Church through the successors of the Apostles. The grace of the Spirit which the Apostles gave to their collaborates through the imposition of hands continues to be transmitted in Episcopal ordination. The bishops and the presbyters build up the Church through Eucharistic celebration which is 'the summit and source of the life of the Church' and in which the Spirit is actively present (DV 8, LG 25).[18]

Our Response to the Spirit Today

We have described the various stages of the Spirit operating in the history of humankind. Now, we shall try to be more specific and see what is the response that we, living in the third millennium have to give to the Spirit who has manifested himself in a very special way through Vatican II. Keeping in mind the role of the Holy Spirit in the world after Pentecost, we need to begin by identifying the areas where the Kingdom is prevented from being realized. Only a Spirit-filled and Spirit-led community can effectively implement them.[19] The following are some measures to be adopted to meet these situations.

a. All the gifts of the Spirit and the role of the Spirit in the fulfillment of the mission of the Church needs a re-interpretation.

b. A renewed effort has to be made to understand the presence of the Spirit in the world in our country in the other religions so that we can allow ourselves to be led by the Spirit in our dialogue with them.

c. A special effort to be made to understand the role of the Spirit in a society that is stamped by the marks of injustice and exploitation.

d. Creation of a sense of openness towards the Charismatic movement can be understood in the broader sense so that all those who are moved by the Spirit and are endowed with the gifts of the Spirit can work together for the Kingdom of God.

e. The gifts of the spirit given to all should be made available for functioning in the concrete situation of the parish. For this, a catechesis of the gifts of the Spirit, especially some extra- ordinary gifts of the Spirit be made available to all peoples. This will enable individuals to give the proper place and importance to some of the more exotic and extraordinary gifts.

The Holy Spirit: Love and Hope of the Church

The Council concludes its marvelous description of the Holy Spirit's divine activity in the Church by saying that the Spirit "renews her and leads her to perfect union with her Spouse.

No other outcome is possible for this history of salvation which is ordained by the Father, realized by the Son Jesus Christ, and carried to perfection by the Holy Spirit, "Lord and Giver of life," for the purpose of "elevating human beings to participate in the life of God" (LG 2).

The pilgrim Church cannot live without "eschatological" tension as part of her eternal destiny. Only then, impelled by that hope for "perfect union," can the Church, working in the midst of human affairs and temporal realities, be the "hierarchical communion of faith, hope, and love" which serves as an effective instrument of Jesus Christ, teacher and redeemer, for communicating to all people his truth and his grace.[20]

Conclusion

Church is the community of those who follow the Lord and proclaim his kingdom. This Church was inaugurated by Christ and is being guided by the Holy Spirit. The council relates the Church and the Holy Spirit by saying that the Church is the temple of the Holy Spirit. Throughout this discussion on the Church and the Holy Spirit, we emphasized the fact that Holy Spirit continues the day of Pentecost daily in the Church through the liturgy and thereby the Father, Son and Holy Spirit are at work to bring forth this One, Holy, Catholic and Apostolic Church. Today in many parts of the world under the influence of the grace of the Holy Spirit, many efforts are being made in prayer, word and action to attain that fullness of unity which Jesus Christ desires (UR 4). Hence, it is a wakeup call for everyone to be instrumental in the hands of the Spirit to carry out the mission of Christ in the church.

Endnotes

[1] Issac Arickappillil, "Holy Spirit in the life of the Church," *Kristujyothi* 14, no.3 (Sept 1998):10.

[2] R. A. Torrey, *The person and the Work of the Holy Spirit* (Grand Rapids: The Zondervan Corporation,1974), 10.

[3] John K Urichianil, "Holy Spirit the main Agent of the Mission of the Church," *Indian Theological Studies* XXXI, no.1 (March 1994):353-355.

[4] Monseñor Oscar A. Romero, The Holy Spirit in the Church, First Pastoral Letter,www.romerotrust.org.uk/sites/default/.../lost%20pastoral%20romero.pdf (accessed October 10, 2016), 2.

[5] John   K Urichianil, "Holy Spirit the main Agent of the Mission of the Church," 356-357.

[6] John   K Urichianil, "Holy Spirit the main Agent of the Mission of the Church," 366-367.

[7] Luis M. Bermejo, *The Spirit of Life* (Anand: *Gujarat Sahitya Prakash*, 1987), 85-90.

[8] Boris Bobrinskoy, "Church and the Holy Spirit in 20th Century," *Ecumenical Review* 52, no.3 (July 2000): 329-330.

[9] John Juellen Bach, *Church: Community for the Kingdom* (Manila: Philippines, 2000), 50-53.

[10] Kurien Kunnumpuram, *The Indian Church of the Future* (Mumbai: St. Pauls Press, 2007), 81.

[11] Kunnumpuram , *The Indian Church of the Future,* 108.

[12] Paul Puthanangady, "Holy Spirit and the Mission of the Church," *Kristujyothi*14, no.1 (March 1998): 3-4.

[13] M. Welker, *God the Spirit* (Minneapolis: Fortress Press, 1994), 12.

[14] Walter Kaspar, *The Catholic Church: Nature, Reality and Mission* (London: Bloombury Publishing House, 2015), 135.

[15] Lycurgus M. Starkey, *The Holy Spirit at Work in the Church* (New York: Abingdon press, 1965), 19-26.

[16] Hans Urs von Balthazar, *Church and World* (US: Heeder and Heeder, 1967), 137-138.

[17] Brian Gaybba, *The Spirit of Love* (London: Cassell Publishers Limited,1987), 177.

[18] Darbello Christus, "Church and the Holy Spirit According to Vatican-II," *Aikya Samiksha* 7, no.2 (Oct 2010):50-51.

[19] Paul Puthanangady, "Holy Spirit and the Mission of the Church," *Kristujyothi*14, no.1 (March 1998):4.

[20] Monseñor Oscar A. Romero, *The Holy Spirit in the Church,* First Pastoral Letter, 9.

The Influence of Bhakti Music of South India on Telugu Christian Hymns

Dusi Ravisekhar S.J.

Introduction

The origin of music is believed to be divine. Musicologists speak about the celestial genesis of music. Every religious tradition employs music heavily in the ritual worship. From time immemorial music has been used as a vehicle of expressing one's deepest devotion to the beloved deity. Music emanates from devotion and in turn enhances the devotion. *"Sangīta gnānamu bhakti vina"* said Sri Tyagaraja, one of the Musical Trinity's of Carnatic music in his composition in Dhanyasi. The South Indian Pre-Trinity[1] period is filled with a galaxy of composers who used music as a powerful means of *bhakti*. Several Indian (Hindu) Saints have used music as a medium of expressing their passionate longing, agony, love, pain and suffering through *bhakti* music. The earliest composers of the South Indian music tradition, namely Alwars, Nayanmars, Jayadeva, Narayanatirtha, Annamayya, Purandaradasa, Ramadasu and Tyagaraja had made use of the powerful instrumentality of music through various musical forms. These outstanding composers from Telugu region had made a great impact by their soul-stirring musical works. The impact of the *bhakti* propagated by these *Vāggēyakārās* or poet-saints in and around Telugu-speaking regions of South India could be felt profoundly through their masterly musical works like *kīrtanās, bhajans* etc.

Bhakti and music go hand in hand. Music always evoked *bhakti* and *bhakti* always embraced music as an effective medium of communication between God and man. Music has been the preferred means of expressing one's devotion in many religions. The Bhagavadgita proposes music as one of the paths *(Bhakti Mārga)* that brings the devotee close to the Nada Brahman. Music facilitates intimacy with the divine, *paramātma*. Indian music system, especially the Carnatic music has served as a powerful vehicle of facilitating profound divine experience. The myriad *rāgās* in Carnatic music expressed myriad emotions of the passionate soul. As different colours in a rainbow give it beauty, the varieties of *rāgās* with their evocative capacities contribute to experiencing devotion from all its varied perspectives.

Every religious tradition in India possesses *bhakti* music and literature. The music and literature of South Indian have played a vital role in propagating *bhakti*. The essence of South Indian *bhakti* music tradition had touched the core of every religion like Buddhism, Jainism, Sikhism, Islam and even Christianity and influenced them in some way or other. The Christianity which originated in the East and enjoyed much patronage in the West practiced its own style of rich sacred music from the beginning. Just as the devotional singing formed part of the ritual worship in Indian temples, in the same way the devotional singing or choirs played vital role in the worship in Christian tradition. There was no worship without music. Initially, the medium of language in the Liturgical worship used to be Latin anywhere in the world. Hence, the music was more in line with the Gregorian music. Gregorian music, which was soul-stirring, was the only prescribed sacred music in the Catholic Church.

Those who accepted Christian faith in India at first used to sing the Latin or English hymns, though they did not really understand.

During the British colonial rule in India, some missionaries promoted the native languages, music, art and culture. They had picked up some skilled writers and musicians to either translate some important biblical works or to produce the original works in the local language or music. Some early Protestant converts from the eastern part of Andhra Pradesh, namely Srikakulam, Vizianagaram, Visakhapatnam and the Godavari coast coming from the educated traditional Brahmin community, accepted the new faith. And when joined the new Christian faith-community, they brought along with them their own rich literary and musical traditions. It helped the early communities to express their faith in the native poetic language and to compose hymns based on the native musical genre like *bhajans and kīrtanās*. This is the radical shift that took place helping the early Telugu Christian community in the 19th century to express their faith and devotion in the indigenous way.

1.   Music in Christian Worship:

Though there are references to Musical instruments in Genesis, they are meant to be for the festive purposes. Book of Exodus 15:1, "Then sang Moses and the children of Israel this song unto the LORD, and spoke, saying, I will sing unto the LORD, for he hath triumphed gloriously: the horse and his rider hath he thrown into the sea." The voices of thousands, in fact over a million, singing this song of praise glorifying Jehovah, must have been glorious. King David, whose period was considered to be the golden period of music, played Harp, a ten-stringed instrument to refresh king Saul and to drive out the evil spirits (I Samuel 16:23). After he became king he used it to sing *kīrtanās* known as Psalms in the Bible. Singing Psalms became then part of the Jewish worship. This was the custom even till the early Christianity when Roman emperors adopted Christianity as the State religion. Gregorian chants were introduced in the worship. Latin became the official medium. Latin hymns were sung across the world. When Martin Luther parted with the mainline church he encouraged language and music of the local and indigenous cultures.

2.   Various Stages in the Evolution

At this juncture, it is important to understand the struggle of early Christians to make sense of their faith. It is vital here to understand how it became a necessity for the new faith to accept the native cultural symbols in order to express their faith in an intelligible way. It is also necessary to probe who were the earliest persons who made such attempts to make the new faith nourishing by adopting the native music models of *bhakti* genre. The struggle was not merely one of the language-problem. It was a question of understanding the new symbols, new culture, new medium and a new world altogether. How to comprehend it? Two stages were identified in this study before the inclusion of *kīrtana* form in the Telugu Christian. These developmental stages can be identified not only in Telugu- speaking regions but also in the neighboring regions of Tamil Nadu and Kerala.

a.   Direct Rendering of the Latin or English Hymns

This is the first stage before the development of *kīrtana* form in Church singing in the early 19th century. When the French and the Portuguese arrived in India, they brought the priests with them to preside over the liturgy[2]. Since Latin was the official language of the church, the liturgy was conducted in Latin. Even the music associated with the liturgy was in Latin and had to be sung in the prescribed form. Until the British arrived in India, it was primarily the Latin-dominated religious ritual and music performed during the liturgy. However after the arrival of the British in India, the mainline protestant Churches[3] started singing the liturgical hymn in English language.

b.   Translations, Improvisations and Adaptations of Latin and English Hymns

This is the second stage before the introduction of the *kīrtana* singing in the Telugu Christian worship. The British made certain translations of the English hymns available in the native language which the native converts sang. Hymns like 'what a friend we have in Jesus' translated as '*prīti gala mana yēsu*', 'Jesus, lover of my soul!' translated as '*yēsu, ātma priyudā*', 'a mighty fortress is our God' translated as '*mā karta gaṭṭi durgamu*', Christmas carol like'Joy to the world' translated as '*hāyi lōkamā! prabhuvacce*'. These are a few examples which show how the early believers translated the English hymns and sang in Telugu. This can be identified as the second stage in the evolution of native Telugu Christian music.

c.   **Early Musical Compositions in the Native Language: Hymns in Western Languages**

From the 11th century onward, a movement of Christian devotional mysticism developed in Germany, which was similar in nature to the *bhakti* movement of South India. This movement arose as a response to the over-institutionalized religion of Western Europe.

Medieval Roman Catholicism placed great emphasis on the mediation of priests and Church in the relation between man and God. It prescribed elaborate public rituals, which were to be conducted by Catholic priests in Latin, the language of the educated elite. Interestingly, as in the case of the South Indian *bhakti* movement, the pioneer of German *bhakti* was a nun, Hildegrad von Bingen. She was followed by several other nuns such as Elisabeth von Schoenau, Mechthild von Magdeburg etc. For them, "the longing for inner spiritual union with Christ found allegorical expression in the form of a mystical wedding of the Soul with the Saviour" as said by Fritz Martini. However, the most important representative of German *Bhakti* was the mystic Meister Eckhart. Wilhelm Goessmann notes, "He emphasized the intense and intimate relation of Man with God: Man must seek detachment, and distance himself from the World, in order to focus his sole attention on divine wisdom and truth."

Eckhart was followed by his disciples Johannes Tauler (1300 – 1361) and Heinrich Seuse. Like the south Indian *bhakti* saints, they expressed themselves in the native language of the common people. This enriched the German language and enabled the Germans to express their innermost spiritual emotions in their mother tongue. They emphasized the need for man to directly experience the divine through personal efforts. These thoughts violently clashed with the teachings of the Roman Catholic Church, which saw itself as the intermediary between God and Man.

The German Reformation led by Martin Luther (1485–1546), gave a great boost to the *bhakti* movement in Germany. Luther, who was himself a gifted poet and a musician, composed numerous congregational hymns in German. These devotional songs, which were commonly known as 'chorals' became immensely popular among the German people. Numerous poets and composers followed Luther's example and composed moving chorals. These included poets such as Nicholas Decius, Philipp Nicolai, and Paul Gerhardt, and composers such as Hans Leo Hassler, Samuel Scheidt, Johann Adam Reinken, and Dietrich Buxtehude. The choral was indeed a great vehicle of Christian devotional feelings.

3.   Attempts to Compose Hymns in Indian Native Languages

Attempts to produce Telugu Christian literature as well as music in the native language can be traced back to 17th Century. Both literature and music in the native Telugu language originated almost around the same time:

> Christian literature in Telugu dates back to early 17th century and most of it is a product of Roman Catholic missionary endeavours. The Italian missionaries of the order of St. Cactano at Goa were sent to Golkonda and Chandragiri under Vijayanagara kings in latter part of the 16th century. They produced catechism in Sanskrit as well as Telugu which are considered to be the earliest Christian works in Telugu. The 17th century Jesuit Robert de Nobili of Madurai mission too is credited with some works in Telugu but no copies have survived. Pingali Ellanarya's *Tōbhya Caritra*, Mangalagiri Ananda Kavi's *Vēdantarasāyanamu*, Mallela Thimmaraju's *Gnānacintāmani* are the earliest creative works with Christian themes. The Roman Catholic missionaries from Europe produced devotional literature in Telugu which included catechisms, summaries of the gospels. However, it is only from the early 19th century that Protestant Telugu Christian

literature became a vibrant tradition with numerous writers and composers like William Dawson, Pulipaka Jagannadham, producing a sizeable corpus of devotional literature.[4]

4.   The Origin of Telugu Christian *Kīrtanās*

The real shift had taken place when the native converts coming from the scholarly background. "Some of the native converts came from scholarly background and were employed by the missionaries in the school, seminaries and printing presses run by them. It was these early converts who shaped the protestant literary tradition in Telugu"[5]

The missionaries initially accepted the natives from Brahmin community who had become very resourceful in the production of Telugu Christian Literature and Telugu Christian music. Since they hailed from a scholarly and devout Hindu religious background, when they started writing and composing on Christian themes they based themselves on the rich *bhakti* musical forms like *bhajans* and *kīrtanās* which were used as vehicles of *bhakti* in both South and North India. Some earliest converts in South India, especially in Tamil Nadu and Andhra Pradesh like Purushothama Choudhary, Pulipaka Jagannadham and Vedanayakam Sastriar belonged to that scholarly class converts whose literary and musical works emanated from their native religious and cultural traditions and which stood on a par with other native composers like Ramadasu, Annamayya and others.

5.   Major Composers of Christian Hymns in South India

It is interesting to note that attempts to compose hymns in the local music styles took place in all three regions, namely Telugu, Tamil Nadu and Kerala almost simultaneously. The British followed the same approach of picking or converting the native talented musicians and writers to create the local tradition. It is surprising to note that in Tanjavore court, a native convert brought out great musical works as a contemporary of Sri Tyagaraja. Similarly, it is found that, in Tiruvananthapuram, Moolan Tirunal Maharaja praised the pioneer musician Mosa Valsalam Sastriar for his native music rendering on the Christian themes. These pioneer- musicians had gradually introduced the local musical forms in the congregational singing of the South Indian Church.

6.   Telugu Composers

It is difficult to identify any Christian literature and music till 17th or 18th centuries in Telugu-speaking regions. Except *Sarvēswara Mahatyam* of Pingali Ellana and *Vēdānta Rasāyana* of Mangalagiri Anandakavi there was nothing noteworthy to mention in the Telugu Christian literature. What is known for certain is that Purushothama Choudhary of early 19th century was the first ever Telugu Christian hymn-writer. He adopted the style of the 17th century *bhakti* poet-saints like Ramadasu, Kshetrayya and Sri Tyagaraja. Pulipaka Jagannadham, a native Brahmin convert and Willian Dawson, a British missionary with amazing Telugu literary standards became the co-founders of the Telugu *bhakti* hymns which they called *kīrtanās*. These three composers are also considered as the Trinity of Andhra Kraistava Kīrtanalu.

a.   Purushothama Choudhary

Purushothama Choudhary is the foremost Telugu Christian music composer of Andhra Pradesh. He produced Christian literature in fifteen different literary forms as well as composed over 200 *kīrtanās* set in Carnatic music *rāgās* and *tālās*. Choudhary's works were rooted in the "indigenous aesthetic, cultural and spiritual discourses."[6] He was a person with profound devotion to God and a seeker of true faith, salvation and *mukti*.

Purushothama's literary accomplishments earned him the title 'kavisārvabhauma', the monarch of Christian literature. Purushothama wrote *Śatakās*, *Prabandhās*, *Yakshagānās* etc. The prominent *kāvyās* written by Purushothama are: *Yēsunāyaka Śatakamu* (1845), *Yēsukrīstu Prabhu Śatakamu* (1845), *Pancacāmarapannamulu* (1845), *Rakshaṇa Caritra* (1846), *Niṣṭāra Ratnākaramu* (1846), *Vigrahanirmānamu*

(1846), *Kraisthava nītiprakāsamu* (1851), *Satyavēdasara sangrahamu, Krīstu Paratatvamu* (1871) and *Satya Bhajana* (1874).

The best known kirtanas of Purushothama are *Trāhimām krīstu nāthā* in Yadukulakambhoji ragam, *Yehōva nā mora lālincenu* in Sankarabharanam, *Nī caraṇamule nammiti* in Sahana, *Ānandamagu mukti in* Surati, *Unnapātuna vaccu cunnāḍu and Entō śrungāramainadi* in Mukhari and *Mangalamē Yēsunaku in* Thodi.

b.   Pulipaka Jagannadham

Pulipaka Jagannadham is the second major native composer of Christian *kīrtanās*. He was born in 1826 in East Godavari district and was brought up by Mr. Garten and later received baptism. After his initial education he became a teacher and worked in Srikakulam. He authored the book '*Nīti Prabhōdhita*' in 1875 which contained 62 poems. He wrote 29 *kīrtanās* which are still sung in the mainline churches today. His composition *Hrudaya maneḍu talupu nodda* in Bhairavi *rāga* and *Adi tāla* is one of the most popular *kīrtanās*:

Pulipaka Jagannadham composed well known *kīrtanās* like *Nāvanni angīkarincumō dēva* in Sourastra *rāga*, *Cūcu cunnāmu nī vaipu* in Khamas *rāga*, *Kalugunugāka* in Pantuvarali *rāga* and many other *kīrtanās* in various other *rāgās*. Jagannadham used wide range of *rāgās* like Ananda bhairavi, Surati, Kambhoji, Hari Kambhoji, Nadanamakriya, Nata, Bilahari, Sankarabharanam, Regupthi, Thodi, Asaveri, Mukhari, Sri Ragam, Neelambari and Madhyamavati. Jagannadham is the contemporary of Purushothama Choudhary. He also hailed from a scholarly and elite background of a learned family. Both his *sāhityam* and *sangītam* presented high proficiency in language and music. His compositions withstood the test of time even after 150 years after their composition.

c.   William Dawson

William Dawson was a British but was born in India. He was the son of Rev. James Dawson who worked in Visakhapatnam for London

Missionary Society. Although a foreigner, Dawson loved the native culture and got interested in mastering the languages. He learnt Telugu, Tamil, Hindi and Sanskrit. He learnt the classical music. He excelled well in literature and music equally. He stood on a par with his contemporary Christian musicians and writers like Purushothama choudhary and Pulipaka Jagannadham.

His language was smooth and flowing. It was rhythmic and captivating. He decked the hymns with beautiful similes and metaphors. Today 14 *kīrtanās* of Dawson are available in Andhra Kraistava kīrtanalu Hymnal. In the *kīrtana* 'Varanāmame śaraṇ amu' we find elegant expressions like, 'sāra hīna samsāra pārāvāra= tāraṇa kāraṇa-taraniyaina krīstu'. Dawson learned music in order to equip himself for the ministry. He gave equal importance to both *sangītam* and *sāhityam*. That's why his *kīrtanās* are filled with *madhura bhakti*. He used traditional Carnatic *rāgās* like Kambhoji, Bhairavi, Surati, Mukhari, Anandabhairavi, Bilahari, Sri Ragam, Nadanamakriya, Maruva, Navaroju etc. William Dawson gets the credit for having brought out the first ever Telugu hymnal in 1844 with the compositions of Purushothama, Pulipaka Jagannadham and himself with the name Andhra Kraistava Kirtanalu.

7.   Tamil Native Christian Composers

A brief account of the pioneering Christian musical works of Tamil Nadu may not be out of place because of the missionary links and common traits we find. This is also essential in order to authenticate the developments in Telugu region with that of the neighboring regions. It was discovered there were three outstanding Tamil Christian *vāggēyakārās*, namely Vedanayagam Sastriyar, Samuel Vedanayagam Pillai and Abraham Pandithar who could be considered as Tamil Christian Musical Trinity in the model of Carnatic Music Trinity and the Trinity of Telugu Christian hymns. All three were great writers and musicians. Besides composing excellent *kīrtanās*, they also produced great literary works.

Vedanayagam Sastriyar, the first of the early Tamil Christian composers was a contemporary of Sri Tyagaraja in Tanjore. He was directly influenced by the compositions of Sri Tyagaraja. Vedanayagam Pillai was the contemporary and a close associate of Gopalakrishna Bharathi who produced Tamil *kāvya Thēmbāvani*. All three have made outstanding contributions for Tamil Christian *kīrtana* genre.

8. Malayalam Composers

In Kerala, one of the pioneers in composing Christian devotional hymns in the native language of Malayalam was Mosa Valsalam Sastriyar. Like Purushothama Choudhury of Telugu Christian tradition, Mosa Valsalam made some substantial original composition in native language of Malayalam using pure Carnatic music.

9. A Critical Analysis of the Radical Shift from Western to Indian Music Styles

As it is said this part discussed how the transition from direct singing of the Gregorian or western music singing to native vernacular singing during the Christian worship had taken place. The shift was not sudden but gradual. It was largely initiated by the missionaries as early as 18th century. The initiation process had gone through different stages. The native converts in the early 18th century sang the hymns in foreign language for worship. In the second stage they translated some of them in their native languages but imitated the western tunes. In the third stage, the natives, primarily those who hailed from educated, scholarly and influential elite communities, started writing hymns in the local vernacular languages like Telugu in Andhra Pradesh, Tamil in Tamil Nadu and Malayalam in Kerala. Hence, they played a vital role in determining the style and quality of singing which continues till today qualitatively influencing the present day compositions.

a.   Early Native Christian Composers' Exposure to *bhakti* Music

The five native Christian composers mentioned above with profound knowledge of Carnatic music, belonged to the age of great Trinity of Carnatic music and one of them Vedanayagam Sastriar was as associate of Sri Tyagaraja. It was noted that he even tried to imitate Sri Tyagaraja in his compositions on Christian themes.[7] Being the classmate of King Serfoji and with the exposure to the court of Tanjore, one should not have any doubt about his capacities for singing and composing in Carnatic style. Dr. Anand Amaladass says that Sastriar maintained *Vāggēyakāra mudra* like Sri Tyagaraja.

b.   The Royal Patronage

It is a well-known fact that the arts flourished by and large in the ancient India due to the royal patronage. The courts of the kings like Tulaja, Serfoji, Swati Tirunal and Sri Krishnadevaraya encouraged the literary and music stalwarts, honoured them and rewarded them greatly. Royal patronage was very essential to survive and flourish in any art during those days. The early eminent native composers enjoyed the patronage and the support of the kings. Vedanayagam Sastriar had a place in the court of king Serfoji. They recognized not only the immense musical and literary knowledge of Sastriar but also the new trend which Sastriar was all set to start in the Christian milieu. Listening to the musical genius of Mosa Valsalam the Maharaja of Travancore Sri Moolan Thirunal invited him to sing in the Travancore court. Purushothama Choudhary was reputed for his musical talent and learning and was employed as a court *vidwān* in Parlakimedi *samsthāna*.

c.   Similarities among the three early South Indian Christian composers

Going by the scholarly background and great length of literary and musical works of the early composers, three of them, namely Purushothama Choudhary for Telugu Compositions, Vedanayagam Sastriar for Tamil Compositions and Mosa Valsalam Sastriar for

Malayalam compositions, some similarities are found from the point of view of the family background, proficiency in literature and music, royal patronage, their experiments, popularity and impact in the society. They were the pioneers who set the trend and tradition for the future in the sphere of Christian music and even literature. We find their trails in today's music and literature of various Churches. And it should be acknowledged that they had set great standards with their educated background and prowess.

10. Radical Shift after the II Vatican Council

The Second Vatican council[8] took place in Rome in 1964 brought about radical changes in certain practices of the Catholic Church. It brought about renewal in the liturgy and worship and clearly spelt out the role of music in the document called 'Sacrosanctum concilium'. It was this Council which permitted the vernacular singing and encouraged the adaptations of the local cultures and traditions. It says,

> In certain parts of the world, especially mission lands, there are peoples who have their own musical traditions, and these play a great part in their religious and social life. For this reason due importance is to be attached to their music, and a suitable place is to be given to it, not only in forming their attitude toward religion, but also in adapting worship to their native genius.... Therefore, when missionaries are being given training in music, every effort should be made to see that they become competent in promoting the traditional music of these peoples, both in schools and in sacred services, as far as may be practicable.[9]

The Vatican Council recommended that the local musical traditions need to be incorporated into the sacred worship and should pay special attention to promoting them. The Vatican council duly acknowledged the importance given in the Bible for music. The Council also recommended that the "Composers, filled with the Christian spirit, should feel that their vocation is to cultivate sacred music and increase its store of treasures."[10] It also prescribed that the music used in the sacred worship should be qualitative and should provide the facility and opportunity for the entire assembly of the faithful to join singing and praising God.

However, what needs to be acknowledged at this juncture is that the Protestant churches, especially in Telugu-speaking regions (even in Tamil Nadu) had already introduced *kirtana*-modelled singing in their sacred worship. By the time Catholic Church permitted the regional singing, hundreds of Andhra kraistava kirtanas were available with excellent music and lyrics, composed in Carnatic music style with classical *rāgās* and *talas*. One can definitely find the influence of these *kīrtanās*/hymns on the emerging Telugu Catholic hymns in the Post-Vatican II era. In fact, some hymns that were already popular in Protestant Churches came to be used in the Liturgy immediately after the II Vatican. They can be easily identified since we sing them even to this day.

1.	*Hrudaya manedu talupu nodda*	Anandabhairavi	Pulipaka Jagannadham
2.	*Na vanni angikarincu mi deva*	Sourashtra	Pulipaka Jagannadham
3.	*Nadipincu na nava*	Kambhoji	Masilamani A. B.
4.	*Devuni stuti incudi*		Ujjiva Gitalu
5.	*Swamina velugu*	Kalyani	Ujjiva Gitalu
6.	*Yesutho teevi ganu podama*	Yamuna Kalyani	Kinsinger
7.	*Cinta ledika yesu puttenu*	Bilahari	Abel N. D.
8.	*Randi yutsahinci padudamu*	Sankarabharanam	Samuel Pakianadham
9.	*Devuni prema idigo*	Anandabhairavi	Gollapalli Nathaniel
10.	*Emmanuelu raktamu*		Harmes H
11.	*Ne Yesuni velugulo nadacedanu*		Ujjiva kirtanalu
12.	*O deva! Na balama!*		Siyonu Songs

Conclusion

One could clearly find the influence of the *bhakti* music in the *kīrtanās* of Purushothama Choudhary, Pulipaka Jagannadham, N.D. Abel, Chetti Bhanumurti, Gollapalli Nathaniel etc. going by the *rāgās* and the literature which he had used. The influence of the same early Christians composers can be found on Telugu Catholic hymns going by the musical and literary frame work. South Indian *kīrtana* form of music has totally replaced every other musical genre whether Western or Gregorian. One can recognize the power of the South Indian musical form namely, *kīrtana* which occupied an irreplaceable centrality in the liturgical music. And there cannot be any other Indian musical form which can be more outstanding than *kīrtana* since *kīrtana* can touch the soul and elevate facilitating deep experience of God. Perhaps, what needs to be done is to reinstate the sanctity of *kīrtana* which it originally had during bhakti period and by reinstating the sanctity of *kīrtanās* of the great early Christian composers, reinstate the sanctity of the worship or liturgy itself which is the real purpose and role of sacred music.

Endnotes

[1] Pre- Trinity period: In the history of Carnatic music, the period before the musical Trinity, namely Sri Tyagaraja, Muthuswamy Dikshitar and Syama Sastri is called the pre-trinity period. It could be roughly fixed as the time from 11 to 17 century A.D. Composers like Jayadeva, Narayana Tirtha, Annamayya, Ramadas etc. were the prominent composers of this period.

[2] Liturgy which is the original Greek word was used of a public work of any kind, not only religious, but in the Septuagint it is applied particularly to the services of the Temple. The word in English is used in two senses: (1) of all the prescribed services of the Church and (2) specifically as a title of the Eucharist (as the chief act of public worship). *Cross F.L. The Oxford Dictionary of the Christian Church, Oxford University Press, 1997, Page 988.*

[3] Protestant Churches: Lutheranism, Zwinglianism, Calvinism would now all be regarded as Protestant and there are, in fact, a large number of denominations, with a considerable variety of beliefs, which are now in a general sense Protestant. All these various denominations are called Protestant Churches from 17th Century reformation movement initiated by Martin Luther. *Cross F.L. The Oxford Dictionary of the Christian Church, Oxford University Press, 1997, Page 1339.*

[4] Negotiating the Spiritual: Purushothama Choudhari and Early 19th Century Christian Literature in Telugu, K. W. Christopher, p. 152

[5] Ibid, p.153

[6] Ibid, p.153

[7] Ibid, p. 249

[8] II Vatican Council (1962-65): ... this council was apparently entirely due to Pope John XXIII, who attributed the idea of convening such an assembly to a sudden inspiration of the Holy Spirit. He defined its immediate task as renewing the life of the Church and bringing up to date its teaching, discipline, and organization, with the unity of all Christians as the ultimate goal. *Cross F.L. The Oxford Dictionary of the Christian Church, Oxford University Press, 1997, page 1682.*

[9] The Constitution on the Sacred Liturgy, Second Vatican Council; Pope Benedict XVI: Catholic World News, 2006.

[10] Ibid,

Khristbhakta Movement

Dialogical Mission of the Church

Jerome Sylvester, IMS

Indian Christians are happy about their presence and contribution in the Nation Building, especially in the area of not only literacy, but of higher education and human formation. Such Christian witness, especially in the cultural ethos and of human freedom and dignity has left its mark for the last two millennia. It is right and just that Indian Christian history be revisited with renewed enthusiasm and zest while we speak of New Evangelization. With a sense of *Children of the soil* the Christian community has to reckon its contributions from the later part of the first millennium.

According to Historians[1] the history of Christianity in India could be traced back to the time of its origin; from the time of St. Thomas, the Apostle of India whose mission had three phases: The Sind Mission in the kingdom of Gondapores, the Malabar Mission and the Coramandal Mission.

The Church in Northern India has to recognize that the cradle of its faith is embedded in the early First Century from the reign of king Gondopores (21-60 AD Ca) whose name the Act of Thomas and Takht-i- Bahi (stone inscription) mention. The recent discovery of coins inscribed with his name[2] stand as evidence of St Thomas's connection to the region East of river Indus.[3] This historical reference acknowledges the connection of St Thomas to the region prior to the Council of Jerusalem (Acts 15, before 50 AD). The controversy of the Gentile Mission and the Apostles gathering at Jerusalem to discuss the matter is also attested in history. So, St. Thomas's mission in North India could be placed prior to 46 A D.[4]

The Malabar Mission keeps up the tradition of St Thomas, the apostle and the arrival of Thomas of Canna (345 AD) with his community of 300 families of Christian believers. Those Christian communities rooted themselves in India ever since. The Coramandal Mission of St. Thomas is evident with the Santhom Cathedral, Chennai.[5] Their adaptation to the cultural ethos of India was different from those who came during later times.

The so called Mission Expansion from Europe and America had a gap of hundreds of years. Since then Church in India had different phase and face. In the later phase, the doctrinal and cultural differences of the European Churches and their allegiance to their polity were predominant and the Church in India was only a sprout of the West in all forms and manners.

The early phase of evangelization was succeeded by the interest of others who visited the region.[6] The following phase of Christian witnessing is associated with the invitation of Emperor Mohammad Jalalhudin, the Akbar, who sought the missionaries' presence and built the St. Mary's Church of Agra for their use.[7] From the last part of the eighteenth century the mission of North West India was called the Prefecture of Golconda. Today it is known as the ecclesiastical Region of Agra. It has grown in strength and vitality during the last three hundred years with the help of many religious congregations and development of several dioceses.[8]

The impetus for the establishment of local Churches came from the teaching of the Holy Fathers from the beginning of the twentieth century. With Leo XIII's clarion call "thy salvation is in the hands of thy sons" a new missionary zeal was awakened. Encyclical of

Benedict XV *Maximum Illud* 1919 rejected the Europeanization of mission. *Rerum Ecclesiae* (1926) of Pius XI, *Evangelii Praecones* 1951 of Pius XII, *Ad Gentes* of Vat II and *Evangelii Nuntiandi* of Paul VI were mile stones. The *Redemptoris Missio* (1990) and the call for New Evangelization by John Paul II changed the attitude towards evangelization. While those who ventured as missionaries in North India in the past worked as Educators and Medical personnel. New missionary efforts have changed much during the last few decades, especially in Varanasi and nearby regions.

The members of the Indian Missionary Society (IMS) are working in and around Varanasi for many decades in a pioneering way through various ministries since 1941. The call of Pope John Paul II for a new response to the emerging situation with a new approach and methodology impelled the missionaries with new zeal for enculturation and to address massive poverty and religious aspiration of the oppressed masses. The response to this inspiration got translated into action and a powerful movement emerged in North India showing great signs of hope to the Church in India especially in Varanasi and with phenomenally large number of Khristbhaktas around Matridham Ashram and at the Christian Ashrams in many parts of Northern India.

The Sprouting of Khristbhakta Movement

The Jan Sewa Ashram, Benipur Mission began to organise prayers (*Satsang*) by Fr. Jerome IMS for the needy and seekers of Christ since Good Friday 1994. In the same year Christmas Vigil was celebrated with large number of seeks. In the following year Satsangs were organised on Lenten Fridays and Easter Vigil was held at Benipur Mission in 1995. As it was becoming a regular feature, at the advice of the Bishop and Superiors the prayer was held on Sunday afternoons at Matridham Ashram since Christmas 1995. The Ashram was a centre of Indian Christian spirituality, open to people of other faiths, and so attracted many who were interested in spiritual renewal.

Later, Swami Anil Dev began to organise outreach programmes in the villages from December 1995. The Jan Sewa Ashram continued with its social ministries and organised lay volunteers for the help the seekers. They also screened the film *Dayasagar* (Life of Christ) in many villages. Many people from the villages began to attend the *Satsang* (in the name of *Changai prarthna*) on Second Saturdays. Since late nineties many seekers began to visit Matridham Ashram. These devotees of Christ Jesus came to be known as Khristbhaktas.

Who are Khristbhaktas?

Khristbhaktas are seekers and followers of Christ, who accept *Yesubhagavan*[9] as their *Satguru* and often draw spiritual nourishment from Christian centres. Most of Khristbhaktas are characterised by their liminal[10] position between Hinduism and Christianity. There are thousands of such devout Khristbhaktas from various walks of life, following a distinct *Way of Life*. During the last few decades the number of Khristbhaktas has increased considerably and it is known as Khristbhaktas Movement.

The social composition of the Khristbhaktas Movement is an expression of the Indian social reality in transition. The Khristbhakta Movement has originated as a religio-cultural response of the poor and weaker sections of people in search of a new identity. Their struggle against caste and class can be well understood in the background of heterodox movements[11] and antisystemic movements.[12] Those who are at the margins negotiate the porous borders in their search for a new identity and empowerment mostly from their local religions to Christianity. Khristbhaktas negotiate the borders of faith and culture for empowerment against social exclusion and marginalisation from their liminal position of Hinduism and Christianity. This fluidity distinguishes the Khristbhaktas from the Christians.

The Khristbhaktas are at the periphery of established culture and conventional faith. The creativity of the movement is in its religio-cultural negotiation in modern times. Negotiating into permeable areas becomes essential for those who experience social oppression and exclusion, both in the cultural and religious realm. Culturally Khristbhaktas practice the traditions of their ancestors with modifications but negotiate other areas of faith for empowerment.[13] The Khristbhakta Movement is a social phenomenon with these religious and cultural roots and the sensibilities of inculturation and dialogue of life which is transformative. The new vision and vibrancy of the movement is bringing changes in their identity and in their social situation. These transformations happen in the way they appropriate faith and the way interpret the Christian message from the Bible in their day today life's struggles. Their simple faith and devotion to Christ can be known from the following description.

The Growth of the Movement - Bhakti of the Cross

Apart from attending the monthly Satsang on the second Saturdays, thousands of Khristbhaktas fast and pray during the forty days of Lent. On Lenten Fridays a few thousand gather for the Stations of the Cross organised in an enculturated way. The route of the of Stations of the Cross was arranged in such a way that the whole crowd was able to move around the Ashram as a *parikrma*, a pilgrim of walking around the Ashram, by carrying Lord in the heart, following the wooden cross carried a few. It began at noon and ended at 3 p.m. with a blessing. There were no pictures or statues to follow the stations. The priests vested in saffron alb passed on a six foot tall, 6 cm diameter wooden cross from the dais to the people to carry and he himself led the procession in silence. The prayers and singing were led from the dais till the Stations of the Cross were completed. Even as the priest reached back to the dais one third of the crowd did not even reach the half the distance. So long was the procession. But people went to their place only after they completed their turns.

Only those who kept fast and took permission could carry the cross. There were many to volunteer. People bowed and touched the ground wherever they were at the concluding prayers and moved ahead. This devotion and meditation on the passion of Christ was an enriching experience.

One of them shared in these words "I am coming to *Satsang* from 1999. I fast sometimes during the *chalisa* [40 days]. I fast on Fridays. When I go to *satti* [vegetable market] I visit Ashram and spend some time in prayer. I have peace in my life. ... We pray every day at home, more than an hour. There were people who were against us for attending the satsang, now they are in difficulties, they are suffering. But we pray for them also, because the Lord said.... In my village we pray together, I mean there are 12 settlements in my village, we are about 15 people who pray. The Lord blesses us." The ethnographic narrative speaks louder than words. It is more important, for him, to follow the teaching of the Lord. Visiting the Ashram fasting[14] on Fridays and praying for the neighbours are some of his activities. He enjoys peace and health of mind and body.

On the Good Friday the Satsang was made more dynamic. The Stations of the Cross started with the enactment of Judgement Scene around 11 o'clock in the morning. The cross was taken from the enacting Jesus by the crowd and carried by different groups through the same pilgrim route. Only those who keep fast for forty days come forward to carry the cross on that day. At the twelfth station, crucifixion was enacted back on the dais and the seven words of Jesus from the cross were preached at length by different person. The service ended with a long session of intercessory prayers. The songs sung during this service are much traditional in theme set to local music. Some of them are heart-rending and emotive. The, oft repeated song, '*oh, how strange is the way you loved, Lord,*' expressed the meaning of Jesus sacrifice on the Cross.[15] Everyone participated in the veneration of the cross at the end of the session. No one would have missed the religious experience in such devote and meaningful Satsang of that day.

Ritual Enculturation

Practice of rituals among the Khristbhaktas is innovative and engendering a new cultural scenario in the society. These new practices primarily address the issue of ritual lowness and social mobility among the subaltern people.[16] Ritual lowness is a social issue in defining oneself, because it manoeuvres into social psyche. As long as there is ritual exclusion or ritual lowness, the person does not experience self-worth. When some people are not allowed into the temples and when no priest officiates their ritual moments, the present practice of prayer and blessing adds new importance to the subalterns and to their identity re-gained in Christ.[17] The ritual negotiation by Khristbhaktas marks the beginning of a change in the religious sphere. The openness of the atmosphere the Satsang where everyone hear the word of God and every religious leader addresses the common concern of humanity from the same platform during the inter-religious prayer are unique liminal moments at Annual Satsang.

Transformative experiences of the Khristbhaktas are celebrated in known rituals like naming the infant, marriage and the blessing they seek at different stages of life. Enculturation takes place through the celebration of Diwali, Christmas and Easter with new meaning and symbolism. This new meaning of rituals among the Khristbhakta, hitherto, interprets human existence differently. The triangular relationship of God, Christ - the sacrament of God and human celebration of life events- leads to a new anthropological vision of rituals. The theology of rituals is understood only in relation to Jesus' life and death, the mystery of incarnation and resurrection that could be a universal symbol for every age and section of people. The celebrations this mystery among Khristbhaktas is simple and unbiased.

The faith in Christ among Khristbhaktas has brought a change in their meaning and relevance of practice of rituals. They have adapted to the changes from within the culture of their community without discontinuity in ritual practises and customs. This negotiation of rituals and customs can very well be called enculturation.

Bible and Khristbhaktas

Khristbhakta Movement drinks more from the word of God. It is a great openness for the subaltern people to hear the word of God. Some have even learned to use the Bible pretty well. Biblical verses are taught and used in Satsang and in village prayer sessions. They use simple methods for interpretation. The methods used among the Khristbhaktas could be identified with the folklore methods known as Folkloristics for the study and interpretation of Christian scriptures. The genre of storytelling, so common to folklore, has been identified as an influential method in creating greater awareness for social change. The hermeneutics developed from the genre of storytelling and the parables from the Gospel have paved a path for people's hermeneutics within the oral traditions. The tools of Folkloristics are keys to interpret the scripture for the empowerment based on knowledge system known among people. The result is subaltern's discovery of their agency for personal transformation and of social change. The Bible and Christian teachings become the Gospel of the Khristbhaktas in a specific way. An example will make the point crystal clear. The focus of discussion on the parable of Good Samaritan is the one who is lying of the ground half dead. The interpretation echoes the cry 'I am the one' on the ground, exploited, excluded, outcaste, the one in need of help. So, the methods of folklores, such as Formulaic Theory and Performance Theory, are used in the biblical hermeneutics among the Khristbhaktas.

The Khristbhakta Movement makes use of endogenous knowledge pattern and cultural resources for its progress. The movement interprets Christian scriptures and message in the social context and lives of its members. The interpretation happens within oral tradition prevalent among ordinary people. These interpretations are articulated in the stories, song and prayers. These interpretations are part of the theologizing in the context of Khristbhaktas, as people's hermeneutics. Thereby, theologizing happens from below with the encounter of cultures in oral tradition.[18] The Khristbhaktas have greater advantage than traditional Christians in the knowledge of the Bible. The easy availability of Bible to the Khristbhaktas engages them to actively participate in their interpretation and expression of their collective consciousness.[19] These interpretations not only become starting points, but also as rung of the ladder to reach particular religious experience based on Christian Scriptures. **They discover a discipleship within biblical understanding, and not as members of a particular confession.**

Sagas: Theology from Below
The sagas of Khristbhaktas are their interpretation of life in the light of their experience as they have joined the Khristbhakta Movement. The explanation they give for their life depends on their personal search. Those who find meaning in their way of interpreting them on the basis of Christ experience do give a theological expression. These simple narrations are foundations to understand their society, their aspirations and their experience in Christ. The sagas are simply narrative theology. They are experience based God-talk. The oral traditions found in folklore have been used by the Khristbhaktas to enrich their religious experience with the use of Bible. Now these interpretations have entered the world of letters, though it remains still as part of the oral genre and a theology emerges from below.

Insights from the Movement
Culling out certain articulations from the life story of Khristbhaktas I am presenting a few reflections on their faith. There are new insights from the discussion on the religio-cultural experience of the Khristbhaktas. Some of them are important for the understanding of theology from the perspective of plurality of religion in India and how a distinctive thought pattern emerges from a particular context.

Faith Appropriation
Some of Khristbhaktas give expression to their personal experience in Christ. Dullu Patel says, "I came with curiosity to see what is

happening, but came back with peace, so I continue to attend.[20] Urmila Patel was ready to face the opposition to go to the Ashram and she says, "In the early days of the Satsang the villagers were not respecting us, but, now they don't put any pressure on us."[21] The fine statement of Prem is "I have become one with the Lord;[22] and Rajwati articulated it as Yesu is my Satguru;[23] and Meera Devi said that she has a new meaning for her suffering, saying "I have learned to bear sufferings. I conduct prayer in my house once a week".[24] Peace, respect, new identity, spiritual fulfilments are some of the points that keep these people with the movement. There are many such testimonies of their experience in Christ.[25]

Many Khristbhakts are no more the same persons after their experience Christ. Urmila Devi[26] has a new-found identity and her outlook on life has changed. She has a new meaning and purpose in life in Christ.[27] Many others have given up their bad habits and have experienced renewal of life in the family and in their society. All these are attributed to the experience of Christ in their life, not to any human power. These simple statements are declaration of faith in Christ. Many of the promoters of Khristbhakta Movement acknowledge that the faith of these people is not just 'spiritual power-tapping'. They are sincere in their belief. It is clear from the number of years each one tells about their participation in the Satsang and the eagerness they show to attend the Satsang. This process of coming to know the power of Christ and growing in the Christian faith is called Faith Appropriation.

The Khristbhaktas also go through a process of 'misappropriation' of all that has stifled his/her self-worth and identity. The new understanding of self as true human becomes a liberative and emancipatory. The process of knowing, understanding, interpreting, and re-interpreting one's own life happens on the basis of their Christ experience and from their liminality of culture and faith. This faith experience of Khristbhaktas gives them a special identity which they long for. This in fact *institutes them into new persons.*

This experience leads them to emancipation and empowerment through self-understanding and self-transformation is called self-appropriation.[28] The Achariya has acknowledged it like this:

> The bhaktas ascend to higher realms of devotion and they experience not only healing from various physical ailments, no matter how terrible and old they might be, but inner healings, freedom from psychological bondage, especially those that are created due to socio-creedal discriminations and oppressions...Consequently, they are freed from various superstitions.[29] In the context of Khristbhakta Movement, the liminality opens up the possibility of new understanding of oneself from both Hindu and Christian heritage, and from the cultural resources. Khristbhaktas break away from the shackles of subjugated self into a liberated self through the foundational experience in *Yesubhagavan*. Appropriation for Khristbhakta is the whole process of approximation of oneself with empowering faith experience in Christ.[30] This appropriation - Christ experience of Khristbhaktas- leads to much further theological reflection in the direction of Christ as the Sacrament of God.

The Christ experience of the Khristbhakta is genuine and life transforming. The faith appropriation among the Khristbhaktas began from their liminal position of their religious and cultural outlook. The interpretation of the foundational experience in Christ is a religious experience leading to self appropriation. This is a significant contribution to the field of theology. Through a process of appropriation of faith, the Khristbhaktas, become also a challenge to the other religious traditions. It is not the case of a rupture from one religious universe and a move to a new one. It is not only faith of the people even the culture is getting transformed in the light of their experience in Christ. The dehumanising values give way to social values of equality and peace.

The appropriation of self-experienced by the Khristbhaktas shapes their identity and self-worth against centuries of wounded history. The sense of reconciliation experienced and expressed by the Khristbhakta helps him/her in social reconstruction, both at the family and societal level. He/she begins to experience certain amount of freedom from money lenders and debt, superstitions, which in due course adds to new dimensions of social change. The reconciliation and peace ushered within the family and neighbourhood by the Khristbhakta are agents of social harmony. These changes are invitation for theological reflections in the field of applied Christology.

Appropriation of faith and self is an alternative theological vision. This interpretation has deeper theological significance for people who search for meaning and purpose in life amid deprivations. In the context of the struggles of life the Khristbhaktas make faith as integral part of their quest for well-being. Their faith becomes more creative and responding to the issues of life. The process of theologizing carries along with it the moral commitment to an egalitarian society to respect and promote every human person's well-being. This is a theological praxis emerging from the solidarity with poor and marginalised in Asia for social harmony and societal change.

Evangelization Vs Conversion

The research reveals that there are a few who are baptised by the Churches. Some of them have been baptised by pastors some years ago.[31] Some people have received baptism from other centres in the recent years. There are some who wish to take *diksha*. But many of them feel more at home with the Satsang and the Ashram. This particular situation has to be examined critically. What is the role of evangelical movements and independent Churches in baptising the local people? The fact is that among the many thousands of Khristbhaktas a hand full are baptised. Some of the Church personnel are anxious about their baptism.

One of the anxious questions of many Christian missionaries ask "Will the Khristbhaktas be baptised?" Answering a similar question Achariya Anil Dev says, "Can we think of a Church without walls and structures, a Church that is Spirit-generated movement rather than an institutionalized religion? Can this be another possibility, *a new way of being Church,* especially in today's religio-political situation of this part of India? We don [sic] not know. We are open to the Lord's promptings, to the movement of the Spirit. For the present we would say as Paul says, "Christ did not send me to baptize. He sent me to tell the Good News (1 Cor. 1:17)"".³² At another centre R.B. Lal asks this question, "Which comes first: the baptism of the Spirit or water? Very often it is the Spirit's work and when people ask for it, I do give."³³ According to Fr. Subhash, "There are some who get baptised. It may increase in the course of time. But the new way of spreading the gospel is coming from the Charismatic Movement, but I am not sure how long it will last."³⁴

Present Scenario

Khristbhaktas have a noticeable presence in the society during the last decades. They live a distinct life of faith and culture. They practise their ancestral rituals in the name of Christ, praying in the name of Jesus and using the Bible. There are community leaders known as *Aguwa*. These Aguwas become the contact between the Ashram and the village Satsangs. As the number and enthusiasm increased among the Khristbhaktas the Matridham Ashram is organising Sunday Satsang and three day annual convention. Even baptised Christians benefit from these events. The *Annual Samelan* for three day is attended by many Christians from the neighbouring States. Christmas is being celebrated in the Ashram and in the villages. Indian feasts like *Deewali*, for Christ the light, *Gurupurnima* for Christ the Satguru, are also celebrated with lots of enthusiasm. Many more thousands participate in these festivities. Apart from the celebration and Satsangs there is three days *Sadhana* every month, which focuses on the training of the local leaders known as Aguwas.

There is considerable number of male participants in the movement. There are many young people in the movement (13-25 years of age 37.30%) and a large number of Middle age people (26-50 years 50.70%) and many children are growing in and through this movement for many years. Citizens above the age of 50 are just

11% only. The future of the movement is significant from the point of this demographic profile.

A few dioceses in North India have opened new Ashrams to help these new seekers of Christ. Presently there are tens of thousands of Khristbhaktas in many parts of Bihar, Delhi, Haryana, Jharkhand, Madhya Pradesh, Uttar Pradesh, and Uttarakhand. Large presence of such members and their way of practising faith in Christ Jesus makes them a recognisable as a Movement.

Some Reflections

The Universal Church and the Church in India look at the Movement as great hope in the field of dialogical mission at a time when the Church is repeatedly asked to be silent about Jesus Christ and his Good News. Theologians call the movement as new way of being Church and the Missiologist consider it as a breakthrough in the mission approach of the Catholic Church in North India. It is akin to new Pentecost.

Today, Khristbhakta Movement is no more an unknown phenomenon in the Church. There are scholars and researchers who discuss and reflect about it. Hence it is matter to be studied and reflected upon from different perspectives in order to enrich the Movement as well as the Church through the Movement.

Every time and everywhere, faith got implanted into culture and became anew again and again in history. Indian religions have seen various forms of cultural adaptation for centuries too. India has accepted Christianity from the time of St. Thomas the Apostle and different rites and confessions too have played their role. Each has made this land as its home with assimilation and incorporation of cultural practices to give expression to life-cycle rituals, feast and festival etc. Khristbhakta Movement is also a native response to Christian Messages. The type of enculturation that happens among Khristbhaktas is from their own initiative and from their cultural practices. How could the Churches and Christians understand the process of enculturation from faith perspective?

Is the faith of the Khristbhakta different and could it lead them to liberation and salvation gained by Jesus Christ through his paschal mystery. What is their relationship to Christ Jesus, the universal saviour? Can faith-appropriation lead to self-appropriation without external articulation in signs and symbols? What can the Church do and how could she assist the Khristbhaktas in their search for universal destiny of humanity?

Some Trajectories

A response to this situation could be drawn from the Acts of the Apostles chapter 15 and the teachings of Vat II. For instance, when the early Church was confronted with new situation, like the expansion among the Greeks, Asia Minor and North Africa, new structure like Apostles, presbyter, deacons and preachers were created and various Councils addressed the issues and gave guide lines. Some of the ancestral practises were changed and the role of Holy Spirit and the new sacraments were introduced. Later through many centuries the Councils have revised and guided in new direction according to the time and cultural changes that happened in this world.

The Vatican II is a moment of grace for our age, the third millennial Church. With lived experience and with the gift of the Holy Spirit the Fathers of the Council have discerned the movement of the Spirit and have drafted the 16 document. The document on dialogue with other religions and cultures is a break through like the Council of Jerusalem. There is still a need to understand the spirit of mission in *Evangalii Nuntiandi* such as evangelical liberation centred on the kingdom values. "It cannot be contained in the simple and restricted dimension of economics, political, social or cultural life; it must envisage the whole *human person*, in all aspects, right up to and including *its* openness to the absolute, even the divine

Absolute..."[35] It also should be followed with the spirit of unity of religions as spoken by Pope Francis in *Evangelii Gaudium* on the topic confession of faith and commitment to society. ""God, in Christ, redeems not only the individual persons, but also the social relations existing between *peoples*". To believe that the Holy Spirit is at work in everyone means realizing that he seeks to penetrate every human situation and all social bonds: "The Holy Spirit can be said to possess an infinite creativity, proper to the divine mind, which knows how to loosen knots of human affairs, even the more complex and inscrutable." Evangelization is meant to cooperate with this liberating work of the Spirit.""[36]... "The great majority of the poor have a special openness to the faith; they need God and we must not fail to offer them his friendship, his blessing, his word, the celebration of the sacraments and a journey of growth and maturity in faith. Our preferential option for the poor must mainly translate into a privileged and preferential religious care." [37]

In the emerging situation of large number of Khristbhaktas, the example of the growth of the good olive tree onto which the new branches are grafted (cf. Rom 11:17-24; Eph 2:14-16; NA 4) is an important metaphor to be grasped by Universal Church. The number further carries in these words 'Jerusalem did not recognize God's movement when it came (Lk 19:42),... some even opposed (Rom 11:28)' but 'when all people will call on God with one voice and serve him shoulder to shoulder (Is 66:23)' a challenge to reckon to. It is time for Christ's faithful to understand this Dialogical Mission, to recognise it and nurture the new olive 'knowing Christ as God's universal love and the source of all Grace.'[38] The spirituality of dialogue that emerges from the Khristbhakta Movement from the osmosis of faith and culture could be called as religious cosmopolitanism, for each respects not only the similarities, but the differences as well and play their role more responsibly toward whole humanity.

Finally, to be sons and daughters of our Father in heaven, he urges whole humanity to live in peace with one another (Rom 12:18) and that is the way to be true children. Let us make every effort to come to know our other brothers and sisters-mothers, the sheep of the other folds of Christ (Jn 10:16a). To love and to share the grace and peace with the sheep of other folds is also the mission of Christ, as the will of the Father of us all.

Endnotes

[1] A.E. Medlycott, *India and the Apostle Thomas*, Chennai: Santhome, 2011. *ACTA THOMAE*, Edessan Tradition, Ecclesial History, Vol III,1.

[2] [Gundaphara-bharata-putrasa] maharajasa tratarsa Avadagasasa. Cf. A.E. Medlycott, *India and the Apostle Thomas*,18.

[3] A.E. Medlycott, *India and the Apostle Thomas*. As history attests, from the time King Gonda Porus and his brother were blessed by St Thomas, the Apostle himself. *Agra Mission, Church History of India*, Vol. II, 419-465.

[4] The story of the healing of the brother of the King goes along with it.

[5] The Seven Churches in Kerala and three churches, the Santhom Cathedral, Little Mount, and St. Thomas Mount, (*Parngi Malai*) in Chennai preserve such a tradition.

[6] Cf. M.K. Kuriakose, *Christianity in India: Source Material*, ISPCK, Delhi, 1982, p. 6; C.B. Firth, *An Introduction to Indian Church History*, Madras 1992, 11.

[7] Fondly known as Akbar's Church.

[8] There are twelve Dioceses spread out in three States of Uttar Pradesh, Rajasthan, Uttarakhand, (URU Region). The upcoming the National Catechetical Directory, Fostering *the Faith of a Pilgrim People* has to reflect on and study these aspects to work out recommendations for its effective implementation. (Chennai, 22nd to 24th September 2015).

[9] Jesus is addressed as *Yesubhagavan* by ordinary people. The expression refers to *Christ of Faith* in theological terms.

[10] Cf. Victor W. Turner, Dramas, *Fields and Metaphors: Symbolic Action in Human Society*, Cornell University Press, London 1974, p. 237. Victor W. Turner, *Ritual Process: Structure and Anti-Structure*, Routledge & Kegan Paul, London 1969, p. 107. Liminality could be a set of transitional qualities of "betwixt and between" defined as states of culture, and society. In his exposition of the theme Victor W. Turner has tried to show that this liminal position in the society as living in the fringes or margins as community as in permanent liminality to be a kind of prophetism. Liminality represents the

midpoint of transitions in a status-sequence between two positions. Presently Khristbhatas are also liminal people.

[11] Religious and cultural movements against the orthodoxy of hegemonic traditions.

[12] Antisystemic movement are discussed in the light of capitalism and the resistance based on class conflicts. Cf. Giovanni Arrighi, Terence K. Hopkins & Immanuel Wallerstein, Antisystemic *Movements*, Verso, London; 1989.

[13] Cf. David Kettle, "Believing without Belonging: Cultural Change Seen in Theological Context", *International Review of Mission* 94 (345) (October 2005) 507-523; Grace Davie, *Believing Without Belonging*, Black Well, 1994. 'Believing without Belonging' is discussed in the Western context as a moral choice in a given situation of the society. This choice is also seen as a strategy with an ethic of obligation to be practical and prudent.

[14] On fasting days they do not eat anything from morning till evening. In general people have only two meals a day, one in the late morning and in the evening some time after the sunset. On the fast days they do not take the morning meal. It is said, they do not eat anything cooked on that day. They can drink water and eat fruit. There are some who keep absolute fast, even not drinking water (*nirjal upavas*).

[15] The song '*he aisan ajeeb kaile pyar haire masih*- oh, how strange you loved, hai re [expression of deep emotion] Messiah. These are sung in Bhojpuri, the native tongue. Cf. *Mukti Bhajan Mala*.

[16] Cf. A. K. Lal and S.N. Tiwary, *The Harijan Elite: A Study of their Status, Networks, Mobility and Roles in Social Transformation*, Thomason Press, Faridabad, 1976.

[17] Cleaning of the place of worship after the visit of certain members of the society or conducting enquiries after suspected pollution of the sacred premises are still in practice in India. e.g. Jagannath Temple, Iyyappan temple.

[18] Jerome Sylvester, "Hermeneutics of Khristbhakta Movement," (Unpublished Doctoral Dissertation.) University of Madras, 2009.

[19] Cf. Maria Arul Raja, "Hermeneutical Engagement of Dalit Location with Biblical World," *Vaihari* Vol.8, No. 4 (Dec, 2003) 22.

[20] Dullu Patel G52MBCr.

[21] Urmila Patel G56FUDp.

[22] Prema- G89FUDp.

[23] Rajpathi Devi- A305FSCp.

[24] Meera Devi- G53FBCm.

^{25} Rama Devi G146FSCp- I was sick and healed. I pray, both morning and evening. It is five years now; Sita Kumari G135FMBCp I have prayed and the Lord gave me the gift of praying for others. I am attending the Satsang for nine years; Prabhavatti G139FMBCm - I feel in my heart that I should be here longer and pray more. So, I wait every month for this day to come to the Satsang. I do prepare to for this day a lot; Rina Patel- G248FMBCp - I was going to Satsang with friends without the knowledge of my Father. He was not a believer. He used to beat me. But, I did not stop. I was still coming for the Satsang. He knew about it. Once, he fell sick and I prayed for him and applied oil and he got well. Now he also joins the Satsang.

^{26} Urmila, "mai ne thume vipathi ki bhatti me parishkrith kiya hai", *Vachan Sudha*.10 / 3 (May-June 2004). Urmila, the fifth daughter of a downtrodden family accepted marriage to a poor lame man in order to escape the hard realities of her family. Her marriage to him was only to save his social-face. Urmila never had any joy in this marriage; rather she experienced more isolation and poverty. Frustration and suffering were not alien to her. It drove her to attempt suicide. She tried it in vain over and over. She tried to immolate herself, drank phenol; even tried to jump into a river. But, even as she suffered, she claims that she heard an inner voice which prevented, and encouraged her to go back home each time. One day, she left the house at mid-night, and sat at the foot of a tree that was believed to be haunted by evil spirits. She imagined that the evil ones would consume her and thereby end her sufferings. She narrates a different experience. 'An old man in white cloth advised me to go home and led me home, but he disappeared as we reached near my house. After a few days, a lady took me to Matridham Ashram for prayer. I prayed to Jesus at *Dharsan Bhavan*. I visited the place a few more times and spent time in prayer and listening to the Word of God in the Satsang. I began to understand the meaning of my suffering and how God was leading me. There was a total change in my life. I did not know that through these sufferings the Lord had been preparing my way to *Mukthi*.

^{27} Since the year 2004, Urmila is a new person with a new found identity, and meaning in her life. When the researcher interviewed her she said that she helped others, and guided them to the *Satsang* at the Ashram. The researcher had been keeping track of this respondent for the last few years in this field of study. She conducts weekly prayer at her home on Fridays these days. The researcher heard her addressing a group of Khristbhaktas at the, Adalpura village, on 15 July 2007. She spoke how she underwent a real and lasting transformation through the Khristbhakta Movement. She was quite articulate and spoke of an inner experience that always motivated her.

[28] P. Ricoeur, *Hermeneutics*, 144ff.

[29] Anil Dev, "*Khristbhakta Movement*". A paper presented in the FABC-OE Meeting, Thailand, July 8-12, 2008.

[30] P. Ricoeur, *Hermeneutics*, 36-37, 158ff.

[31] G13MSCp Kishori Lal 65 He and his family were baptized by some pastor a few years before in the river Ganges.

[32] Anil Dev, "Khrist Bhakta Movement: Its Origin and Dynamics," *Jeevadhara* 38/227 (2008) 440.

[33] P337MUDr R.B. Lal 58, interviewed on 16/04/2006.

[34] P339MUDr Fr. Subhash 56, interviewed on 14/08/06.

[35] EN §33.

[36] EG §178ff.

[37] EG §200.

[38] NA §4.

Principle and Foundation in the Ecological Context of South Asia

Amala Arockiaraj S.J.

While sitting on the bank of river Cardoner, Ignatius was given deep insight into how all creatures came from God in Christ and returned to God in Christ. The impact was so great that he said, "If there were no Scriptures to teach us these matters of faith, he would be resolved to die for them solely because of what he has seen" (AB, No.29.9). He wanted to communicate his God experiences with those who were disposed to it. "The true shape of the rose is already in its bud; the mature shape of any embryo is already in the DNA of its first multiplying cells. Analogously, my authentic self…is already in my concrete, existential self with all my determinants."[1] The Principle and Foundation invites us to one of the foundational experiences of Ignatius, to discover God's project for us and cooperate with God in that project. God works with us to turn our chaos to make us one with cosmos. Today's ecological crisis is also an invitation from God to check our value system and set proper order. Let us briefly discuss on today's ecological crisis, reasons for it and look at it from the perspective of the Principle and Foundation.

Ecological Crisis today

Ecology deals with the intricate relationships between the living organisms and their living and non-living surroundings. In 1935, A.G. Tansley coined the term 'eco-system' and defined it as 'the system resulting from the integration of all the living and non-living factors of the environment'. The eco system is the basic functional unit in ecology. The components of ecosystem are: Biotic [Producers, Consumers (Herbivores and carnivores) and decomposers.] and Abiotic: Organic and Inorganic substances and climatic conditions. As producers are dependent on soil- nutrients and geo-chemical cycles, the consumers are related to producers and among themselves in the form of food-chains and food webs. There are complex interactions in 'eco-systems' and in spite of advanced science and technology, the intricate relationship between species and abiotic components is not well understood. Naturally, there exists equilibrium between the eco-systems and geo-chemical cycles (Hydro cycle, Nitrogen cycle, Carbon cycle, Phosphate cycle...etc) called 'ecological balance'. When this balance in nature is disturbed, we get into crisis called 'ecological crisis'[2].

In the ecological pyramid, human beings are 'consumers' and they depend on plants and animals. Other than 'natural calamities' (reasons are not yet understood well), only human beings are responsible for the ecological crisis as they are endowed with 'freedom' and 'reasoning power'. While the planet earth remains finite for centuries, the human population has increased exponentially causing the imbalance in production and consumption rates. In addition to this, in the name of 'development', human beings have exploited the nature without looking into future consequences. Some of the ecological crises which have attracted the world-wide attention are:

1. Air Pollution (Climatic Changes – Global warming, Acid rain, Ozone-layer depletion, Photo-chemical smog...etc)

2. Water Pollution (Toxic chemicals, management of waste water, thermal pollution, Eutrophication, water borne diseases...etc)

3. Land Pollution (Problems of solid wastes, Desertification, soil erosion, Fertilizer and Pesticide pollution...etc)

4. Deforestation (Loss of forest cover, extinction of species and loss of bio-diversity, destruction of wildlife habitats…etc)

5. Depletion of non-renewable fuels and minerals.

6. Sharing of Natural Resources (Water disputes, Construction of Dams, Minerals… etc)

This ecological crisis can be compared to a man sitting on a branch of a tree and cutting its trunk. Human being 'digging its own grave' is the apt term to describe ecological crisis caused by humans. The modern man is turning against himself. The threat to ecology from industry witnesses the fall of human person and the world.[3]

Reasons for Ecological Crisis

Environmental problems started haunting us from the time of Industrial Revolution of the 18th century. Rapid industrialization was accompanied by unlimited exploitation of natural resources. Man got at his disposal all sorts of machinery tools to help him in works like mining, deforestation etc. During the time of industrialization, the idea of development was understood in a narrow sense, that is, only in terms of material progress. It failed to notice other aspects of human life and environment. Man started using technology to assist him in his craze for wealth, power and pleasure. In the rapid economic growth and development, people and nature were looked upon as 'objects' to be exploited. Most developmental program have ignored to assess the possible impacts on natural resources, giving priority only to economic aspect. Ecological problems in India can be classified into two broad categories: a) those arising from poverty and under development and b) those arising as negative effects of the very process of development[4].

The root cause of all environmental crises is the present value system that considers earth and all its products as things to be plundered and exploited. In a world of globalization and market economy, monetary benefits occupy the top place in the hierarchy of values whereas truth, honesty and love are kept below. The ecological crisis is a moral issue.[5] There is an erosion of traditional values and dominance of consumeristic culture. Various legislations, conferences and environment developmental program could not bring out the desired change. In this context, there is a need for reordering of values both at the individual and global level.

Principle and Foundation and Ecology

St. Ignatius says that the purpose of the Spiritual Exercises is to overcome oneself and to order one's life, without reaching a decision through some disordered affection.[6] His aim is to help the individuals to free him/herself from undue attachments and make proper decisions in life so that the individual chooses what is conducive to his/her real happiness and growth. It is clearly stated in the Principle and Foundation: "We ought to desire and choose only that which is more conducive to the end for which we are created". He is calling for 'ordering' one's value system, thereby one's life. While talking about the effectiveness of Ignatius' Principle and Foundation, Fr. Kolvenbach says,

> He [Ignatius] avoids exclusive attention to any one line of thought: an anthropocentrism independent of God and the environment, a theocentrism that pretends to ignore creatures and all created things, a biocentrism that would ignore the Creator and the call to collaborate with him in relationship with the environment. Ignatius understands clearly that if God and the human person are not in a proper relationship this will have serious consequences in the biosphere. He invites the retreatant to '...an exclamation of wonder and surging emotion, uttered as I reflect on all creatures - the heavens, the sun, the moon, the stars, and the elements, the fruits, the birds, fishes and animals - on how they have allowed me to live and have preserved me in life.[7]

The concept of 'sustainable development'[8] can be traced to the phrase 'we ought to use these things to the extent they help us...' As we know, that the principle is 'that which is first' and 'foundation' is the basis; this Principle and Foundation culminates in contemplation to attain love, where the retreatant is invited to find 'indwelling and labouring God.'

> I will consider how God dwells in creatures; in the elements, giving them existence; in the plants, giving them life, in the animals, giving them sensation; in human beings, giving them intelligence; and finally, how in this he dwells also in myself, giving me existence, life, sensations and intelligence...[9]

> I will consider how God labours and works for me in all the creatures on the face of the earth; that is, he acts in the manner of one who is labouring. For example, he is working in the heavens, elements, plants, fruits, cattle, and all the rest – giving them their existence, conserving them, concurring with their vegetative and sensitive activities and so forth.[10]

What we have become aware of 'the inter-relatedness or inter-dependence' by ecological crisis today was already realized by our mystic Ignatius.

At the time of Ignatius, environment was not threatened as it is today, and Ignatius and his contemporaries did not have to address environmental issues. However, his Spiritual Exercises has got excellent insights to help us address the ecological crises that we are facing today. It invites us to renew our relationshipwith nature by imbibing the spirit of a reverential and loving attachment. "In the time of Ignatius humanity was not in possession of powerful means, which today threaten the environment. Yet, Ignatius understands clearly that if God and human persons are not in proper relationship this will have serious consequences in the biosphere."[11] And in Ignatius' world-view nature and all its elements have got a very special place. For Ignatius, world is charged with the Grandeur of God. "Clearly Ignatius takes the world with utmost seriousness. It is the indispensable medium, the locus in and through which God comes to us and we in turn move to God"[12]. "If creation can lead us to God, it is because it is, in its own way, the language and revelation of God. It bears the mark of God". Ignatius writes, "'The same divine Sprit is present in all' and 'All the good which is sought in creatures is present with greater perfection in Him who created them"'[13]. So, the spirituality and world-view of the Principle and Foundation rightly invites every human person to find reflections of God in nature and to show reverence and respect.

As long as humans cannot control their inordinate desires, there is no solution for ecological crisis. The spirit of indifference of the Principle and Foundation can free us from greed and help us to make use of nature and natural resources with equanimity and love. Also, when in modern times human persons and communities are driven by the wrong concept of development, every person with the spirit of Ignatian world view has to enlighten the world, through whatever means possible, about a new mode of development respecting nature and people.

Ignatius was gifted with various visions, apparitions and gift of tears. At the end of his life, he understood that the attitude of 'submission and reverence' is more important than the other graces. He clearly perceived that such an attitude of reverence was God's gift.[14] When we have an attitude of 'reverence' towards all creatures, we will not treat them as 'objects' or be slaves of 'use and throw culture'.

South Asian religious traditions towards harmony[15]

Not only Ignatius, but also most of Indian religious traditions are calling us to work towards harmony. Let us briefly look into the scripture and traditions of major religions with respect to ecology. Vedic worshippers recognized the universal, moral and cosmological order and called it 'Rta'. Varuna the god was considered the promoter of Rta[16]. All the five primal elements were perceived as deities who nourish life and they nourish in return. The same respect for nature was ascertained in Bhagavat Gita, as it says, "entertain the gods and let the gods entertain you... He who enjoys what is given by them without offering it to them, is indeed a thief" (B.G: III: 11 & 12). The entire universe is seen as God's dwelling place where all beings are interrelated with each other. Gita invites us to see the divine Lord in all beings and beings in the Lord. (B.G: VI:30) A wise man is called to perform action unattached, desiring the welfare of the world. (B.G: III:25). All of us are called to participate in the divine work of keeping all beings in life and harmony. Some animals were treated as close associates of deities: snake on Siva's neck, white bull as Siva's Vahana, Garuda as Vahana for Vishnu, Peacock as vahana for Murugan, Rat as Ganapathi's vahana, Krishna as Goapala...etc.

The root of Islam is 'slam' meaning 'being in peace' and 'being a member of wholeness'. According to Quran, God is seen as the creator of all things (Qr 6:102), human beings are created from soil and soil has the characteristics of sky, air, fire and water. Hence, human beings are related to all other beings. (Qr 23:12) In Islam, creation of the universe is considered as an open book which points to the Creator. The Islamic faith stresses on improving the condition of the Earth at the hands of humans and humans are the vice regents of God on Earth.[17] Quran invites every Muslim to respect and follow the laws of nature (Qr 7:55-57).

To find answer to the miseries of the world, Siddartha left his house and family at the age of 29 and attained enlightenment under the pipal tree. He became the Buddha. He envisaged that the entire universe is a system of law composed of striving creatures continually passing from one form of existence and taking shape in another. In 'Dhamma', he summed up his entire teachings which is the law of nature. The eight-fold path of Dhamma aims at getting rid of Ignorance of the law of nature. The eight-fold path is divided into three parts: Sila (abstention from unwholesome actions), Samadhi (Practice of concentration) and Panna (wisdom). The real purpose of Sila and Samadhi is to lead to wisdom which frees us from all ignorance and attachments.[18] Buddha's main teaching was a call to universal harmony. Harming other beings, starting from humans to tiniest creature, must be avoided at all cost.

According to Jainism, the universe consists of an infinite number of souls (jivas) enmeshed with matter: Not only are gods, human beings, animals and insects believe to be inhabited by jivas, but also plants of all species, earth and stones, and everything derived from the earth, rivers, ponds, seas and rain drops, flames and all fires and gases and winds of every kind. Thus, the whole universe is full of life.[19]

The popular harvest festival Pongal (in Tamilnadu) Sankranthi (in Andhra Pradesh) Onam (in Kerala) brings out the 'gratitude' of human beings to sun, earth, animals and other beings which were instrumental to get the produce. It brings out the intimate relationship of human beings with other creatures and a clear manifestation of our 'inter-relatedness'.

Among the tribals, "Navakhani" (the harvest festival) is an expression of gratitude to God and ancestors. The "Karam tree" is associated with the redemptive act of God and "Sal tree grove" serves as worship symbol. In August, when the whole surroundings are green, Hariari festival is celebrated invoking God's blessings to protect their crops.[20] Some tribals celebrate 'Sohrai', the cattle feast, to acknowledge the benefits received from the cattle.

In India, most of the mountains and rivers are named after 'deities' and considered as 'sacred'. Rivers are considered 'holy' and taking a dip in them cleanses the devotee from his sins. No worship is possible without the natural elements such as fire and water. Leaf, flowers and fruits are part and parcel of Indian worship.

Christianity, particularly the Church, had a dualistic view till the Vatican II. Withdrawal from the evil world in order to cultivate virtue in the soil of religion was encouraged from the beginning of Christianity[21]. However, Vatican II had changed this view. It views work as sharing in creation and redemption in Christ. "Human being, created in the image of God, shares by one's work in the activity of the Creator..." The work of the human person is treated as 'the gospel of work'[22]. The phrase, 'subdue it, and have dominion' (Gen 1:28) is not interpreted as to "exploit and destroy" but to show 'reverence and love' as Evangelium Vitae presents it: "To defend and promote life, to show reverence and love for it, is a task which God entrusts to every man, calling him as his living image to share in his own lordship over the world"[23]. The real state and fact of human being is well described in the book of Job: "Naked came I from my mother's womb, and naked shall I return; the Lord gave, and the Lord has taken away; blessed be the name of the Lord"[24] While offering the first fruits, Deuteronomist, invites the offeror to recall all the deeds of God and be grateful to all the blessings[25]. While calling for the preservation of Environment, Pope John Paul II said that humankind was commissioned by God to act as a steward of the earth's resources and guardian of God's creative work.[26]

Steps towards harmony....

- Article 51(g) of the Indian Constitutions states "It shall be the duty of every citizen to protect and improve the natural environment, including forests, lakes, rivers, and wild life and to have the compassion for living creatures". The National Education Policy, 1986 stresses on the role of education "about" and "for" the environment.

- EIA (Environmental Impact Assessment) is imposed to ensure a sustainable environment.

- In response to the signs of time, Jesuits in GC 34 recommended to Father General to make a study how Jesuit apostolate can respond to ecological issues. Retreats based on Ecology, Seminars and workshops, Programmes such as Tarumitra, Tree plantation, Water shed, Conservation of energy...etc. are undertaken in various provinces.

- Other religious congregations, NGOs, environmentalists and other voluntary organizations continue to promote awareness and work towards sustainable environment.

Conclusion

Ignatius proposes the 'Principle and Foundation' as the starting point to reach the goal of "Finding God in all things" (Contemplation to attain Love). The Principle and Foundation leads us to seek the Divine in all beings. Further, he also valued the attitude of 'loving reverence' above all the graces. In a world of crisis, we are called to set order for oneself and help others to have an attitude of 'reverence' to put an end to our 'ecological crisis'. The Principle and Foundation is in tune with our South Asian religious and cultural traditions. It goes beyond the 'Ahimsa' (Non-violence) principle of Mahatma Gandhi. The tribals have their life inter-woven with nature. Let us join hands to re-discover our roots and live in harmony with nature!

Endnotes

[1] Tetlow, Joseph A., "Ignatius Loyola: spiritual exercises" New York, 1999, 53.

[2] Cf. The text books, A.K., "Environmental Chemistry", Third Edition, Wiley Eastern Ltd, 1994 and Sharma, J.P., "Comprehensive Environmental Studies", Laxmi Publications, New Delhi, 2004.

[3] Redemptor Hominis, 1979.

[4] Rosencranz A,Divan S, and Noble Martha, "Environmental Law and Policy in India", Tripathi Pvt Ltd, 1991, 9.

[5] Pope's Peace Message, January 1, 1990.

[6] Annotation No.21.

[7] Our Responsibility for God's Creation" *The Very Rev. Peter-Hans Kolvenbach S.J.* Address at Opening

of Arrupe College, Jesuit School of Philosophy and Humanities, Harare / Zimbabwe, August 22, 1998.

[8] World Commission of environment and Development has adopted the following principle for sustainable development, "that current generations should meet their needs without compromising the ability of future generations to meet their own needs".

[9] Spiritual Exercises, 235.

[10] Ibid, 236.

[11] Leo D'Souza, S.J., "Environmental considerations in the Spiritual Exercises", Ignis 2005:2, 29.

[12] Schineller Peter, "St Ignatius and Creation Centred Spirituality", *The Way*, Vol.29, January 1989, 47.

[13] Cusson G, S.J., "Biblical Theology and the Spiritual Exercises", 59.

[14] Munitiz Joseph A. S.J.(Ed), "The Spiritual Diary of Saint Ignatius Loyola", Inigo Enterprises, London, 1987. Nos: 156(2), 157(2), 159(2).

[15] Here it is understood as "consistent actions" w.r.to maintaining natural rhythm or ecological balance.

[16] De Smet R and Neuner J (Ed), "Religious Hinduism" St. Paul's, 1997,33.

[17] http://www.speednet.com.au/~keysar/ecology.htm

[18] Jerome John, "Discernment in Buddhism", Ignis, 1999:1,24-31.

[19] Basham, A.L., "Jainism" in R.C. Zaehner (ed): *The Concise Encyclopedia of Living Faiths*, 1971, 257.

[20] Lakra, John. S.J., "Tribal Spirituality: A way of Life", Catholic Press, Ranchi, 2006,59-60.

[21] Patmury, J., "Mission and Ecology: Rejection or Redemption of the World?" in "Dimensions of Mission in India" Mattam, J and Kim S, (ed), St. Paul Press, 1995,125.

[22] Encyclical Laborem Excerns (1981), Nos:6 &12.

[23] Evangelium Vitae, Section 42 (1995)

[24] Job 1:21, RSV, TPI, 1980.

[25] Deut 26:5-10

[26] Pope's regular audience, Vatican (CWNews.com).

Igniting the Young Minds

Bala Bollineni, S.J.

Accompanying young people as they build their lives today for a bright tomorrow is not an easy job. Nelson Mandela once said, *'The youth of a country are a valued possession of a nation. Without them, there can be no reconstruction and no development programme. Without them, there can be no future.'* True to these words, there is one person who has been untiringly accompanying thousands of young people for the last 45 years in preparing the leaders for a better tomorrow. He is none other than Fr. Jojayya Pudota, S.J..

I have been blessed with the good fortune of journeying with this 87 years old saintly Jesuit Priest for the past four years. He is an erudite biblical scholar, down to earth theologian, an illuminated writer, inspiring teacher, thought provoking preacher and committed youth minister. A man with such impeccable character and credits could boast of himself to the skies, but he remains unpresuming and continues to render yeoman service to the world even in the evening years of his life. I shall proclaim that it is nothing but a pure grace of God to be associated with this noble man.

Here, I wish to reflect and share particularly about Fr. Jojayya's fundamental philosophy towards youth work and his note-worthy contribution for the development of young people, most specially the rural youth. For any person to journey with the young people and accompany them all through life is neither an easy task nor unchallenging. It certainly has its own demands. To understand the place and importance of youth in a civilized society, to have deep convictions that are born of a context, to make conscientious efforts for the growth of the young – all these play a vital role in preparing transforming leaders.

Fr. Jojayya being a conscientious man has ultra carefully assessed his strengths and dedicated himself in empowering the youth through his teaching and writing. He himself hailing from a rural background is particularly aware of the needs of the victims of exploitation and social inequality that lie beneath the garb of caste and religion in India. One of his main approaches to abate and redress such growth stunting elements is to form the young minds. The means that he employed for formation of the young are: conducting leadership camps, Bible courses, writing youth guidance books and running a youth magazine namely 'Chaitanya Vani'.

It is not an exaggeration to say that this limping and round-shouldered wise man has formed, empowered and transformed thousands of young people, particularly the rural young students. This is being done regularly and dutifully, free of cost, with great devotion and dedication during not one but more than four decades. For the last four years, I have been closely witnessing of the impact that he created in the lives of many. Assuredly, such noble work from this humble man has given the opportunities for many young students to grow into mature and responsible adults.

Through his relentless and sustained efforts the timid became courageous, passive turned into active, dull headed changed to intelligent, the low self-esteemed moved to high self-esteemed, the self-centered progressed to other centered. It is humbling to see this silent positive revolution in local communities. Compassion and competence have always been well balanced with firmness and frankness in the way he approached the young. With his extraordinary skills he inspires and challenges the youth to be real catalysts in nation building. These are not my additions of praise to this man of God but the heartwarming testimonials from the transformed. Being closely associated with him for last four years and meeting the people who are associated with him in training the youth, and most satisfyingly, sharing and listening to him one to one about the youth ministry, I perceived that the following unwritten and unexpressed goals that he set for himself are noteworthy for any formation, accompaniment and empowerment of youth.

Firstly, in order to promote the holistic development of a young person, the youth animators should aim to emphasize the process of *'Becoming'*. The youth needs to be helped to deepen their personal relationship with their personal God; to be close to people, nature and oneself via study, reflection, discussion etc.; to develop a deeper understanding of the self and the complexities of the world. In all of Fr. Jojayya's work with youth, we can vouch for this process as a starting point.

Secondly, in the process of becoming a holistic person, the young should be drawn to a responsible participation in the life and mission of the community in which they live. This is simply *'Belonging'*. Here the youth are engaged into action to belong. They are provided with opportunities to share their ideas, encouraged to involve themselves in community activities where they get a sense of 'we' and 'ours' rather 'I' and 'myself'. In this process their qualities, gifts, talents, energy and power are unearthed, sharpened and channelled for cooperative and collaborative participation. The atmosphere of responsible freedom and friendliness nurture the youth to reveal the people and community they live in, and identify with them. Along with Fr. Jojayya when I attended the leadership camps for rural high school students, it is evident for me that his methodology and approach enabled the students to rise up and shine through.

Thirdly, the process of becoming and belonging to this world should have a natural lead towards 'Transforming and Serving'.

Once the youth realize that they are part of this global family and that they have a responsibility to play in making this world a place of peace, harmony and prosperity. Becoming, belonging, transforming and serving simply means: nurturing one's potential and preparing oneself to work for justice, serve those in need, pursue equality, defend the life, dignity, and rights of all and sundry.

Fr. Jojayya emphatically stresses that we are children of God, born in his image and likeness. We cannot deviate from the very purpose of being transformers and servers. Fr. Jojayya injects this spirit of serving in all of his endeavours towards preparing the young to be men and women for others. He assiduously works to help young people integrate faith and life, develop life-affirming Gospel values, develop skills for serving others and advocating for social change, and become personally involved in action.

Working with and for youth is primarily an exercise of building relationships -- relationships that allow young people to know adults who care about them and who are willing to walk as fellow pilgrims on a life-long journey of integrity. Relationships are difficult to build if one is not present to the people with whom one is building the relationship. Therefore '*be there*'. Being present in the lives of young people is essential to unleash their potential to discover, grow, transform and serve.

"You will be my Witnesses…":

A Challenge and Invitation

P. R. John S.J.

Introduction

To preach the gospel is the mission of the Church (Mt 28:16-20). Paul, the Apostle wrote: "I am not ashamed of the Good News; I do not boast of preaching the gospel, since it is a duty which has been laid on me. It is a responsibility which has been put into my hands" (1 Cor 9:16). And yet honestly, I cannot give you a blue print of, what sort of witnesses (evangelizers) can we be in the present context of the Universal Church and Church in India, in particular. The world is changing and together with these fresh challenges crop us staring at us in our faces, at times making us wonder which way to turn: secularization, non-religious movements, religious fundamentalism, globalization, media and consumerist culture, science and technology. "All the more so because we are not living in a time of changes but are experiencing a true epochal shift, marked by a wide-ranging "anthropological" and "environmental crisis" (*Veritatis Gaudium*, no. 3). Besides, a certain tiredness of witnessing to Jesus Christ and his Kingdom values is wide spread in the Church. Pope Francis calls it "Cooling of Charity". The challenge and invitation seem to be, witnessing is more than to be as administrators in schools and colleges, parishes, social and health center and presiding over the liturgy. It is more of 'working together' and 'communing together'. If anyone wants to be a relevant 'shepherd with the smell of sheep,' (*Evangelii Gaudium*, no. 24) he/she must begin 'to know' the sheep at a 'deeply personal' and 'communitarian level'. I do not think programs, models and concrete workable proposals produce witnesses, but rather is the "living" and "work" places where people impact us.

Vatican Council II, before talking about its hierarchical structure, presents the Church as the *People of God*. It is the people of the new covenant with the law of God written in their hearts. (cf. Jer 31:31-34). Peter calls it "a chosen race, a royal priesthood, a holy nation… who in times past were not a people, but now are the People of God." (1 Pet 2:9-10) The people are priests participating in the priesthood of Christ, offering not only Christ's sacrifice as his body, but themselves. The presbyters only have a ministerial or service role.

In this article, I shall begin with the few concerns in formation of clergy and religious. Second, I shall propose four priorities which might shape our way of being witnesses: 1. Civic and Political Leadership, 2. Marginalized-focus Formative Emphasis, 3. Inter-religious Dialogue, and 4. Peace and Reconciliation Strategy.

Formation: To be witnesses?

In *Veritatis Gaudium,* the Pope Francis writes:

> This vast and pressing task requires, on the cultural level of academic training and scientific study, a broad and generous effort at a radical paradigm shift, or rather – dare I say – at "a bold cultural revolution". In this effort, the worldwide network of ecclesiastical universities and faculties is called to offer the decisive contribution of leaven, salt and light of the Gospel of Jesus Christ and the living Tradition of the Church, which is ever open to new situations and idea. Today it is becoming increasingly evident that "there is need of a true evangelical hermeneutic for better understanding life, the world and humanity, not of a synthesis but of a spiritual atmosphere of research and certainty based on the truths of reason and of faith. Philosophy and theology permit one to acquire the convictions that structure and strengthen the intelligence and illuminate the will… but this is fruitful only if it is done with an open mind and on one's knees. The theologian who

is satisfied with his complete and conclusive thought is mediocre. The good theologian and philosopher has an open, that is, an incomplete, thought, always open to the *maius* of God and of the truth, always in development, according to the law that Saint Vincent of Lerins described in these words: annis consolidetur, dilatetur tempore, sublimetur aetate (Commonitorium primum, 23: PL 50, 668)".[1]

How are we to understand the urgency of Pope Francis' invitation? Let us look at some of the Challenges faced in Formation:

a) *Lack of Inner Freedom:* Formators must understand that there are men and women who are incapable of the kind of inner freedom needed to make the full Exercises (retreats, recollections etc...).

b) *Care-fronting authority:* One place where the authority issue and the relationship with God interact is on the question of whether to pray or not and why. Why do I pray? Should I pray? Who is going to be God? This struggle goes on at many levels. Second place, sexuality is an area where the relationships between self and God, superiors, peers, and others interact and become entangled. Open and honest dialogue with the Lord about every issue, including one's actual sexual and erotic feelings and fantasies, is the royal road to inner freedom and integrity.

c) *We are all cultural addicts:* All of us have subconscious caste and ethnic stereotypes that we imbibe with our mother's milk, as it were, and that condition many of our reactions to other people. Many of these cultural expectations and values are not only contrary to Christian values and hopes but also obstacles to the development desired by our presbyteriums/institutes for its men and women. Our formation will have to be intercultural and countercultural and be experienced as such if our young men and women are to become the kind of clergy/religious our documents describe.

The urgent need is, to think out of box. I am more interested in looking at the generational changes which will offer clues to understand the challenges in formation better. Younger generations are different in three very important ways. *First,* they have a lesser level of identification with their religious traditions/rituals both in sacred and secular realms. Nothing to be alarmed that is how younger people interact with the world. *Second,* they have a thinner religious formation (new converts), and thus lack an inchoate (undeveloped) grasp of doctrines beyond what is being argued at the present moment. *Third*, their religious understanding has been formed in an age dominated by the religious right.[2] It means "no religious preference" (strong sense of motivation/option). If there is no "religious preference" then it affects the formation. Then it poses a huge challenge the way we look at formation.

I consider the goal of formation is to bring about healthy **integration** between its **spirituality** and **apostolate**. Most of us Christians and many others too are quite accustomed to hearing and using phrases like 'the spiritual life', 'spiritual things', 'spiritual direction' and in more recent times 'spirituality'. These phrases have long been important, even central, expressions in our Christian lives and Christian teaching and preaching. Up to comparatively recent years the reference of these phrases tended to be, largely, to the practices of prayer, meditation, devotional reading, self-denial and ascetical practices, Mass and the sacraments and pilgrimages. Many referred to these practices as being the main elements of their 'spiritual' lives. Today, however, many Christian teachers and writers see this way of characterizing the spiritual life as being rather too narrow and, hence, as being split off from the moral, social and political dimensions of the Christian life.[3]

The stage of theological formation is chiefly meant to help the students to acquire, "*a thorough and a contextual grasp of the faith of the Church*", to develop certain facility in the methodology of doing contextual theological reflections, to interiorize the theological insights thus gained in their personal life, and to effectively communicate it in their socio-pastoral ministries in accordance with the mission of the Church, to be at the service of the Church and the wider world. If we are preparing men and women for mission then they need to have a passion for mission. They need to dare to risk their lives for the sake of Christ.[4] Pope John Paul affirmed, "A fire can only be lit by something that is itself on fire...(we) have to be on fire with the love of Christ and burning with zeal to make him known more widely, loved more deeply, and followed more closely" (Ecclesia in Asia, n. 23). Pope Francis said during the October Synod: "How often, instead of making Lord's words our own, have we peddled our own ideas as his word! How often do people feel the weight of our institutions more than the friendly presence of Jesus! In these cases, we act more like an NGO, a state-controlled agency, and not the community of the saved who dwell in the joy of the Lord."[5] To conclude, it is important to remember, the future of mission is not in Christians' hands, though they do have a part to play. Hence, we need to,

1. Emphasize less the quantity of growth and more the quality of witness, to increase not number but Christian commitment and discipleship;

2. Practice mission not as sending missionaries from North to South, West to East, but as mutual witnessing for transformation of the whole person and the whole society, each in it's own location;

3. Be firmly rooted in the Christian tradition and be open to creative change;

4. Encouraging study of different sacred scriptures would be a good training for the priesthood. When priests know about other faith, they might just become less fanatical about their own religion.[6]

5. Promote worship in a way that is both contextual and universal.

6. Build up the church as a community of justice and peace.

7. To be faithful to the loving mercy of God.[7]

Priority One: Civic and Political Leadership

South-Asia is a continent with a rich diversity of cultures and religions. We celebrate, not just tolerate, the interreligious differences in Asia, especially when it concerns life and praxis. It echoes Pope Francis' idea of witnessing our faith in a particular "concrete lived reality". The task of the Church in India takes this dimension seriously and articulates its mission as the building up of the Reign of God and of the Church as its symbol and servant. The dynamic nature of the Kingdom of God has been described well by George Soares-Prabhu:

> The core message of Jesus contains an *indicative* which epitomizes all Christian theology and an *imperative* which sums up all Christian ethics. Its indicative is the proclamation of the kingdom, that is, the revelation of God's unconditional love. It imperative is a call to repentance, that is, the demand that we open our hearts to this love and respond to it by loving God in the neighbour...

> When the revelation of God's love (the Kingdom) meets its appropriate response in man's trusting acceptance of this love (repentance), there begins a mighty movement of personal and societal liberation which sweeps through human history. The movement brings *freedom* inasmuch it liberates each individual from the inadequacies and obsessions that shackle him. It fosters *fellowship*, because it empowers free individuals to exercise their concern for each other in genuine community. And it leads onto *justice*, because it impels every true community to adopt the just societal structures which alone make freedom and fellowship possible...

> The vision of Jesus is theological, not sociological. It spells out the values of the new society (freedom, fellowship, justice), not the concrete social structures through which these values are realized and protected. To elaborate these is our never-to-be-ended task – for no "perfect" society is possible in history. One cannot fully actualise the vision of Jesus: one can merely approach it asymptotically! Ultimately, then, the vision of Jesus indicates not the goal but the way. It does not present us with a static pre-fabricated model to be imitated, but invites us to a continual refashioning of societal structures in an attempt to realize as completely as possible in our times the values of the Kingdom. The vision of Jesus summons us, then, to a ceaseless struggle against the demonic structures of unfreedom (psychological and sociological)

erected by mammon; and to a ceaseless creativity that will produce in
every age new blueprints for a society ever more consonant with the
Gospel vision of man. Lying on the horizons of human history and
yet part of it, offered to us as a gift yet confronting us as a challenge,
Jesus' vision of a new society stands before us as an unfinished task,
summoning us to permanent revolution.[8]

The Reign of God is defined not in terms of just celebration "For the
kingdom of God is not food and drink but righteousness and peace
and joy in the Holy Spirit" (Rom 14:17), which the FABC expresses it
in terms of the three-fold dialogue of the Good News with the many
poor, the rich cultures and the thriving religions of Asia. Ultimately,
what we are seeking is, the transformation of cultures and religions.
Certainly, Catholic Social Thought with an interreligious perspective
fosters such a social transformation. Our core mission is to prepare
future leaders and citizens, men and women for others, for lives of
service.

We, in India, are motivated, despite the number of hurdles
from the present government, to develop our institutions into a
comprehensive "social project" that approaches its teaching, research
and outreach missions, not as narrow educational enterprises but,
as way to live out our vision of moulding men and women 'for' and
'with' others in a rapidly changing India. The prime motive of such
an endeavour is to train young men and women to engage in the
"humanization of the world." In this endeavor, the Shepherds have
to be the signs and agents of intrinsic unity among the followers of
Jesus as People with 'one heart and one mind' to bring to fruition
the dream of Jesus.[9] The Church needs to open up in a big way to
women in leadership in the Church. The Old Testament story of
Miriam (Micah 6:4) as a powerful but nuanced example of a woman
leader. From the mouth of Paul, the Apostle, we hear the stories
of women in leadership: Phoebe (Rom 16:1-2), Prisca and Aquila
(Acts 18:26), Andronicus and Julia (Rom 16:7). This is enough to see
women as apostles and deacons, co-workers, teachers, missionaries,

proclaimers of the Gospel, benefactors and hard workers, exercising authority and deserving recognition.[10]

In India, the Church has many educational institutions. If we have to be at the cutting edges of social transformation, we have to form the laity to be in the realms of civic and political leadership. "Political responsibility belongs to every citizen and, in particular, to those that have received the mandate to protect and to govern" says Pope Francis.[11] Real change normally starts from below (context-sensitive/ contextualizing education). So, we have to be with the subaltern groups, their concerns and struggles. But at the same time the real challenge is to make sure that both rich and poor benefit from our service, after all God's project of love encompasses everyone. This is difficult. The dominant groups will not often be ready to offer us space. We have to be therefore more competent and gifted so that they cannot ignore us. We have to be ready for struggle at this level too, though it may have political overtones. Therefore, the need for networking with the people of goodwill towards this project is more than evident. It won't be an exaggeration to say that the church in India has to be more secular (embracing every religious perspective and not particularly fanatic about any one dispensation) the more we will be accepted, especially in cultural circles.

The Church, has a very powerful mechanism to develop common platform to launch into such an endeavour, namely a well honoured, time tested, spirituality packed Indian Constitution which affirms, that the aim of civil society is to secure liberty, equality, fraternity and justice for all the citizens. These are spelt out in terms of fundamental rights. The fundamental rights include the liberty to practice and propagate any religion of one's choice (Art.25). Besides this general protection of liberty of religious profession and practice, the Constitution also protects the right of minority groups, including religious ones, to protect and promote their identity through appropriate means like schools and other development institutions. In our desire for evangelization, we need to foster and defend human rights as one of the principle concerns of human liberation (Vat II, DH 2).

The church in India can operate at all three levels which correspond to our traditional *social, educational* and *pastoral apostolates.* The present need may be to move away from an exclusive ecclesiastical focus in all these and work for and with other believers and with all people of good will. Authentic transformation will come only through participation in the struggles of the poor, reflection on such experience and personal transformation through conversion and interiorization. For us Christians, Jesus remains an enduring model of leadership. Analyzing his characteristics as leader, these are the qualities that strike the observers.

> Jesus was a man of integrity, who was authentic, generative, compassionate, forgiving and straightforward. As a minister, he listened to people, responded to what he heard, created and communicated a vision, included all in his community, and empowered people and communities to implement that vision.[12]

Applying this model to Christian leadership Sofield and H. Kuhn go on to say:

> The Christian leader is a person of integrity who is generative, compassionate and who communicates hope and joy. The Christian leader listens to people, creates a vision with those people, responds to the needs of the Christian community, especially the alienated and marginalized, works collaboratively with others in responding to those needs, expands the concept of ministry, and supports the gifts and ministries of the laity and those who influence their values.[13]

The best practices and projects to be implemented in the churches in India are:

1. To encourage social analysis in our institutions (some institutions have introduced) so that we do not pass the social doctrine of the Church as only information, rather we create social critics who will be at the service of civic and political leadership.

2. To create a platform for like-minded people who vibrate with our "social project". While respecting our service to the Christian folk, we need to dialogue on common issues that affect the humanity at large and with a special focus on poor and oppressed.

3. To engage in qualitative research, reading, writing, speaking in public forums (media) on our 'social project' and inviting the alumni to be co-creators in or vison and mission.

4. To experiment Philosophy and theology studies in public spaces (Doing Public Theology).

5. To take migration issues in a big way.

6. To promote public governance journalism/law and Humanities as a priority in our schools/colleges.

7. To promote collaboration and networking with like minded Civil Society Organizations and groups.

8. To express 'prophetic anger' and to challenge exclusive religious nationalism which preaches intolerance. To be passive and to keep quiet out of fear or other reasons is to quench the Spirit that continually works to transform the world.[14]

Priority Two: Marginalized-focus Formative Emphasis

Education is the master key to one's overall development. It becomes even more pertinent in the life of the poor and the marginalized as education is the only way to enter into livelihood options and other resources of life. Formal and technical education equips the poor and the marginalized to acquire skills and technical knowhow to enter into job market which is the most important necessity for survival. At the same time, it opens their mind up to the existing social, economic, political and cultural realities which is in most instances anti-poor and anti-marginalized. India offers two important and immediate contexts in which one must see the role of education in the life of the marginalized: It has to counter unbridled corporate economic system which has privatized every form of social function, very particularly education system; It has to deal with rightwing political governance supported by religious fundamentalism like Hindutva (*Political Hinduism/Ram Temple*), both of which are intrinsically anti-poor and anti-marginalized. And there is very close, unholy nexus between these two operations which render the poor and the marginalized further discriminated and excluded.[15]

Worst effects by the draconian realities are Dalits, Adivasis, Minorities, poor OBCs (other economically marginalized communities like fisher people, some artisan communities whose expertise have been replaced by automation and machination like weavers, etc.). They are targeted and subjected to multiple forms of oppression, exploitation and discrimination. Their livelihood options are so limited, circumscribed and even snatched away from them. As a result, the gap between the caste people and casteless (Dalits and Adivasis), majority and minority people, rich and poor, and other ostracized segments have been widening day by day. They must be our target people for all our ministries, especially education ministry. The context beckons us to commit ourselves for their liberation. It is with these unfortunate lot that we are called to "transform the world together".

The CBCI on its part has articulated in clear terms the education policy in February 2006. It mandates:

> To evolve an Education Policy that focuses on providing quality and relevant education to the marginalized, especially the children of our Dalit and Tribal brothers and sisters. It also broadens the narrow focus on personal academic development and emphasizes the holistic and fuller development that meets the challenge of modern culture and society, and its demand for higher levels of competence. This makes it imperative for us to bring about several significant changes in the planning and organization of our institutions, so that our education retains its Catholic identity and promotes genuine personal development and excellence.[16]

Some best practices can be:

1. We have clear admission policy for Dalits, Adivasis, minorities, rural poor and first generation, etc.

2. Some institutions have the practice of following up the rural, first generation, poor Dalit and Adivasi students in the academic performance. Since most of the students from these categories are far below in education compared with other students, it is not enough that we admit them. We need to also follow them up with supplementary tutorial helps until they close the gap with other students.

3. Many institutions set apart sizable amount of money as scholarship for the socially and economically weaker students. Besides the available government scholarship and other endowment scholarships which are properly utilized by deserving students, there are also institutions which set apart management scholarship which has been great help to many poor, Dalit and Adivasi students in the past.[17]

Priority Three: Inter-religious Dialogue

Many religions in the world are no longer regarded as rivals to evangelization but as a field of lively and respectful interest and fostering friendship. Surely, the thought of religious pluralism is a growing and increasingly important feature of many societies. The very plurality invites people to harmony, overcoming the social division. Religious pluralism is not confined to the domain of a few specialists. It is deeply connected to the inseparable values of faith, humanity, justice and love. If the church centers inhabit this world made up of different religious contexts, then it affirms the Kingdom values. Our teachings and sermons should expose the theme of other cultures and religions to foster critical awareness, innovation and inventiveness. The Asian theologians speak of

The fruits of the Spirit perceived in the lives of the other religions' believers: a sense of the sacred, a commitment to the pursuit of fullness, a thirst for self-realization, a taste for prayer and commitment, a desire for renunciation, a struggle for justice, an urge to basic human goodness, an involvement in service, a total surrender to God, and an attachment to the transcendent in their symbols, rituals and life itself, though human weakness and sin are not absent.[18]

Inter-religious encounter can be a prime educational tool, leading to enhanced intercultural competency. We need to contextualize religious experience historically. We cannot understand ourselves, as individuals and members of society, unless we understand the past. Contextualizing religious experience historically can help avoid the narrow focus on idealized versions of the truth (Satya). The benefits of a historically informed religious perspective are not only useful but necessary. This emphasis has received particular attention since *Nostra Aetate*, one of the most influential documents of Vatican II, also shares this emphasis as it stresses finding shared values among difference, as a way.

All men [women] form but one community. This is so because all stem from the one stock which God created to people the entire earth (cf. Acts 17:26), and also because all share a common destiny, namely God. His providence, evident goodness, and saving designs extend to all men (cf. Wis 8:1; Acts 14:17; Rom 2:6-7; 1 Tim 2:4).

Pope Francis has stressed the need for interreligious encounter to establish shared spiritual values, and to move out into genuinely shared action for the benefit of all.

An attitude of openness in truth and in love must characterize the dialogue with the followers of non-Christian religions, in spite of various obstacles and difficulties, especially forms of fundamentalism on both sides. Interreligious dialogue is a necessary condition for peace in the world, and so it is a duty for Christians as well as other religious communities. This dialogue is in first place a conversation about human existence or simply, as the bishops of India have put it, a matter of "being open to them, sharing their joys and sorrows". In this way we learn to accept others and their different ways of living, thinking and speaking. We can then join one another in taking up the duty of serving justice and peace, which should become a basic principle of all our exchanges (EG, no. 250).

Human existence cannot be reduced to the rational domain. Life experiences are necessarily ambivalent and multivalent. The Universal Church believes that faith and reason complement one another, has particular competency in interreligious encounter, since it takes faith (and other religious experiences) seriously. For the Asian Church mission simply means "being with the people, responding to their needs, with sensitiveness to the presence of God in cultures and other religious traditions, and witnessing to the values of God's Kingdom through presence, solidarity, sharing and word" (FABC V, art. 3.1.2). Preaching and witnessing are not two separate much less exclusive ways of missionary activity; they are two forms and ways of bringing the good news of salvation in Christ.[19]

We need to talk of "dialogue of experience". The "dialogue of experience" must include not only specifically spiritual experience, but other experiences - especially the experience of the marginalized and powerless. We need to address the following questions too: How can we avoid imposing one particular version of interreligious dialogue? How do we honor and include the experience of practitioners of indigenous religions which do not have scriptures? How can interreligious dialogue be meaningful in a secularized context? Or with religious partners who do not see the value of dialogue? What can dialogue achieve with regard to religious issues and about religions? Is inter-religious dialogue necessary? If yes, to which aim and in whose interest?[20]

Experience is suggesting that the vital questions raised in dialogue cannot be answered until the parties involved *do* something together. This involves a change from content to method. A healthy "dialogue of life" is more compelling than the dialog of intellect. Experience of working together has to be done first. Out of that shared action, theological reflection emerges, responsive to and shaped by social need. For dialogue at these levels we need, not so much the clerics, who have a special function within the Church, but the people who live in the (secular) world. We have to declericalize and secularize the Church at this level. The Church needs to be a facilitator.[21] Addressing other religious leaders in Chennai in February 1986, John Paul II said:

> By dialogue we let God be present in our midst; for as we open ourselves in dialogue to one another, we also open ourselves to God... As followers of different religions we should join together in promoting and defending common ideals in the spheres of religious liberty, human brotherhood, education, culture, social welfare and civic order.[22]

Priority Four: Peace and Reconciliation Strategy

We live in a world of growing violence. The cry for peace is heard all over. Peace-building and reconciliation have become the need of the hour. Education for peace is a priority for the church in India because India continues to be a major conflict prone area in the country. We need to focus on promoting peace across all areas of our educational ventures, including the teaching-learning process. A culture of peace must imply more than a theoretical vision and understanding that impresses itself. It should reach out to persons and groups, communities and societies, nations and states, and indeed our entire world. This culture must also spell itself out as a practical process that impacts all these levels of human activity and endeavors.

How can an education for peace be made meaningful and integral to our present system? This calls for developing concrete methodologies to promote peace and reconciliation which implies that we are aware of the dynamics of violence at the socio-cultural-politico-religious level and diagnose the motives, intentions and dubious attempts at consciously promoting violence and disharmony. In a world rife with injustice and inequality this demands a serious and explicit pedagogic commitment to create critical consciousness, which is concerned with justice and freedom. This will motivate our students to learn alternative ways of conflict resolution rooted in people's lives, cultures, values and attitudes.[23] Pope Francis emphatically says:

> Peace in society cannot be understood as pacification or the mere absence of violence resulting from the domination of one part of society over others. Nor does true peace act as a pretext for justifying a social structure which silences or appeases the poor, so that the more affluent can placidly support their lifestyle while others have to make do as they can. Demands involving the distribution of wealth, concern for the poor and human rights cannot be suppressed under the guise of creating a consensus on paper or a transient peace for a contented minority. The dignity of the human person and the common good rank higher than the comfort of those who refuse to renounce their privileges. When these values are threatened, a prophetic voice must be raised (EG, no. 218).

Let me share with you my experience: Karwan e mohabbat (A journey of atonement and love) that made me understand **gifts** (Jesuits, non-Jesuits and 50 NGOs), **ministry** (contextualizing theology or inter-religious liberative action) and **mission** (a journey of atonement and love - "reconciliation and justice"). The *karwan* team headed by a renowned social activist Harsh Mander journeyed across Assam, Jharkhand, Karnataka, Delhi, Uttar Pradesh, Haryana, Rajasthan and Gujarat. Vidyajyoti, College of Theology joined the *karwan* from Delhi in Tilak Vihar having a public meeting and sharing with the 1984 anti-Sikh riots' victims. Students from Vidyajyoti were part of a team and, there were several journalists, social activists, columnists, photographers, and a scientist, in the team. I was present with the *Karwan* both in Delhi and in Ahmedabad. The brothers were fondly called by the co-pilgrims as singing priests because of their ability to sing socially awakening songs and nukkads. Speaking about the presence of brothers, John Dayal says:

> The group was the richer with seven brothers from the Catholic Theologate, Vidyajyoti, joining us. ... who enlivened our evenings with their dholak beats, songs and hymns. I was at least twice the age of the eldest of these scholastics, but they knew far more of systematic theology and the Gospels and narrations, and Acts of the

Apostles. Back and forth we went, sometimes connecting my life experiences and theirs, seeking patterns and arguments, we decided that the journey's experiences were changing our perceptions and our understanding of theology.[24]

The *karwan* team of men and women were from different walks of life with the unity of hearts and minds. As we shared our joys together, we were ready to share the challenges together as well. The most painful moment for us was to listen to and feel with the parents who had lost their sons in a cruel way unjustly. To console them was the most difficult thing for us. One of them was a father who had lost his son, a victim of violence by the *gau rakshaks*. He was troubled not only because of the loss of his son but he was in great agony because he was forced to take the buried body after a week which is a sacrilegious act in the religion he belonged to.

Karwan e Mohabbat, a prophetic movement of Mr. Harsh Mander taught me to redeem our theological education in India at the root level so that our priestly training goes into the head and heart of our future priests, precisely because during these past 25 years (there had been different activities in the past too like joining peoples movements, world social forum, Netarhat issues) our young priests are more under the influence of "NEW GEN" atmosphere than what they are expected to be for the Church and for the people of God. This is due to the arrival and rapid dissemination of digital technology in the last decades of the 20th century. Even though Vidyajyoti participation in *Karwan e Mohabbat* is a small initiative, meeting and mixing with the simple and the humble (even facing the saffron brigade at Alwar, Rajasthan) in this vast sub-continent is a challenging and contemporary re-reading of the ministry of Jesus, and it speaks volumes for those who are prepared to hear and understand the signs of the time. What we need to remember is we are not alone in the journey of collaboration and networking (VG, no. 4, d) but which we share with so many men and women who are consecrated to the service of others.

Conclusion

To conclude, the future is characterized by un-imaginable challenges that surpass our present-day theological tools of mission. Pope Francis encourages us to "march towards a missionary transformation of a Church that 'goes forth' (VG, no. 3; EG, no. 20) ...this vast and pressing task requires, on the cultural level of academic training and scientific study, a broad and generous effort at a radical shift, or rather-dare I say-at "a bold cultural revolution" (VG, no. 3). There is no return to the past, none of the past mission methods, models and paradigms will fulfill the goals of mission. A new way of being witnesses has to be explored: formation in secular space, to engage ourselves in civic and political leadership, authentic presence in inter-religious spaces and to be catalysts in promoting peace and reconciliation. The life of Christ our Lord, poured into us by the Holy Spirit as a sharing in the divine life itself, enters the hearts of men and women into the very heart of the world. Pope Francis says, "It is not by proselytizing that the church grows but by attraction" (EG 15). "For truth is not an abstract idea, but is Jesus himself, the Word of God in whom is the Life that is the Light man [woman], the Son of God who is also the Son of Man (VG, no.1). As witnesses, we are invited to share Christ-life with the others in and through our lived experiences. The Light of Christ interprets these experiences and energized by the dynamism of Christ's love (EG, no. 264). In particular, when the Gospel is preached to the poor (EG, no. 197, 212, 213), through our life service, then the Holy Spirit authenticates our desire to be his witnesses. I end with the words of FABC:

> The "small flock" of Jesus should not be timid or fearful among Asia's billions...He journeys with us just as he did with his disciples on the way to Emmaus (Lk 24: 13-32). At every Eucharistic celebration, he keeps opening our eyes and warming our hearts with the fire of love for a New Evangelization in Asia.[25]

Endnotes

[1] Pope Francis, *Veritatis Gaudium,* no.3.

[2] William A. Barry, "Jesuit Formation Today: An Invitation to Dialogue and Involvement," in *Studies in the Spirituality of Jesuits* 20/5 (November: 1988), 3f.

[3] Bill Cosgrave, "Understanding Spirituality Today," in *The Furrow* (November 2017), 593.

[4] James H. Kroeger, "FABC: Asia Urgently Needs Renewed Evangelizers," *SEDOS Bulletin,* Vol 45, no. ½ (Jan-Feb 2013), 30.

[5] As Quoted in Christopher Lamb, "Faith is neither a doctrinal system or social activism," *The Tablet* (3 November 2018), 24.

[6] Susunaga Weeraperuma, *Clarity is the only Spirituality* (New Delhi: Finger Print, 2018), 16.

[7] See Noel Davies and Martin Conway, *World Christianity in the Twentieth Century* (London: SCM Press, 2008), 288-93.

[8] George Soares-Prabhu, "The Kingdom of God: Jesus' Vision of a New Society," D.S. Amalorpavadass (ed), *The Indian Church in the Struggle for a New Society* (Bangalore: NBCLC, 1981), 600, 601, 607.

[9] Vimal Tirimanna, (ed.,) *Harvesting From the Asian Soil: Towards an Asian Theology* (Bangalore: ATC, 2011), 161.

[10] Jessie Rogers, "Women in Church Leadership Roles: Biblical Perspectives," in *Furrow* (July-August, 2018), 409.

[11] https://zenit.org/articles/the-theme-of-the-2019-world-day-of-peace-is-good-politics-at-the-service-of-peace/, accessed on 08.11.2018.

[12] Loughlar Sofield and Donald H. Kuhn, *The Collaborative Leader.* (Notre Dame: Ave Maria Press, 1995), 40.

[13] *Ibid.*

[14] Raj Irudaya & Vincent Kundukulam, "Challenges of Religious Nationalism in India Today: A Theological Response," ITA Statement 2018 (unpublished).

[15] See, Walter K. Anderson & Shridhar D. Damle, *The RSS: A View to the Inside* (New Delhi: Penguin, 2018), 63-76.

[16] Refer also, CBCI, *Policy of Dalit Empowerment in the Catholic Church in India: An Ethical Imperative to Build Inclusive Communities* (New Delhi: CBCI, December 2016).

[17] Some ideas of A. Selvaraj from JHEASA Annual Conference held at Dhyana Ashram, Chennai on Oct 19-20, 2018.

[18] "Theses on Interreligious Dialogue" in John Gnanapiragasam and Felix Wilfred (eds), *Being Church in Asia,* Vol I. Manila: Claretian,1994, 13.

[19] D. S. Amalorpavadass, "Approaches in Our Apostolate Among Followers of Other Religions," *Mission Theology for Our Times* no. 3 (Bangalore: NBCLC, 1978), 30.

[20] Kizito Chinedu Nweke, "The Necessities and Limitations of Inter-Religious Dialogue," in *Exchange* 46 (2017), 131.

[21] Michael Amaladoss, "Models of the Church and the Concept of Ministry," in D.S. Amalorpavadass (ed.,) *Ministries in the Church in India: Research Seminar and Pastoral Consultation* (New Delhi: CBCI, 1976), 370.

[22] *Origins* 15 (1986) 598. For similar sentiments see John Paul II's address to leaders of other religions in New Delhi after the publication of *Ecclesia in Asia:* "The Interreligious Meeting", *Vidyajyoti Journal of Theological Reflection* 63 (1999), 884-886.

[23] Some ideas of Binoy Jacob from JHEASA Annual Conference held at Dhyana Ashram, Chennai on Oct 19-20, 2018.

[24] Harsh Mander, Natasha Badhwar & John Dayal, *Reconciliation: Karwan E Mohabbat's Journey of Solidarity through a Wounded India,* (New Delhi: Manipal Technologies Limited, 2018), 60-61.

[25] James H. Kroeger, "FABC: Asia Urgently Needs Renewed Evangelizers," *SEDOS Bulletin*, Vol 45, no. ½ (Jan-Feb 2013), 32.

భారతమిత్రం

కతోలిక వార పత్రిక

అక్టోబరు 7, 1990

సంపుటి: 47 ✳ సంచిక: 37 ✳ ఎడిటర్: ఫాదర్ బి. బల్తాజార్ ✳ సాలుసంద: 25 పైసలు ✳ పేజీలు: 8

సరికొత్త కతోలిక తెలుగు బైబులు ఆవిష్కరణ
ఫాదర్ పూదోట జోజయ్య S.J. కు సన్మానం

విజయవాడ: గుంటూరు, సరికొత్త కతోలిక తెలుగు బైబులును
సెప్టెంబర్ 19వ తేదీ, సాయంత్రం 6.45 గంటలకు, విజయవాడలోని
గునదల వార పుణ్యక్షేత్రం ఆవరణలో అలంకార పీఠాధిపతులు నవ
కాండ్లో ఆర్చిబిషప్ [కి సామినేని ఆరుళప్పగారు ఆవిష్కరించి, తొలి
[పతిని తెలుగు పీఠాధిపతుల సంఘాధ్యక్షులు – వెల్లూరు బిషప్ [కి
పి.సి. బాల్సామ్య గారికి అందించారు.

అంతకు ముందు గునదలవార పుణ్యక్షేత్రం ఆవరణలోకి
[పవేశించిన పీఠాధిపతులందరిని అక్కడ వేచివున్న వేలాదిమంది భక్తులు,

తొలి [గంథము తొలి [పతిని విడుదలచేసే పి.పి.సి.సి. డైరెక్టర్ బిషప్
పి.సి. బాల్సామ్యగారికి అంటజెప్పున్న ఆర్చిబిషప్ ఎస్. ఆరుళప్పగారు.

సన్మానం అందుకున్న పుణ్యకురు సమారాధనలు ఫాదర్ పూదోట జోజయ్య
SJ గారిని అభినందిస్తున్న డైమల్ కమిషన్ డైరెక్టర్ బిషప్ గారిలతోసహా.

మతస్థులు, గురువులు కొరల భార్యలగా ఎప్పించారు, పీఠాధిప
విష్వాసిలకాగ సన్మానించిన బహుళ అందంగం విజయవాడ [కి
[కిసోన్ మధ్యాగారు పీఠాధిపతలు, పరిశుధుల ఆశ్వాస పని
కార్య పీఠాధిసంఘంలోవారి గుర్తుల బయలుపరిచి పిల్కిరంది
ఆ అర్చన [మహిమ [పైబిల్ నాట్ల 1ఆరాధనగ ఎవారు కొ
నార్చించిన [కి బి. జబ్బారా ఆలంచిన వర్త పనలు అంద

అందించారు... బిషప్ [గనియా పీఠాల [పధాన్యవిద్యాయిని, కౌస్టర్
కమిటి అధ్యక్షులు [కి బాల్సామ్యు గారు బివర్లం కృషిని, కార్యవర్గ
సభ్యులను [పశంసించారు.

బైబులు ఆవిష్కరణముందుగా, గుంటూరు బిషప్ [కి గరి
వారిగారు బైబులును ముద్రించేందుకు జరిగిన కృషిని మురందారు.
బైబులు తొర్కితీరి అందున్న బివర్ పి.సి. బాల్సామ్య గారు తెలుగు
బైబులు అనువాదంను కృషిని ల్పహించారు. అనంతరం బైబులు పాత
నిబంధన అనువాదముల, వేదముత్కరైన ఫాదర్ పి. జోజయ్య గారిని
కాలనాతోసా, పాలసుకృంతోను సత్కరించారు. అతను అరిసి సత్కా
రానికి ఫాదర్ జోజయ్యగారు కృతజ్ఞతలు తెలుపులు, ఫాదర్ నైజ
గార్స్ [సేరలంలో ముఖల్మైన ఉన విరలాల కొరక సంవేశినందుకు
ఆనందాస్ను [పకటించారు. [కి బి. క్రస్పియన్ వందన సమర్పున,
జగమ్మరు గీతాలావన ఆవంతరం పీఠాధిపతులు అందరూ హార్లైన భక్తి
లను నివేనందించారు, ఈ కార్య[కమున ఫాదర్ టి. మన్రెడ్డి, మోని
గ్నర్ కుల్ కాంతరలింకల్, ఫాదర్ వారంఘుని జోతే గార్ల
విర్యూలతోన్ ఆశిరింది... [కి పద్మల అంటలోని ఈ కార్యమునంచం
సమ్మమొక్కమునగా వ్యవహరించారు, సుమారు 4000 మంది [పజల,
పండమంది గురువులు, మూదపందల మంది మహాన్యలు ఈ కార్య
[కమంలో పార్ల్సార్లు.

The release of the Telugu Bible
with the completed version of
Fr. Jojayya Pudota's translation
of the Old Testament
September 19, 1990

పూదోట జోజయ్య స్వామి రచనావలోకనం

గుజ్జల అంతోని పీటర్ కిశోర్, ఎస్.జె.

పరమ పూజ్యులు జోజయ్య స్వామి సుదీర్ఘ కాలం ఇటీవల వరకు నిర్వహించిన విద్యార్థి శిబిరాలలో నేను 8,9,10 వ తరగతుల (1977–1980) విద్యార్థిగా పాల్గొనడం; అప్పటినుండి వారి ద్వైమాస పత్రిక చైతన్యవాణి పాఠకుణ్ణి కావడం; వారి బైబులు కరస్పాండెన్స్ కోర్సులో పాల్గొని బైబులు జ్ఞాన సముపార్జనకు ఓనమాలను దిద్దటం; ఆంధ్ర లొయోలకళాశాలలో ఇంటర్మీడియట్ విద్యార్థిగా (1980–1982) అప్పుడు ఆయన మార్గ దర్శకత్వంలోఉన్న AICUF లో సభ్యుణ్ణి కావడం; ఆయన జీవితం కలిగించిన ప్రేరణంతో దేవుని పిలుపు మేరకు నేను కూడా ఏసు సభలో చేరడం; ఆయనతో కలిసి ఆంధ్ర లొయోల కళాశాలలో దాదాపు 20 వసంతాలు జీవిస్తుండటం; ఆయన రచనలను చదివి, కొంతవరకైనా వాటిని అర్థం చేసుకోనగలిగే అదృష్టానికి నోచుకోవడంత వీటన్నిటిని నాకు దేవుడిచ్చిన పరమ వరములుగా నేను భావిస్తుంటాను. ఈ సాన్నిహిత్యంతోనే జోజయ్య స్వామి సాహిత్య క్షేత్రంలో విరబూసిన ఆధ్యాత్మిక, విద్యార్థి హిత వాఙ్మయ పుష్పాలను వింగడించి లేశమాత్రంగానైనా పరిచయం చేయడానికి వినయపూర్వకంగా ప్రయత్నిస్తాను.

బైబులు పూర్వ నిబంధనము - అనువాదం

జోజయ్య స్వామి 1976 వ సంవత్సరం మార్చి – ఏప్రిల్ నెలల చైతన్యవాణి సంచికలో అప్పటికి రెండున్నర సంవత్సరాల వయసున్న ఆ ద్వైమాసిక పత్రిక మీద నిర్వహించిన సమీక్షా ఫలితాలను ప్రచురిస్తూ, వాటిలో వచ్చిన ఒక సూచనకు సమాధానంగా "ఈ సంపాదకుడు ఒంటిగాడు. ఇతని ప్రధాన కార్యం గూడ చైతన్యవాణిని ప్రచురించడం గాదు. **బైబులు పూర్వ వేదాన్ని తెలుగులోకి అనువాదం చేయడం.**" అని చెప్పారు. అదే విధంగా పదిహేడు సంవత్సరాలు అలుపెరుగని అకుంఠిత కార్య దీక్షతో కతోలిక తెలుగు బైబులు పూర్వవేదం అనువాదం పూర్తిచేశారు జోజయ్య స్వామి. దేశవిదేశాల్లో వారు

సముపార్జించిన వేదాంత విద్య, ఆంధ్ర విశ్వకళా పరిషత్తులో వారు అందుకున్న ఎమ్.ఏ. తెలుగు పట్టా ఈ అనువాద మహా యజ్ఞంలో వారికి ఉపకరించాయి. జాను తెలుగులో అలతి అలతి పదాలతో, అచ్చతెలుగు పలుకుబడి, జాతీయాలతో జోజయ్య స్వామి చేసిన బైబులు అనువాదం తెలుగు బైబులు అనువాదాలన్నిటిలో ముందు వరసలో ఉంటుంద నటం అతిశయోక్తి కాదు.

రచనల విస్తృతి, పరిధి

జోజయ్య స్వామి తన రచనలకు ఎంచుకున్న ముఖ్య విషయం బైబులు విజ్ఞానం. తన జీవితకాలంలో క్రీస్తు దాసునిగా క్రీస్తు ప్రబోధాలను అసంఖ్యాకంగా తన చిన్న చిన్న పుస్తకాల ద్వారా కథోలిక క్రైస్తవ విశ్వాసులకు దాదాపు 50 ఏళ్లుగా అందుబాటులోకి తీసుకొస్తున్నారు. బైబులు పుస్తకాల పరిచయం వంటి మౌలిక వ్యాస తరంగిణితో మొదలై జ్ఞానస్నానం,దివ్య సత్ప్రసాదం, అంత్యగతులు, దేవమాత పట్ల భక్తి తత్పరత, కీర్తనామృతం తదితం అంశాలపై సాధికారికంగా, జైపదేశికంగా వ్యాసాలను వెలయిస్తున్నారు.

తాను ఏసు సభకు చెందిన గురువు కావడం వలనా, విజయవాడలో ఏసు సభ నడుపుతున్న ఆంధ్ర లొయొల కళాశాలలో నివసిస్తుండడం వలనా విద్యార్థి, యువజనలో కం పట్లస్వామికి మక్కువ ఎక్కువ.క్రైస్తవ పాత్రికేయునిగా చైతన్య వాణిని, విద్యార్థిహిత గ్రంథమాలలను 46 ఏళ్లుగా నిరంతరాయంగా ప్రచరిస్తూ యువతకు దిశా నిర్దేశనం చేసే వ్యాసాలు పుంఖాను పుంఖాలుగా రచిస్తున్నారు. ఈ మధ్య కాలంలో అందరి నోళ్ళలో నానుతున్నవ్యక్తిత్వ వికాస శిక్షణను ఏనాటినుంచో జోజయ్య స్వామి తన వ్యాసాల్లో నిర్వహిస్తున్నారు.

ప్రధానంగా 12 సంపుటాలుగా వెలువడిన బైబులు భాష్యం జోజయ్య స్వామి రచనల భాండాగారం. ఆధ్యాత్మిక సత్యాల లోతులను స్పృశిస్తూ, సామాజిక అలసత్వం, రుగ్మతలను సుతిమెత్తగా మందలిస్తూ సాగిన ఈ సంపుటాల్లో విషయ చర్చ ఈ క్రైస్తవ తరానికితారకమంత్రం. ముఖ్యంగా కథోలిక క్రైస్తవులు అవధానంతో ఈ పన్నెండు సంపుటాలూచదివితే చాలు, వారు తమ విశ్వాసం గురించి తెలుసుకొనవలసినదంత తెలుకుంటారు.

బైబులు భాష్య సంపుటావళి విహంగ వీక్షణం

1972 లో మొదలైన చిన్ని పుస్తకాల సమాహారం 2003 నాటికి 157 సంచికలుగా విస్తరించింది. వీటిలో 60 పుస్తకాలు అంతకు ముందే బైబులు గ్రంథమాల శీర్షికన పల ముద్రణలు పొందాయి. ఈ సంపుటావళి మొదటి ముద్రణకు వ్రాసిన ఆముఖంలో

నాటి విజయవాడ పీఠాధిపతి మల్లవరపు ప్రకాశ్ ఏలినవారు ఇలా రాశారట "తెలుగు కతోలిక శ్రీ సభకు బైబులును, క్రైస్తవ సిద్ధాంతాలను అర్థం చేసుకోవలనన్న కోరిక గల క్రైస్తవేతరులకు ఫాదర్ జోజయ్య గొప్ప వరమని నేను భావిస్తున్నాను. సరళమైన స్వచ్ఛమైన సామాన్య ప్రజలకు అర్థమయ్యే తెలుగు భాషలో రచింపబడిన ఈ పుస్తకాలను చదివి, ఆధ్యాత్మిక జీవిత వికాసానికి, క్రైస్తవ సిద్ధాంతాలను లోతుగా అర్థం చేసుకోవడానికి వీటిని వినియోగించుకోవాలని కోరుతున్నాను". ఈ పలుకులు సర్వదా శిరోధార్యం.

ప్రథమ సంపుటిని రచయిత బైబులు పరిచయం, బైబులు సమాచారం, బైబులు పఠనం అనే అంశాలతో ఆరంభించారు. ఇందులో ప్రేరణ, బైబులు సంస్కృతి, మూల భాషలు, అనువాదాలు, రచనోద్దేశం మొదలైన మౌలికాంశాలను విపులీకరించారు. వెనువెంటనే బైబులు గ్రంథాలన్నిటి సారాంశం, వివరణ వస్తాయి. ఆపైన పూర్వవేదంలో ఆదిదంపతులు, యోసేపు, నిర్గమనం, యోబు, తోబీతు తదితర పూర్వవేద కథలు దర్శనమిస్తాయి. "బాధామయ సేవకుడు" శీర్షికన క్రీస్తుకి అన్వయించే ఈ దృగ్విషయానికి రచయిత కావించినరూపకల్పన మహోదాత్తమై వ్యాసం. పిమ్మట బైబులు భక్తుల గురించి, ఇతర ధ్యానాల గురించి కూలంకషంగా వివరించాక జోజయ్య స్వామి యేసు ప్రభువు చేసిన పర్వత ప్రసంగంలోని అష్ట భాగ్యాలను విశ్లేషించడంతో ఈ సంపుటి ముగుస్తుంది.

ఇక రెండవ సంపుటంలో పాపం, పాపవిముక్తి, దైవ సాన్నిధ్యం వంటి వేదాంత భక్తి విషయాలతో పాటు క్రైస్తవ నాయకత్వం, సాంఘిక న్యాయం, సేవకు పిలుపు, కుటుంబ జీవితం తదితర ఆచరణాత్మక అంశాల విశ్లేషణలున్నాయి. చివరలో బైబులు గ్రంథంలోని మొత్తం 150 కీర్తనలకూ సంక్షిప్త వివరణ అందించారు జోజయ్య స్వామి. మధ్యలో సహోదర ప్రేమను గూర్చి రచయిత ప్రస్తావించిన భావాలు అమోఘం. తలపుల్లో, మాటల్లో, చేతల్లో సోదర ప్రేమ, క్షమలను గురించి వర్ణిస్తూ, ఇదే వరసలో బైబులు సువిశేషాల్లో పౌలు యోగి వ్రాతల్లో సోదర ప్రేమ అంశాలను చదువరులకు ఆకళింపు చేశారు రచయిత. అన్ని సత్కార్యాల కంటే సోదర ప్రేమ గొప్పదని, క్రైస్తవ సాధకులు ఈ పుణ్యసాధనలో బహుజాగరూకత వహించాలని స్వామి ఉద్బోధించారు.

తృతీయ సంపుటం మరిన్ని గంభీరమైన వేదశాస్త్రాంశాలను ఆవిష్కరించింది. వీటిలో ఎడారి మునుల సూక్తులు, పునీత ఇగ్నేషియస్ సూక్తులు వేద సూత్ర ధ్యానంలో తరగని పెన్నిధులు. క్రైస్తవ వేద బోధ గురించి స్వామి అభిప్రాయాలు ఈ సంపుటిలో 9వ అధ్యాయంలో కనిపిస్తాయి. ఇదే అధ్యాయంలో భారత దేశంలో వేద బోధ స్థితిని

రచయిత సమీక్షించారు. 'సన్మనస్కుల' శీర్షికతో ఇందులో కనిపించే దేవదూతలను గురించిన సమాచారం విజ్ఞానదాయకం. మొదటి అధ్యాయంలో బైబులు ప్రవక్తల గురించిన్న వివరణను స్వామి అత్యంత కుశాగ్రబుద్ధితో రచించారు. ఈ సంపుటి మధ్యలో ఈ వేదశాస్త్ర బోధ విశ్లేషణ సరసన "పని" అనే శీర్షికన క్రైస్తవులంతా, ఆ మాట కొస్తే మానవులంతా తలదాల్చ వలసిన హిత బోధ చేశారు. మంచి మరణం గురించిన స్వామి బోధనామృతంలో వేదాంత విషయాలే గాక, మరణం విషయంలో క్రైస్తవ భక్తుల వైఖరి ఎలా ఉండాలనే అభిప్రాయాలను కూడా ప్రబోధాత్మకంగా స్వామి వివరించారు.

నాలుగవ సంపుటం అంతటినీ జోజయ్య స్వామి క్రైస్తవ భక్తి తత్పరతకు హృదయ స్పందన అనదగిన "ప్రార్థన" కు కేటాయించారు. ఈ సంపుటం తెలుగు క్రైస్తవ సాహిత్యంలోనే ప్రార్థన విపులీకరణలో అనర్ఘ రత్నమని చెప్పకతప్పదు. ప్రార్థనల రకాలు, క్రీస్తు ప్రార్థనం, ప్రభువు నేర్పిన ప్రార్థనపై వ్యాఖ్యానం, బైబులు భక్తుల ప్రార్థనలు, ఆత్మ శోధన వంటి అంశాలపై జోజయ్య స్వామి ధ్యాన పూర్వక వివరణలు ఇందులో ఉన్నాయి. ఈ సంపుటంలో బాధ తత్త్వం అనేది ప్రభువు సిలువ మార్గంపై ధ్యానం, సిలువపై ప్రభువు పలికిన సప్త వాక్కుల సందేశం, మొత్తంగా యిది క్రీస్తు సిలువ హింసల గురించి ధ్యాన పూర్వక ప్రార్థనావేశాన్ని పఠితల మనసుల్లో స్థాపిస్తుంది.

ఐదవ సంపుటం ముఖ్యంగా భగవంతుని అస్తిత్వం, అవతారమూర్తి క్రీస్తు వ్యక్తిత్వాలపై, ప్రబోధాలపై దృష్టి సారించింది. ఇందులోనే పీడిత తాడిత దళిత మానవులకోపు తీసుకున్న క్రీస్తు హృదయాన్ని రచయిత హృద్యంగా వివరించారు. తండ్రిగా, తల్లిగా దేవుని గుణలక్షణాలను గురించి రాయడంలో భాగంగా బైబులు పుటల్లో దేవుని గురించిన ఐదు పోలికలనుత కాపరి, వరుడు, తోటమాలి, తండ్రి, గృహ నిర్మాణకుడు – చదువరులు అర్థం చేసుకానేలా స్వామి వివరించారు. క్రీస్తును గురువుగా ఎంచి మనం క్రీస్తు అడుగు జాడలలో ఆయనను అనుచరిస్తూసాగడమే శిష్యలక్షణమని స్వామి వివరించారు.

క్రైస్తవ దళితవాదాన్ని జోజయ్య స్వామి బైబులును ఆధారంగా చేసుకుని సోదాహరణంగా వివరించారు. దళితుడుగా, దళిత పక్షపాతిగా, దళితుల పట్ల ఆదరాభిమానాలు కనపరచిన క్రీస్తు వైఖరిని బహు సమర్థవంతంగా జోజయ్య స్వామి వెలయించారు. బహిష్కృతులను స్నేహితులుగా స్వీకరించి, వారితో సహపంక్తిభోజనాలు చేసి, వెలివేతకు గురైన దళితునిగా హింసాత్మక మరణం పొందిన క్రీస్తు ఈ అధ్యాయంలో సాక్షాత్కరిస్తాడు. జోజయ్య స్వామి, గురువుగా తన పర్యటనల్లో దళితక్రైస్తవులను సమాదరించిన వైనమంతా ఈ అధ్యాయంలో అక్షర రూపం దాల్చింది.

ఆరవ సంపుటం శీర్షిక "క్రీస్తు జీవిత పరమార్థం." ఈ సంపుటంలో 'క్రిస్టాలజీ' సారాంశాన్ని జోజయ్య స్వామి తన అనుభూతులతో రంగరించి వివరించారు. క్రీస్తు జీవితంలోని ఘట్టాలన్నిటినీ కరతలామలకం కావిస్తూ తిరుహృదయ ప్రాశస్త్యాన్ని అభివర్ణించారు. క్రీస్తు అనుభవించిన హింసల పరమార్థం, మొత్తంగా ఆయన మూర్తిమత్వంలోని రమ్యత కళ్లకు కట్టినట్టు, హృదయ గోచరం అయ్యేలా రచించారు. క్రీస్తు దివ్యనామావళి మొత్తం 17 బిరుదుల సారాంశాన్ని, శాస్త్ర విషయాలను ఇక్కడ పూసగుచ్చారు రచయిత.

ఏడవ సంపుటాన్ని జోజయ్య స్వామి పవిత్రాత్మకు కేటాయించారు. ఆత్మ అనుగ్రహించే ఏడు వరాలను, విశ్వాసుల్లో ఆత్మడు చేసే కార్యాలను చర్చించారు. ముఖ్యంగా సమకాలీన క్రైస్తవలోకంలో సర్వేశ్వరుడు ఆరంభిస్తున్న ఉజ్జీవ కార్యాల్లో ప్రముఖమైన పవిత్రాత్మ ఉద్యమం,దాని ఆవశ్యకత, ప్రాధాన్యతలను రచయిత విశ్లేషించారు. అపోస్తలుల కార్యాలగ్రంథంలో పవిత్రాత్మని చొరవ, కార్యాచరణలను వివరించారు. ఉత్తర భాగంలో 'పాప పుణ్యాలు' అధ్యాయంలో ఏడు మూల పాపాలు, నాలుగు నైతిక పుణ్యాలను గురించి, క్రైస్తవుల ఆధ్యాత్మిక జీవితంలో కలిగి ఉండవలసిన స్పృహ పరిజ్ఞానం, ఆచరణలను గురించి స్వామి ఉపదేశించారు. అరిషడ్వర్గాలను బైబులు దృక్పథంలో వివరించి హితబోధగావించారు.

ఎనిమిదవ సంపుటం ప్రధానంగా కతోలిక విశ్వాస సంప్రదాయాలను, వాటి అంతరార్థాలను కూలంకషంగా వివరించింది. దివ్య సత్ప్రసాదం, పాస్క, జ్ఞాన స్నానం, పాపోచ్చారణం, కీర్తనామృతం తదితర శ్రీసభ సంబంధిత అంశాలు ఈ సంస్కారాల, ఆచారాల పట్ల క్రైస్తవులకు, క్రైస్తవేతరులకు అవగాహన కలిగిస్తాయి.

ఈ వివరణనే కొనసాగిస్తూ 9 వ సంపుటంలో వివాహం, గురుపట్టం, తిరుసభ, క్రీస్తు వర్రప్రసాదం వంటి క్రైస్తవ సంస్కార సంప్రదాయాలను గురించి స్వామి వివరించారు. ఈ సంపుటిలోనే 30 వివిధ అంశాల గురించిన బైబిలు దృష్టాంతాలు, హితబోధలను చదువుకోవచ్చు. ఈ జ్ఞాన బోధకు సహాయకరంగా బైబిలు వ్యక్తుల కథలను ఉటంకించి వాటి ద్వారా నేర్చుకోదగిన పాఠాలను స్వామి వివరించారు.

పదవ సంపుటంలో దేవమాత భక్తి బోధను స్వామి హృద్యంగా రచించారు. ఇది కతోలిక క్రైస్తవులకు మరికన్యలకు అత్యంత ప్రీతి పాత్రమైన విభాగం. ఆ పునీత మాత తత్త్వం, వ్యక్తిత్వాలను మనోహరంగా స్వామి ఆవిష్కరించారు. చివరి అధ్యాయం అంత్యగతులను గూర్చి వర్ణిస్తూ క్రైస్తవ విశ్వాసులకు మరణం గురించిన మౌలిక విషయాలను అవగతం చేస్తుంది. ఈ సంపుటిలో బైబులు క్విజ్ ప్రశ్నలు మన సంఘాల్లో బైబులు పరిజ్ఞానం పెంపొందించుకునే జిజ్ఞాసకు తోడ్పడతాయి. 'భక్త

విజయం' అధ్యాయంలో మరొకసారి బైబులుభక్తులు దైవ సేవలో సాధించిన విజయాలు, నెరవేర్చిన కార్యాలను తెలిపే కథలున్నాయి.

ఇక పదకొండు, పన్నెండు సంపుటాల్లో కలగూర గంపగా బైబులు జ్ఞాన సముపార్జనకు దోహదం చేసే వివిధ అంశాలు ఉన్నాయి. ఇవి ఖండికలుగా జోజయ్య స్వామి ఆయా సందర్భాలను పురస్కరించుకుని రాసిన వ్యాసాలు.

ఇవిగాక వేరు వేరు పుస్తకాలుగా జోజయ్య స్వామి నాలుగు సువిశేషాల మీద వివరణలను; అపోస్తులుల చర్యలు, పౌలు భక్తుని లేఖలు, యోహాను దర్శన గ్రంథాల మీద వ్యాఖ్యానాలను ప్రచురించారు. వీటిలో ప్రతి అధ్యాయానికి ఆరంభంలో బైబులు ఆలోకనాలను రచయిత పొందు పరచారు. బైబులును నేరుగా చదివి ఆ మీదటనే వ్యాఖ్యానాలను చదవాలన్నది రచయిత అభిలాష, నివేదన. చదవరులకు అటు బైబులు పొండిత్యం, భక్తి మార్గానునరణం అనే రెండు ఉద్దేశాలతో జోజయ్య స్వామి ఈ వివరణలను, వ్యాఖ్యలను రచించారు. పాటించ శక్యంగాని ఉపదేశాలను బలవంతంగా జనసామాన్యంపై రుద్దే ప్రయత్నం ఇక్కడ కనిపించదు. వీటిలో కనిపించే ఉపదేశాలన్నీ ఆచరణాత్మకంగాఉంటాయి. ఇలాంటి వ్యాఖ్యానాలు కతోలిక క్రైస్తవులకు ఇంతవరకు అందుబాటులో లేవు. వీటిలో కనిపించే ప్రశ్నలు ఆత్మ పరిశోధనకు, పురోగతికి చాలా ఉపయోగపడతాయి.

తపోభ్యాసాలు – మనేసా

పునీత ఇగ్నేషియసు లోయోలా గారు ఏసు సభ స్థాపకులు. ప్రాపంచిక జీవిగా ఉన్న ఆయన పారమార్థిక జీవిగా మారుతున్న క్రమంలో ఎదురైన దివ్యానుభూతుల అక్షర రూపమే ఆయన రచించిన 'తపోభ్యాసాలు' అనేగ్రంథము. ఈ గ్రంథం కతోలిక ఆధ్యాత్మి కతకు మేలి మలుపు. ఇది ఏసు సభ సభ్యుల మత జీవితానికి పునాది. దీనిని జోజయ్య స్వామి తన ఆధ్యాత్మికతనంతటిని రంగరించి తెలుగులోకి అనువదించారు. ఈ గ్రంథంలోని అంశాలను 'మనేసా' అనే మరో పుస్తకంలో జోజయ్య స్వామి క్రైస్తవుల మేలు కొరకు ధ్యానాలుగా మలిచారు. ఇందులోని 21 అధ్యాయాలు ఈ ధ్యానాలకు వివరణలు. ఆత్మ శోధనం, పంచేంద్రియ ధ్యానం, తటస్థభావం, సదసదాత్మ వివేచనం వంటి పునీత ఇగ్నేషియస్ భావాలు, సూచనలు భక్తులకు ఇందులో దొరుకుతాయి.

రచనల్లో ఆవిష్కృతమైన ఆత్మ

ఆర్ద్ర హృదయంతో, స్వీకరణ భావంతో జోజయ్య స్వామి రచనలను చదివిన వారి మనోఫలకంపై చటుక్కున చెరగని ముద్ర వేస్తుంది స్వామి ఆత్మ. తండ్రివలె హితవు పల

కడం, ఉపాధ్యాయునివలె బుద్ధి గరపడం, గురువు వలె ఆధ్యాత్మిక ప్రబోధం గావించడం, స్నేహితునివలె నచ్చ జెప్పడం – ఇదే వారి వైఖరి, వాలకమూను. జోజయ్య స్వామి రచనలు ప్రధానంగా ప్రబోధాత్మకాలు.

క్రైస్తవ జన బాహుళ్యంలో పేరుకుపోయిన నిర్లిప్తత, నిక్రియా వాదం, స్తబ్ధత అన్తమానం జోజయ్య స్వామిని కలచి వేస్తూనే ఉన్నాయి. కొండకొమ్ముపై నుండి దొర్లుతున్న బండరాయిని అడ్డుపడి ఆపే ప్రయత్నం దుస్సాహసంగా కనబడుతుంది. అయితే జోజయ్య స్వామి అపారమైన మనోధైర్యం, అభినివేశం కలవారు కనుక క్రైస్తవుల్లోని ఈ నులివెచ్చనితనాన్ని నిరంతరాయంగా తన రచనల్లో నిరసించారు. ముఖ్యంగా క్రైస్తవుల్లో గ్రంథపఠనాభిలాష లోపం స్వామిని కలచివేస్తూనే ఉన్నది. "మన వాళ్ళకి పుస్తకాలు చదివే అలవాటు లేదు", అని బేల నవ్వుతో ఆయన పలికిన ప్రతిసారీ ఆ మాటల వెనక ఉన్న లోతైన ఆవేదన బయటికి తన్నుకు వస్తుంది.

స్వతహాగా మృదుభాషి, స్నేహశీలి, భేషజాలకు దూరంగా ఉండే సరళస్వభావి అయిన జోజయ్య స్వామి వ్యక్తిత్వం, ఆత్మ ఆయన రచనల్లో కొట్టవచ్చినట్టు కనిపిస్తుంది. జోజయ్య స్వామికి దైవదత్తమైన ఉపదేశక, కాపరి ప్రేషితవరాలున్నాయి. ప్రేమ, శాంతి, సంతోషాది ఆత్మ ఫలాలు కూడా స్వామిలో పుష్కలంగా వ్యక్తమవుతాయి. శ్రీసభ సంస్కారాలు, వాటి అంతరార్థం, ఆత్మ అనుగ్రహించే వరాలు, భక్తులు నడుచుకోవలసిన రీతి రివాజులను పదేపదే తన రచనల్లో ప్రస్తావిన్తూ వారంతా సత్రైస్తవులుగా రూపుదిద్దుకోవలనే తపన, ఆర్తి ఆయన రచనల్లో కొట్ట వచ్చి నట్లు కనిపిస్తాయి.

కాపరి హృదయంతో బాటు ఉపాధ్యాయునిగా జోజయ్య స్వామి ఆత్మ వారి రచనల్లో ప్రతిబింబిస్తుంది. చాలా వ్యాసాలకు చివర్లో పునర్విమర్శ, చదివినది తలకెక్కిందో లేదో సరిచూసుకోడానికి ప్రశ్నలు కనిపిస్తాయి. చెప్పినదే పదేపదే చెప్పి ఒప్పించే అధ్యాపక లక్షణం ఈ రచనల్లో ప్రస్ఫుటంగా కనిపిస్తుంది.

విశ్వాస సమర్ధక సాహిత్యం

విశ్వాస సమర్ధక సాహిత్యం (అపాలజెటిక్స్) అనేది తనకంటూ స్వతంత్ర ప్రతిపత్తి కలిగినసాహిత్య విశేషం. క్రీస్తు శకం తొలి శతాబ్దంలో వేదహింస చెలరేగిన కాలంలో క్రైస్తవులు రెండు రకాలుగా స్పందించారు. మొదటి రకం వారు తమ విశ్వాసం కొరకు ప్రాణత్యాగం చేసిన వేద సాక్షులు. రెండవ కోవకు చెందిన వారు తమ విశ్వాసాన్ని లోకానికి వివరించి, సమర్ధించడానికి అనేక రచనలు చేసిన క్రైస్తవ మేధావులు. ఈ రచనల సారాన్ని సోదాహరణంగా జోజయ్య స్వామి సామాన్య విశ్వాసులకు

అందుబాటులోకి తెచ్చిన తీరు ప్రశంసనీయం. విశేషించి ప్రొటస్టెంటు క్రైస్తవులు కతోలి కవేదంతంగ విభేదించే అంశాల్లో వారి వివరణలు కొంతాసమ్మితంగా, నమ్రతంగా ఉంటాయి. ఎక్కడా "నేను చెబుతున్నాను, మీరు వినండి" అనే ధోరణి కానరాదు.

శైలి, భాష, ఉక్తివైచిత్రి

జోజయ్య స్వామి భాష సరళ గ్రాంథికం, శిష్టవ్యావహారికం. ఈనాటి ప్రామాణిక పత్రికాభాష కలగలిసిన కదళీపాకం. రచనా రీతిలో ఉట్టి పడే సొబ్రాత్రం, ఆత్మీయత చదువరులను కట్టిపడేస్తాయి. చలం రాసినంత అలవోకగా ప్రజల భాషలో జోజయ్య స్వామి రాశారు. 'వుండే కాద', తేపతేపకు, 'మొదు వారిన కార్రు', 'పాలుమాలి', 'పెద్ద యెలుగున' ప్రభువని 'కొండాడాలి', 'తెలివిడి', 'యెదబెట్టు', 'కుస్తరింపు', 'పోస్కొలు రాయుకల్లు', 'దిడీలున', 'చెలమ', 'జాబు' మొదలైన వదాలు ఇక్కడ తప్ప నేడు మరెక్కడా కనిపించవు. వీరికి మాత్రమే సొంతమైన 'ప్రాణిపోషణానురక్తి', 'మేర మర్యాదలు', 'నేత్రవినీతి', 'భగవదనుభవం', 'వశవర్తిని', 'అంతర్నివాసి' తదితర ప్రయోగాలు చదువరులను అలరిస్తాయి. 'కొమ్ము కాస్తాడు', 'కోప తీసుకుంటాడు' మొదలైన ప్రయోగాలు దీనబంధుడైన భగవంతుణ్ణి చదివేవారికి సన్నిహితం చేస్తాయి.

జోజయ్య స్వామి ప్రయోగించే "యడాగమాలు" ఆహ్లాదాన్ని కలిగించి, మనసును మురిపిస్తాయి. 'ఆ యమ్మ', 'ఈ యాత్మ' మొదలైన ప్రయోగాలు ఆత్మీయతను పెంపొందిస్తాయి. "పదియాఱ్జులు" ఈ కోవలోనిదే. పాతకాలం తెలుగు పండితునిగా జోజయ్య స్వామి శైలిలో పాత వదప్రయోగాలు మిణుకు మిణుకుమంటూ ప్రత్యక్షమవుతుంటాయి. (ఉదా:- ప్రాత, పిత (తండ్రి). "ఇలాటి" అని ఆధునికులు రాసే పదాలు ఈ వ్యాసాల్లో "ఈలాటి" అని ఉంటుంది. ప్రార్థన అని మనం సాధారణంగా చెప్పేది, జోజయ్య గారి "జపం" (ప్రార్థనం") అవుతుంది.

అంతగా ప్రాచుర్యం లేని సామెతలు జోజయ్య స్వామి రచనలలో తళుక్కున మెరుస్తుంటాయి. ఇలాటిదే "ఎరుగక తిని అరుగక చస్తిని." మనుషుల్లో పేరాశను ఎత్తిచూపే మరొక సామెత "కడుపు నిండినా, కళ్ళు నిండవు."

"నజరేతు ఊరి వాడు" అనే ప్రయోగం జోజయ్య స్వామి వ్యాసాల్లో నజరెత్తూరి వాడు" అయి కూర్చుంది. దావీదుకు బత్షెబ "ప్రక్క ఇంటి ఆడగూతురు". "ఐదవసారి" అనేది "ఐదవతూరి". నూత్న, ఆత్మము మొదలైన విలక్షణ పదప్రయోగాలు ముచ్చట గొలుపుతాయి. "కొబ్బరి" జోజయ్య స్వామి భాషలో "కొబ్బెర".

అదేసమయంలో వాడుక భాష ముఖ్య సూత్రాలైన జంట దీర్ఘలు (తండ్రీ, క్రీస్తూ), విభక్తి ప్రత్యయాల సమర్థవంతమైన ఉపయోగం, వాక్య నిర్మాణ శైలి మొదలైన వాటిని జోజయ్య స్వామి అలవోకగా అత్యంత ప్రతిభావంతంగా నిర్వహిస్తున్నట్లు కనబడుతుంది.

ప్రేషితులు, దేవద్రవ్యానుమానాలు, అప్పురసాలు, పిత్రు పాదులు, వారసం, సన్మనస్కులు తదితర పదజాలం విశేషించి తెలుగు కథోలిక క్రైస్తవులు ఉపయోగించేవి. అయితే కథోలికేతర క్రైస్తవులను కూర్చుని చదివించి అలరించే బైబులు సత్యాలు ఈ వ్యాసాల్లో కోకొల్లలు. అంతర్నివాసి అంటే క్రైస్తవునిలో కాపురముండే దైవాత్మ. పాలుమాలిన అంటే సోమరితనం.

నన్ను చకితుణ్ణి చేసిన ఒక పదచమత్కారం, బైబులు భాషలో దేవుడు తన వారితో "నేను మిమ్మల్ని నా అరచేతిలో చెక్కుకున్నాను" అన్న మాటకు జోజయ్య స్వామి వాడిన రమ్య ప్రయోగం, "మిమ్ములను నా వొంటిపై పచ్చ బొడిపించుకుంటాను". ఇది చదివినప్పుడు నా మేను పులకరించింది. పుస్తకాలన్నిటా స్వచ్ఛమైన వచన కవిత్వం ఎదురై మనోల్లాసం కలిగిస్తుంది. సన్మనస్కుడు మరియమ్ముకు వినిపించినది "మంగళ వార్త." అచ్చ తెలుగు నుడికారం ఇది.

స్త్రీవాదం, దళిత పక్షపాతం

జోజయ్య స్వామి వ్యాసాలు బోధనాప్రధానాలు. అలాగే అవి కరుణారసప్రధానాలు. మనసమాజమంతటా వ్యాపించి ఉన్న లింగ, కుల, జాతి, వివక్షలు స్వామిని ఎంతో కలవరపరుస్తాయి.

స్త్రీ పక్షపాతం వీరి రచనల్లో సముచిత స్థానం పొందింది. "బైబుల్లో స్త్రీలు" అనే శీర్షికన ఏకంగా ఒక పుస్తకమే బైబులు మహిళల గురించి రాసి ప్రచురించారు. బైబులు భాష్యం మొదటి సంపుటంలోనే బైబులు సుదతులు కొందరి విశ్లేషణాత్మక వివరం గ్రంథస్థం చేశారు. ఐదవ సంపుటంలో "క్రీస్తూ, స్త్రీలూ" అనే అధ్యయనంలో క్రీస్తు దృక్పథంలో స్త్రీల గురించి జోజయ్య స్వామి రాసిన వ్యాసం తెలుగు అభ్యుదయ, సంస్కరణ రచనలో అజరామరంగా నిలిచిపోతుంది. భ్రూణ హత్యలు, పురుషాధిక్యత, వరకట్నం, గృహహింస, అవకాశాల్లో, వేతనంలో అసమానత, వ్యాపార ప్రకటనల్లో స్త్రీల చిత్రీకరణ, చదువు నేర్పించక పోవడం మొదలైన సమకాలీన అనాచారాలను చెబుతూ, క్రీస్తూ తన జీవితకాలంలో స్త్రీల పట్ల ఎలా ప్రవర్తించారో జోజయ్య స్వామి హృద్యంగా చిత్రీకరించారు.

ఐదవ సంపుటంలోని "దళిత క్రీస్తు" అధ్యయనం మొత్తంగా తెలుగు వారికి చేరవలసిన సమాచారం. స్త్రీవాదం క్రిందికి రాదుగానీ, మరియమాత పట్ల భక్తి

తత్పరత జోజయ్య స్వామి వ్యాసాల్లో ఉట్టిపడుతుంటుంది. ఆ తల్లికి రక్షణ చరిత్రలో ఉన్న విశిష్ట హోదాను వారు సహేతుకంగా బైబులు పరంగా నొక్కి వక్కాణించారు.

జోజయ్య స్వామి తాను నమ్మిన యేసు ప్రభువు వలె కరుణాంతరంగుడు. దీన జనోద్ధరణ, దీన బంధుత్వం స్వామి మనసులో వేరు పాతుకున్న వట వృక్షం. దళిత పక్షపాతం, దళిత పీడకులను నిర్ద్వంద్వంగా ఖండించడం ఈ వ్యాసాల్లో అడుగడుగున కనిపిస్తాయి. సాంఘిక న్యాయంపైన నా విద్యార్థి దశలో వారు వెలువరించిన 'నరికి నరుడు తోడేలు' పుస్తకంలో కూడా ఇవే భావాలను జోజయ్య స్వామి సునిశితంగా ఎక్కడ లేని ఆర్తితో, ఆవేదనలతో వెల్లడించారు. సమాజ శ్రేయస్సుకు దోహదం చేసే ఈ భావాలు అందరికి శిరోధార్యాలు.

మధ్యయుగాల భక్తి వేదాంత మథనం, పితృపాదుల ఆలోచనామృతం

మరి దేనికోసమో కాకపోయినా, రెండవశతాబ్ది మొదలుకొని మొన్నమొన్నటి వరకూ తమ ఉపదేశామృతాలు చిలకరించిన పితృపాదుల, క్రైస్తవ తత్త్వవేత్తల బోధనలుగురించి కొంతైనా తెలుకోవడానికి ప్రతి ఒక్కరూ జోజయ్య స్వామి రచనలను చదవవలసిన అవసరం ఎంతైనావుంది. అసలు మొదటిగా జోజయ్య స్వామి ఆ మహానుభావులందరి ఆలోచన జీవధారలను ఎంతగా ఆపోసన పట్టారో, చెప్పుటానికి వారి వ్యాసాల్లో కొల్లలుగా కనిపించేఆ ప్రస్తావనలే సాక్ష్యం. సమయానుకూలంగా పూర్వ క్రైస్తవ వేదాంతుల అభిప్రాయాలను, ఉవాచలను తన రచనలలో జోజయ్య స్వామి ఉదాహరించారు. ఆంబ్రోసు, అగస్టీను, ఆన్సెల్మ్, అంతియోక పురి ఇగ్నేష్యస్, గ్రెగోరి, యెరూషలేము సిరిల్, వివిధ జగద్గురువులు, ఇరెనియస్, డయొనీఖ్యస్, క్రిసోస్తం, బోన్హోఫర్, కిర్క్ గార్డ్, సిప్రియన్ ఇలా అనేకమంది పునీతులు, పితృపాదులు, తత్త్వవేత్తలు ఈ వ్యాసాల్లో సాక్షాత్కరిస్తుంటారు. ఈ వ్యాసాలు అసలు క్రైస్తవ వేదాంతుల్లో ప్రధానంగా ఎవరెవరు ఏమేమి చెప్పారు అనే సమగ్ర సమాచరం అందిస్తా, చదువరులకు అవసరమైన అవగాహన కలిగిస్తాయి. "ఎదారి మునుల సూక్తులు" అనే మొత్తం శీర్షిక తన బైబులు భాష్యం 3 వ సంపుటంలో పొందుపరిచారు జోజయ్య స్వామి.

ఇదంతా ఒక ఎత్తు అయితే క్రైస్తవ భక్తి మేధావిగా జోజయ్య స్వామి వ్యాఖ్యానాలు, వివరణలు మరొక ఎత్తు. ఆత్ముడు ఇచ్చే వరాల గురించి, పరిశుద్ధాత్మ పరిచర్య, పరిశుద్ధాత్మ ఉత్సవం ఇటీవలి పెంతెకోస్తు ఉద్యమం గురించి; జ్ఞానస్నానం, దివ్యసత్ప్రసాదం, పాపోచ్చారణం మొదలైన క్రైస్తవ సంస్కారాల గురించి; నాయకత్వం, సోదరప్రేమ, పిలుపు, సంపదలు, వివాహం, కుటుంబ జీవితం వంటి ఆచరణాత్మక

అంశాల గురించి; ప్రార్థనలు, యేసుక్రీస్తు మహోపదేశాలు మొదలైన అంశాలను కూలంకషంగా చర్చించారు. జోజయ్య స్వామి నాలుగవ సంపుటంలోని "బాధాతత్వం" అధ్యయనం భక్తుల హృదయాల్లో చెరగని ముద్ర వేస్తుంది. ఇకపోతే జోజయ్య స్వామి వ్యాస పరంపర శ్రీసభ మతాచార సరళికి కరదీపికలు. గురుపట్టం, పునీతమాత, తిరుసభలో గృహస్థుల పాత్ర మొదలైనవి గురువులకు సైతం మార్గ దర్శకాలు కాదగిన వివరణలు.

మరోవెపు పటిమ, గరిమగల బైబులు వ్యాఖ్యాతగా బైబులు అంశాల వివరణాత్మక ఉపదేశాలు పఠితలకు, ఆత్మానందం, ఆత్మిక క్షేమాభివృద్ధి కలిగిస్తాయి. ఈ కోవలో 3వ సంపుటంలోని పునీత ఇగ్నేషస్ సూక్తులు మణిమకుటాలు.

చారిత్రిక దృక్పథం

జోజయ్య స్వామికి ఏసు సభ సభ్యునిగా వాటికన్ కౌన్సిళ్ళ ఆదేశాలు, జగద్గురువుల సందేశాలు తెలిసి ఉండడంలో ఆశ్చర్యం లేదు. అయితే ఆయా చారిత్రికాంశాలపై స్వామికి ఉన్న పాండిత్యం అపారం. అందరికీ అర్థమయ్యే రీతిలో కథోలిక క్రైస్తవుల విశ్వాసాన్ని, ఆచారాన్ని శాసించే వివిధ కౌన్సిళ్ళ ముఖ్యాంశాలను ఈ వ్యాసాల్లో జోజయ్యస్వామి సందర్భోచితంగా పొందుపరచారు. క్రైస్తవ సంఘ చరిత్ర గురించిన సద్గాలదృక్పథాన్ని మణి కిమచ్చుకున్న వారుగా రచయిత అక్కడక్కడా ఆయా పరిణామాలను ప్రస్తావిస్తూ తన అభిప్రాయాలను, వ్యాఖ్యలను పొందు పరిచారు. ముఖ్యంగా లూతరు లేవనెత్తిన సంస్కరణ ఉద్యమం, సంస్కరణ వాదుల సైద్ధాంతిక నేపథ్యాలను నునిశితంగా పరిశీలించి వ్యాఖ్యానించారు. ఈ మధ్యకాలంలో తిరుసభనంతటినీ చుట్టబెడుతున్న పెంతెకోస్తు ఉద్యమాన్ని చక్కగా విశ్లేషించారు.

మనోవైజ్ఞానిక విశ్లేషణలు, నైతిక ప్రబోధాలు

జోజయ్య స్వామిలో సమర్థవంతుడైన సైకాలజిస్టు దాగి ఉన్నాడన్న సత్యానికి ఆయన వ్యాసాలు తిరుగులేని తార్కాణాలు. ఫ్రాయిడ్ మొదలగు వారి మనోవైజ్ఞానిక ప్రతిపాదనలను ప్రస్తావిస్తూ వాటికి క్రీస్తులో ఇవ్వగలిగిన జవాబులను విపులీకరించారు. ఇక నీతి సూక్తుల విషయానికొస్తే పాపాన్ని గురించి, నీతి న్యాయాల గురించి, మంచి మన్ననల గురించి, మర్యాదల గురించి జోజయ్య స్వామి మనసారా ఈ వ్యాసాల్లో బోధించారు. హితబోధ, వాత్సల్యం, దయ ఈ వ్యాసాల్లో చిప్పిల్లుతూ ఉంటాయి. "సద సదాత్మ విచారము" అనే శీర్షికన ఉత్తమ వ్యక్తిత్వ వివేచనాంశాలను పాఠకుల ఎదుట తేటతెల్లం చేశారు వ్యాసకర్త.

చైతన్యవాణి

యువత పాలిట చైతన్య రథం జోజయ్య స్వామి 46 ఏళ్లుగా (ప్రచురిస్తున్న చైతన్యవాణి ద్వైమాసిక పత్రిక. "ఆనో భద్రా: (కతవో యాంతు విశ్వత:" అనే ఋగ్వేద వాక్కు ఈ పత్రికకు ఆత్మ. ఈ పత్రిక 1973 జూన్ లో జన్మించింది. చైతన్యవాణిని జన చైతన్య బాణీగా మలిచే సదుద్దేశంతో జోజయ్య స్వామి పత్రిక ఆరంభమై నడుస్తున్న రెండున్నర సంవత్సరాలకే చైతన్యవాణిపై సమీక్ష తలపెట్టారు. ఈ సందర్భంలో ఆయన రాసిన విన్నపం ఆయన వ్యక్తిత్వానికి తిరుగులేని సాక్ష్యం. "సమీక్ష శాస్త్రీయ పద్ధతిలో జరగాలి. ముఖస్తుతి కోసం ఇచ్చకాలు (వ్రాయవద్దు. ఒక్కో (ప్రశ్న జాగ్రత్తగా ఆలోచించి చూచిమీ అనుభవానికి వచ్చిన అంశాలు మాత్రమే చెప్పండి. మీ సొంత అభిప్రాయాలు వ్యక్తం చేయడానికి జంక వద్దు. కటువుగా ఉన్నా నిజం చెప్పడానికి వెనుకాడవద్దు." సునిశితమైన సమీక్ష (ప్రశ్నలు పదహారింటిని జోజయ్య స్వామి ఈ సంచిక (జనవరి – ఫిబ్రవరి 1976) లో (ప్రచురించి పాఠకుల అభిప్రాయాలను కోరారు. కాని వచ్చిన స్పందన(ప్రోత్సాహకరంగా ఉందని చెప్పలేము. 1350 మంది పత్రికను అందుకోగా 100 మంది మాత్రమే సమీక్షలో పాల్గొన్నారు.

ఇక ఫలితాలను చైతన్యవాణి మార్చి – ఏప్రిల్ 1976 సంచికలో జోజయ్య స్వామి విశ్లేషించిన తీరు ఆయన కూలంకష దృష్టిని, విశ్లేష (ప్రతిభను ఎత్తి చూపుతున్నది. శీర్షికల్లో 'మనన మాలిక' అత్యంత జనాదరణ పొందినట్టు తేట తెల్లమయ్యింది. లైంగిక జ్ఞానం శీర్షిక గురించి "యువతీ యువకులకు లైంగిక జ్ఞానం (ప్రత్యేకంగా రచనలద్వారా నేర్పవలసిన అవసరం లేదేమో" అంటూ వచ్చిన ఓ ఉపాధ్యాయని అభిప్రాయాన్ని ఉన్నదానిని ఉన్నట్లుగా ముద్రిస్తూ – "ఇక్కడ ఒక్క విషయం స్పష్టం చేయాలి. మన యువతీ యువకులకు లైంగిక జ్ఞానం అట్టే తెలీదు. అసలు పెద్దవాళ్లకూ తల్లిదండ్రులకూ గూడ ఈ విషయాలు సరిగా తెలియవు. అనుభవం కొద్దీ పోతుంటారు అంతే. తెలిసిన తల్లిదండ్రులు కూడ తమ పిల్లలకు లైంగిక సత్యాలు నేర్పరు. (ప్రాయమొచ్చేకొద్దీ యువతీ యువకులు కుతూహలం ఆపుకోలేక పాడు పుస్తకాల నుండీ పాడు స్నేహితులనుండీ లైంగిక విషయాలను గూర్చిన మురికి సంగతులన్నీ నేర్చుకుంటారు. తరువాత ఈ రంగంలో నష్టపోయేది విశేషంగా ఆడపిల్లే. అందుచేత ముందుగానే మన యువతీ యువకులకు శాస్త్రీయ పద్ధతిలో ఈ సత్యాలు నేర్పడం అత్యవసరం" అంటూ జోజయ్య స్వామి చెప్పిన సమాధానం అక్షర సత్యం. తాను నమ్మిన ఈ సత్యం కొరకు, యువతీయువకుల (శేయస్సు కొరకు ఆ తరువాత కూడ జోజయ్య స్వామి ఈ శీర్షికను జయ(ప్రదంగా కొనసాగించారు. మొత్తమ్మీద సమీక్షలో

పాల్గొన్న పాఠకులు పత్రికలోని సరళమైన జాతీయమైన భాషను, ఉత్తమ వ్యక్తిత్వ సమపార్జనకె చైతన్యవాణి చేస్తున్న కృషిని ప్రశంసించారు. ముఖ్యంగా యువత తమలోని ఆత్మన్యూనతా భావాలు, ఇతర మానసిక సంక్లిష్టతలు దూరం చేసుకోవడానికి చైతన్యవాణి ఉపకరిస్తుందన్నారు. ఒకరైతే "ఈ పత్రిక చదివినప్పుడెల్ల గద్ద పెరుగుతో గుటక త్రాగినట్లు, తుమ్మెదలు తేనెను గ్రోలినట్లు, ఓ పండితుని వద్ద విద్య నభ్యసించు తున్నట్లు వుంది" అని రాశారు. ఆలోచన శక్తిని, సేవాద్యుక్థాన్ని పెంపొందించు కోవడానికి, వ్యాసరచనల, వక్తృత్వపు పోటీలకు వెళ్ళడానికి, ఈ పత్రిక ఈ నాటికీ ఎంలైనా తోడ్పడుతునే ఉన్నది.

"చైతన్యవాణిలో కొన్ని బైబులు విషయాలూ, క్రైస్తవ మత విషయాలూ ప్రవేశ పెట్టమని చాలా మంది అడుగు తున్నారు. కాని ఈ పత్రిక మన విద్యా సంస్థల్లో చదువుకొనే అన్ని మతాల విద్యార్థులకూ ఉపయోగపడాలని సంపాదకుని ఆశయం. క్రైస్తవ మతాంశాలను ప్రచురించే ఇతర పత్రికలు చాలా వున్నాయి కదా!" అని పత్రిక ఉద్దేశాన్ని తేట తెల్లం చేశారు జోజయ్య స్వామి.

చైతన్యవాణి మీద సమీక్షకు జోజయ్య స్వామి చైతన్యవాణిలో "ఈ వరకే ప్రచరితమైన శీర్షికలు కొన్ని పుస్తకరూపంలో వెలయించాలనుకొంటున్నాం. మీ వుద్దేశం ప్రకారం ఏ యే శీర్షికలు ఇందుకు తగినవి?" అని ఓ ప్రశ్న అడిగారు. దానికి వచ్చిన జవాబులను బట్టి తదనంతరకాలంలో వెలయించినవే "విద్యార్థిహిత గ్రంథమాల" లోని 17 పుస్తకాలు. అవి వ్యక్తిత్వాన్ని గుర్చి చెప్పే 'లోచూపు'; పెద్దల మాటలనుండి 'ఏరిన ముత్యాలు'; నైతికాంశాల నువివరించే 'నైతిక మార్గం, నైతిక విలువలు', 'హితోపదేశాలు', 'చైతన్య దీపం', 'మెరపు తలపులు', 'వెలుగుబాట'; నీతికథల సమాహోరాలు 'నీతికథలు', 'ప్రబోధ కథలు', 'దిష్టి కథలు', 'ప్రేరణ కథలు'; మర్యాదా మన్ననలను తెలియజేసే 'మంచి అలవాట్లు'; విజయ సూత్రాలను తెలియజేసే 'గెలుపు బాట', 'విజయ పథం', 'ఆత్మ విశ్వాసం'; ఆత్మ పరిశీలనకు ఉపకరించే 'ఆత్మవలోకనం'. ఈ పుస్తకాలన్నీ ఎళ్ళ తరబడి ముద్రితమవుతూనే ఉన్నాయి. విద్యార్థులకు ఈ పుస్తకాలు ఎంత మేలు చేస్తున్నాయో చెప్పటానికి ఇంతకంటే వేరే రుజువు అక్కరలేదనుకుంటాను.

"ఈ సంపాదకుడు ఒంటిగాడు ఇతని ప్రధాన కార్యం పత్రికను ప్రచురించడం కాదు... అన్నివ్యాసాలూ తానే వ్రాయాలంటే ఇతనికి తలబరువవుతుంది..." అని పలుకుతూ రచనలు చేయగల వారిని జోజయ్య స్వామి విన్రమంగా తమ రచనలు పంపమని ఆహ్వానించారు. సమీక్షరాసి పంపిన వారిలో పదిమందికి బహుమతులు కూడా నిర్ణయించి అందజేశారు. ఆడంబరాల జోలికి పోకుండా, పొదుపుగా అమూల్యమైన

చైతన్యవాణి ప్రబోధాన్ని 46 ఏళ్లుగా నిరంతరాయంగా కొనసాగిస్తున్నారు జోజయ్య స్వామి.

చైతన్యవాణిలో ధారావాహికంగా చిరకాలం నడిచిన ఇతర శీర్షికలు వేటికవే తెలుగు భాషకు మణిహారాలు. తెలుగు సామెతలూ, మానవస్వభావం, తెలుగు జాతీయాలు, కబీరు ప్రార్థనలు, తుకారాం ప్రార్థనలు, బౌద్ధ, ముస్లిం ప్రార్థనలు మొదలైనవి. వీటిపై ఎంఫిల్, పి.హెచ్.డి., పరిశోధనలు జరగవలసి ఉంది. ప్రత్యేకించి "మనన మాలిక" పూర్తిగా ఆయా దేశకాల సంస్కృతులకు చెందిన మాన్యుల జీవిత కథనాల చైతన్య గుళికలు. సూక్తి ముక్తావళి ధారావాహికంలో ఆర్యసూక్తులకు లఘువ్యాఖ్య జోడించిన ఖండికలు నిజంగా మేలి ముత్యాలు.

గాంధీజీ, మదర్ తెరెస్సా తదితరులు చైతన్యవాణి సంచికల్లో నిరంతరాయంగా దర్శనమిస్తుంటారు. వీరేశలింగం, గరిమెళ్ల సత్యనారాయణ, సత్యజిత్ రాయ్, రవీంద్రనాథ్ ఠాగూర్, మోక్షగుండం విశ్వేశ్వరయ్య, ఆంగ్సాన్ సూకీ, తుమ్మల సీతారామమూర్తి, చార్లీ చాప్లిన్, రాజ్ కపూర్, శరత్, కన్ఫ్యూషియన్, టంగుటూరి, సి.వి.రామన్, పి.టి. ఉష, అంజయ్య...ఇలా ప్రాచీన, సమకాలీన ఆదర్శ మూర్తల సంక్షిప్త జీవిత చరిత్రలు చైతన్యవాణిలో జోజయ్య స్వామి కలం నుండి జాలువారాయి.

వేమనను జోజయ్య స్వామికి అభిమాన ధ్యాన వస్తువుగా చైతన్యవాణి శీర్షికలు తేట తెల్లం చేస్తున్నాయి. వేమన మానవతావాదం, వేమన వాడిన ఉపమానాలు, హేతువాదం, పొడుపుకథలు, విలువలు ఇలా వేమన్నవాదంలోని అనేక పార్శ్వాలను ఆయన స్పృశించారు.

"చైతన్యవాణి సమీక్ష" అనే శీర్షిక ధారావాహికంగా పాఠకులను పలకరించి జోజయ్య స్వామి భావాలను ఉదహరిస్తూనే, పాఠకుల అభిప్రాయాలను కూడా ఆహ్వానిస్తూ సాగుతున్నది. అనేక పుస్తక సమీక్షలు సమకాలీన సాహిత్య దర్పణాలుగా ఈ సంచికల్లో దర్శనమిస్తాయి. మరోక ప్రశస్తమైన అంశం విద్యార్థులు చిన్న చిన్న అంశాలపై రాసిన చిరు వ్యాసాలు. జోజయ్య స్వామి ఆంధ్ర దేశమంతటా, క్రైస్తవ పాఠశాలలను సందర్శిస్తూ విద్యార్థులు రచనా కౌశలాన్ని వెలికి తీసే సదాశయంతో చిన్న చిన్న వ్యాసాలు వారిచే రాయించారు. వాటిలో కొన్నిటిని ప్రతి చైతన్యవాణి సంచికలోనూ కనీసం నాలుగైదు పుటలలో ప్రచురించారు. పిల్లచే వ్యాసాలు రాయించిన అంశాలు చప్పనాతి తనం, నాకు నచ్చిన సామెత, నేను మహానందం చెందిన రోజు, నేను చేసి న కొంతపనులు నాలోని మంచి గుణం మొదలైనవి. అవకాశమున్న ప్రతి పేజీలోనూ మహానుభావుల ఆలోచనాధారకు అద్దం పట్టే చిన్న చిన్న సూక్తులు, ఉవాచలు కనిపిస్తుంటాయి.

ఈ చిన్ని వ్యాసంలో చైతన్యవాణి క్షీర సముద్రాన్ని సమగ్రంగా మధించడం అసాధ్యం. అసలు చైతన్యవాణి పత్రికే జోజయ్య స్వామి మేధోమధనం. ఇందులో వారు స్పృశించని విషయం లేదు, ప్రస్తావించని ప్రఖ్యాత వ్యక్తి లేదు. యువతకు, సాహిత్యం, తత్త్వశాస్త్రం, నీతి, ప్రబోధం, వినోదం, ఒకటేమిటి, విస్తృత పరిధి గలిగి, మేధోమథనానికి ఊతమిచ్చే చైతన్య సాగరం చైతన్యవాణి.

2019 మార్చి- ఏప్రిల్ చైతన్యవాణి ఈ సత్యానికి తిరుగులేని సాక్ష్యం. ఇందులో జంతువుల పట్ల కరుణ, యవ్వనదశలో మానసిక సమస్యలు, ప్లాస్టిక్ వాడకం, దర్శనీయ స్థలాలు మొదలైన శీర్షికలు జోజయ్య గారి బహుముఖ పరిజ్ఞానానికి తార్కాణాలు. ఇటీవల చైతన్యవాణిలో ధారావాహికంగా వారు అందిస్తున్న తెలుగు జాతీయాలు శీర్షిక వారి తెలుగు భాషా ప్రియత్వానికి, అందరూ మంచి భాష మాట్లాడాలన్న ఆయన తాపత్రయానికి నిదర్శనాలు.

చిన్ని పుస్తకాలు

మనస్సులో ప్రేరణ కలిగినంతనే ఆలోచించినదీ, ఇతరత్రా గ్రంథాలనుండి, బైబులు నుండి సేకరించినదీ గ్రంథస్తం చెయ్యడం జోజయ్య స్వామి పని తీరు. అలా రాసిన చిన్న చిన్న వ్యాసాలను చైతన్యవాణిలో ప్రచురించడమో లేక చిన్న పుస్తకంగా అచ్చొత్తించడమో కద్దు. ఇలా ప్రస్తుతం ఉనికిలో ఉన్న చిన్న పుస్తకాలు పాతిక పైగా ఉన్నాయి. వీటన్నిటిలోను తాను సమాజంలో ఒక సమస్యను చూచినపుడు, బైబులు నుండి ఒక తలంపు తన మనస్సులో మెరసి నప్పుడు, ఆ భావాలను సమకాలీనుల అవసరాలకు అన్వయించడంలో జోజయ్య స్వామి చూపే బుద్ధి కుశలత తేట తెలుంగ కనిపిస్తుంది. అసలు ఈ చిన్న పుస్తకాల్లోనే గాక బైబులు భాష్యంలో చోటు చేసుకున్న వేదాంత బోధ విషయంలో కూడా ఆయా కాలాలలో పెద్దలు చేసిన ఉపదేశాలను, తన కాలానికి అనుగుణంగా వ్యాఖ్యానించి మెప్పించడంలో జోజయ్య స్వామి సిద్ధహస్తులు.

వ్యాసరచన

కావ్యమైతే ఆరంభం, అవసానం, సర్గల ఎత్తుగడలు, శబ్ద చమత్కారాలు, వస్తువు తదితర విషయాలుంటాయి. రచయితలు తమ రచనా ప్రయోజనాన్ని దృష్టిలో పెట్టుకుని సాహిత్య ప్రక్రియలను ఎన్నుకుంటారు. అంతేగాక తమ రచనలు చదివే వారి అక్షరాస్యత, ఆసక్తి, అవసరాలు తదితర విషయానుకూలంగా రచనలు చేస్తారు. సాహిత్య ప్రయోజనం హృదయోల్లాసమైతే ప్రౌఢ పద్యప్రక్రియ ఉండనే ఉంది. జోజయ్య స్వామి రచనా ప్రయోజనం క్రైస్తవుల, యువతీ యువకుల మేలుకొలుపు. దానికనుగుణంగా ఆయన ఎంచుకున్నది

వ్యాసం. ఋతు వర్ణన, ధీరోదాత్త నాయకుడు, అష్టవిధ నాయకల ఆపసోపాలు, ఇవేవీ జోజయ్య స్వామికి పట్టవు. నేరుగా మెత్తమెత్తని మాటలతో సూదిమందు చదువరుల మనస్సుల్లో దింపడానికి ఛందోబద్ధత, అలంకారాల చెరసాలలో బందీకావడం జోజయ్య స్వామికి సరిపడవు. ఒకటే తపన, ఒకటే ఆర్తి, ఆవేదన. తన చదువరులను మరోప్రపంచం మెట్టెక్కించాలి. భావంలో సౌకుమార్యం, భాషలో మార్దవం, అభ్యుదయ కవితా లక్షణం ఆయనకు అనుంగు తమ్ముళ్ళై వర్తించాయి. ఆయన రచనలు మనస్సుకీ ప్రగతికీ మంచి గంధంలా పరిమళించే మానవత్వానికి పట్టుగొమ్మలు. క్రైస్తవలోకం కునారిల్లుతున్న తిమిరంతో సమరం ఆయన జీవితధ్యేయం.

భాషని, శైలిని తనకు అవసరమైన రీతిలో మలుచుకున్నారే గానీ వాటికోసం తాను వెంపర్లాడలేదు. వ్యావహారికానికి దగ్గరగా ఉండే గ్రాంథికంలో ఈయన రచనలుంటాయి. విషయం తేట తెల్లం చేస్తూ నొప్పించకుండా, నిదర్శన సహితంగా హితబోధ గావించడం స్వామి శైలి. దేవోక్తుల నిర్దోషత్వము, మత విశ్వాస సనాతనత్వము, స్త్రీ పక్షపాతం, దరిద్రనారాయణోద్ధరణాభిలాష, నాగరికత, వేదాంతము, విద్య, యువతలో ఉదాత్తభావాల సృష్టి ఇవి జోజయ్య స్వామిని ప్రేరేపించి వారి రచనా వ్యాసంగంలో సాక్షాత్కరించిన విశిష్టాంశాలు. కథలురాసి గొప్ప వారై పోయిన వారున్నారు. పద్యాలు రాసి గండపెండేరాలు తొడిగించుకున్నవారున్నారు. నవలలు రాసి వన్నెకెక్కిన వారున్నారు. వ్యాస ప్రక్రియకు పెద్ద పీటవేసి బైబులు భాష్యం పేరున బైబులు సత్య వేదానికి టీకా తాత్పర్యాలు రాసి సమకాలీన క్రైస్తవ సాహిత్యంలో చిరస్థాయిగా నిలిచిన వారిలో పెద్ద పీట వేయించుకున్నవారు ఒక్క జోజయ్య స్వామే. వ్యాస ప్రక్రియకు అపూర్వ సాహిత్యగౌరవం తెచ్చిపెట్టి తెలుగు భాషామతల్లి ఋణం తీర్చుకున్నారు ఈ తెలుగు బిడ్డ. ఆంధ్ర సాహిత్యంలో చిలకమర్తి, పానుగంటి, కందుకూరి తదితరుల సరసన క్రైస్తవ వ్యాసకర్తగా నిలవదగిన దిట్ట ఈ ఘనోట. క్రైస్తవ సాహిత్యాకాశంలో జోజయ్య స్వామి ధ్రువతార.

తదేక మనసుతో, తన జీవితమంతా వెచ్చించి జోజయ్య స్వామి సృష్టించిన ఈ సాహిత్య సంపద తెలుగు వారికి తర తరాలకు తరగని పెన్నిధి. అందరికి అందుబాటులో ఉన్న ఈ సంపదను వినియోగించుకొనగలిగిన వారు ధన్యులు.

పరమహంస జోజయ్యస్వామి

కె. జోబ్ సుదర్శన్

రెవ. ఫాదర్ పూదోట జోజయ్య స్వామి సర్వసంగ పరిత్యాగి కావున సన్యాసి; ప్రత్య క్షము గాని అర్థాలను బుద్ధిచేత చూచువాడు కావున దీర్ఘదర్శి; బైబులు వేదాధ్యాయి కావున శ్రోత్రియుడు; తనను సమీపించు వారిచేత అధ్యయనము చేయించువాడు కావున ఉపాధ్యాయుడు; సత్త్వోన్నత సంప్రదాయాదులను గ్రహింపజేయువాడు కావున ఆచార్యుడు; దీక్ష గలిగినవాడు కావున దీక్షితుడు; పావన హేతువు కలవాడు కావున తీర్థుడు; జ్ఞానముగలవాడు కావున ముని; తపము గలవాడు కావున తపస్సి; జ్ఞాన పారము చేరినవా డుకావున ఋషి; ఇంద్రియ నియమము గలిగినవాడు కావున యతి; మనో వాక్, కర్మదండ ములు కలిగిన సన్యాసి కావున త్రిదండి; సంసారమును జయించినవాడు కావున జినుడు.

సంపన్న కుటుంబీకులైన పూదోట మరయ్య. చిన్నమ్మ దంపతులకు గుంటూరు జిల్లా కనపర్రు గ్రామంలో 1931వ సంవత్సరం ఫిబ్రవరి 15 న ముగ్గురు అక్కల తరువాత ఏకైక పుత్రునిగా జన్మించిన కారణజన్ముడు జోజయ్యగారు. ఒక్కడే కొడుకు గన క చదివిస్తే అటూ ఇటూ వెళ్ళిపోయి తమకు కాకుండా పోతాడన్న భయం వల్లనేమో ఈ బాలుణ్ణి చదివించడానికి తల్లిదండ్రులు ఇష్టపడలేదు. జీవితాంతం కలం పట్టి సాహిత్య సేద్యం చేసిన జోజయ్య స్వామి బాల్యంలో, తరుణ ప్రాయంలో హలం దున్నాడు. ఈ హాలికుడు సత్కవిగా రూపాంతరం చెందిన తీరు మనోజ్ఞం. యేసుస్వామి కరుణా వాత్సల్య లీలకు రమ్యమైన తార్కాణం.

కనపర్రు సస్యక్షేత్రాలలో వ్యవసాయంలో పశుపోషణలో నిమగ్నమై, అంతరంగం లో ఏదో అలజడి చేత ఉక్కిరిబిక్కిరి అవుతున్న కాలంలో జోజయ్య స్వామిని ప్రభువు దర్శించాడు, స్పర్శించాడు. నీ విధ్యుక్త ధర్మం వేరే వుంది అంటూ వెన్నుతట్టాడు. అక్కడ మొదలైంది జోజయ్య స్వామి సనాతన ధర్మ, సారస్వత ప్రస్థానం. నేటికీ అప్రతిహతంగా ఏసుసభ సభ్యునిగా అరవై మూడు సంవత్సరాల, అభిషిక్త గురువుగా యాభై మూడు సంవ

త్సరాలూ సేవలందించారు జోజయ్య స్వామి. బాల్యంలో తల్లిగారితో కలిసి గోవాలో నిక్షిప్త మైన ఫ్రాన్సిస్ జేవియర్ పునీతుల వారి రక్షిత దేహాన్ని దర్శించుకున్న పుణ్య, సమయంలో తల్లి చేసిన ప్రార్థనా ఫలితమే ఈ ధన్యతకు పునాదులు వేసి ఉండవచ్చు.

విద్యాభ్యాసానికై పంతంబట్టి విశాఖలో ఉపాధ్యాయురాలిగా ఉన్న పెద్దక్కగారి దగ్గరికి తరలిపోయిన జోజయ్య స్వామి పాఠశాల విద్య సంపన్నం గావించి, మదరాసు లోయోలాలో ఇంటర్ కోసం వెళ్ళారు. అక్కడి ఫాదర్ల ఆధ్యాత్మిక జీవనానికి ఆకర్షితులై గురు జీవనానికి అంకితం కావాలని నిశ్చయించుకున్నారు. ఆంధ్ర విశ్వకళా పరిషత్తులో తెలుగు ఎం.ఎ. పట్టభద్రులైనారు. తదనంతరం 1955 జూన్ 14 న ఏసుసభ సభ్యునిగా ఆధ్యాత్మిక శిక్షణ ఆరంభించి 1965 మార్చి 27న అభిషేకం పొంది గురుజీవితానికిశ్రీకారం చుట్టారు జోజయ్య స్వామి.

విద్య, వైరాగ్యం, ఆముష్మిక విచక్షణ అనే మూడు లక్షణాలు జోజయ్య స్వామిలో మూర్తీభవించాయి. పాండిత్యం, యాజకత్వం, మానవత్వం ఈయనలో వెల్లివిరిసాయి. యేసు క్రీస్తు దివ్య నామ సంకీర్తనమే అఘమర్షణ మంత్రం జపించి పరిశుద్ధాంతరంగు డైనాడు. బైబులు వేదాన్ని పలుమార్లు పారాయణం చేసిన స్వాధ్యాయి ఈయన. ఈయన క్రైస్తవ వాఙ్మయ యాజక సేవాఫలాలు అనశ్వరమై ఆచంద్ర తారార్కమై వెలుగొందుతాయి.

పుంఖావ సరస్వతి

నిరంతర కఠోర పరిశ్రమతో, అధ్యయనంతో పరిపుష్టమైనది జోజయ్య స్వామి అంతరంగం. ఆ ఊట నుంచి ఉబికి వచ్చిన బహుగ్రంథ సముదాయం ఈయన తెలుగు క్రైస్తవ భక్తకోటికి ఇచ్చిన వారసత్వ సంపద. రోమ్ నగరంలో రెండున్నర సంవత్సరాలు బైబులు శిక్షణ, హీబ్రూ భాషాధ్యయనం ఈయన పవిత్ర బైబులు గ్రంథం అనువాద కార్యక్రమానికి దోహదకారులు. బైబులును శిష్ట వ్యావహారికంలో పండిత పామర మనోరంజకంగా, ఆధ్యాత్మిక క్షేమదాయకంగా తెనిగించి, మాతృమూర్తి అయిన శ్రీసభకు సమర్పించి జన్మ ఋణంతీర్చుకున్న ధన్యజీవి జోజయ్య స్వామి. బైబులు ఆధ్యాత్మిక జ్ఞానాన్ని ఆపోసన పట్టి, ఆంతర్యాలను విశ్లేషించి బైబులు భాష్య గ్రంథావలిని రచించిన అపర బృహస్పతి. ఐదుదశాబ్దాలుగా పుంఖాను పుంఖాలుగా పుస్తకాలు, వ్యాసాలు వెలయించారు. దివ్య నామావళి, బైబులు దృష్టాంతాలు, జ్ఞానస్నానం, పాపోచ్చారణం, క్రీస్తు, కడగతులు, దేవుని ఆత్మ, వాళ్ళిద్దరూ ఒకే వ్యక్తిగా ....., విజ్ఞాన బోధలు, కీర్తనామృతం, భక్తవిజయం, బైబులు పోటీలు, బాధాతత్త్వం, మన్నేసా, బైబులు భక్తులు మొదలైనవి కొన్ని మచ్చుతునకలు.

ఋత్విజుడు

"యాజయన్తి ఋత్విజ" అని ఆర్యోక్తి. జోజయ్య స్వామి దివ్య పూజలను క్రమం తప్పక భక్తి నిష్ఠలతో ఆచరిస్తూ అన్ని క్రైస్తవ సంస్కారాలనూ శ్రద్ధాభక్తులతో నిర్వహిస్తూ శ్రీసభను సేవిస్తున్నారు. క్రైస్తవ పవిత్ర మతాచారాల, పూజాదికాల పుణ్యఫలాన్ని ఇతోధికంగా క్రైస్తవ జన బాహుళ్యానికి పంచుతున్న ఋత్విక్కు ఈయన యాజి, లేక గురువు గా శ్రీసభకు చేసే శుశ్రూషక రెండు పార్శ్యాలు. ఒకటి యాజకధర్మమైతే రెండవది ఉపదేశ అనుగ్రహ భాషణాలు. జోజయ్య స్వామి అవిశ్రాంతంగా ప్రయాణాలు చేస్తూ పల్లెపట్టుల్లో క్రైస్తవ బుధజనావళికి యేసు స్వామి దివ్యప్రబోధాలు కర్ణామృతంగా వినిపిస్తూ తరిస్తూ ఉన్నారు. అభిషేకం పొందిన తరువాత మొదటిసారిగా స్వగ్రామంలో పూజాబలి నిర్వ హించిన తరుణంలో వీరి తల్లి "నా కొడుకు నా ఇంటికే కాదు, లోకానికే వెలుగునిచ్చే సామిలోరు" అని ఆనందాశ్రువులు చిప్పిల్లుతూ మురిసి పోయిందటా.

"చైతన్య" పూరిత పాత్రికేయుడు

విద్యార్థిలోకంలో నిద్రాణమై ఉన్న సృజనాత్మక, కథనాత్మక ప్రతిభలను వెలికి తీసే పరమావధిలో భాగంగా విద్యార్థుల కోసం జోజయ్య స్వామి గత 40 సంవత్సరాలుగా "చైతన్య వాణి" పత్రిక ప్రచురిస్తున్నారు. విద్యార్థుల కోసమే వీరు 'విద్యార్థిహిత గ్రంథమాల' వెలయించారు. లోచూపు, నీతికథలు, ఏరిన ముత్యాలు, నైతిక మార్గము, మనస్తత్వ శాస్త్రజ్ఞులమనుగడ, ప్రబోధ కథలు, మంచి అలవాట్లు, ఆత్మావలోకనం, తల్లిదండ్రులుగా ఉపాధ్యాయులు, దీప్తి కథలు, నైతిక విలువల, హితోపదేశాలు, గెలుపుబాట, విజయపథం, ప్రేరణ కథలు విద్యార్థి లోకానికి జోజయ్య స్వామి అందించిన ఆణిముత్యాలు. ఆంధ్ర లాయోలా కళాశాలలో అధ్యాపక జీవనాన్ని ప్రారంభించి దీనికి మించిన ఆధ్యాత్మిక జీవ నమున్నదని గ్రహించి స్వచ్ఛంద పదవీ విరమణ గావించి పత్రనా రచనా వ్యాసంగానికి సంపూర్ణంగా తరలిపోవడం క్రైస్తవ సాహిత్య కళామతల్లికి అనేకానేక ఆభరణాలు సమకూ డేందుకు హేతువయింది. శతాధిక గ్రంథకర్తగా స్వామి సన్నుతికెక్కారు.

నవయుగ తెలుగు క్రైస్తవ ప్రవక్త

జోజయ్య స్వామి కతోలిక సమాజాన్ని అపరిమితంగా ప్రేమించారు. దేవుని నుండి ప్రసరించే అత్యంత శ్రేష్ఠ వరాలు వారికి దక్కాలని ప్రగాఢంగా అభిలషించారు. అందువల్ల వారి రచనల్లో హెచ్చరికలేగాక, ఆశాభావమూ, ఆదరణా ప్రతిధ్వనిస్తాయి. వారు క్రైస్తవ ప్రజానీకం యొక్క అత్యున్నత అభ్యున్నతిని, క్షేమాన్ని ఆకాంక్షించారు. వారు మానవ పరిజ్ఞానం, సిరి సంపదలు, జీవపుడంబం తదితరాలపై నుండి దృష్టి మరల్చుకుని

సర్వేశ్వరునిపై ధ్యాస నిలపాలని ఆయన తపించిపోయారు. సర్వేశ్వరుని విమోచనాత్మక దీవెనలు వారు పొందేలా, ఆయన నిబంధన షరతులకు కూడా విధేయంగా ఉండాలని పదేపదే ఉద్బోధించారు.

ప్రజల పాపంపట్లా, నిర్లక్ష్యధోరణిపట్లా జోజయ్య స్వామికి లోతైన క్షోభ్యత ఉంది. ఆధ్యాత్మికతను చులకన చేస్తూ, శుష్కాచార ధోరణుల్లో మునిగితేలే విధానాన్ని వారు తన రచనల్లో అడుగడుగునా నిరసించారు. సర్వేశ్వరుని ప్రజల్లో కనిపించే రాజీ ధోరణులు, నిర్లిప్తతలు, నటనలు, సంజాయిషీలు వీటి పొడ జోజయ్య స్వామికి ఎంతమాత్రం గిట్టవు.సర్వేశ్వరునికి నీతి న్యాయాల పట్ల ఉన్న ప్రేమలోను, ఆయన ప్రజల ఉదాసీనత పట్ల ఉన్న ద్వేషంలోనూ జోజయ్య స్వామి పాలుపంచుకున్నట్టుగా వేరెవరూ చెయ్యలేదు. కతోలిక సమాజం కనుపరిచే మొక్కుబడి భక్తిని జోజయ్య స్వామి ఎడతెగక సవాలు చేశారు. నిశితంగా, తీక్షణంగా కాక సున్నితంగా, వేదనా భరితంగా, కాంతా సమ్మితంగా ప్రజల నామకార్థ మతభక్తిని అధిక్షేపించారు.

సర్వేశ్వరుడు తన బైబులు ఉపదేశాల్లో వెల్లడించిన కీలకమైన మాటలకు ప్రజలు హృదయ పూర్వక విధేయత చూపేలా వారిని ప్రోత్సహించడానికి జోజయ్య స్వామి విశ్వ ప్రయత్నం చేశారు. దేవుని పట్ల ఆయన నిబద్ధత సంపూర్ణం. ఉడికీ ఉడకని భక్తి, మధ్యేమార్గం జోజయ్య స్వామికి సరిపడవు. సర్వేశ్వరుని ప్రజల మధ్య ఆయన రాజ్యం, ఆయన నీతి న్యాయాలు పరిపూర్ణంగా వెల్లివిరియడం చూడకపోతే జోజయ్య స్వామికి నెమ్మది లేదు. ఆయన ఆర్తి, ఆవేదన అదే.

జోజయ్య స్వామి ధీరోదాత్తుడు. అపారమైన మనోబలం ఆయన సొత్తు. అందుకే సర్వేశ్వరుని ప్రజల ఆధ్యాత్మిక స్థితిని చూసి జోజయ్య స్వామి నిరుత్సాహపడి మిన్నకుండి పోలేదు. ఆ ప్రజల పూర్వ క్షేమస్థితి పునరుద్ధరణ, వినూత్నీకరణల పట్ల అభిలాషను, హెచ్చ రికలను పదేపదే వ్యక్తపరిచారు. అదే సమయంలో ఆయన రచనల్లో ఆయన ఒంటరితనం, గూడుకట్టుకున్న దుఃఖం ద్యోతకమవుతుంటాయి. బైబులు కాలాల్లో ప్రవక్తలందరిదీ ఇదే స్థితి. అయితే నిజమైన దైవ ప్రవక్తకు ఎంత ఆమోఘంగా దేవుని మనిషి అనే గుర్తింపు ఉం టుందో అలాటి గుర్తింపు భక్తిపరులైన కొద్దిమందికి జోజయ్య స్వామి పట్ల భద్రంగా ఉంది. ఈ నవయుగ తెలుగు ప్రవక్త సందేశాన్ని నిర్లక్ష్యం చేయడం నేటి ప్రజానీకానికి ప్రమాదహేతువు. గతంలో పూర్వవేదంలో దేవుని ప్రజలు చేసిన పొరపాటు ఇదే.

ప్రవక్త, యాజకుడు కూడా

పూర్వవేదంలో అధికభాగం ప్రవక్తలకు, యాజకులకు అనివార్యంగా గిట్టని పరిస్థితి ఉండేది. ఆ కాలంలో ప్రజల దుర్నీతికి, శుష్కాచార పరాయణతకు వ్యతిరేకంగా నిలవడంలో యాజకుల అలసత్వం ప్రస్పుటంగా కనిపించేది. జోజయ్య స్వామిలో యాజక, ప్రవక్త ధర్మాల మేలికలయిక కనిపిస్తుంది. ప్రజల వైపునుండి సర్వేశ్వరునికి యాచనలు, ప్రభువు వైపు నుండి ప్రజలకు హెచ్చరికలు, ఇలా యాజక ప్రవక్తగా నేటి కాలంలో జోజయ్య స్వామి తరించారు.

వీరి రచనల్లో సృష్టికర్తగా, విశ్వనాథునిగా దేవుని స్వభావాన్ని జనసామాన్యానికి కరతలామలకం చేశారు. అవినీతిని, అన్యాయాన్ని సహించలేని సర్వేశ్వరుని పవిత్రతను జోజయ్య స్వామి తన వ్యక్తిత్వంలోను, రచనల్లోను కూడా ప్రతిబింబించారు. అలాటి ఆమోఘ పవిత్రతలో సైతం సర్వేశ్వరునిలోని దీర్ఘశాంతం, జననీజనక ప్రేమ జోజయ్య స్వామి తన రచనల్లో ఆవిష్కరించారు.

నిబంధన ప్రజల్లో నిరంతరం తొంగి చూస్తున్న అవిధేయతయత, ద్రోహబుద్ధి, విగ్రహ పూజ, దుర్నీతుల విషయంలో దేవుడనుభవించే విచారంలో జోజయ్య స్వామి కూడా భాగం పంచుకున్నారు. తన తరం వారి ఆధ్యాత్మిక దివాలాతనానికి, వారికి చక్కగా అందుబాటులో ఉన్న దైవ వరప్రసాదానికి జోజయ్య స్వామి వారధులు నిర్మిస్తూ వచ్చారు. కేతలిక్కుల అపారమైన ఆధ్యాత్మిక సాహిత్య సంపదను, అంటే మధ్యయుగాల వేదాంత భక్తుల ఆలోచనామృతధారను నేటి పరితులకు దోసిళ్లతో పంచారు.

అన్నిటికి మించి తన బైబులు భాష్యంలో సత్యవేదమైన బైబులు సారాంశాన్ని ఏదీ చేజారిపోకుండా కూలంకషంగా వివరించారు. అదే సమయంలో తనపై గాక భక్తుల దృష్టిని అస్తమానం దైవగ్రంథం వైపే ఉంచేలా పాటుబడిన విన్రమతా మూర్తి జోజయ్య స్వామి.

దేవుడు పంపిన మనిషి

బైబుల్లో విశ్వేశ్వరుడు తన పక్షంగా మాట్లాడేందుకు మనుషుల వద్దకు ఎవరిని పంపాలని చూస్తున్నాడు. "నేనున్నాను, నన్ను పంపు" అని జోజయ్య స్వామి వచ్చాడా అనిపిస్తుంది. ఇలా వెళ్తానన్న రాయబారితో ఆ ప్రభువే అన్నాడు, "నీవు పోయి ఈ జనులతో ఇట్లనుము – మీరు నిత్యము వినుచుందురే గాని గ్రహింపకుందురు. నిత్యము చూచుచుందురు గాని తెలిసికొనకుందురు."

దైనందిన ఇహలోక వ్యవహారాల రణగుణ ధ్వనుల్లో చెవులు దిబ్బెళ్ళుపడి కొట్టు మిట్టాడుతున్న వారికి జోజయ్య వాణి చెవిటివాని ముందు శంఖరావమే. అయితే తన విధి, దైవాజ్ఞ మేరకు జోజయ్య స్వామి ప్రవచనాల ద్వారా, రచనల ద్వారా అవిశ్రాంతంగా సందేశ ప్రవాహం వెలువరిస్తూనే ఉన్నారు.

జోజయ్య స్వామి దీర్ఘదర్శి (seer). ఆధ్యాత్మిక అవలోకనం, జనుల యథార్థస్థితి స్పష్టంగా చూడగలిగిన కుశాగ్రబుద్ధి ఈయన. క్రైస్తవ సమాజ రుగ్మతలను ఎరిగి ఇదే పరిస్థితికొనసాగితే వాటిల్లనున్న పరిణామాలను ముందే వీక్షించి జనసామాన్యాని తట్టిలేపాలన్న తపన జోజయ్య స్వామిలో కనిపిస్తుంది. బైబుల్లో ఇలాటి వ్యక్తులను "ప్రవక్తలు"అన్నారు. దేవుని మనస్సు గ్రహించి, దేవుని ఆత్మ మూలంగా పలకడం జోజయ్య స్వామి నియామకం. ఈయన దేవుని మనిషి, సర్వేశ్వరుని సేవకుడు, ఆత్మమూర్తుడు, కావలివాడు, వైతాళికుడు.దేవుని ఆత్మను తమలో నిలుపుకుని మనుషులకు ప్రబోధాలు చేసిన దైవ వార్తాహరుడు. దైవజ్ఞాన ప్రత్యక్షత, విలక్షణ వ్యక్తిత్వ వ్యాపకాలు జోజయ్య స్వామి ప్రవృత్తులు.

సర్వేశ్వర సేవలో నిమగ్నం కావడానికి జోజయ్య స్వామి ఇహలోక చింతన పరిత్యజించారు. వ్యక్తిగత సౌకర్యం, కీర్తి కాంక్ష, విశ్రాంతి తదితరాలకు మోకాలొడ్డి సర్వేశ్వం సత్యప్రవచన సేవకు జీవితం ధారవోశారు. ప్రవక్తగా ఉండాలంటే దేవునితో దైనందిన సన్నిహిత సంబంధం ఉండాలి. నిరంతర పరిశ్రమ, నిబద్ధత, కాడి క్రింద మెడ పోనిచ్చే సేవతత్పరత, సాత్వికం జోజయ్య స్వామి నైజాలు. తన సాటివారిని మానవదృష్టితో గాక దైవదృష్టితో చూచిన పరమ భాగవతుడు మన జోజయ్య స్వామి.

ఈయన శాస్త్రి. బైబులాది గ్రంథ పరిజ్ఞానమంతటినీ జీపోసన పట్టి దాన్ని తాను జీర్ణం చేసుకుని సుబోధకంగా మనవంటి సామాన్యులకు అలతి పదాల్లో విప్పి చెప్పిన ఉపాధ్యాయుడు. "అంతరంతశ్శరీరే శాస్త్ర రూపా వాణియన్యేతి అంతర్వాణీ" అనే ఆర్యోక్తి ప్రకారం జోజయ్య స్వామి శరీరమందు శాస్త్రరూపమైన సరస్వతి గలవాడు.

దైవ విద్యలో అందెవేసిన చేయి జోజయ్య స్వామి. ఈయన యోగి, వివేకి, శీల సంపన్నుడు. గీర్వాణ సాహిత్యంలో ప్రథమగణ్యుడు, ఆంధ్ర భాషా పటినిష్ఠుడు. ఆరోగ్య శాస్త్రము, మనో విజ్ఞానశాస్త్రము, ధర్మశాస్త్రము ఎరిగిన ఉచితానుచిత విచక్షణా దక్షుడు. ప్రాచీనతత్త్వవేత్తల మనోభావాలను మధించి వారి విచారధారను నేలకు రప్పించిన అపరభగీరథుడు. ఇంతకుముందు నుడివినట్టుగా బైబులు సత్యవేదాన్ని ఆంధ్రీకరించిన పుణ్యాన క్రైస్తవవేద రహస్యాలన్నీ వీరికి జిహ్వాగ్ర గతం. సర్వేశ్వర హృదయం ఈయన

బాసికం. నిష్కళంకమైన భక్తి ఈయన నిలువెల్లా పూసుకున్న చందనం. క్రైస్తవ జన సంస్క రణాభిలాష ఈయన పట్టిన అసిధారావ్రతం. శమదమాలే ఈయన పాదరక్షలు.

బైబులు భాష్యం సంపుటాలు జోజయ్య స్వామి మూలంగా మనకబ్బిన అపురూప దైవజ్ఞానసిరి. తెలుగు కతోలిక లోకానికి అందిన వారసత్వ సంపద. జన సామాన్యం, మరి ముఖ్యంగా యువత వీటిని పారాయణం చేయవలసిన ఆవశ్యకత ఉంది. ఇందులో విద్యాసంస్థల పాత్ర చాలా ఉంది.

1. గృహాల్లో, విద్యాలయాల్లో ఈ గ్రంథాలను విద్యార్థుల చేత చదివించడం ఒక ఉద్యమంగా చేపట్టాలి.

2. కళాశాలల్లో ఈ భాష్యాలు ఆధార గ్రంథాలుగా నర్టిఫికెట్ కోర్సులను రూ పొందించి విద్యార్థులను ఆ కోర్సులు పూర్తిచేసేలా ప్రోత్సహించాలి. ఇవి ఇచ్చికం గానీ, తప్పనిసరిగానీ చేయవచ్చు.

3. పాఠశాలల్లో, కళాశాలల్లో గతంలో ఉండి ప్రస్తుతం కాలంచెల్లిన మతబో ధన తరగతులు (కతోలిక విద్యార్థులకు) పునరుద్ధరించి, వారానికోసారి బైబులు భాష్యం సారాంశం పాఠ్యాంశంగా బోధించాలి. బ్రదర్లను, సిస్టర్లను ఇందుకు ఉపయోగించవచ్చు.

4. వార్షిక సెమినార్లు నిర్వహించి రెండు మూడు రోజులపాటు భాష్య గ్రంథా లను విద్యార్థులకు పరిచయం చేయాలి. కార్యశాలలు నిర్వహించి ఈ గ్రంథాలను బోధించి చదివించి, చర్చలు, గోష్టులు, వక్తృత్వపోటీలు, వ్రాత ప్రయత్నాలు విద్యార్థుల చేత చేయించాలి.

వయోజనులు, గృహస్థులు కూడా ప్రభావితం అయ్యేలా కతోలిక విద్యార్థుల తల్లిదం డ్రులకు ఈ గ్రంథాలతో పరిచయం ఏర్పరచాలి. మతగురువులకు రాష్ట్రవ్యాప్తంగా ఈ గ్రంథాల ఎరుక, అవగాహన కల్పించాలి.

"సాత్వికులు ధన్యులు" అని యేసు ప్రభువు ఉవాచ. జోజయ్య స్వామి పరమ సాధుజీవి, సనాతనుడు. నమ్రత, వినయం, సంస్కారం, మృదుభాష ఈయనకు ఆభరణాలు. ఆడంబరాలు, ఆర్భాటాల పొడగిట్టని అరుదైన వ్యక్తిత్వం ఈయనది. ఎంత దూరమైనా సాధారణ ప్రయాణ సాధనాలలోనే వెళ్ళే సామాన్యుడు. నిరంతర ఉపవాస దీక్షాబద్ధుడు. సాటి ఏసుసభ గురువు వయసులో ఎంతో చిన్నవాడైనప్పటికీ అతని సముఖంలో తన అవిధేయతలు క్రమం తప్పక ఒప్పుకుంటూ అతని ఆశీస్సులు కోరిన భక్తుడు జోజయ్య స్వామి. ఇది ఏసుసభ వారు పాటించే ఒక సత్సంప్రదాయం.

గోవాల నిర్మిత రజ్జువు. శిఖ యజ్ఞోపవీతం వంటి బాహ్యాలంకారాలకేం గానీ, జోజయ్య స్వామి మనోదండ, వాగ్దడ, కర్మదండ ధారియైన పరమ హంస, పరమనిష్ఠా గరిష్ఠుడు.

"అందరికీ జీవితాంతం సుద్దులు నేర్పి, నేనే భ్రష్టుడినైపోతానేమో, కావుననా శరీరాన్ని నలగగొట్టుకుంటూ అదుపులోకి తెచ్చుకుంటూ జాగ్రత్త పడుతున్నాను" అని 'వరి. పౌలు' చెప్పిన మాటలనే జోజయ్య స్వామి తనకు శిరోధార్యంగా, తారకమంత్రంగా మలుచుకున్నారు. మనోవాక్కాయ కర్మలా జోజయ్య స్వామి పరమ భక్తుడు, పరమ హంస.

లోయోలా – నిర్మలా విద్యాసంస్థలు వినుకొండ.

సి.వి. కృష్ణయ్య,

ఆంధ్రదేశమున గుంటూరు జిల్లాలో వినుకొండ ఒక మారు మూల ప్రాంతము. ఇది గుంటూరుకు దాదాపు 90 కిలోమీటర్ల దూరములోనున్న పట్టణము.

ఇది పలనాడుకు దక్షిణభాగ ప్రాంతము. గుంటూరు జిల్లాలో బాగా వెనుకబడ్డ ప్రాంతమేదంటే వెంటనే వినుకొండని చెప్పేస్తారు. ఉద్యోగస్థులు ఇక్కడకు రావడానికి భయపడతారు. కారణమేమంటే ఇక్కడ వర్షాలు తక్కువ. ఎండలు ఎక్కువ. త్రాగడానికి వాడకానికి నీళ్ళు దొరికేవి కావు. ఇది ఆనాటి వినుకొండ పరిస్థితి. ఆనాడు వినుకొండకు పట్టణస్థాయిలేదు. నేడు మనకు మార్పు స్పష్టముగా కనిపిస్తుంది.

15వ శతాబ్దములో జీవించియుండిన శ్రీనాథ మహాకవి తన చాటువులలో నాటి పలనా టిసీమ స్థితి గతులను వివరిస్తూ ఆశువుగా చెప్పిన చాటువును గమనిస్తే ఆనాటి పలనాటి సీమ మన కళ్ళముందు ప్రత్యక్షమవుతుంది.

> చిన్న చిన్న రాళ్ళు చిల్లర దేవుళ్ళు
> నాగులేటి నీళ్ళు నాపరాళ్ళు
> సజ్జజొన్న కూళ్ళు సర్పంబులను తేళ్ళు
> పల్లనాటి సీమ పల్లెటూళ్ళు.

పై పద్యమును పరిశీలించినట్లతైతే అక్కడ చిన్న చిన్న దేవాలయాలు, నాపరాళ్ళు, నాగులేరు తప్ప ఏమీ లేవని, ప్రజలు సజ్జ, జొన్న కూళ్ళే తింటారని, ఎక్కడ చూచిన పాములు, తేళ్ళు కనిపిస్తాయని విదిత మవుతుంది. వినుకొండది కూడా ఆనాటికి అదేస్థితి.

> మరొక చాటువులో అచ్చట వరియన్నము దొరకదని చెప్పుచూ
> జొన్నకలి జొన్న యంబలి

జొన్నన్నము జొన్న పిసరు జొన్నలె తప్పన్
సన్నన్నము సున్నసుమీ!
పన్నుగ పలనాటి సీమ ప్రజలందరకున్

అని అంటారు. పలనాటి సీమలో జొన్నన్నము, జొన్నకలి తప్ప సన్నన్నము లేదని అంటాడు శ్రీనాథ మహాకవి.

మనకు స్వాతంత్ర్యము వచ్చిన తరువాత గూడ చాలా కాలము వరకు చెప్పుకోదగ్గ మార్పు రాలేదు. సాగర్ డామ్ నిర్మించినప్పటికిని 1984 వరకు కాలువలకు నీరివ్వడం జరుగలేదు. నీరులేని అప్పటి పల్లెలను, వినుకొండను మనమూహించుకొనవచ్చును.

ఈ ప్రాంతములో వినుకొండకు సమీపాన చాత్రగడ్డపాడులో 1895లో జన్మించి 1971 వరకు జీవించిన జాషువా మహాకవి ఆంధ్రదేశములో పేరు ప్రఖ్యాతులు గడించిన కవికోకిల. వారు తమ ఖండ కావ్యములలో వినుకొండ సీమను వర్ణించినారు. ఆనాటి ప్రజల జీవన విధానమునకు గూర్చి ప్రస్తావిస్తూ

సుంకుబట్టిన కంకిసురిగి వర్షము లేక
ఎండిపోవగ జూచి యేడ్చువారు.

అని వర్ణించినారు. వినుకొండలో వర్షములు తక్కువని, అదునులో వడవని, సుంకుబట్టిన కంకి వర్షము లేనందు వలన గింజ పట్టక నిలువునా ఎండిపోగా రైతులు దుఃఖితమతులవుతారని వర్ణించినారు. అట్లే సమాజములోని అసమానతలు, కులమత భేద నిరసనము ఆయనసాహిత్యములో మనకు కనబడతాయి.

ఆనాటి దళితులు పడుతున్న కష్టములను గూర్చి గబ్బిలము కావ్యములో హృదయమునకు హత్తుకొనునట్లు జాషువాగారు వర్ణించినారు.

విద్యవైద్య సౌకర్యములు లేక వినుకొండ ప్రజలు పడుతున్న కష్టములు ఆనాడు వర్ణనా తీతము. అటువంటి వినుకొండ ప్రాంతము మీద జేసుసభ గురువుల దృష్టిపడినది. ఆంధ్రప్రదేశ్ రాష్ట్రము అవతరించకముందే వారు ఆంధ్రమున కరుదెంచి పలు అభివృద్ధి కార్యక్రమములు చేపట్టిరి గాని నామమాత్రముగనే యుండిరి.

అటువంటి పరిస్థితులలో జేసుసభ గురువులు ఫాదరు దేవయ్యగారు మధురై ప్రావిన్సు నుండి 1953లో ఆంధ్రమున కరుదెంచి విజయవాడలో ఆంధ్రాలోయోలా కళాశాలను స్థాపించి 1954 జూలైలో తరగతులను ప్రారంభించిరి. అదే సమయములో ఫాదరు

బాలయ్యగారిని విజయవాడలోని ఫాదరు దేవయ్య గారికి సహాయకులుగా నియమించిరి. వీరు కూడా మధుర (ప్రావిన్సు నుండి విజయవాడ వచ్చిరి. అప్పటి నుండి జేసునభా గురువుల సేవలు వెలుగులోనికి వచ్చినవి.

అక్కడ విజయవాడలో లాయోలా కళాశాలను, గుంటురులో లాయోలా పబ్లిక్స్కూలును (ప్రారంభించిన తరువాత, ఫాదరు పాపయ్యగారికి గుంటురు లాయోలా పబ్లిక్ స్కూలు బాధ్యతలనప్పగించిరి. తరువాత ఫాదరు బాలయ్యగారు వినుకొండపై దృష్టి సారించిరి. విద్యా వైద్యరంగాలలో మిక్కిలి వెనుకబడియున్న వినుకొండను పరిశీలించి వెనుకబాటు తనకికి విద్య, వైద్య సౌకర్యములు లేకపోవుటమే కారణమని నిర్ధారణకు వచ్చిరి.

వారు 1962లో మొట్ట మొదట వినుకొండకు వచ్చి పల్లెపట్టులను గమనించి, పరిస్థితున వగాహన మొనరించుకొనిరి. ఫాదర్ బాలయ్యగారు వెంటనే కార్యాచరణకు బూనుకొనిరి. 1965లో గుంటురు జిల్లా కలెక్టరు గారిని కలసి వారి (వ్రాతపూర్వకానుమతితో చెక్కవాగు ఒడ్డున కుడియెడమల గల భూమిని సేకరించి భవన నిర్మాణములనొనరింప సమకట్టిరి.

1965లో ఫాదర్ బాలయ్యగారు చిన్నవైద్యశాలను, 1966లో నిర్మల బాలికోన్నత పాఠశాలను (ప్రారంభించిరి. 6వ తరగతి నుండి 10వ తరగతివరకు బాలికల విద్యకొఅకు ఈ పాఠశాలను స్థాపించి, విజయవాడ నిర్మలా సిస్టర్స్ యొక్క మదర్ సుపీరియర్ అనుమతితో సేవ కొఅకు సిస్టర్సును వినుకొండ తీసికొని వచ్చిరి.

ఒక (స్త్రీ విద్యావంతురాలైతే ఒక కుటుంబం విద్యావంతుల కుటుంబ మవుతుందన్న మహాత్మాగాంధీగారి వాక్కుననుసరించి ఫాదరు బాలయ్య గారు మొదట బాలికల పాఠశాలను స్థాపించి, తరువాత 1968లో సెయింట్ మేరీస్ (ప్రథమిక పాఠశాలను (ప్రారంభించినారు. 1971లో బాలుర కొఅకు లాయోలా ఉన్నత పాఠశాలను స్థాపించినారు. అట్లే వైద్య సౌకర్యము కొఅకు 1974లో సెయింట్ జేవియర్స్ హోస్పిటల్సును (ప్రారంభించినారు. ఈ సంస్థలన్నియు బాలబాలికలుకు విద్య నేర్పుతూ, (ప్రజలకు వైద్య సౌకర్యము గలుగజేయుచూ అనతి కాలములోనే మంచి పేరు (ప్రతిష్ఠలు సంపాదించుకొన్నవి.

లాయోలా విద్యాసంస్థలు
జేసునభాగురువులైన ఫాదరు బాలయ్యగారు 1971 జూన్ నెలలో 6,7 తరగతులతో లాయోలా ఉన్నత పాఠశాలను వినుకొండలో (ప్రారంభించిరి. ఆనాటికి (ప్రాంగణమంతా

నివాసయోగ్యము కాక చెట్టుపుట్టలతో, రాళ్ళ రప్పలతో నిండి, భయంకరమైన జనసంచారము కూడ లేని ఊసరక్షేత్రము. అటువంటి భూమిని కన్నుల కింపుగా, మనస్సునకు ఆహ్లాదకరంగా చెట్లను నాటి, పెంచి, మంచి మంచి నిర్మాణాలు గావించి ఒక దివ్య క్షేత్రముగా తీర్చిదిద్దిన ఘనత ఫాదరు బాలయ్యగారికి, జేసుసభా గురువులకే దక్కుతుంది.

గత 47 సంవత్సరములుగా అవిరామ కృషి ఫలితముగా సంస్థ ఇంతటి ఉన్నత దశకు చేరి త్వరలో స్వర్ణోత్సవ వేడుకలకు గూడ సిద్ధమగుచున్నది. ఇంతటి ఉన్నత స్థితికి జేరడానికి శ్రమించిన పెద్దలను ఒక్కసారి స్మరించుకుందాము.

వినుకొండలో లాయోలా ఉన్నత పాఠశాల ఇంతటి ఉన్నత స్థితికి చేరడానికి కారణాలు జేసుసభాగురువులు, ప్రధానోపాధ్యాయులు, ఉపాధ్యాయులు, కార్యాలయ సిబ్బంది. ప్రారంభములో సిస్టరు రొబర్టా, సిస్టరు ఆల్ఫ్రెడా, ఫాదరు క్రీస్తురాజు గారి పర్యవేక్షణలో సాగినది. తదుపరి ఫాదరు మరియదాసు, ఫాదర్ జేమ్సు, ఫాదర్ శౌరిరాజు, ఫాదర్ మరియన్న, ఫాదరు ఇన్నారెడ్డి గారు ప్రధానోపాధ్యాయులుగా నుండి పాఠశాల అభివృద్ధికితమవంతు కృషి చేసినారు. ప్రస్తుతము 2005 నుండి ఫాదరు రవి సెబాస్టియన్ గారు పాఠశాల ప్రధానోపాధ్యాయులుగా నుండి అభివృద్ధి పథముల్లో నడుపుచున్నారు. ఉపాధ్యాయులు, కార్యాలయ సిబ్బంది నిరంతరము శ్రమిస్తూ పాఠశాలకు మంచి ఫలితములనందించుచున్నారు. 1976 నుండి పాఠశాలకు ప్రభుత్వ గ్రాంటు లభించి ఎయిడెడ్ పాఠశాలగా పరిగణింపబడినది. పాఠశాల మూడు పువ్వులు, ఆరుకాయలుగా అభివృద్ధి చెందుచున్నది.

దాదాపు 350 మంది విద్యార్థులు నివసించుటకు అనువైన పెద్ద హాస్టలు బిల్డింగ్ 1980 లోనే నిర్మింపబడినది. వినుకొండ పరిసరాలలో పల్లెటూళ్ళు ఎక్కువ, పల్లెపట్టులలో నున్న విద్యార్థులు మంచి చదువు కొఱకు లాయోలాలో చేరి ఈ హాస్టల్లో నివసించేవారు. నామమాత్రపు చెల్లింపులతో హాస్టల్లో అన్ని వసతులను ఫాదర్సు వారికి సమకూర్చే వారు. ఈ పాఠశాలలో మంచి హాస్టల్ వసతుల వలన ఆనాడు ఎందరో విద్యార్థులు చదివి మంచి అభివృద్ధిని సాధించినారు. వారిలో మన స్థానిక ప్రజాప్రతినిధి శ్రీ గోను గుంట్ల ఆంజనేయులుగారు కూడ ఒకరు. డైరెక్టర్ క్రిష్ అనగా జాగర్లమూడి రాధాకృష్ణ గారు గూడ లాయోలా విద్యార్థియే.

వార్డెన్స్‌గా ఎందరో ఫాదర్స్, బ్రదర్స్ పనిచేసి పాఠశాలను, హాస్టల్‌ను ఎంతో ఉన్నత స్థితికి తెచ్చినారు. ఆనాడు పాఠశాలలోగాని, హాస్టల్‌లోగాని సీటు దొరకాలంటే పెద్దరికమెండేషన్ లెటర్స్ అవసరమయ్యేవి.

ఎందరో ప్రధానోపాధ్యాయులు పనిచేసి పాఠశాలను అభివృద్ధి చేసినప్పటికిని, ఫాదరు జేమ్సు గారు చేసిన కృషి కొంత ప్రశంసనీయము. వారి కాలంలో సింగిల్ సెక్షన్స్‌గా నున్న పాఠశాల డబల్ సెక్షన్స్‌గా రూపు దిద్దుకున్నది. పాఠశాల నూతన భవనములనుసంత రించుకొన్నది. కకావికలమై మెట్ట పల్లాలతోనున్న గ్రౌండ్‌కు వందల ట్రక్కుల మట్టిని తోలించి చదరము చేయించి, ట్రాక్‌లను నిర్మింపజేసినారు. సెంట్రల్ జోన్ ఆటలపోటీలను జరిపి జిల్లాస్థాయిలో పేరు ప్రతిష్ఠలను సంపాదించినారు. ఫలితాలలో 100కి 100 శాతము 3సార్లు సాధించి అవార్డులను అందుకొన్నారు. అంతియే కాక మేరీమాత గుహాలయమును,లాయోలా విగ్రహమును ఆవరణలో ప్రతిష్ఠించినారు. ఈ విధముగా పాఠశాల ఆవరణ రూపురేఖలను మార్చినారు. ఫాదరు మరియన్న గారు గ్రౌండులో మంచినీటి ట్యాంకును నిర్మించి మంచినీళ్ళను గ్రౌండ్ అంతా సరఫరా యగునట్లు చేసినారు. ప్రధానోపాధ్యాయులందరూ ఎదో ఒకనిర్మాణమును చేస్తూ పాఠశాల అభృద్ధికి పాటుబడినవారే.

కాంపౌండ్ సుపీరియర్స్‌గా ఫాదర్ అడక్కల్, ఫాదర్ ఛాండీ, ఫాదర్ వేదరత్నం, ఫాదర్ అంటోనీ, ఫాదర్ జోసఫ్‌రాజ్ మున్నగు వారు పాఠశాల భౌతిక పరిస్థితులను మార్చుటకెంతయో కృషి చేసినారు. దాదాపు 45 ఎకరముల కాంపౌండ్ చుట్టు ప్రహరీ గోడ నిర్మింపబడినది. లక్షల రూపాయల వ్యయముతో మంచి ఫాదర్స్ హౌస్ నిర్మింపబడినది. నేడు లాయోలా ఉన్నత పాఠశాల అన్ని వసతులతో మంచి ఫలితములతో ఆదర్శ వంతమైన విద్యా సంస్థగా వెలుగొందుచున్నది.

ఇటివలన ఇంగ్లీష్ మీడియం పాఠశాలను గూడ అదే కాంపౌండ్‌లో ప్రారంభించినారు. ఫాదర్ బాలయ్య గారు పాఠశాల సమీప గ్రామమైన నాగిరెడ్డిపల్లెలో గ్రామీణులకు పని కల్పించే నిమిత్తము పలకల ఫ్యాక్టరీని స్థాపించి, వారికి పనిని కల్పించి దారిద్ర్యమును పారద్రోలుటకు ప్రయత్నించినారు. దానికి బ్రదర్ బాలస్వామి, ఫాదర్ జ్ఞానదేవన్, మరియు ఫాదర్ నందనస్వామి బాధ్యులుగా నుండి నిరుద్యోగ సమస్యను కొంత వరకు పరిష్కరించినారు.

జేసుసభాగురువుల కార్యకలాపములు ఒక్క లాయోలాకే పరితమకాలేదు. వినుకొండ నడిబొద్దున జీవాలయమును స్థాపించి వినుకొండకే ఒక కళను దెచ్చినారు. అట్లే జీవాలయములో ఒక ఇంగ్లీష్ మీడియం పాఠశాలను ప్రారంభించి విజయవంతముగా నడుపుతున్నారు.

అంతేగాక వినుకొండ చుట్టుప్రక్కల గ్రామాలలోని బిష్వప్ పాఠశాలలను వారి యనుమతితో స్వీకరించి శివాపురం, కొండ్రముట్ల పాలెం, జాలపాలెం, పమిడిపాడు గ్రామాలలోని ప్రాధమిక పాఠశాలను సమర్ధవంతముగా నడుపుచూ పర్యవేక్షించుచున్నారు. గ్రామీణ ప్రాంత విద్యార్థులను ప్రగతి పధములో పయనింపజేయుచున్నారు.

జేసుసభ గురువులు తాము స్థాపించిన సంస్థలను ఇంతటి అభివృద్ధి పధములో పయనిం పజేయుటకు కారకులైన రీజినల్ సుపీరియర్స్ ఫాదర్ బాలయ్యగారు, ఫాదరు యు.యస్. పాల్ గారు, ఫాదర్ కురియాకోస్ గారి సేవలు మరువలేనివి. అట్లే ఆంధ్రమున మొదటి ప్రొవిన్షియల్ ఫాదర్ బోస్కోగారు, ఫాదర్ శాంతియగో గారు, ఫాదర్ జోసెబాస్టియన్ గారు, ఫాదర్ పోతిరెడ్డి యాంటోని గారు, ఫాదర్ అమల్ రాజ్ గారు చేసిన కృషి అద్వితీయమైనది. ఈ విధముగా జేసునభా గురువులు అటు ఆర్థికంగా ఇటు సామాజికంగా ప్రజలలో మంచి మార్పును దెచ్చుటకు ప్రయత్నించి సఫల మనోరథులైరి. ఆనాటి లాయోలా విద్యార్థులెందరో నేడు దేశ విదేశాలలో ఉద్యోగము చేయుచున్నారు. ఈ ప్రాంతము గూడ అభివృద్ధి జెందినది. ఈ పరిణామానికి కారకులైన జేసుసభా గురువులెం దరో మహానుభావులు అందరికీ వందనములు.

నిర్మలా విద్యాసంస్థలు

జేసుసభాగురువులైన రెవరెండ్ ఫాదరు బాలయ్య గారు వినుకొండ ప్రాంతముపై తమ దృష్టిని సారించిన తరువాత మొట్టమొదట 1965లో నిర్మలా కాంపౌండును ఏర్పాటుచేసి అందులో చిన్న వైద్యశాలను ఏర్పాటు చేసినారు. తరువాత 1966లో 6,7,8 తరగతులతో నిర్మలా బాలికోన్నత పాఠశాల ప్రారంభింపబడినది.

పాఠశాల మరియు వైద్యశాలను నడుపుటకు సిస్టర్సు కావలసివచ్చినది. వారి సేవలు అవసరము గనుక ఫాదరు బాలయ్యగారు విజయవాడలోని నిర్మలా సిస్టర్సు సుపీరియర్ గారి అనుమతిని బొంది నలుగురు సిస్టర్సును వినుకొండకు ఆహ్వానించిరి. నిర్మలా సిస్టర్సు సుపీరియర్ గారు ఆనాటికి బాగా వెనుకబడియున్న వినుకొండ ప్రాంతములో

సేవ చేయుటకు నలుగురు సిస్టర్లను పంపినారు. వారిలో ఇద్దరు పాఠశాల కొఱకు మరి ఇద్దరు సువార్త సేవ కొఱకు వచ్చిరి. వీరు 1965లో పంపబడినారు.

నిర్మలా సిస్టర్స్ కొఱకు దాదాపు 45 ఎకరములు భూమిని ప్రభుత్వ అనుమతితో స్వీకరించి, కొంత భూమిని కొని, నిర్మాణములు గావించి సిస్టర్సుకు ఇవ్వబడమైనది. అప్పటికాప్రాం తము నిర్ణీవమై యుండెను. లక్షలాది రూపాయలు వెచ్చించి దాని రూపు రేఖలను మార్చి నవారు ఫాదరు బాలయ్యగారు.

తరువాత చిన్న పిల్లల విద్య కొఱకు 1968లో సెయింట్ మేరీస్ ప్రాథమిక పాఠశాల నెలకొల్పబడినది. ఈ రెండు సంస్థలు నాటి నుండి నేటి వరకు దినదిన ప్రవర్ధమానమై వెలుగొందుచూ స్వర్ణోత్సవములను గూడ జరుపుకొన్నవి. 1968లోనే గ్రామీణ ప్రాంత బాలబాలికల కొఱకు మంచి వసతి గృహము కూడ నిర్మింపబడినది.

అంతేగాదు విద్యార్థుల తల్లిదండ్రులలో నున్న ఆంగ్లభాషాభిమానమును గమనించి ప్రాంగ ణములో నిర్మలా ఇంగ్లీషు మీడియం పాఠశాలను గూడ 2010లో సిస్టర్లు ప్రారంభించిరి. నేడు ఒక ప్రాథమిక పాఠశాల రెండు ఉన్నత పాఠశాలలతో ప్రాంగణము అలరారుచున్నవి.

అంతేగాక 1974లో సెయింట్ జీవియర్స్ హాస్పిటల్స్ను లక్షలాదిరూపాయల వ్యయముతో నిర్మించి, అప్పటి ముఖ్యమంత్రి శ్రీజలగం వెంగళరావుచే ప్రారంభోత్సవము చేయబడినది. సిస్టరు ఫ్లోరెన్సు డాక్టరుగా నుండి దశాబ్దము పాటు చేసిన సేవలు చిరస్మరణీయములు. సిస్టర్స్ సహాయ సహకారాలతో ఫ్లోరెన్స్ చేసిన సేవలు నిర్మలా సిస్టర్స్కు మంచి పేరు ప్రతిష్ఠలు సంపాదించి పెట్టినవి.

నిర్మలా, లాయోలా పాఠశాలలు పేరు ప్రతిష్ఠలు సంపాదించడానికి ఫాదరు జోజయ్యగారి సేవలు కూడా దోహదపడినవి. 1976 నుండి 2016 వరకు ప్రతి సంవత్స రము లాయోలా, నిర్మలా విద్యార్థిని విద్యార్థుల కొఱకు లీడర్షిప్ కాంప్లను నిర్వహిస్తూ వారిలో దాగియున్న అంతర్గత శక్తులను వెలికిదీసి పదును పెట్టే పనిని ఫాదరు జోజయ్య గారు నిర్వహిస్తుండేవారు. దాని వలన విద్యార్థిని విద్యార్థులలో ఎంతో చైతన్యము గలిగినది. వారా తరగతులను నిర్మలా బాలికోన్నత పాఠశాలలో నిర్వహిస్తుండేవారు.

రెవరెండ్ ఫాదరు జోజయ్యగారు మంచి విద్యావేత్త, కథోలిక సాహిత్యమును, భక్తితత్త్వాన్ని బాగా అధ్యయనము చేసిన సాహితీపత్ర. ఆయన కతోలిక బైబిలును ప్రకటింపజేసినారు. అది 1851 పుటల బృహత్తర గ్రంథము. దానికనుబంధముగా 482 పుటల నూతన

నిబంధననూ కలిపి మొత్తము 2333 పుటల గ్రంథము. దీనితో ఆయన తన జీవిత ధ్యేయము నెరవేరినట్లు భావించినారు. చాలా విశాలహృదయులు అంతేకాదు వారు చైతన్యవాణి యను పత్రికను గూడ నడిపినారు. ఇది విద్యార్థినీ విద్యార్థులకెంతగానో ఉపయోగకరముగా నుండెది. లీడరుషిప్ క్యాంప్ లో విద్యార్థినీ విద్యార్థల మనోభావాలను, రచనలను గూడ ఈ పత్రికలో ప్రచురిస్తుండేవారు.

ఈ విధముగా ఫాదరు జోజయ్యగారు విద్యార్థినీ విద్యార్థులలో నైతిక విలువలను, మంచి క్రమశిక్షణను, గురుభక్తి, దేశభక్తి, మాతృభక్తి, మున్నగు మానవతా విలువలను వారి యందు పెంపొందింప చేసేవారు. విద్యార్థినీ విద్యార్థులు నిర్భయంగా సభలలో ఏదైనా మాట్లాడి, చెప్పగలిగే నాయకత్వ లక్షణాలను సైతము వారియందు వృద్ధి చేసేవారు. వారు విద్యార్థల కొఱకు నీతి కథలు, మంచి అలవాట్లు, బైబులు మహోత్తుల కథలు వ మున్నగు మంచి పుస్తకాలను రచించి ప్రకటింపచేసినారు. వీని వలన ఆదర్శ భావాలతో ఉత్తమ భావిభారత పౌరులుగా విద్యార్థినీ విద్యార్థులను తీర్చి దిద్దేవారు. ఈవిధముగా అటు లొయోలా, ఇటు నిర్మలా విద్యా సంస్థలో ఫాదరు జోజయ్యగారికి విడదీయలేని సంబంధమున్నది. వారి సేవలు కొనియాడదగినవి.

నిర్మలా విద్యా సంస్థలో స్త్రీల కొఱకు పాఠశాలలోనే టైలరింగ్, చిత్రకళ, ఎంబ్రాయిదరీ ప్రవేశపెట్టిన ఘనత ఫాదర్ బాలయ్యగారికే దక్కుతుంది. వీటన్నిటినీ సిస్టరు ఎమ్మా పర్యవేక్షించేవారు. ఆనాడు స్త్రీ విద్య కొఱకు పాటుబడిన ఫాదరు బాలయ్యగారికి ఒక సమస్య ఎదురైనది.

ఎక్కడో ఊరికి దూరంగా స్థాపింపబడిన పాఠశాలకు పిల్లలను ఎట్లు పంపించాలన్న భావనతో ఊగిసలాడుతున్న తల్లిదండ్రులకు ధైర్యము గలిగించుటకై ఆడ పిల్లలకుమాత్రమే బస్ సౌకర్యమును ఏర్పాటు చేసి వారి చింత దీర్చి విద్యార్థినులను ఆకర్షించినవారు ఫాదరు బాలయ్యగారు. ఆనాడు బస్ సౌకర్యము వినుకొండలో ఒక్క నిర్మలా విద్యాసంస్థలకు మాత్రమే ఉన్నది.

అటు తెలుగు మాధ్యమ పాఠశాల ఇటు ఇంగ్లీష్ మాధ్యమ పాఠశాలలు మరియు సెయింట్ జేవియర్స్ హాస్పిటల్ అన్ని అభివృద్ధి వధములో సేవాధర్మముతో నడుపబడదానికి, అభివృద్ధి చెందదానికి ఎందరో నిర్మలా సిస్టర్స్ కృషి చేసినారు. వారి సేవలు చిరస్మరణీయములు.

అటు ఫాదర్సుగాని, ఇటు సిస్టర్సు గాని వారు సేవ కొఱకు మాత్రమే ఉద్భవించిన పుణ్యమూర్తులు. వారు నిరంతరము ప్రభుసేవా పరాయణులై ఆయనయందే దృష్టినిలిపి,

వివాహములను త్యజించి సన్యసించి, దీనజనసేవయే ప్రభుసేవగా భావించి సేవించు ధన్య జీవులు. ఎక్కడ వెనుకబాటు తనముంటే అక్కడే వారు ప్రత్యక్షమై ప్రతికూల వాతావరణవ మును గూడ లెక్కింపక దీనజనులకు సేవలందించుటకు ముందుకు వస్తురు. అట్లే నిర్మల సిస్టర్సు కూడా వారి సేవలను కొనసాగించినారు. వారి సేవలు నిరుపమానములు.

పాఠశాలకు, హాస్పిటల్సుకు సేవలందించిన నిర్మల సిస్టర్సులో సిస్టరు రాబర్టా, సిస్టర్ సెలీన్, సిస్టరు ఆల్ఫ్రెడా అన్నమ్మ, సిస్టరు దోరా, సిస్టరు మేరీ, సిస్టరు రాణి, సిస్టరు ఆనీ మున్నగు వారు అందించిన సేవలు మరువలేనివి.

సిస్టరు ఆల్ఫ్రెడా, అన్నమ్మ ప్రధానోపాధ్యాయులుగా నున్నప్పుడు, సెక్షన్సు పెంచడం, గ్రౌండ్ బాగు చేయించడం, సిమెంటు కోర్టులు వేయించడం, ఆవరణమంతా మొక్కలు నాటించడం మొదలైన అభివృద్ధి కార్యక్రమాలు బాగా జరిగినవి. తరువాత వచ్చిన సిస్టర్సు అందరూ ఇతోధికముగా అనేక సౌకర్యముల నేర్పాటు చేసినారు.

పాఠశాల, హాస్పిటల్సును సిస్టర్సు అభివృద్ధి చేస్తే, ప్రాంగమంతా అభివృద్ధి చేసిన సిస్టర్సు సేవలు గూడ మరువలేనివి. వారు ప్రాంగణ సుపీరియర్స్‌గా మరియు ప్రొవిన్షియల్స్‌గా నుండి అందించిన సేవలు గూడ చిరస్మరణీయములు.

మదర్ సుపీరియర్స్ సిస్టరు ఇరిదె, సిస్టర్ గాబ్రియేలమ్మ, సిస్టర్ సిల్వానా, సిస్టర్ బ్రిజిట్, సిస్టర్ సెలీనా, సిస్టర్ ఏంజల్‌మేరీ, సిస్టర్ క్రిష్టనా, సిస్టర్ విల్మా మున్నగువారు ఎంతో శ్రమపడి ప్రాంగణ భౌతిక పరిస్థితుల అభివృద్ధికి దోహదపడినారు. అంతేగాక ప్రొవిన్షియల్ ఆంజెలికా, ప్రొవిన్షియల్ లటీషియా, సిల్వానా మున్నగు వారిశుభాశీస్సుల తో ప్రాంగణము వన్నెకెక్కినది.

నేడు వినుకొండలో ఎంతో పేరెన్నికగన్న నిర్మలా సంస్థలు నేటి అత్యున్నతి స్థితిలోనుండ ఎటకుఉపాధ్యాయులుగా, నర్సులుగా, ప్రధానోపాధ్యాయులుగా మదర్ సుపీరియర్స్‌గా, ప్రొవిన్షియల్స్‌గా పనిచేసి సంస్థల పురోభివృద్ధికి విశేషముగా కృషి చేసి, ప్రజాసేవయే పరమా వధిగా భావించి సేవించిన నిర్మలా సిస్టర్స్ అందరికీ వందనములు.

వారి మనసులు నిర్మలములు, వారి మాటలు నిర్మలములు, వారి చేతలు నిర్మలములు, వారి జీవితములు ధన్యములు.

Contributors

AMALA AROCKIARAJ, S.J. holds a Ph.D in Chemistry from Yogi Vemana Universaity, Anantapur. Presently he is the Principal of YSSR (Loyola) Degree College, Pulivendla. He has transformed the rocky hilly terrain into a hub of ecological garden. He has planted 10,000 trees to emphasize the urgent need to care for our common home (earth).

BALA BOLLINNENI, S.J. is the founder-director of YES-J (Youth Empowering Service-Jesuits). He is a Counsellor based in Andhra Loyola College, Vijayawada. He did his M.A. from Heythrop College, London. Currently, he assists Jojayya Pudota in his works.

C. V. KRISHNAIAH, is a retired teacher at St. Xavier's High School, Vinkonda, Guntur Dt. He has written articles especially related to Vedanta and Bhakti tradition in Hindu philosophy.

DUSI RAVISEKHAR, S.J. has Ph.D from Potti Sriramulu Telugu University, Hyderabad. He is a trained Carnatic Musician. He has been the Director of Kaladarshini and Rector of Andhra Loyola College. He has composed liturgical hymns and produced dance dramas. He has written a few articles in local magazines.

GORANTHALA JOHANNES is a Priest belonging to the Order of the Discalced Carmelites. He obtained a Licentiate degree in Sacred Scripture from the Pontifical Biblical Institute, and then a Doctorate in biblical theology from the Gregorian University. He taught Scripture for seven years at Jyothirbhavan, a theological institute, Kochin. He has authored several articles in these past years. He served six years as the OCD Provincial in Andhra Pradesh, and CRI President for four years. At present he is serving their Order as One of the General Assistants in charge formation and of South Asia, in Rome.

GHATTAMANENI JAYARAJ, S.J. is a young Jesuit Priest holds M.Sc in Statistics and currently pursuing M.Th studies in Systematic Theology at Jnana-Deepa Vidyapeeth, Pune.

G.A.P. KISHORE, S.J. has a Ph.D in Telugu Literature and Linguistics from Potti Sriramulu Telugu University, Hyderabad. Presently he is the Principal of Andhra Loyola College, Vijayawada. He has published a few books and articles.

JEROME SYLVESTER is a member of Indian Missionary Society, living in Varanasi. He is the Director of Gyan Bharati, the IMS Regional Theologate which is an extension centre of Vidyajyoti College of Theology, Delhi. He holds a doctorate from Madras University on the Krista Bhakta Movement, Varanasi.

JOB SUDARSHAN is a layman. He has a BSc from Andhra Loyola College, Vijayawada and MSc from Andhra University, Vishakapatnam. He carried his research in Delhi University. He served as Professor and Head of the Department of Ethics and Religion, Andhra Loyola College for 10 years. He has a text book of Value Education and has distinguished himself as a good teacher and a role model to thousands of students.

JOSEPH SEBASTIAN, S.J. did his doctorate in Missiology at the Pontifical Gregorian University, Rome. He was the founder director of Kaladarshini, an Institute of Fine Arts and Culture. He was the Rector of Vidyajyoti College of Theology and currently serves as Spiritual Animator at Urbaninum, Rome.

JOSEPH RAJAKUMAR, S.J. is a professor of Systematic theology at Vidyajyoti College of Theology, Delhi. He has doctorate from Johannes Gutenberg-University Mainz, Germany. He is the author of *Rediscovering Rebirth and Discipleship in Baptism*, (2017). Currently,

He is the director of Depth (Distance Education Programme in Theology).

MICHAEL AMALADOSS, S.J. is a well-known Indian theologian concerned with the inculturation of the Christian faith in the multi-religious world of India. He has written 32 books in English – 10 of them translated into one or more other languages – and 2 in Tamil, edited 9 books and written 480 articles in various languages (till Dec. 2018). He has also set music to about 150 hymns in Tamil. He worked as Principal and Rector in Vidyajyoti, Delhi (1976-1979). Special Assistant to the Superior General of the Jesuits, Rome (1983-1995); Consultor to three Pontifical Councils, Rome. He was the Founder-Director of the Institute of Dialogue with Cultures and Religions, Chennai (2003-2018).

NIJA VARA, MSGN completed her M.Th at Jnana-Deepa Vidyapeeth, Pune. Currently, she is based in Eluru and teaches as Visiting Faculty at Vijnananilayam, Janampet, Eluru.

PETER EMMAUNUEL has completed M.Th from St. Peter's Pontifical Seminary, Bengaluru. He is the Rector of Pratiksha Seminary, Archdiocese of Delhi. He is pursuing his doctoral studies at Vidyajyoti College of Theology.

PUDOTA RAYAPPA JOHN, S.J. (P. R. John S.J.) holds a Doctorate in Historical-Dogmatic Theology from Leopold – Franzens University, Innsbruck, Austria. Currently, he is the Principal of Vidyajyoti, College of Theology and teaches Systematic Theology. He has published a book and edited three books: *Indian Faces of Jesus* (Anand: Gujarat Sahitya Prakash, 2012), *Prathishta: Faith the Foundation of our Future* (Delhi: ISPCK, 2013), *Searching Christology through an Asian Optic* (Delhi: ISPCK, 2017) and *Fundamentalism in Religions* (Delhi: ISPCK, 2018). He has published many other articles and book reviews.

RUDOLF C. HEREDIA, S.J. has his doctorate in sociology from the University of Chicago and taught sociology at St. Xavier's College, Mumbai, where he was the founder director of the Social Science

Centre. He worked as the Director of the department of research at the Indian Social Institute. He has published in various journals like the Economic and Political Weekly. The well known work of Heredia is *Changing Gods: Rethinking Conversion in India*.

SUNDARI NAGOTHU, MSI (Nirmala Sisters), has completed M.A Christianity at Mysore University and M.Th in Missiology from Jnana Deepa Vidyapeeth, Pune. She has taught systematic theology from 2000 to 2002 at Catholic Theology Institute, Bomana, Port Moresby in Papua New Guinea. She was Provincial Councillor (2005-2012) in charge of Pastoral and Catechetical Ministry & Lay Associates of MSI, Coordinator of Formation, (Provincial House, Nirmala Niketan, Vijayawada). From 2012- 2018, she was a Member of General Direction, Rome, General Councillor in charge of Ongoing Formation and Lay Associates of MSI. Currently she is based in Machilipatnam, Andhra Pradesh.

VALAN C. ANTONY, S.J. is a professor of Scripture at Vidyajyoti College of Theology, Delhi. He has a Licentiate from the Pontifical Institute of Biblical studies in Rome and a PhD from Jesuit School of Theology of Santa Clara University (Berkley Campus), USA. He is a visiting faculty in many theologates: Regional Theology Centre, Anekal, Karnataka, Gyan Bharati, Varanasi, Holy Family Major Regional Seminary, Julandhar, Mater Dei, Goa. He has authored many articles and delivered many lectures. He is a well known priest-preacher in the parishes of Archdiocese of Delhi.

VICTOR EDWIN, S.J. holds a doctorate in Islamic Studies from Jamia Milia Islamia, Delhi. He is the professor of Systematic Theology at Vidyajyoti College of Theology, Delhi. He is the editor of *Salaam*, Journal of Islamic Studies Association, Delhi. He has many edited volumes and articles to his credit. He engages in Christian-Muslim dialogue.